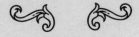

A DAUGHTER'S SECRET

WITH HER MOTHER BACK, Jenny knew she would have to take on again the role of Good Jenny: Esther's polite, poised, well-bred daughter. But a deeper feeling arose in her. Still the child was hurt by her mother's inability to love her warmly. She knew that Esther, for all her attentiveness to Jenny's education and etiquette, could never really love her as she longed to be loved. Too much distance had grown between them. There was the new baby in the family. There were Esther's trips abroad. And now there was a man. Jenny, however, wanted something for herself.

Standing by herself in the library, she made a decision. She would fight her mother and win. Before her mother's eyes she would remain the perfect Jenny; in her secret world she would get what she wanted.

HarperPaperbacks
by Erin Pizzey

The Snow Leopard of Shanghai
The Consul General's Daughter

Erin Pizzey

First Lady

HarperPaperbacks
A Division of HarperCollinsPublishers

HarperPaperbacks   *A Division of* HarperCollins*Publishers*
10 East 53rd Street, New York, N.Y. 10022

Copyright © 1987 by Erin Pizzey
All rights reserved. No part of this book may be used or reproduced in any manner whatsoever without written permission of the publisher, except in the case of brief quotations embodied in critical articles and reviews. For information address HarperCollins*Publishers*,
10 East 53rd Street, New York, N.Y. 10022.

A hardcover edition of this book was published in 1987 in Great Britain by William Collins Sons & Co. Ltd.

Cover photo by Herman Estevez

First HarperPaperbacks printing: December 1991

Printed in the United States of America

HarperPaperbacks and colophon are trademarks of HarperCollins*Publishers*

10 9 8 7 6 5 4 3 2 1

DEDICATION

This book is dedicated to all the people who saw us through several dreadful bankrupt years: to John Munday, for his lovely covers; to Derrick Searle and John Blake, for their diligence and commitment; to Peter Lavery, whose years of encouragement kept me going; to John Faure, our lawyer and the most eligible bachelor in America; to David Morris, John Elford, and Alan Cohen, whose combined efforts have kept me out of trouble in England; to John Gianardi who kept our family healthy even when we couldn't pay; to Jim Downey and all at Kaune's food shop, who fed us when we had no food; to Dr. Tom Smith, who took care of our numerous animals; to Barry from Armstrong Pest Control, who kept us free from black widows; to Anthony Concoff for cutting our hair when it was long but money was short; to Joe Boyle at Computerland, who made the work on the manuscript possible; to Genevieve Leach for all her help; to Wilfred Padilla who fixed our cars and gave us credit; to Don McTeigue at New Mexico Federal Savings and Loan, who kept a roof over our heads; to Annette Hernandez at the First Interstate Bank; and to Jeff Flook, our friend and helper. I wish to dedicate this book especially to Marjory Chapman, who believed in my writing and commissioned this book, and to my agent Christopher Little, who kept the faith. Also to my husband Jeff Shapiro upon whom I utterly depend. Thank you and God bless you all.

Where love rules, there is no will to power; and where power predominates, there love is lacking. The one is the shadow of the other.

—Carl Gustav Jung

PROLOGUE

Jennifer Jensen stood by her son Benjamin's grave. What had been a tall, handsome boy of nineteen now lay in a hole beside a pile of thick New Mexican soil. The pink rays of the setting sun lightly touched the ranch which had once belonged to her great-grandfather. The open grave darkened in the shadows.

Tomorrow, Jenny would have to explain the incident which had torn through the heart of Santa Fe, New Mexico: the incident which had taken her son's life. Tomorrow, journalists were going to arrive for a press conference at Jenny's home, the Governor's Mansion. Tomorrow, they would expect good reasons for the occurrence of the upheaval. Tomorrow, Jenny would announce her decision.

Jenny looked down at her beloved son. The last memory she had, a haunting vision, was of his eyes looking at her, trustingly and unsuspectingly, just before the bullets hit.

Where had it all gone wrong? Why did this nightmare have to happen? Jenny had to know.

She looked at her folded hands. Held in those hands was a locket, a mourning locket. Jennifer opened it gently. Inside was pressed a small plait of fine gray and black hair, the hair of her great-grandmother Lilla. Jenny stood staring at the locket, hoping that it might give her an answer. Surely it must contain the answer. It had been Lilla, after her arrival in America all those years ago, who had started the lives which had led to Jenny's life. Perhaps, Jenny thought, if she could understand those lives, she could understand her son's death.

A wind blew across the land and strands of her own auburn hair covered Jenny's eyes. She shut her eyes and, for a moment, felt she was entirely alone—alone by the grave, alone in the huge universe which now felt empty to her. The whisper of the wind, the call of the evening birds in the trees, even the sound of her own breathing, all withdrew to a distance, leaving Jenny alone behind the darkness of her closed eyes.

Her mind, however, allowed her no solitude, no comfort, no peace. Memories and images forcibly intruded into her private darkness. Her thoughts replayed the events which had led to this tragedy. Her head filled with her earlier dreams, her young hopes, her fulfilled ambitions of political power. Jenny opened her eyes. Before her lay the dead fruit of her decisions.

The pain was too great. If only to quiet her nightmarish thoughts, Jenny had to discipline her mind. As her eyes stared intently at the grave, a fresh and fleshy wound in the red, New Mexican earth, she pushed her mind back beyond her childhood, back before her birth, back to every detail she had ever known and had ever heard of her ancestors, back to the beginning. For a moment, a brief yet peaceful moment, the immediate agony of Jenny's life gave itself over to the past. From the past, Jenny demanded her answer. She sighed. The past, whispering in her ear like the cool evening breeze, told her its truths.

BOOK ONE

Lilla
1881

❦ CHAPTER 1 ❦

The bell over the door rang piercingly in the Gott-steins' shop in Middletown, New Jersey. Lilla Braff was startled. She had been shuffling aimlessly through the rows of dry goods. Lilla did not feel well today. Her belly was swollen with her first child and she felt sick to her stomach. Pregnancy did not suit Lilla Braff. Her body, she assured herself, was not designed to carry babies.

Lilla's young body was as diminutive as it was shapely. Her hair was shiny black, smooth, and entic-ingly long. Her face, though small, had fine well-proportioned features. Every night, Lilla thanked God for the favor He had done her by not giving her a nose which could be easily recognized as Semitic. From a distance, she might be mistaken for a gentile.

The noise of the bell made her jump and a pang of nausea rose from her stomach to her throat. She turned her head quickly and eyed the newcomers to the Gottsteins' shop. Immigrants, Lilla thought. More immigrants. She recognized the sheepishness in their eyes. She recognized the fear, the anticipation, the hope. From across the room, Lilla thought she could even smell their smell, as if they had brought with them the smell of their homeland, a sourness which now seemed foreign and dirty compared to the clean smell of America.

Lilla wrinkled her nose. The smell was too familiar. She had smelled it on herself and on Reuben, her husband, and on all the other people who had made the voyage by boat to America. Having smelled it once, Lilla had promised herself that she need never smell it again. Now, against Lilla's will, it resurrected memories of the trip to America a year ago.

Lilla and Reuben Braff arrived on a boat from Russia, bringing with them the money from the sale of their home. The voyage itself seemed a protracted nightmare to Lilla, but it marked the end of what had been an even longer, apparently endless, nightmare—her youth of poverty.

Her mother had died when Lilla had been a mere toddler. Her father had never been much of a provider for the family. When his wife died, he handed over the raising of the young Lilla to his elder daughter and left the two girls alone most of the time in their meager home in the countryside, while he wandered the large Russian cities, looking for odd jobs. Occasionally, he remembered to send money home to them.

Childhood, then adolescence, meant only one thing to Lilla: boredom. Every morning the sun rose predictably, the daily chores of running the small house called her incessantly, and each evening ended predictably with trying to fall asleep despite the niggling hunger of a never-adequately-filled stomach.

The sole source of amusement in her life she found in drawing. From an early age, Lilla noticed her talent for creating, with paper and pencil, images of the props in her dreary world: a sleeping cat, a broken jar, a beam of light through a dusty window.

When Lilla was sixteen, she met someone who promised to change her world. An art student from the university in St Petersburg was spending his summer in the country. Every day he walked through the fields, set up his easel, and painted his studies of haystacks, farmhouses, rain clouds, and sunsets. One humid, summer evening, as Lilla was walking home from the local shop with a loaf of crude, heavy bread in her hand, she met the student as he was returning from a day of sketching. "I'm an artist too," she announced, after he had introduced himself to the beautiful girl with long, black hair.

The next day, by agreement, she met him in the fields and showed him some of the better drawings she had saved. "Very good," he said. "But I'll show you how to make them even better." Taking a sharpened stick of charcoal between his long, pale fingers, he scraped the lines of Lilla's drawings with the charcoal's edge. Lilla watched as her drawn shapes gained depth and life. Here was a man who could teach her a lot. And, Lilla quickly decided, here was a man she could love, a man who could take her away forever from the dreariness of her country life.

All through July, Lilla spent her days with him. He taught her the tricks of perspective and shading. She watched him paint his studies of the countryside. As he painted he talked to her, telling her of life in the great city, of the fashionable clothes women wore, of the delicacies they ate, of the magnificent homes they lived in. With each passing day, Lilla's feelings of love grew, love for the artist, and love for what she imagined to be the big world beyond the confines of the hills around her.

By August, Lilla had made her decision that this would be the man to liberate her. To ensure that she would hold him forever, she gave him the only things she had: her love and her body. These presents he accepted gladly. In return, he promised her his never-dying love. Then September came and he was gone. There were no explanations, no goodbyes, no parting kisses. Instead, Lilla walked to the harvest fields one crisp, windy morning and found that he simply was not there. As she had expected, he had returned to St. Petersburg. And he had left her behind.

In the late autumn, Lilla's sister married a farmer. The small house was sold, and she moved into a cramped spare bedroom at the newlyweds' farm-house. Her life there became one of almost complete servitude. Monotony returned to her with what seemed unbearable permanence. Her love was gone. So were all hopes of ever finding a life of fashion, art, comfort, luxury—of freedom.

It was then Lilla made a very practical decision: she would make her own way out, in the person of Reuben Braff. Reuben had been raised in Lilla's village. All through his childhood he had gazed with adoration at Lilla's smooth, white face, but his shyness had prevented him from ever breathing more than a polite greeting to the girl his heart longed for. When his father had died, Reuben, the only child, had been left to care for his widowed mother, Rebecca, and to take up the post of village cobbler.

For Reuben Braff, Lilla felt nothing but indifference. She saved her passion for the memories of her artist. As far as Lilla was concerned, Reuben was a short, hardworking, Jewish peasant bore, like all the other Jews in her village. In his quiet way, however, Reuben was a dreamer, a natural wanderer. He spoke all over town of his eagerness to venture out into the world, to leave behind the growing animosity toward Jews in Russia, to begin a new life in a new land. With a dogged determination, Reuben spoke always of America. In Reuben, Lilla saw a ticket to the fulfillment of her own ambitions for freedom.

She let it be known to Reuben that her eye was turned favorably in his direction. Reuben, already so enamored with the creature he thought to be beyond all earthly beauty, needed little encouragement. A speedy courtship led to an immediate proposal of marriage. But this time, Lilla took no chances. This time she saved her body until *after* the wedding ring sat securely on her finger.

Once married, Lilla set about encouraging all of Reuben's dreams. America, she avidly agreed, would be their future. The sooner they left Russia, the better. Only Reuben's devotion to his mother stood as the last chain which bound them to their home. Rebecca had never approved of Lilla. She recognized the girl to be ambitious, single-minded and unloving. But she knew her son well enough to recognize how useless it would be to argue with his captivated heart.

After much intimate and skillful persuasion, Lilla finally had Reuben convinced: the best thing for them to do would be to leave his mother behind, set up a home in America, then send for Rebecca later. The old woman, Lilla assured her husband, was far too feeble to endure the voyage without a safe home there first. Full of dreams for America and love for his wife, Reuben agreed.

Lilla left the packing to her husband. She wanted to take with her as few mementoes as possible, the reminders of her misery. She kept for herself only one item—a small, gold, heart-shaped locket which had been her mother's. This she wore around her neck at all times, a single treasure from the days when she had had a mother to love her. Any other possession she would be only too glad to see rot in the Russian soil.

Reuben sold his cobbler's shop and his house, moved his mother into a cousin's farm, promised her regular letters and a boat ticket once he was rich in America, and at last—*at last*—took Lilla away forever from the tedium of the farmland.

On the boat, crossing the Atlantic, Reuben doted and fussed over Lilla as if she were made of porcelain. He organized their existence on the boat so that, despite the miserable state of the vessel, his wife was spared needless discomfort. Once the ship docked at Ellis Island, his heart trembled with quiet anxiety. Would they be accepted or would they be returned?

Given the fact that they were both in passable health, they were overjoyed to find themselves accepted and on dry land at last. Lilla took a deep breath. The air was fresh and smelled excitingly of wealth. It was then, having breathed a new and different air for the first time, that Lilla became aware of her smell, of Reuben's smell, of the dusty weary smell of all the other immigrants.

Reuben dropped to his knees in the middle of a bustling thoroughfare and kissed the ground. Lilla, though thrilled to have her dreams fulfilled, was embarrassed by Reuben's display of emotion. She tapped him impatiently on the shoulder. Reuben got to his feet, cleared his throat and said, "Let's find lodgings."

Within days they had walked from the city, where the slums overpowered the few rich areas, to the green and lush countryside. Lilla had given up insisting that they had to live in New York City itself. In her mind, the city embodied all the fashion and luxury she had ever imagined, but she soon saw the money they had with them would only provide the first month's rent in an overpriced cockroach-infested tenement filled with old-smelling immigrants. Reuben argued they would be better off setting themselves up in the country first. They could always move into the city once they were rich, or at least she could visit it from time to time. "I didn't come all the way to America just to get stuck in another country village," Lilla complained, but in the end she gave in.

Together they made their way past the homes of the very rich, spread out along the New Jersey coast. The sea air, the rich were advised, would keep those whom God had blessed so mightily from experiencing the plague, scarlet fever and the Spanish flu which regularly decimated the less fortunate immigrants, crouched in the hovels in the city.

Slowly, Lilla and Reuben Braff moved from village inn to village inn. Reuben, handy in all manual tasks, earned their board by shoeing horses or banding and mending the casks used by innkeepers; saving money for when they found the right land to buy. Reuben insisted he and Lilla share a room alone. Other visitors, desperate to save a few cents, shared two families to a room, but Reuben was fiercely protective of his wife.

At night, exhausted from a good day's work, Reuben lay down beside Lilla. Occasionally, she allowed him to make love to her. He, always slightly in awe of his wife's beauty after the great joy of knowing her body, would lie looking at her, softly lit in the candle-light. "To be given such a blessing," he would whisper. "A man couldn't ask for more." She would roll away from him, wondering why the man beside her was Reuben, and not her artist.

Every day the dawn filtered predictably into the little white room. Lilla, first awake, saved the candle. The quarters offered little privacy so, with no alternative, she stood fully in Reuben's view in front of the wash bowl, running a cloth over her shoulders and under her arms. Reuben loved to watch her. Her white buttocks turned slowly rosy as the impudent sun lay warm fingers on her body. Her trim breasts retained their firmness unstretched, as yet, by childbirth. Reuben vowed to himself that he would soon change that. Her stomach was taut, and below her navel grew a thick, ash-colored patch of hair. The sight of that alone made Reuben want to lie with his face buried in the soft-scented mound which now, he reminded himself, belonged to him. But Lilla, he knew, would never allow him to do such a thing. Ever mindful of his wife's wishes, Reuben contented himself to look, if not to touch.

"These are strange days," he said. "It will soon be autumn and the cold will set in. We must find a place for the winter."

"Good," said Lilla. "Maybe now you can build me a house of my own."

"You shall have it," Reuben promised gallantly, and they moved on.

By now Reuben had saved sufficiently to buy a horse. The one he chose was a young mare he called Beauty. Along with her, the owner let him take a rickety old trap. Within days, Reuben had mended the wheels and painted the trap black to match his mare. Now, villages and towns flew by as the Braffs sat behind Beauty, looking for a place to live.

Finally, they came to a place Reuben felt might be home, at least for the winter. "I must be near water," he said. Water meant fish—always a good, free dinner when times were hard. Middletown consisted of a few houses crouched around a church, a small synagogue and a shop. Reuben tied Beauty to the rail outside the shop and helped Lilla to get down. Looking around the village square, Reuben could see that the tall trees, standing so proudly, must indicate a good supply of water. Over by the church, he could smell the rank odor of a forge. He could hear the clang of a smithy working on bands of steel. "There's work here," he said. "I'll be cobbling the town's shoes in no time. Come on," he said, tilting his head toward the Gottsteins' shop. "Let's go in and meet our neighbors."

So Lilla came into the Gottsteins' shop for the very first time, with the smell of the boat, the smell of Russia, still on her clothes and in her hair.

Now, begrudgingly pregnant after Reuben's persistent efforts to expand his family, her stomach turned by the kicks of the life inside her, Lilla's nose was confronted once again by the smell she wanted to forget forever. The immigrant smell seemed sour to Lilla's delicate nostrils and it served only to increase her nausea. Quickly, she clutched her handbag, pushed past the people in the doorway, and walked out of the Gottsteins' shop into the fresh air.

The sudden metallic ping of the bell drew Joseph

Gottstein out of the back room and into the dusty interior of the shop which was the love of his life. All he saw of Lilla was her back as she fled the store.

❦ CHAPTER 2 ❧

"Yes?" Joseph Gottstein said pleasantly to his customers. "Can I help you?"

Vincent Cooper stared at Joseph. Vincent stood tall and looming. He suddenly felt very much a gypsy. What was he doing without a house, without a roof for his wife when this man before him was so obviously prosperous?

Joseph knew that desperate look on a man's face. "Don't worry," he said. "I was the same."

Vincent Cooper blinked hard. He felt the veins in his head constrict. A blinding headache threatened to block his vision. Suddenly, for the first time since he closed the door of his farmhouse in Sligo, he felt at home. Why he should feel at home in the presence of this small, dark man, he didn't know. Mary Cooper, whose soul was so interwoven with her husband's, took his hand. "Darling," she said in her soft, lilting brogue. "Darling, let us sit for a while and catch our breath." She smiled at Joseph. "We have come a long way and very fast."

"I know." Joseph was busy looking for glasses on the cluttered counter. "The trip from Poland was far enough. We've been here two years." His eyes shone. "I have a house, a beautiful baby boy, and my wife.

Ah," he said, "here we are," fishing out three glasses from under a pile of red ribbon. "Wait. I'll bring tea and some of my wife's applecake." He disappeared into the back of the shop.

Vincent sat down on a bale of fabric. Mary gave him a quick hug. "We'll be all right," she whispered into his ear.

Vincent buried his face between her ample, warm breasts. The familiar, sweet, mown-grass smell of her reminded him of the field around the farmhouse in Ireland, hazy and golden in the setting of the sun. The larks gliding and sailing in the evening wind, the long, tremulous ears of the curious rabbits taking themselves so seriously and talking to each other like elder statesmen . . . He wished he could hold that minute forever and lie always in the soft warm shape of the woman he loved.

Joseph coughed apologetically. He was struck by the tableau before him. He had seen so many forlorn couples, often with wide-eyed children, pass through the village. This man and woman, however, touched Joseph Gottstein especially deeply. "Here." He put a glass of warm tea laced with sugar into Mary's hands. "Drink this," he said to Vincent. "You'll feel better. We Jews survived the crossing on Russian tea."

Vincent sipped the tea loudly, then grinned. "I'm sorry," he said. "I'm not a mewling man, but somehow your shop suddenly made me feel at home. My granny ran the local shop in Sligo when I was a lad. I'd nip in from school and she'd give me a piece of her homemade gingerbread. She's dead now, God rest her soul. Just as well she's not alive to see her great-grandsons all fighting the English. I'm too old to fight, but my boys—they're proud of old Ireland. My family have always been mercenaries, you know. We fought with the Scots at Culloden. The bastard English razed Scotland to the ground." Vincent had a lost look on his face, as if the pain of worry for his boys' safety could only be borne by telling the terrible story of the rape of Ireland and its sister, Scotland, to whomsoever he should meet.

Joseph nodded. "We all left our mother countries," he said. "All of us here, refugees taken in by this huge place called America. We have to help each other. If we don't we will die, either from disease or from the Indians." He shook his head.

"Indians?" Vincent laughed. "I didn't know there were any Indians in New Jersey."

"There aren't." Joseph laughed back. "I guess my mouth gives me away. You see, I am staying here for a while until I save enough money then I hope to take my family West. I hear there is good, fertile land out West. For we Jews to create a ghetto is to create more persecution. We had enough of that where we came from. We must learn to assimilate and to cooperate with the gentiles."

Vincent smiled. "The Irish and the Jews always cooperate," he said, and laughed. "Both bloody sentimental people, you know." He sipped his tea. "I think we'll get along well," he said. "From now on, I think we'll call this town our home."

Joseph held out his hand and shook the big man's hand warmly. "You'll like it here. Different kinds of people coming from different places. But everyone looks after everyone else. We all need a helping hand at first."

"Why did that woman leave when we came in?" Vincent asked. "She certainly left in a hurry."

"Oh, that's Lilla Braff. Nice woman, but she has a hard time fitting in. Don't be offended. She's just a little shy. Her husband's a good friend to have. You'll meet him. Reuben Braff. You need any help, you just ask Reuben." Joseph smiled. "Come on," he said. "Let's go home and surprise Ruth. It's not often she has a visitor. We'll see what she can manage for dinner."

Ruth Gottstein was surprised but pleased. She immediately bustled Mary off into the kitchen. "That Joseph!" she said. "Not a word of warning." Her son, Danny, lay in a wooden cradle by the black, pot-bellied stove. He was drawing his knees up to his chest and crying.

"Can I?" asked Mary, eager to feel a baby in her arms again.

"Of course." Ruth frowned. "He's just three months old, and every night he cries."

Mary smiled at Ruth's anxious face. "Don't worry," she said. "A drop of mint tea on a piece of cloth. Let him suck it. Does wonders for his stomach. It's the colic, and it will leave after the third month. My, but you're a beautiful baby," she crooned.

"Sit down." Ruth removed a pile of fresh washing from a chair.

"Thank you." Mary sat back and held the little baby to her neck. She smelled the familiar smell of the baby's neck. "There is no smell quite like that in the world," she said.

Ruth smiled. "Yes. I never noticed that smell until I had Daniel."

"I don't think women do notice, until they have a baby of their own." Mary looked slyly at Ruth. "I'm nearly too old to conceive, but when I hold a baby, I still get broody. No doubt, as soon as I am settled, I'll take to knitting little socks." She gently kissed the velvet soft cheek of the baby, as he lay contentedly across her bosom.

Ruth, for the moment, was staring into various pots which bubbled on the stove. Mary rested and watched the woman at home in her kitchen. That was what Mary missed the most: her own kitchen, with the old rocking chair, had been her domain, and in it she had raised her family. Many had been the time she had sat alone at her kitchen table, praying for the safety of her husband and sons as they went off into the night to fight for the freedom of their Ireland.

All this was over for Mary and Vincent. She sighed. The boys would take their chances, but she could have a kitchen again, without fear of losing the man she loved.

Ruth added rice to a pot and pulled the heavy metal plate from the top of the stove. The coals glowed red, and the room seemed to pulsate with warmth and security. Tired from traveling, Mary fell asleep with the baby snuggled safely in her arms. Poor thing, Ruth thought, as she reached into the bread oven. Poor thing. At least we were young.

For a moment, recognizing the exhaustion on the face of this newcomer to America, Ruth's memory was thrown back to her own arrival in the new and unknown land. She remembered the relief she felt when she saw the American coast, offering refuge for herself and the few relations who managed to escape the Czar's cruel troops. God had been good to her, and even if He only gave her a son, without the blessing of a daughter, she would be a happy woman.

When Danny had been born, her first prayer had been answered. He was a beautiful 8 lb 6 oz, black-haired, wailing baby. "A blessing on his head!" cried the women in the room. "Such a beautiful boy!" Ruth had lain back, well pleased, with a smile on her lips, her baby at her breast and her forehead still moist from Joseph's kiss. She had never seen Joseph cry before. As she sank slowly into a deep cloud of peace, she found the sight comforting. "Such a man," she had said to God. "I'm a lucky woman, indeed."

Ruth's thoughts were cut short as Vincent Cooper put his head through the doorway. "I'm just off to unhitch the horse," he said.

Ruth smiled at him. "Good," she said. "Dinner will be ready in twenty minutes."

Vincent glanced at his sleeping wife. "She needs the rest," he whispered.

Ruth nodded. "You can stay here. Don't spend your money at the inn. We have a room. Danny can sleep in our room with us."

"That's very kind of you." Vincent was touched.

Ruth looked at him. She had a mischievous twinkle in her eye. "Don't thank me. Just wait till Miriam, the rabbi's wife, hears we are entertaining *goyim*. That will keep her busy for weeks." She laughed, and Vincent laughed too. "Go and tell Joseph I've said you can stay."

The Jewish community kept strictly to themselves. Mort the rabbi saw to that, and the rabbi's wife seemed to have eyes everywhere. Sometimes Mort thought she had an extra pair which lived independently of her large, cumbersome self. "I see," she would tell her husband at night as they lay pale, like prawns, on their marital bed. "Ruth Gottstein is best of friends with that Catholic, Mary Cooper."

"Well . . ." The rabbi was tired of the conflict between the women in his congregation. "They are nextdoor neighbors, dear."

"Nothing good will come of it," Miriam warned him darkly.

"No, dear." Mort was hoping to heave himself up on top of his sofa of a wife and, with any luck, he might just get time to climax before she fell asleep, snoring so hugely he would feel he was astride a huge vessel awash in a storm. "Remember," he said as he struggled, "it's a double *mitzvah* on the sabbath." Snores drowned his efforts. Defeated, he collapsed by her side. Miriam, he thought, did not like sex. Not like little Molly Parkington. She had plenty of time for sex and she too was a Catholic. With that guilty secret on his heart, Mort fell asleep with his hand protectively over his crotch.

CHAPTER 3

Nothing ever deterred the ordinary, everyday happiness of the small Gottstein family in Middletown, New Jersey. Little Danny Gottstein grew in the sunny streets of a town where everyone knew his name. Every Friday night, Ruth lit two candles and Joseph, Ruth, and Danny broke bread, passed the wine, and blessed the President of America. At the synagogue, the ancient, fervent prayers swayed the wall-hangings which depicted refugees from terrible times praying to God and thanking Him for their deliverance. Ruth prayed quietly for the birth of a daughter every week but, as the years slipped by, she accepted her loss and waited for the advent of a daughter-in-law.

Meanwhile, Danny's legs and shoulders grew. Lovingly, his mother fed him *kasha varnishkes* and *kugel*. She made her own gefilte fish every week. "Gefilte fish is good for the brain," she would say. "Eat a little something." Both men in her life would laugh. Joseph Gottstein, in particular, loved Ruth's cooking. At the synagogue and at his store he bragged about his wife until his boasting became something of a local joke.

Father and son spent weekends camping and fishing. "Come with us, Ruth," Joseph begged once. Ruth smiled her shy quiet smile. "No," she said. "In the old country, men and their sons had time together. How does a man become a man if all he has is the company of women? You go; I'll bake with Mrs. Cooper."

Mary Cooper, by this time, had settled safely and happily into small-town life. Vincent had built a sturdy, comfortable house nextdoor to the Gottsteins'. From the very first day of their meeting, Mary Cooper and Ruth Gottstein became steady, loving friends and they spent time with each other almost daily.

When Danny Gottstein had reached the age of eight years old, news of a baby came to a family on the other side of the growing Middletown.

Lilla Braff did not want another child. Her first pregnancy (to her it now seemed an eternity ago!) had produced a son, Benjamin. Four months later, she had found herself despairingly pregnant again with her second child, Isaac. Two years after that, Naomi was born. Two more years passed, and her second daughter, Bea, had joined the Braff family.

Lilla had never wanted children in the first place. Carrying them stretched her body in what seemed an unsightly fashion. Tending to their incessant demands took away the time she wanted to devote to herself and to her art. In the eight years since her first pregnancy, she hadn't had time so much as to pick up a sketch pad.

Only Ben, her eldest son, brought any joy to her life. As a baby, he breastfed happily. As a toddler he contented himself sitting beside her and humming little songs, while she struggled with the housework and changing the nappies of the younger babies. When she had a moment to spare, Lilla would amuse herself by lying on the floor beside Ben. They tickled each other and rolled on the ground with laughter. As a young boy, Ben grew quiet and shy but, from the thoughtful look in his eye, Lilla knew that he understood her—her secret thoughts, her yearning for freedom, her frustration with Reuben. Ben and Lilla shared a secret understanding with each other, a silent confidence which excluded the rest of the family.

Intercourse was not something that Mr. and Mrs. Braff normally practiced. Lilla felt little need for sex. If she wanted a new table or perhaps some ribbons from the Gottsteins' shop nearby, she allowed Reuben a brief moment of pleasure. He, so glad to share a few intimate minutes with his adored wife, ran quickly to the store next morning. "Ay men!" Lilla would laugh with her small daughters. "Wait till you marry. They all want only one thing, dears. Learn to ration them like I do. Never," she said, "never allow a man to think he has any rights."

"But Mama," Naomi, the more forceful and precocious of the daughters would say, "mommies and daddies should love each other. Shouldn't they?"

"Love?" Lilla always sneered at that question. "Love—that's moonshine. That's for when you are little. No, there are men to love, then there are men to marry. I married your father because I knew he would keep a roof over my head and pay the bills. The man I truly loved was an artist." Here, Lilla always put on a mournful face. "When I met your father—well, that was different. Your father is the marrying kind."

Reuben made a steady yet meager living in Middletown making shoes for the community but he was certainly not yet wealthy enough for Lilla to contemplate setting herself up alone as a woman of independent means. She could only wait.

Lilla felt as if she lived in a prison, and confirmation of the new pregnancy seemed only to add another brick to her cell. Most of all, she was dreading having another girl. Girls meant dowries, and in those days Lilla and Reuben had little enough to spare without having to afford someday marrying off another girl. Another mouth to feed right now, was problem enough. When Lilla Braff knew that indeed she was pregnant again, she burst into tears. Reuben tried to comfort her. He was a small, nervous man, afraid of everything and everyone. The flight from Russia broke what little nerve he had had. Leaving behind his mother had made him feel disoriented and afraid. Lilla, however, made up for any aggression her husband lacked.

"I shall go and find a woman I've heard of, and get rid of it," she said to her horrified husband.

Reuben argued, "A baby is a gift from God."

"Well, God can have it back again." Lilla was adamant.

At a set date, she arrived at the doorway of the woman who, it was whispered, would do the vile deed. She paused for a moment. In her pocket was the exorbitant sum of five dollars. Much against Reuben's wishes, he had parted with the money to calm his hysterical wife.

The cottage seemed clean enough on the outside. Lilla suddenly felt like running but too much was at stake, particularly the pride she felt for her surprisingly girlish breasts. Those breasts were her guarantee of her husband's fidelity. Lilla never trusted any man sexually; she had been betrayed once. Now, young, lascivious women abounded. Leaving their old lands, they were bent on husband-hunting in the New World—especially the gentile women with their yellow hair, blue eyes, and predatory little hands. Lilla shuddered. The thought of being left manless and poor, with her family to take care of, filled her with fear. This year, trouble from earlier immigrants who had not fared well in America had left many dead. Women had been raped and mutilated by angry, disillusioned immigrant men. Young women had sometimes been spared death but the older ones tended to be raped—then killed. Lilla knew her looks were no longer girlish. Having four children had aged her.

Standing before the door, Lilla breathed in deeply to steady herself. She had heard dreadful stories of attempted abortions gone wrong. She hoped there would be no pain. Getting rid of the baby, she reminded herself, was a necessity. She had to free herself from one more chain before it was too late and she found herself spending the rest of her life in captivity.

She knocked resolutely on the door. To her surprise, it was no old shrew with scalpel in hand who greeted her. She was momentarily sure she had come to the wrong address. "Come in, dear." The elderly woman was gray-haired and kindly.

Lilla was astonished. "Do I have an appointment with you?" she stammered.

"Yes. You are Lilla Braff?"

"I am."

"Come along, then."

As she followed the stocky woman down the neat clean hall, Lilla felt bewildered. She knew that if either of them were found out, she risked getting flogged, but this woman would pay for the deed with her life. Lilla expected the woman to be a heartless mercenary. For the moment, she suspended all judgment, and let the events carry her where they would. She, Lilla, was opting out. As if she were a puppet, she entered a small, tidy room.

The lady said, "I must remain nameless for now, dear. You understand. How pregnant do you think you are?"

Lilla mumbled, "About seven weeks, I think."

"All right. Let's get on with it. Have you ever attempted to rid yourself of a child before?"

Lilla hung her head. "Yes. The last one. I took quinine. All it did was make me go deaf for a few months."

The lady smiled. "That's an old wives' tale. It

rarely works. Do you use vinegar with cotton to prevent conception?"

"Yes, I do, but it has never served me well."

The lady frowned. "I know," she said. "I was a nurse in England. I lost my beloved sister after seventeen births. Ten of her children died in infancy; only seven survived. She married a bad man." The lady's mouth was bitter. "I saw her struggle on that last pregnancy, and I held her in my arms as the light faded from her eyes. She was in agony. Just too weak to give birth another time . . ." She cleared her throat. "But then, let's not dwell on the past. Now, are you sure you want to give this baby up?"

"Yes." Lilla was vehement. "I'm sure."

The lady didn't argue. She knew that fierce look in a woman's eye when a pregnancy was an inconvenience and the baby, if born, would suffer for it.

Not that Betty Thompson, in private, approved of all the abortions she completed. Often she could talk a woman out of her fear and panic, and send her home calm and resolute. Here, in a new country, deprived of loving grandparents, deprived also of maiden aunts and bachelor uncles, only too willing to share the burden of a new baby, it was no wonder women became desperate.

What no one in Middletown knew was that she had been forced to slip away from the Lancashire town of Ashton-under-Lyne where she had "helped out" women from the mills and the factories. She had started out as a midwife, having learned from her mother the ancient folklore from the English countryside. Red raspberry tea leaves were good for a pregnant mother. She saw that her charges drank the tea every day during the month before delivery. She kept a bottle of lavender packed in beeswax to apply to an aching head. She kept yarrow and shepherd's purse by her side to control bleeding.

Betty was well-pleased with her life until the day she lost her sister. As her sister lay dying in her arms, Betty made a vow to her Catholic God: "I'll help those who can't help themselves. I'll use my herbs to save the lives and the sanity of those women who can't—or don't want to—carry the child within them."

She worked on a douche of herbs to clear the womb and flush the fetus out without scarring the body. The usual method, used by money-haggling old crows in the village of Ashton, was to use a mix of carbolic soap and water. This mixture tore the delicate lining of the womb and would sometimes flush the fetus—though often the method failed and the baby, in a delicate state of development, lost its eyes and was born permanently blind. The method which Betty developed often failed too, for when a baby is determined to survive, it will survive, but at least it was born unharmed. Failure or not, Betty's method ensured that the mother going through the procedure felt only a little discomfort, instead of the usual great, rolling agony caused by the carbolic.

Betty gestured to a chair by a neat board in the center of the room which had a clean white sheet over a piece of bright pink rubber underneath. "Here," she said to Lilla. "Take this nightgown and put your clothes on the chair. I'll be back in a minute."

By now, Lilla was very frightened. Her friend Vanessa had died from infection caused by a different abortionist's failed attempt. Lilla had watched Vanessa wither slowly away, and had helped change the putrid, stinking bandages between her friend's legs at the very end, when Vanessa could do nothing for herself but cry.

"Don't worry." Betty smiled warmly at Lilla. "My method doesn't hurt and there is no infection. I use herbs. Simple, honest herbs." Lilla looked relieved. "I'm just going to get us both a nice pot of tea," she said. "Have you ever had tea from a teapot?" Lilla shook her head. "Well," Betty continued, "a pot of good Lancashire tea, thick enough to line a man's hat with, and enough sugar to keep the military for a year, is just the ticket. You get ready, and it will all be over before you've time to say 'Bob's your uncle'."

Lilla could hear Betty's determined feet making their way toward the kitchen. Slowly, she took off her clothes. Her mother's golden locket hung between her breasts. When she was naked, she gazed down at the alabaster-white belly with the dark bush of pubic hair below. For a moment she felt compassion for the scrap of life about to be torn so rudely from its refuge. But then she remembered her belly, huge and tight. She feared the advent of another varicose vein, and she remembered the sickness which had accompanied the last three unwanted pregnancies. Silently, she cursed Reuben for his male need to rut. Restlessly, she donned the simple white shirt and lay down, staring at the ceiling.

Betty opened the door carrying the tray of tea. She put it down on a little table by the neat, white window and went to a small cubbyhole in the wall. "All I'm going to do," she said, "is to use this rubber douche filled with herbs and warm water. It will feel a little uncomfortable, but you will lie still for ten minutes. Then I'll help you stand up over that pail." Lilla nodded. So far it didn't seem too bad. She was used to douching. She, like so many women of her time, used douching after intercourse as a form of contraception.

When the douche-bag was empty, Lilla felt a warm, slightly burning sensation as the purging herbs did their work. Betty held Lilla's hand. "Tell me about your husband," she said.

"There's nothing much to tell," Lilla replied. "He's just a man in a woolly suit who makes shoes. That's all he does. Back in Russia we had a nice little house near my sister. Now we have no one. I thought everything would be wonderful once we got to America, but I'm beginning to think I'd rather risk the Czar and his troops than live in this godforsaken place. Why die in the hands of these foreigners when at least, if you got raped back home, it was by one of your own?

"In Russia I used to paint pictures for my sister, and sometimes we'd go over to a neighbor's house. At night we all played piano and danced. Here, all the singing and dancing is done at night by the whores. I even envy them sometimes. At least they are free and," she lowered her eyes, "they get paid." She glanced up at Betty. "They get paid for what I have to do to keep a roof over my head."

Betty nodded. "The day will come," she said, "when women will make their own decisions over their bodies. The day will also come when more women will choose whether to marry or not. I only hope," she said bleakly, "that when we get what we ask for, we will use it responsibly."

Lilla nodded furiously. "I want that day to come," she said.

Betty smiled at her stern, pinched client. "Have you considered that your husband might love you very much?"

Lilla's mouth dropped. "That's the problem. He does love me very much," she said. "But I don't love him. I loved a man a long time ago. He was an artist from St Petersburg. I loved him with all my heart." Tears formed in her eyes. "You see, with him I was myself. Gay, abandoned, and . . ." She blushed. "I've never told anyone this before. I gave myself to him. Nobody, not even Reuben, knows about that."

Betty squeezed her hand gently. "I'll never tell," she said.

"He said he wanted to marry me. I waited and I waited. He never came back again. He's probably married to some beautiful city girl by now." She made a face. "So I married Reuben. Good, kind, boring Reuben."

Betty shook her head. "Well, at least you have a man who wants to love and protect you," she said. "This is no place for a young mother on her own."

"I know . . . Can I stand up now?"

"All right. Let me help you." Slowly, Betty lifted Lilla to her feet.

The potion left Lilla's body and cascaded into the jug. A rush of blood and mucus descended with it. "Do you think it's all gone?"

"I hope so," Betty said. "Occasionally you get what I call a 'meant-to-be' child. They don't let go, ever. But I hope, for your sake, it's gone. If not, I'll give you back your money and you pray for a good birth. I'll be there to help you."

"Thank you." Lilla was suddenly touched by this big, kindly woman.

Betty put her hand on Lilla's shoulder and said, "I'll say goodbye. After you've dressed, please leave by the back door. We have sufficiently nosy neighbors to chart my whereabouts. If you're ever asked, just say you were here consulting me about a certain women's condition, will you?"

"Yes," Lilla promised, "I will."

That night, as Betty was making ready for bed, she sat up before her small, bright fire, drinking a cup of tea. "Well, Prince," she said, patting her small puppy on the head. "We'll see that one again soon. That baby's a sticker, like a burr on a boat. It'll live, whether she wants it to or not."

❧ *CHAPTER 4* ❧

As the small life grew inside Lilla's belly, there was little peace in the Braff household. Lilla, frustrated and upset by her unwanted pregnancy, fumed at Reuben, who tried to comfort her. He tried to placate her with presents. He tried humor. He tried love. But Lilla was implacable.

Reuben felt his wife's heart harden against him. All he could do was watch impotently as her eyes gazed with affection only toward Ben, their eldest son.

One day, early in the summer, a few months before the baby was due, Reuben heard of a small farm-holding, twenty miles west of Middletown. His shoe trade was beginning to expand, but Reuben missed the soil. As a youth, he lived on his father's few acres, and he always felt a deep affinity for the soil which clung to his fingers and muddied the bottom of his trousers.

He loved the little house he built for his family. Often, at night, he walked around the square, single-story cabin, and admired his handiwork. He and Moses Ephraim, a good neighbor, felled and carried trees from the forest behind Middletown. Putting down a floor was the easy part. Building walls, fitting the logs one upon another, took time but they worked, those men, like Trojans. Mud and straw filled the gaps and kept the cabin warm and airtight. Reuben's masterpiece was his chimney. He carefully built a huge range for his wife to cook the meals which bound a Jewish family together.

Lilla might complain, but was as competitive as all her friends, and her cooking was a source of great pride to her. At the small synagogue, also a cabin of logs, she helped prepare the communal food for feasts and high holidays. There she met Ruth Gottstein with her boy, and other mothers. The fact that the Braffs had a house with a big, fine, tiny chimney which glittered in the sunlight made her the envy of the town, but Reuben felt the need to move on. He was an inventive man, and shoemaking did not satisfy his country soul.

"How would you feel about moving to a new house?" Reuben addressed his family one Friday night. He chose Friday particularly because he felt he wanted the occasion to be blessed by the light of the sabbath candles. His four children sat clean and washed in front of him. His very pregnant wife sat in her chair before a huge bowl of *kasha* and a platter proudly bearing a large salmon, caught specially for her by Ben, her special Ben.

Reuben had already taken a day off to see the property. He talked to the farmer, who was taking his family West, like so many others. "I'm off," the farmer said. "I hear I can claim land out there—far more than I've got here."

For Reuben the place was a paradise. Lush trees stood by a large pond in front of the two-story brick house. A pretty white porch encircled the place, and behind the house was a hay barn. To Reuben, the farm resembled a beautiful gentile woman. No Jew, to his knowledge, would dream of owning such a *goyishe* place. All his friends in Middletown lived in log cabins, not very different from the hovels they inhabited in the Old Country before they were hunted and persecuted by the soldiers. Of course, there were the rich in the village, but they chose to spend their money on fine clothes and carriages.

Reuben felt a flutter of love around his heart. All his life, from the time he was a small boy, he wanted a share of what he considered was available in the real world. He resented the continual grumbling of the Jewish community against the *goyim*. He resented just as much the persecution by the fair-haired boys with their cold blue eyes when they caught a Jew on the way to study the Torah at the synagogue. When Reuben was seventeen, he vowed that someday he would leave the enclave of the Jewish community and live alone, free to share friendships between man and man.

He was eager to talk to this tall, serious man who wanted to take his family far away. They would risk the danger of Indian ambushes and attacks by predatory animals as they trekked westward through deserts and forests, looking for the promised land.

After some hard, but friendly, bargaining, Reuben made an appointment to bring his wife to see the property on the next Sunday. Now he sat at Friday night's dinner, waiting for Lilla's approval. "How many rooms does it have?" was Lilla's first question.

"Four," Reuben was happy to answer. The children were immediately keen. Ben, particularly. He was a sturdy boy of eight. Unlike his thin father, Ben was a stocky boy. A shock of black hair hung over his wide, questioning, brown eyes. "I'd love it," he said firmly. Then he checked his mother's face to see if he had contradicted her wishes. Lilla's face remained blank for the moment. She turned to Ben as if waiting to hear his thoughts. Ben decided it was safe to show his feelings. "I don't like this town. The Irish boys fight all the time. I want to go to a school where I don't have to spend all my time fighting. Is there a synagogue over there?"

"We'll still come to the synagogue here," Reuben answered. "The farm is about twenty miles away. We'll ride here any time we need to. There's so much land we can keep all the horses we want."

"And ducks?" Bea, a tiny little three-year-old, was the apple of her father's eye.

"Yes, *shaynalah*, my pretty little one." Reuben leaned forward to pinch her round cheek. "You can have ducks and hens and whatever you want. You see"— Reuben looked at his wife—"I am a family man. I really feel we should live on our own land, and I should be responsible for feeding and caring for my own family, like we did in Russia. I know how to sheer and spin wool. You and the girls can make clothes. I can skin and tan hide for boots and coats. Ben and Isaac can help me grow vegetables and wheat. You can bake and pickle. Remember the old days?" He looked earnestly at his wife. "We all lived by the seasons then. Now, women are forgetting the old skills. Mothers in this town get the bread and butter from the store. Imagine." He shook his head. "Our milk comes from the man down the road now. I miss a cow. I miss tilling and ploughing and planting. All I do all day is sit and make shoes for ladies who complain."

Lilla was thinking. This pregnancy was taking its toll on her, both mentally and physically. Four bedrooms would at least give her some space from her noisy, insistent children. She really did not like or sympathize with their quarrels and misunderstandings. Even her Ben was beginning to fight with the local boys, and Bea whined a lot. But what really attracted her to the whole idea was the realization that she could legitimately have a bedroom of her own. All she needed to do was claim a female sickness and she would never again have to succumb to her husband's advances. She knew Reuben well enough to know that if she presented her case well, whatever the cost to himself, he would leave her alone.

Lilla put her hand on Ben's neck and ruffled his hair. "Let's go and see it." Ben smiled at his mother. She smiled back sweetly and began to carve the fish.

The family made the ride to the farm on the bright, sunny Sunday. Much to Reuben's delight, Lilla gave her consent to move. Reuben finalized the deal with the previous owner, and the Braff family prepared to leave.

Lilla was already enormous. She had another three

months to go in her pregnancy, but she felt she might give birth at any moment. Meeting Ruth Gottstein at her husband's store one day before the big move, Lilla boasted about her new house. Joseph Gottstein listened with interest. "Can you supply kosher meat and chickens?" he said.

"Oh, I think so." Lilla was aglow with happiness. She had always envied Ruth Gottstein, who sat at a small, rickety table doing the bills. Ruth's boy, Danny, played among the sacks of flour.

Joseph, calm and neat, bore no resemblance to Lilla's nervous and erratic husband. "I'll help you move," Joseph offered.

"Thank you," said Lilla. "Reuben will like that. We leave when the baby is six weeks old."

Ruth looked sympathetically at Lilla. "Who is at hand for the birthing?" she asked.

"Betty Thompson, the English nurse." Lilla flushed in guilty remembrance. "I only met her once to make the arrangements."

Ruth smiled. "She is really very, very good. Does Miriam know you're having a gentile for a midwife, instead of our own Eva?"

"If she knows, I don't care. At least Betty can keep her mouth shut. If old Eva is present, the details are all over town by the next morning. Anyway, it's none of Miriam's business. Not that she doesn't make everything her business." Lilla snorted. "She'd take charge of the moon if she could." Ruth and Joseph laughed. "You can laugh." Lilla was stern. "You ought to hear what she says about you and your friendship with that Irish couple next door."

Joseph looked surprised. "Does she really talk about that?"

"Yes. You should hear her."

"Well." Joseph drew himself up. "I came to this country to get away from such bigotry. I want to live my life according to the Torah, not according to some rabbi's wife."

Ruth nodded. "The Coopers are nice people, and Mary is like a grandmother to Danny. We need all the friends we can get in these troubled days. Come, Danny, time for food." Lilla smiled at Ruth and Joseph, and left the shop like a merchant vessel, full sail. "I do feel sorry for her," Ruth said when Lilla had gone. "I know this child was unwanted. Isn't it odd how I so much want another child, and she can have them like popping puppies?"

Joseph drew his wife to him. "I know," he said. "It is a shame. But we have a good life together and the boy," he said, glancing fondly at Danny who was engrossed in building a castle out of a pile of corn. "He will give you many grandchildren. Come. Let's go and eat."

❧ CHAPTER 5 ❧

The baby's entry into the world, after the arduous and miserable pregnancy, was definitely unpleasant and unwelcomed. It was a very good thing that Eva, the Jewish, and somewhat squeamish, midwife, did not witness the birth. Instead it took all of Betty's strength and will to keep a calm head during Lilla's shrieking.

Lilla always had difficult births. She did not have the solid, stoic temperament of her forebears. Every twinge caused her to scream and rant against God and her husband. If she was not cursing the Almighty, she was swearing against the lot of women, forced to bear children. "Come on." Betty was getting exasperated. "Do give over. It's not as bad as all that. And if you'd stop yelling and start concentrating on pushing, the baby would be here a lot sooner."

Lilla writhed in pain. Betty was busy with a large poultice of herbs. "Lie back now," she said, "and this should do the trick." Indeed, the deep, warm poultice spread warmth and comfort through to the baby struggling to be born.

Soon, Betty was ready to catch the little form as the head emerged from its mother's body. A thin wail escaped the newborn's mouth. "Oy!" Lilla exclaimed. "Another girl!"

"But she's beautiful. Look at her delicate hands." The baby's blue-black eyes stared blindly into Betty's smiling face. "There's a love," she crooned. "Let me bathe her." She carried the baby over to a table and immersed the small body in warm water. The tiny girl-child waved her legs appreciatively. She liked the feeling. "Here, dear." A few minutes later Betty handed a clean, sweet-smelling baby to a disgusted Lilla.

Lilla stared down at her fifth child. "I don't want to breastfeed her," she said, pulling away from the baby's searching mouth.

"Well, you'll have to for the first few days. The baby needs your secretions for protection from diseases. But Mrs. Schwartz is in milk. Her baby died a few weeks ago, and I'm sure she'll be glad to feed the little one. She's short of money after the funeral. I'll visit on my way home."

An apologetic cough advertised Reuben's presence. Worried and disheveled, he had waited all day long, wringing his hands and wincing, as his wife labored away in the next room. "Is she all right?" he asked Betty.

"She's fine. Doing well, and you have a beautiful baby daughter."

Reuben strode over to his wife's bed. His eyes were moist. He put his arms around Lilla and kissed her. *"Baruch ha'shem,"* he said. "Blessed be His Name. Another girl." Gingerly he picked up the baby, and clumsily he took her tiny face between his two fingers. "Look," he said delightedly. "She looks just like you."

He remembered the day Ben had been born, when he heard the words, "You have a son." He felt as if his head were full of stars. A year later, he experienced that joy again when Isaac, his second son, was born. Then he remembered the birth of his first daughter Naomi. If he had been bowled over by the birth of his sons, he was knocked flat by his daughter. By the time she was born, Reuben was already established as the best shoemaker in Middletown, and he needed to work long hours at his last. Lilla was perpetually cross and cranky. After she had been in labor for twelve hours, Ben ran over to the shed where Reuben made his shoes crying, "Daddy, Daddy! We have a girl! Come quickly!" As he walked the few yards to the house, Reuben felt a sense of curiosity. He hurried into the house and into the marital bedroom. "Lilla," he said smiling. "A girl!"

Lilla was pleased it wasn't another boy. Ben was all

she could want in a son. Isaac, she largely ignored. At least a girl would keep her company, someone to dress and undress. Naomi was born with a mass of black hair. The midwife Eva grinned. "Here," she said. "Hold your little girl."

Reuben did not like Eva. She was a twisted, little crone with black teeth. He took Naomi into his arms. Naomi was lying quietly. Her eyes were open and unfathomable. Reuben took the baby to the oil lamp. The yellow shadow caused the baby's skin to glow golden in the light. He gazed at her tiny fingers and at her tiny, pink ears. He had always been ashamed of his pendulous earlobes, but this little girl had the prettiest ears in all of Middletown. "She's perfect," he said, moving back to the bed. "Lilla, she is perfect."

Lilla nodded tiredly and said nothing.

"I'll make her the prettiest pair of shoes in America," Reuben said.

Lilla laughed. "And make me a pair to match."

Eva cackled. "She'll make a fine wife for some young man. I'll be there to birth your grandchild."

Reuben frowned. The idea of any young man being near his daughter disturbed him. "Get along," he said. "I have a lot to do. Here." He handed Eva a golden half dollar.

Eva grinned, a malicious light shining in her eyes. Huh, she thought. Jealous already, and the child is only a few hours old. At Bea's birth, Reuben found himself growing no fonder of Eva. He was glad that his newest baby had not been delivered by that horrid old crone.

Lilla grimaced. "Just as long as she doesn't end up like me," she said in disgust. "Where are the children?"

"They're at the rabbi's house. He's waiting to hear the news. He'll be sad not to get the extra cash for circumcision, but then another girl is a fine thing to have in the family." The baby felt safe and at home in her father's welcoming hands. Gently, Reuben replaced the baby in her mother's arms. The child felt the sharpness of her mother's body. She smelled the sourness of a woman who could not love, and she began to cry.

Reluctantly, Betty had to leave. She was tired but, as she walked to her cottage in the trees, she was also triumphant. What had been a small clot of living tissue was now a fully grown, healthy baby. "Thank you, Lord," she prayed on her way home. She stopped at Mrs. Schwartz's house. Could she possibly wet-nurse a baby for a mother who had no milk? Mrs. Schwartz was large and energetic. The loss of her own baby left tearstains on her round warm face. "I'll be glad to," she said to Betty. "My arms feel so cold without my child. You bring her over tomorrow. I'll keep her until she can eat rice."

Betty was relieved. At least her newborn would stay with this nice kind woman for the next months until she was able to eat solid food. Betty, from years of experience, knew that those first six months were vital in forming a child's temperament. Her little baby was going to be safe.

The move to the farmhouse was fraught with hysterics. Lilla realized at the last moment she would be even more of a prisoner in the new life Reuben was offering, tucked far away from civilization. When she was pregnant, the idea of living in the country in a two-story house was attractive. But the reality facing her now was very different. "You can always take the trap," Reuben tried to comfort her. "Ben's nearly old enough to drive you. Or I'll take you in to visit your friends."

They were all packed up to leave. Joseph Gottstein and Vincent Cooper sat patiently with Reuben Braff at the table in the Gottsteins' store, all waiting to help. The remains of a large meal supplied by Ruth lay in front of the men. "Shall we just go quickly to say goodbye to the little one?" Reuben asked his wife. As yet, the baby had no name. Since she was taken to Mrs. Schwartz, the wet-nurse, Reuben had made efforts to see his little daughter as often as he could, but he greatly minded her absence from his own home. He always loved to hold his children and to feel their warm bodies moving against his chest.

Lilla was not inclined to make the journey across to Mrs. Schwartz's house to say goodbye to a baby who didn't even know her. She was just relieved to get her figure back and have time to pack her clothes without attending to the tedious demands of a baby. "Reuben," she said. "I'm still not well. You go over and tell Mrs. Schwartz we're leaving now, and that you'll pick up the baby in six months' time."

Reuben was shocked by Lilla's attitude. He had been more affected by the birth of his last baby than he had ever been by the others. He resolved to call the girl Nora, after his much loved grandmother. "Nora," he whispered, whenever he visited her at Mrs. Schwartz's. He could swear the baby understood him. He put his index finger into the baby's tiny hand. The little fingers closed. Nora's rosebud mouth blew appreciative bubbles. Her long, brown eyelashes fluttered and she fell asleep holding fast to Reuben's hand.

Reuben was no surprise visitor to Mrs. Schwartz's house. Unbeknown to Lilla, he often visited on his way home from work. He loved to sit with Nora pressed close to his chest and tell her all about the shoes he was making for the people of Middletown. In the first week of her stay, he had made her a pair of velvet slippers with minute, pearl buttons. Mrs. Schwartz clucked cheerfully around them both.

Today, Reuben went alone once again to Mrs. Schwartz's house and held his daughter in his arms. He told her all about the new house, and he promised the baby he was getting a goat for her and, soon, he would come for her. "I'll visit you and I'll think of you." He always felt he had missed out in the lives of his other children. He had been too busy working. He missed the first words, the first steps. Lilla was not the sort of mother to treasure them for him, either. This time, he promised himself, I'll be there.

Kissing his Nora goodbye, and thanking Mrs. Schwartz for her help, Reuben Braff hurried off to tie on the last piece of bedding before the traps set off for the farm.

CHAPTER 6

Ben was the first of the Braff family to push open the farmhouse door and enter the hall. Reuben followed.

He swung Lilla into his arms and carried her across the threshold. "There," he said. "Here is your house."

Although they had all visited the farm on several occasions, they had never seen it without furniture. Naomi, with Bea holding tight to the edge of her skirt, ran up the wide central staircase built of solid pine. The previous owner had obviously loved this house. The staircase was well-constructed. The girls ran in and out of the bedrooms.

Lilla ran up the stairs. She made for the room in the far corner of the landing. "This one," she said to her startled family, "this one will be mine." Reuben hung his head. Lilla had told him she intended to have her own room. He didn't understand why her announcement should so embarrass him.

The children looked astonished. "You mean," Isaac asked incredulously, "you mean you're not going to share a room with our father?"

"That's just what I mean," Lilla said blithely. Then, seeing the look on Ben's face, she softened. "It doesn't mean that I don't love your father," she said. She floated down the stairs and put her small hand on Ben's shoulder.

"Let's go and see the barn," said Reuben.

Lilla smiled at Reuben. "I don't want to see the barn," she said. "I want to see my kitchen where I shall cook lovely meals for my darling husband. Come on, Reuben," she said. "Let's explore."

Reuben felt a glow of contentment sweep over his soul. Here he was with his new brick house, his beautiful wife, and his lovely children. Outside the front door was his own cart with two gray horses and Beauty awaiting patiently the arrival of Vincent and

Joseph not far behind. Reuben followed Lilla into the large square kitchen that sat at the back of the house. The previous owner had been justly proud of it. All the counters and kitchen cabinets were made from hand-carved teak. The wood glowed soft and red from many years of wax polish. "He got it from a Chinaman," Reuben said. "They brought in a load of wood from the Orient. Look, Lilla," he said, opening the cupboards. "He lined them all with cedar wood. You'll never get flies in here."

Lilla was pleased. Wait, she thought. Just wait until Joseph Gottstein sees all this and tells Ruth. Lilla felt a moment of hatred as she imagined Ruth's lovely face. Silly cow, thought Lilla. Fat, uninteresting, *old* silly cow. "Come on, darling." She smiled at Reuben. "I can hear the others coming."

Together, arm in arm, they walked from the kitchen, passing the parlor on the way. Vincent and Joseph arrived within half an hour of each other. Both were full of admiration for the little farm. Reuben took them on a tour of the grounds. "Whew. You can raise a few cows on these acres," Vincent Cooper remarked when he looked at the hay barn. "That's a good roof the man put up."

"Yes." Reuben was pleased. "He was from Holland. He told me that he built this barn in the Dutch style. You know, I really do wonder what a little Jew-boy from the Old Country is doing walking around a farm that belonged, till today, to the *goyim*." Suddenly, he very much wished that his mother could see him. There was still no news of her. The last he had heard, from another immigrant who had arrived in Middletown a year ago, was that she was alive and well. Though it agonized Reuben at the time, he had learned to bear his father's death, years ago, but the thought of his mother's death some day was unimaginable. Every Friday night, when Lilla lit the candles, he said a prayer for his mother's safety. Quietly, without telling even Lilla, he was putting money away a little at a time. As long as he could believe that one day he could send for his mother to join him in this new land he loved even more passionately than he had loved Russia, he could cope with the thought of her absence.

But now, standing in the quiet of the hay barn, he felt close to Joseph and Vincent. They had all arrived in America from far corners of the world. They had helped to build each other's houses in Middletown, just as they had all cooperated with the other men in the village and cut wood for the long bleak white winters ahead. "Ah well," said Reuben, "I'll miss you both, but I'll be in town several times a month, and we can play cards."

"Sure," Joseph grinned. "And you can stay the night at my place."

"Yeah. That'll be nice." Reuben laughed. "Lilla can't nag. I meant that as a joke, of course."

"A joke?" Vincent grinned. "My Mary was furious. The last time we played poker, I lost!"

"Huh. Wait till the rabbi's wife finds out you taught two Jews to play poker." Reuben laughed.

"Well"—Vincent looked at Reuben with a twinkle in his eyes—"We'll say I'm an honorary Jew, shall we? Without the operation, of course." The three men were laughing loudly when Lilla called them for lunch.

Slowly, by the end of November, Reuben began to master farming the American way, and the children responded to life on the farm like daisies planted on a compost heap. Vincent came down with Joseph in the autumn to help harvest the field of wheat. The children picked the apples and pears in the fruit orchard, and it was Ben's job to place each piece of fruit on the huge racks which ran the length of the barn. Vincent was a source of amazement and fascination to Ben, full of stories about his former life in Ireland.

Vincent was in an amiable mood on his second visit. He and Ben were digging up potatoes. The rich earth turned easily. Vincent put his huge shoulders behind each thrust of the fork. Ben squatted and pulled the large, earth-smelling potatoes from the ground. He loved the smell of the autumn earth, but Vincent missed the smell of his own Irish soil. American earth, in all its richness, lacked the smell of peat.

Vincent missed cutting his peat for the winter from the bog at the back of his farm in Ireland. Every year, he and his boys used to take their hoes and cut the peat into neat squares. Every year, the men of the Cooper family used to stake the peat against the wall of the farmhouse. The whole family rejoiced the night of the first fire. Mary always used to cook a special meal—Vincent's favorite—roast pork, which came from his own pigs. Much as he mourned each pig he slaughtered, he knew the meat would keep them through the long, cold winter. Added to the huge dish of roast pork, with its brown crust of crackling, Mary made a dish of roast potatoes and a stuffing which Vincent would swear could only have been made with the help of the angels. But it was Mary's gravy which made the boys vow they would never look at another woman, unless she were able to make a gravy to match. Deep brown, and so thick you could stand a serving spoon in its depth, the jug of gravy was passed hand to hand. In reverent silence the boys waited for their father, the head of the household, the lord and master of the family, to give his verdict. Mary always smiled at this point. Lord and master he might be to the boys and to the outside world, but she knew she ruled supreme in the home.

Vincent, much older than Reuben or Joseph, found the transition to the new land hard. He was as Irish as the peat he dug. The smell of the peat fire carried in the smoke the history of Ireland. To him, Ireland was indeed the land of Angels. True, she was being raped by the English, but then Ireland, eternal and terrible in battle, would bide her time and then, like the great dinosaurs which lay deep beneath the bogs, she would rise up and shake the invading British off her soil.

All these stories he shared with Ben. "I'll leave my bones in the soil here," he told the boy. "But you and your people will never settle."

"No." Ben was always very sure of this fact. "I want," Ben said, "to see Jerusalem." He sighed. "I always dreamed I'd become a *bar mitzvah* there." He made a face. "The Middletown synagogue is not exactly how I'd seen it."

Vincent laughed. "Well, that's why I don't worry about buildings: buildings can be burned, villages can be sacked. But what you have in here," he tapped his heart, "that's where God is. It doesn't have to be in a synagogue or a church."

"Does that mean you're not a Christian?" Ben asked, still not fully reconciled to the fact that he felt so close to a man who was not Jewish.

"That's why I'm not anything," Vincent answered. "Just a lover of God."

The pile of potatoes grew. Vincent, Ben, and Reuben moved the pile to the back of the barn. Vincent showed Reuben and Ben how to earth them up. "Cover them well with sand," he said, "and then they won't grow green." The men of the Braff family were learning.

The first few months on the farm, though productive, were very difficult. Reuben and his children all worked hard. Lilla, however, was content to spend most of her time in her room. She deplored housework. She had done enough cleaning as a child in Russia, she reckoned, to last her a lifetime. Naomi was now getting old enough to do some of the chores around the house. The girl swept and dusted and polished with her younger sister, Bea, tagging along, busily pretending to help. With the girls working in the house, Nora still in Mrs. Schwartz's care, and Isaac and her Ben helping Reuben outside, Lilla found the demands on her time easing. Occasionally, as she sat in her room, she resumed the diversion she had laid down years ago: her drawing. Perched at her window, she sketched the trees, the barn, the sun glinting on the top of Ben's head as seen from above, the fields beyond the barnyard, and the chimneys of a big house distant across the fields.

Reuben grew increasingly aware just how much he missed any intimate contact with her as she suffered, apparently endlessly, from her mysterious womanly complaint. Still, Reuben could never imagine life without his beautiful Lilla.

As often as he could, he found reason to visit Middletown on the pretext of some bit of business or other. During these visits, he would spend as many hours as possible at Mrs. Schwartz's house, hugging and playing with his baby daughter, Nora.

During one particular trip to Middletown, Reuben found himself in a chance meeting with the rabbi. Reuben had not intended to discuss his private life with him, but, in the end, Reuben was surprised to hear himself discuss deeply personal feelings which seemed to express themselves through their own will. The rabbi was hardly surprised, nor was he unaccustomed to discussing such matters with other men: sexual love was very much a part of the laws of Jewish life, and sexual union was considered a great blessing in marriage. "You see," Reuben said with great difficulty, "my wife has been suffering from a certain condition. She says she can't have intercourse."

The rabbi looked at Reuben. "My dear fellow," he said, putting an arm around Reuben's shoulder, "they all say that."

Reuben was amazed. "Not my wife," he said firmly. "She wouldn't lie to me. We've always had a perfectly good marriage."

Mort punched him lightly on the shoulder. "Go and see Molly Parkington. She'll give it to you for a dollar."

"You mean you go to a whore?"

The rabbi sighed. "Reuben," he said gently, as if he were addressing a small child. "Yes, I do. And so does half the town. It satisfies the need to release myself without having to spend the next day feeling guilty because my beloved Miriam goes about with a smile on her face that reminds me of the first Jewish Martyr. I pay for what I want. And that is that."

Reuben shook his head. "I don't believe half the men in town go to her. What about Joseph Gottstein? He seems to have a good wife."

The rabbi snorted. "That's very true. He's a lucky man. I don't know." He looked down wistfully at Reuben. "I don't know what's happening to women these days. Back in the old country, they had their place. Now they are turning into warriors."

Reuben took his leave and he politely thanked the rabbi for his advice. On the way over to Mrs. Schwartz's, he comforted himself. I'll never go to a whore, he promised himself. My Lilla's all I want, even if I never get to share her bed again. I'll be faithful to her. With that promise, he cheerfully went to visit his little daughter.

Only once during the early months on the farm, did Lilla go to Middletown with Reuben to visit Nora. Lilla found the baby sticky and crotchety. Nora did not recognize her mother and wanted to spend no time in her arms. Lilla took this as a personal insult. "She'll get used to you," Reuben pleaded in the trap during the ride back to the farm.

"If she's so happy there, why don't we leave her with Mrs. Schwartz for good? After all, she's more attached to her than she is to me."

Reuben, however, could not entertain the thought of not having his Nora come to live with him as soon as she was weaned. With each of his visits, he watched Nora grow and change. His Nora, at nine months, was a perfectly formed little woman. She still had a protruding stomach and was making brave efforts to pull herself up on the ample Victorian chair which filled Mrs. Schwartz's overstuffed living room.

When Nora was weaned at eleven months, Reuben succeeded at last in convincing Lilla that it was time for their youngest daughter to return home. In preparation for the great day, Reuben went to work building a new crib for Nora. "What's wrong with the old one?" Lilla asked.

"Nothing." Reuben smiled at his wife. "I just feel like making a present for her. She has such a sweet smile, you know, and . . ." He stopped. He realized his wife resented the child. He learned to hold his tongue.

The day for Nora's return finally arrived. It was heralded by a huge wind blowing from the distant sea, sending large white clouds scudding across the sky. Gulls, blown off course, landed on the farm chimney and complained loudly as Reuben cleared the trap. Then, with his wife beside him, he set off to Middletown to retrieve his infant daughter.

At Mrs. Schwartz's house, Lilla snatched Nora abruptly from her familiar cradle in the spare room. Nora did not much enjoy being held in her mother's arms. Mrs. Schwartz's arms were plump like pillows. Her double chin was a soft place to snuggle. Her great breasts were a comfort when Nora cried or fell down. Lilla's arms were thin, and her wrist bones prominent. It felt like being embraced by a scarecrow. The wind on the ride there had pulled the pins out of Lilla's hair, which covered the little girl like the mane of a horse. Nora was not used to horses.

Once when Nora was in her pram, a huge black horse had wandered across the square and stuck its inquisitive nose into her face. Dumb with fright, she could see up the tunnels of its nostrils. Even more terrifying were the huge teeth. The horse was a good age, and the teeth were yellow. It blew a friendly greeting to the baby. Nora, drenched in the massive sneeze, opened her mouth and screamed. The horse, mildly surprised, ambled off. Mrs. Schwartz had come out to find Nora nearly hysterical. "Poor child," she had said, taking Nora into her arms. "Nora, my poor baby. What on earth can have happened to have upset you so?" Wrapped in the warmth of the ample body, Nora had breathed deeply and, reassured by the warm musky odor of the woman who had fed her, she had fallen asleep from exhaustion.

Now, three months since her horrifying encounter with the horse, Nora found herself in the arms of an unknown woman. She recognized her father and she wriggled with joy when she saw him. She sensed something was wrong because Mrs. Schwartz was crying and her largely silent husband, Mr. Schwartz, was comforting her. "I'll bring her back to visit." Reuben was sad to see the wet-nurse cry. Reuben and Lilla, with Nora in her arms, climbed back into the trap to return to their farm.

"Come along." Lilla was bored with the whole scene. "She's only a wet-nurse," she remarked as they set out.

"I know." Reuben flicked the reigns. "But she loves Nora."

But now, even Nora's name did not seem safe. "That's another thing," snapped Lilla. "I don't see why we have to call her by your grandmother's name. She's been dead for years."

"Because it honors my grandmother," Reuben explained. "It's the Jewish custom to name a child after a dead relative. You know that."

"But Nora's a horrible name. I hate the sound of it."

"It's a lovely name," Reuben held firm.

Lilla soon grew bored with the entire discussion.

"Call her what you like," she conceded in the end. "Just see you keep her quiet."

"Oh, I will," said Reuben as he looked down at Nora in her mother's arms.

Nora felt very afraid of this woman who held her so clumsily. The black hair that whipped over her little body reminded her of the horse's mane. Lilla tried to talk to her, but Lilla's teeth looked sharp and cruel. Nora started to shriek. "Oh, I give up!" Lilla snapped. "She won't stop that awful noise. You take her."

Reuben stopped the wagon and took Nora in one arm. Holding her against his chest, he grasped the reins in his other hand and called the horses into motion. But Nora was still frightened, still upset by Mrs. Schwartz's absence and by the sharpness in her mother's voice. She cried on and she did not stop until she fell asleep, unable to sob any longer.

⚓ CHAPTER 7 ⚓

During the winter, Lilla was reluctantly busy in the kitchen. Even though Naomi and Bea managed most of the cleaning, Lilla was still left with the task of cooking and with no other women around to compare her cooking to, she found it a singularly unrewarding job. Nora spent her days in the corner of the kitchen, in the new cradle which Reuben had built especially for her. She was only left in the cradle because Lilla's impatience with her daughter worried Reuben.

One evening, he came home from a day's work outside to find his little baby bruised. "How did this happen?" he asked Lilla, seeing a blue, swollen lump on Nora's head.

"Mommy hit her," Naomi said loudly. "Mommy hit her. She's always hitting her."

Lilla was furious. "Naomi," she said, "you must be mistaken. You know she fell down the stairs. I was just comforting her."

"No, you weren't." Naomi was the fiercest of all the children. Long ago she had given up placating her fickle mother. Naomi stood motionless at the kitchen table. She said a quick prayer, asking God to avert her mother's wrath from the dinner table.

"I don't want to see Nora hurt like that again!" For once Reuben was really angry. He picked up Nora from the floor and left the room. During dinner that night he could be heard in the barn, banging and sawing. Lilla didn't dare disturb him. Never before had she seen him so firm and determined. She put his dinner in the oven of the big black range and waited. She did not even scold the children. They, knowing there had been yet another scene, crept quietly to bed.

Nora was in the barn with her father. Reuben put her in the hay cart and wrapped her in a horse blanket. Rosey, the large and very pregnant cow, looked on lovingly from the next stall. Nora did not want to go to sleep at all. She sat with her fat hands full of hay. When she was fussy because she was hungry, Reuben went across to the vegetable racks and chose a fine, big, red apple, still fresh from the autumn harvest.

Wiping it carefully on his jacket, he handed it to Nora and continued his labor of love. She sucked on it enthusiastically.

By midnight, Nora was asleep in the hay cart, her bruised head forgotten. Reuben had finished his pen. He carried Nora to her crib in the girls' room, then he carried the pen to the kitchen. Lilla was waiting for him in her nightdress. Reuben looked at her sharply. "Why," he asked, "are you waiting up?"

"I just thought I'd keep you company," she said sweetly. "Here." She moved gracefully to the stove and bent over. A familiar surge of lust shot through Reuben's groin. Her small, tight buttocks always made him want to place his hands on either cheek and thrust and thrust until he was spent. "I've kept your food warm," Lilla smiled. "Your favorite. Chicken and *kasha.*" She sat down beside him at the large kitchen table. "Eat," she said. She picked up his spoon and dug it into the mound of *kasha*. The old, familiar smell of the buckwheat groats and onions transported Reuben back to his childhood home. Every sabbath, from when he was tiny, his mother would take the family's only silver spoon and feed him *kasha*. Lilla leaned toward him. "Here," she said. "Try it." She pushed the spoon gently into his mouth.

Reuben moaned with pleasure. He felt his saliva well into the back of his throat. The hot smell of the roasted groats filled his head with a well-remembered perfume. He opened his eyes and saw the swell of Lilla's firm breasts. The gold of the locket glinted excitingly between them. Engorged with food and lust, Reuben forgot himself completely. He reached for his wife, and they fell to the floor. As he lay between her legs, thrusting for his life, he was unaware of Lilla's face, staring blankly at the ceiling. I'll have to do a bit more of this, she thought, if this is what keeps him happy. After all, there are plenty of *shiksas* who would do anything for a house like this. The moon nodded through the window and cast a cold, imperious glance at Reuben's bare buttocks.

Lilla was up early the next morning. She bustled and sang around the kitchen. Reuben, out in the barn with his very pregnant cow, felt a deep sense of loneliness. Somehow, the events of the night before had left him internally homeless. True, Lilla had been sweet and appreciative. He remembered the smile on her face after he was spent.

He had walked Lilla to the door of her bedroom and had winced when she'd said, "I do hope I'm not pregnant again."

Immediately, Reuben felt like a monster and a betrayer. "I didn't hurt you?" he asked anxiously.

"No," she said.

"Did you enjoy it?"

"Of course," said Lilla and kissed him a stony farewell for the night.

Now, in the bright, innocent sunlight, alone with his cow, Reuben felt guilty. His cow looked at him with benign soft-lashed eyes. She blew her warm haystack breath over his face.

Reuben took her head into his arms and kissed her broad nose. "Why can't women be more like you?" he said.

The cow rolled her eyes and flicked her tail.

Reuben could see the calf moving inside her huge, extended stomach. "Not long now," he said.

"Reuben!" Lilla called across the courtyard. "Come and eat!"

Reuben left the barn and stood for a moment, looking across the fields. Winter had arrived. Slowly and inexorably, her grip had changed the surrounding countryside. Her icy fingers had stripped the leaves off the trees. If she is merciful this year, thought Reuben, we can get to know the neighbors. Maybe Lilla could find a friend. Reuben sighed. Slaked lust and guilt made bad bedfellows.

A gust of wind blew his hat to the ground. His cow called and Reuben ran back to the barn. Rosey looked at Reuben with pain in her eyes. "Ach," Reuben smiled. He ran his hands over her belly. He put his ear to the cow's side. "All quiet," he said. He patted Rosey's warm flanks and felt the urgent ripple of a contraction. Rosey heaved a sigh and looked hopefully at Reuben's face. "Don't worry," he said. "I'll get Ben and you'll be fine." Rosey heaved again, and Reuben raced back to the house.

"Ben!" Reuben yelled. "Rosey's in labor! Come! Come quickly!"

From her new pen, Nora looked up lovingly at her father. Reuben swung the girl into his arms.

"No!" Lilla was immediately angry. "Put her down," she said. Hands on her hips, she glared at Reuben. "She's too young to see anything so disgusting. Don't be silly, Reuben."

Reuben looked into the metallic darkness of his wife's eyes. At times unbidden, he remembered the same look in the eyes of a snake, poised to strike him in the woods of his childhood. "But we're farmers, Lilla," he said. "There's nothing wrong with seeing a calf born."

"Maybe you're a farmer," she said, "but I never said I wanted to be a farmer's wife!" The words came out so suddenly that Lilla surprised even herself. Reuben stood, staring at her speechlessly. "Go on," she said in a lower voice. "Take the boys out. But leave Nora here. Watching a birth is not the sort of thing for my daughters. Give her to me." She held out her arms.

Nora clung to Reuben and started to cry.

Ben stood by the back door with his father. He watched his mother's face. She's right, he thought. She's not a farmer's wife. She deserves more. How could anyone as beautiful and graceful as his mother bear to live like this? "Come on, dad," he said, "let's go."

Reuben handed Nora to Lilla. "Maybe you're right," he said.

Naomi, with Bea's hand in her own, turned to her mother. "I'm going to see the calf born," she said firmly. She looked at her father. "You're a coward. You let mother do whatever she likes. You're afraid of her, aren't you?"

Reuben stared at his forceful daughter. "No," he said. "I'm not afraid of your mother. I love her. How can you say such things? And in front of your sister?" He turned to Bea. "You want to stay in here with your mother, don't you?"

"Oh, I'm tired of all this," Lilla snapped. She looked down at Nora sobbing in her arms. "Take her. Do whatever you like. And take Bea and Naomi, too. I don't care. I'm going to go upstairs and lie down." She pushed Nora into Reuben's arms. "I have a headache. Go away." Lilla put a small white hand to her brow.

Rosey's loud bellow caused Reuben to clutch Nora in his arms and leave the house. Naomi, Isaac, and Ben ran behind him. Ben followed slowly, unsurely.

Alone, Lilla stood in the hall. Her life, she felt, was a trap. She loved the house, but the people in it were not part of what she expected from the universe. As a little girl, she had always imagined herself sitting some day in elegant drawing rooms talking to well-dressed people about politics, books, and art. When she had married Reuben, she had stood at his side with a vision of their life together. In her vision, she had seen Reuben making sufficient money for them to live in a tree-lined street in a solid house in the city with a parlor full of good furniture and lined with books. In the corner of the parlor, near the baby-grand piano, was her easel with a delicate watercolor of a vase full of spring flowers . . .

Lilla walked up the stairs to her bedroom. Instead, she thought, she had five children, all alien to her—even her Ben seemed to be growing away from her—and a husband who turned out to be a farmer, more interested in his cow than in the neighbors across the wintering fields.

Lilla pushed aside her drawing pad and took her seat by the window. Far across the fields, she could see the smoke from her nearest neighbor's house, the big house with the chimneys which she sometimes sketched: the house where, Lilla had learned through gossip, the Witney-Hays lived.

She heard the Witney-Hay family was British, and rumor also had it they had left England in a hurry over gambling debt, and that they had "fast" friends. They believed in the new ideas, even in the emancipation of women. Mrs. Witney-Hay had been seen in bloomers once on a visit to Middletown. Lilla had seen her go past in a hansom cab. Mrs. Witney-Hay was driving herself, a massive, gray-haired lady. Lilla had particularly noticed her hands: powerful hands which maintained a grip on the reins at once relaxed, yet completely in control.

Lilla sat by the window, thinking about those hands. Suddenly she wanted very much to know Mrs. Witney-Hay. I'll walk over and leave a note, she thought. My brown dress with the green velvet cloak, she promised. The green velvet always stirred her sexually. The velvet fell around her and brushed her arms with such a soft, caring gentleness Lilla felt loved by the cloak.

In the beyond of her childhood, there had been little human caring, only the efforts of her older sister who struggled to look after her once her father went off to the cities. Her mother's death had left Lilla with no soft arms to hold her. She had inherited instead only the locket and a driving ambition to succeed: to leave the hard, dark, earth-encrusted life and to soar into the soft, warm world of silver and furs . . .

But, for now, the green cloak would suffice. Lilla changed hurriedly and left the house.

Nora was perched on the railing of the stable. Isaac, her devoted brother, held her firmly. Bea and Naomi crouched beside Reuben. "Is anything happening?" Ben whispered. He held Rosey's head in his arms and kissed her nose.

"Yes," Reuben grinned. "Push, Rosey! Push!" Rose grunted loudly. "Everybody!" Reuben stood up. "Let's all push."

Rosey heaved a strained moan. Slowly, the birth

canal opened and a white caul emerged. Reuben took the sack into his hands and then, as the children shouted encouragement, he pushed his hand deep into the cow and gently pulled the calf toward him. "Push, Rosey!" Naomi and Bea clapped their hands.

A moment later, Reuben had the calf securely in his arms. He pulled away the remaining covering and took the calf across the floor to Naomi. "Here, darling," he said. "He's yours. Look at his face."

Naomi smiled at her father. She looked into the calf's brown eyes so like her own, and she put her hand on his head. "Mine," she said contentedly. "Mine."

Reuben carried the calf back to its mother. Ben looked at his father. He felt puzzled. Why did his father, so different from Lilla, seem at home here in the barn? In the house, he always looked out of place. He watched Reuben walk over to a bucket of water and immerse his clever, capable hands. The weak, winter light caught the man and the children in its pale shadows.

After the excitement of the birth, the other children were silent for a moment. Ben looked at Isaac, his brother, so like his father, never questioning. Naomi, fiercely loyal to Reuben, sat beside little, fat Bea. Then Ben looked at Nora. Everyone looked at Nora. She had such a glow to her eyes, such an alert look on her face, and she brought such light into her life, that Ben felt torn between the two worlds. He loved his mother and he loved her stories of the great cities and huge events she dreamed of. He also, he realized, loved the peaceful predictability of his father's world. Which world, Ben wondered, would be his?

Rosey was licking the calf with her huge, pink

tongue. Ben heard the front door of the house slam. Mother must be going out, he thought.

Reuben dried his hands on a piece of sackcloth. "Your mother needs some fresh air," he said. "A walk will do her good. Come on. Let's all go and drink tea."

☙ *CHAPTER 8* ❧

Lilla stood nervously by the imposing front door. Visiting the Gottsteins or the rabbi's wife was one thing, but standing before the Witney-Hays' house was another. Apart from Betty Thompson, who frequently visited her little charge Nora, Lilla knew no English people. As if watched by an unseen presence, the front door swung open. A parlor maid stood before Lilla. "Yes?" she said.

Lilla was surprised. She assumed, at least, this was a parlor maid. Certainly, in the novels Lilla had read, the heroine usually had a variety of servants. The dashing hero was always dropping his top hat into the waiting hands of a butler or a maid. "Is Mrs. Witney-Hay home?" Lilla said at last. "If not, I'll leave a note . . ."

"Susan?" A melodious voice called from another room. "Susan, do we have a visitor?"

"Yes, ma'am. A lady is here to see you."

"Bring her in," the voice commanded. "I could do with a visitor in this godforsaken place."

Lilla followed the maid into the hall up to a large mahogany door. Susan pushed open the door, already ajar. Lilla stood in the doorway and stared at the woman who sat regally, by an open fire, in a large chair. "Come in," said Mrs. Witney-Hay. "Do come in, my dear. I've been very bored all day. I'm delighted to see you."

Lilla blushed; then she realized all her life she had waited for this moment, for this room. This was the room she had dreamed of, even as a child. This was the room Lilla *belonged* in, with the walls of books, the thick Persian carpet, the polished mahogany furniture. And this woman, with her craggy, kindly face, was home for her. "Thank you," Lilla said. "Thank you very much."

"Tea?" Mrs. Witney-Hay asked. Lilla nodded. Susan curtsied and then left. "Well, dear. We're neighbors, aren't we?"

"Yes." Lilla nodded. "We are."

Mrs. Witney-Hay inclined her head. "I heard from my gardener, who chats with your husband." Lilla grimaced. How like Reuben to gossip with servants. "You're the Braff family. You used to live right in Middletown, and now you're stuck out here in the boondocks, like me."

"Yes." Lilla smiled tentatively. "Before that we came from Russia. Then we moved to Middletown. Then I had five children, and we decided a country life was what they needed. We still have to find a school, but they do love the farm. Of course," she paused, "it's difficult for me." Lilla looked intently into her neighbor's pale, alert, blue eyes. "I am an artist. But with a family, there's hardly any time, and there is very little intellectual company to be found here in the middle of nowhere."

Mrs. Witney-Hay smiled and nodded. "Never mind, my dear," she said. "You know me now. Do call me Amelia. And your name?"

"Lilla." Her name left her like an arrow and plunged itself into Amelia Witney-Hay's heart. Lilla felt a small trembling in her soul. A soaring feeling of excitement chilled her body. The top of her head felt as if it were about to lift and float to the ceiling. Amelia, she said to herself. Lilla smiled at her new friend. "I am glad to have a friend."

"Oh, you shall have many," Amelia said. "We have a woman's group that meets here every week." Amelia's blue eyes became intense. "These are the women of the new persuasion."

"You mean women's suffrage?"

Amelia laughed. "Not just that, Lilla dear. There's a whole new world out there. Not just for men and families, but also for women who want to live any way they please. Look at me," she said. "I chose not to have children. My time is my own. If I wish to read all day, I read. If I wish to travel, I travel."

"What about your husband?" Lilla asked. "Doesn't he mind?"

Amelia leaned forward and put her square hand on Lilla's knee. "My dear child. We are husband and wife in name only."

A jolt of electricity shot through Lilla's body. The hand sat heavy and warm on her knee. A rising sense of panic and joy filled her cold, sharp body. For the first time in her life, she sat in the presence of the one thing she had longed for: genuine freedom. "Oh, Amelia!" she cried, "how wonderful!"

"Wonderful, indeed." The woman laughed. Then she said, "And I must—if I may comment personally—congratulate you on your voice. Your husband, my gardener tells me, still sounds like a foreigner. But your accent sounds perfectly American. You must have worked very hard."

Lilla bowed her head proudly. She had worked hard. But never, she thought, had she heard a sound so charming as Amelia's British accent.

At that moment the maid reentered carrying a butler's tray. "Tea, ma'am."

"Thank you, Susan." The hand withdrew from Lilla's knee and the warmth seeped out of Lilla's body. "Milk and sugar, dear?"

Lilla nodded, feeling a million miles away. If only Ruth Gottstein could see me now, she thought. And Miriam. Lilla was already planning a triumphant visit to Middletown to announce her new friendship. Maybe one day, she thought, sitting by the side of this handsome woman, who was now carefully pouring a thin stream of yellow liquid into a waiting white, virginal porcelain cup . . .

"Here you are, Lilla." Amelia passed the cup across to Lilla. "An English cup of tea: Earl Gray. I think you'll like it."

Lilla took a sip. The slightly smoky liquid ran down the back of her throat and connected itself to her stomach. There it settled and waited for the rest. Lilla relaxed. Her first proper, English tea (not thick and heavy like the tea at Betty Thompson's) tasted wonderful.

"I'll give you a box to take home." Amelia smiled. "Now tell me all about your family."

Both women sat by the fire in the evening shadows, and Lilla told Amelia everything there was to tell about her life.

* * *

It was dark when Lilla came home. Reuben, in his wife's absence, had made supper for the children. They sat, full of cabbage soup laced with spicy pork sausage, in a contented silence. Reuben had decided a while ago that *kosher* food was not for him or his family in their new life. "We are Americans," he lectured the children repeatedly. "We do what Americans do."

Hearing Lilla's step on the porch, the children looked up nervously. Lilla opened the door of her own house and smiled a huge, warm smile at her hall. "Rugs," she whispered to herself. "Lots of rugs and a piano." Hearing the children in the kitchen, she floated across the floor.

Reuben stood up. "Lilla," he said. "I was worried."

Lilla looked at him. "You needn't have been," she said, removing her green, velvet cloak and letting it slide to the floor. "I've been visiting with my friend Amelia." Lilla stood in the green puddle at her feet.

"I'm so glad," Reuben said. "At last you have a friend."

"Yes." Lilla nodded. "She will be a good friend for me. She's a writer. Did you know that?"

Reuben shook head head. "No, I didn't. But I'm glad for you. Her gardener says she has women visitors without their men."

Lilla snorted and then frowned. "Why not?" she said. "There's a new world out there. And, Reuben, please do not hobnob with the servants."

Reuben hung his head.

"Anyway." Lilla smiled at her children. "There's a good school nearby. Amelia told me all about it. We can start all of you at lessons on Monday, and I will visit Amelia every Monday afternoon." Her gaze fell on Nora.

"Don't worry, darling," Reuben said quickly. "I'll look after Nora for you."

Lilla turned and walked up the stairs to her bedroom, her head full of plans for what life would become.

❧ *CHAPTER 9* ❧

Soon there was talk in Middletown. Miriam, the rabbi's wife, met Ruth with Danny by her side in the Gottsteins' shop. In among the yellow, tallow candles hanging from the ceiling, Miriam practically engulfed Ruth with her rage. "She's been seen," Miriam spat, "sitting by herself with that woman, that gentile woman from England! And"—she dropped her voice—"she actually boasted to me that she attends meetings with other women to talk about books and politics. Since when have books and politics been subjects for decent women?"

Ruth sighed. "Miriam, if Lilla has at last found some happiness and made a good friend, I'm happy for her. Last time we were over to see them, Lilla was a changed woman. Why, she's even put on a little weight. Reuben looks so happy. The children love their school. Even little baby Nora has lost her frown. Anyway, where's the harm in a little talking? Mary and I talk all the time."

Miriam's mouth took a sour, downward turn. "We're losing our old ways, mixing with other people. Soon we'll lose our own God."

Ruth raised her eyebrows. "No, we won't," she said. "You don't become a pagan just by talking to gentiles!" She laughed. Then, seeing the weariness on Miriam's face, she grew serious. "Miriam, you look awful. Is something wrong?"

Miriam grimaced. "Have you heard?" she said quietly.

Ruth nodded. "About Molly Parkington? Yes, I'm afraid I did hear. I didn't want to believe it."

Miriam shrugged. "Everybody knows. I'm the laughingstock of Middletown. Mort has humiliated me in front of all the synagogue. How could he do this to me? How could he go to a—a—" She could not make herself say the dreaded word. "Well, you know what kind of woman I mean," she said at last.

Ruth felt sorry for this angry, fat woman. "It's a terrible thing." She shook her head. "I'm sorry." She looked Miriam in the eye. "If I were in your situation, I'd wonder if Joseph and I were truly both working at our marriage," she said softly, trying to be tactful.

Miriam looked outraged. "I'm a wonderful wife," she said, drawing herself up. "Don't tell me what to do."

"Please," Ruth said. "Don't get me wrong—" She turned away. One of the members of the huge Kearney family was demanding attention in the store. The Kearneys were a large, sprawling Irish family with a father perpetually drunk and the mother always pregnant. They were a target of endless local gossip and a continual source of shame to Mary and Vincent Cooper who tried their best to control the family's frequent drunken quarrels. Ruth had to admit she loved them all, even Big John, the father. He lurched into the shop every Friday, usually penniless, and laid his huge forearms on her counter to wheedle free groceries out of her. "A handsome woman, you have there," Big John would bellow at Joseph. "Mind I don't carry her away some dark night." Big John made Joseph nervous. Ruth laughed and blushed. "Don't ever worry about Big John," she would say to her husband. "It's men like the rabbi you have to watch."

Today the customer was Matthew, the eldest son of the Kearney family. Ruth served him as she watched Miriam leave the shop.

Later that night, as she lay in Joseph's arms, she whispered, "Do you think we work enough at our marriage?"

Joseph hugged his wife. "You're the best wife in all the world," he said. Ruth fell asleep, content.

✌️ CHAPTER 10 ✌️

The Monday afternoon women's meetings became a happy and regular routine for Lilla. She found herself feeling more and more as if Amelia's house were her own home. Week after week she attended the meetings, and the weeks turned quickly into months, then years. Before she knew it, five years had passed and Lilla realized very little in her life had changed. The meetings brought to her, as she had hoped, an enticing breath of wind from the exciting world beyond the confines of a small New Jersey town, but she herself was still trapped.

Lilla found solace in the company of the women who surrounded Amelia Witney-Hay. Sarah Harding seemed to be the most dominant woman in the group, but even when Sarah was lecturing them all on the need for independence, Lilla was aware that Amelia listened with a detached sort of amusement. Sarah was very slim. She had been born in Louisiana on a rich, lush plantation. Often, during a meeting, she would explode with rage at the treatment of the black servants and the slaves who, until thirty years ago, had been whipped and abused by the plantation foremen.

Sarah was usually accompanied by her friend, Semprina LaFé, a beautiful, middle-aged woman, half-French and half-African. Lilla had caught her first glimpse of a black person when she and Reuben had arrived in New York. But to sit next to a woman who came partly from France and partly from Africa was so exotic that Lilla spent several hours with the children looking up France and Africa in a book of geography. Semprina was a quiet, gentle woman and she would raise an elegant eyebrow when Sarah expounded too long for everyone else's comfort.

The thing which excited Lilla most was not the politics. In fact, Lilla was not at all sure she agreed that men should no longer protect women because women should protect themselves. Amelia and Sarah both had private incomes, or so Lilla imagined. Political statements, she felt, came easily to women so unencumbered by husbands and children. But what excited Lilla most was their wealth, their travels, their freedom from the demands of a family.

Semprina seemed to act as a companion for Sarah, and they both lived in a very stately house nearby. Sometimes, if Amelia felt like a change, she would take Lilla over there in her hansom cab. Lilla was amazed to find the two women lived in Spartan simplicity. Not only were they new women, but they also lived a new life. Lilla longed for the comfort of Amelia's home as she sat on the small wooden chairs, looking at blank windows unadorned by curtains of any sort, eating brown wheat biscuits from stark, white china.

Sarah often berated the women who claimed to be domestic reformers: women who wanted changes in the law to give them equality but who also asked for recognition that a woman in the home needed to be valued for the work she did. "But this makes sense," Lilla once dared to argue. "I find that now the children are at school and Reuben is busy selling his produce during the days, I am often alone and isolated. I wish someone would appreciate me for just being *me*."

Sarah looked at Lilla. "Well, you say you want to be an artist, don't you? Then be one. Paint your paintings, show your work, and let the world know you for the artist that you are."

Lilla had indeed been taking more active measures to resurrect her artistic aspirations than merely sketching from her window. Reuben had made her a large easel which sat in her parlor, the room which also housed a small upright piano.

Today Lilla stood before the easel, struggling with a painting. She tried her hardest to concentrate, to lose herself in the intense process of applying the paint to the canvas, but concentration proved difficult. Nora, now an active six-year-old, was away from school. She was beginning a cold and her ear ached. She was whining. Lilla tried to ignore her and to apply the delicate brush strokes which would eventually turn into a portrait of her mentor and friend, Amelia. Willfully blocking out the noise Nora was making, Lilla turned her mind to Amelia, their mutual friends, and the alluring life she tasted during her visits to Amelia's elegant house.

Lately, the meetings had ceased to be enough. Hearing about the women's thrilling lives was one thing, but more and more Lilla wanted to experience the thrills for herself. Instead, as the years rolled by, she felt the constraint of her own family life holding her prisoner in its demanding bosom. Sarah and Semprina came and went as their meetings, rallies, and political activities called them: Sarah always had a new outrage to report.

Lilla, looking at the portrait, felt a stab of envy for the freedom enjoyed by the other women in the group, a freedom she could admire only from a distance. How was she supposed to paint, to express her own artistic nature, when Nora seemed intent on distracting her mind?

"Mommy," Nora whined. "My ear hurts." She squirmed on the piano stool and wagged her head from side to side.

"Just a minute," Lilla said, focusing firmly on the canvas before her. "I'll take care of it in a minute. Let me just finish painting the face."

She dabbed her brush in a smear of red paint on her palette, then carefully raised the brush to the corner of Amelia's lips. She touched the lips on the painting with the brush and found her own lips rising in a smile. Amelia has a lot to smile about, Lilla thought as she dabbed the canvas. She has her freedom. Lilla's life, however, seemed increasingly less free. True, all the children were away at school all day. But Reuben, Lilla felt, seemed perfectly content for Lilla to spend the rest of her time at home alone. It was his contentment which so bothered Lilla. How could he not notice how much she minded being trapped at home with only her Monday afternoons to look forward to? How could Ben not notice? How could her whole family not notice? Lilla felt as if her entire family conspired somehow to keep her home, bored, and dissatisfied. It was different with Amelia's husband. He seemed to admire Amelia's freedom. Why couldn't Lilla have married a man like him?

Lilla saw little of Reginald Witney-Hay but, occasionally, she could see him arriving back from a journey on a ship. She watched, jealous of her friend's attention to this rakish man. "He's good for a laugh," Amelia explained. "but someday he's going to go too far."

"Too far" was when Reggie Witney-Hay gambled yet again on the boats. He was an inveterate liar and a cheat, but he brought a whole new world into Lilla's life. She had never met a real rogue, a man who openly boasted of his female conquests and nights in the brothels in Shanghai. Often, on his frequent sallies into opium dens, he commandeered opium pipes. Lilla remembered the first time she had met him, on a Monday afternoon, just after his return from yet another trip to the other side of the globe. "A moment, my dear," he had said, after being introduced to her. He had left the room, then returned, handing Lilla a particularly beautiful ebony pipe. "Smell," he had said, putting the bowl under her nose. "Smell the Orient. Smell the opium."

Lilla, still shy, had sniffed while Reggie told her of the opium dens. The musky sweet smell had climbed into her nostrils and she had indeed imagined herself lying side by side with Amelia in a room exactly as Reggie described. She had envisaged a small Chinaman bent over the pipes, coaxing them to life. The liquid had bubbled in her imaginings, and then the pair of women had flown, their souls in union, across the bat-filled night, soaring over a Chinese ornamented garden described in the book on China Amelia so kindly lent to her.

Reggie's full mouth, under his dense black moustache, had broken into a smile. "Will my little bird ever fly?" he had said, one eyebrow lifted. He had laughed as a red tide of arousal spread from Lilla's chest to her face.

Full of the memory, Lilla now stood in front of the easel with the brush in her hand and began to cry. Most of what she felt was confusion. Her two worlds did not seem to have a bridge between them. Lately she felt more and more ill at ease trying to span the worlds herself. Reuben's presence, she had to admit, she now felt to be barely tolerable.

He would listen at night to Lilla, and she knew he was bored by her talk. Reuben did not read books. If he read at all, it would be a manual on crop-rearing or cow-breeding. He had two topics which were fluent. One was his mother, Rebecca, who had written and was arriving shortly to live with them. The other was his plans to go West with the whole family.

The West of America was booming. Reuben was fast getting disillusioned with the banks of Middletown. As he prospered, he wanted to extend the farm. Reuben was a builder by nature. His head was always filled with dreams of hayricks, more Dutch barns, and extensions to his house. He needed to build a new room for his mother, but the bank refused to give him credit. He tried other lending institutions but, despite his excellent credit record, they also refused him. On a visit to the rabbi yesterday Reuben had asked why.

Lilla wiped the tears from her eyes and continued to paint. Nora was now tinkling annoyingly on the top notes of the piano, impatient for her mother's attention. Lilla ignored the child and tried unsuccessfully to keep her thoughts on what she was doing. Last night's dinner conversation still haunted Lilla. She could not force from her mind Reuben's recounting of his conversation with the rabbi.

The rabbi had shaken his head. "Don't you know?" he had said. "There's a document out that says unless you're a 'white Jew'—that's an Astor or a Rothschild in New York—no credit is to be given 'to those'," he quoted, " 'of Hebraic persuasion'."

"I don't believe it." Reuben had been horrified. "You mean even here in America, our new country, we are discriminated against?"

Mort had looked at Reuben. "To be a Jew is to suffer," he had said.

Reuben had briefly visited the Gottsteins and then left for home. That, he had thought, settles it. We're going West to a new world where everyone is equal.

Then, last night at the dinner table, Reuben had sat his family down and explained his dreams and his plans. He had put his case passionately to his wife.

"The Gottsteins, the Kearneys, and Mary and Vincent Cooper all want to go. Betty Thompson asked me today if we needed a nurse. Please, Lilla. We have no more future here. I want to do more for Ben and Isaac than just be a farmer on a few acres. The girls need good husbands with land, not pocket handkerchiefs. Let's go."

For Lilla, the idea of boarding a train with Reuben and the children seemed like a nightmare. Rosey and her—now large—bull would accompany them on separate cars of the train, along with whatever chickens and ducks could be crated. Even her brand-new, upright Steinway made with polished cherry wood could go, Reuben promised.

Lilla had listened and remained silent. How could she tell him that, to her, leaving her friendship with Amelia would be worse than death?

Lilla looked at her painting and yawned. She was exhausted. She had spent the sleepless night by the window staring across the trees at the light in Amelia's window. She could imagine Amelia sitting upright in bed, reading. Books by great men like Cicero, Amelia read in the Latin. She could also read in French and Italian. Sometimes, if Lilla stayed a little late, Amelia would read sonnets in the original Elizabethan language for her. When Amelia read her poetry, Lilla felt like a small child at a party. Amelia, to Lilla, was a never-ending banquet of information and delight.

Now, they kissed goodnight before Reuben left. Lilla treasured the moment when she approached Amelia to put her lips on her soft warm skin. Amelia always smelled of roses. Reuben's beard always smelled of hay.

Wiping her eyes again, Lilla tried to train her attention solely on her painting. Suddenly, as she tenderly brushed the inner hollow of the left eye, Nora banged loudly on the lower register of the piano. Lilla's back seized up and a knot of pain shot across her forehead. The brush splashed the eye, instantly making the face a grotesque mask. Any concentration, any composure Lilla had struggled to maintain, she now lost.

Lilla lashed out at Nora, who fell from the piano stool to the floor. Reuben was in Middletown selling his produce and Nora had no one to turn to for protection. Nora knew to run when her mother was in one of her rages. The child fled the house into the barn where she knew her mother would never follow. The cowpats stuck to her dainty shoes. Once safe with the young bull, Jack, she waited for her father's return.

Lilla put down her brush and sat down in a chair before her ruined painting. She stared at it and was overcome by a grief which seemed to spring upon from somewhere deep within. What was she to do? Would she be forced to go West with her family and leave her only true friend? She cried until her eyes ran dry. Then, wiping her nose with her handkerchief, she resolved that, at least for now, there was only one thing to do: tomorrow she would trust her friend with her dilemma. Amelia would know what to do. Amelia always knew what to do.

"Reuben is thinking of going West with a group of our friends to buy land in New Mexico or California," Lilla said simply. She bit her lip as she waited for a reply.

Amelia looked concerned. "But, Lilla. What will you do out there?"

Lilla put her hands together and looked at them, folded in pious prayer. What she really wanted to do was throw herself into her friend's arms and lie there like a protected, pampered child. Amelia looked solemnly at Lilla. She had been waiting for a number of years now for exactly this moment. Reggie was to be seen less and less. He had found himself an acrobatic mistress in Manila, so Amelia was without a companion in her life.

Lilla was still young and beautiful. Amelia wanted to travel and she needed a companion. A plan was forming in her mind. "Well," she said, "maybe the men are just pipe-dreaming. Men do like to talk, you know."

Lilla shook her head. "No, it's not like that. The women are just as keen as the men. All except me. I know I'm not made for frontier life. It was hard enough settling here. The first shack we had nearly killed me. Now, Reuben's mother is arriving in five weeks. I'll have to give up my bedroom and move in with the girls."

Amelia put her head on one side. "Don't you share a room with your husband?"

Lilla looked down at her clasped hands. "No, I don't." She faltered. "Ever since I had Nora, I swore I couldn't risk another pregnancy. So we live separately. Except when he has absolutely *got* to," she said hurriedly.

"I see." Amelia was amused. "Well, I have a little surprise planned for you, dear. As your mother-in-law is coming, when she is settled in, why don't you and I join Sarah and Semprina in New York? There is a meeting of the Female Moral Reform Society going on there. I think Sarah wants a chance to argue with them. We needn't necessarily attend. But there is someone else I'd like you to meet—Mrs. Rubenstein. Her salon is famous, and I'll introduce you to several good women painters. I understand she'll be holding one of her art shows. Perhaps we could even enter a painting of yours in the competition."

"I'd love that!" Lilla's fingers were dancing on her lap. "How marvelous! I'll ask Reuben."

Amelia frowned. "You will tell Reuben, my dear."

Lilla laughed. "All right. I'll *tell* him."

All the way home, Lilla hummed to herself.

To her surprise, Reuben raised no objections. "If it will make you happy, dear," he said, "go with my blessing."

Only Ben looked upset. Never before had his mother gone away. Lilla gave him a hug. "You're a man now," she said. "About to leave school and work for your father."

Nora, very quietly, felt enormously happy. Time away from her mother was time to be treasured.

༄ CHAPTER 11 ༄

The idea of Lilla, or indeed of any wife, leaving her home and family and going to a sinful city like New York appalled Miriam. She sat at breakfast with Mort and harangued him. "You're still the rabbi," she scolded. "You must stop this nonsense. Lilla Braff is out of her mind." Miriam sucked a huge draft of tea from her glass.

Mort was weary of the whole subject of Lilla Braff. A man has enough to do fighting with his soul over his need for Molly Parkington's thin thighs than to argue with his wife at breakfast. "I don't see why you women get so upset over Lilla."

"You don't see why?" Miriam's pendulous breasts shook with anger. "You don't see why? I'll tell you why. It's women like Lilla who give young girls ideas before their time. It's women like Lilla who make men feel lust in their hearts." Miriam's voice began to climb. "Did you see her at Betty Thompson's birthday party?" Mort flinched. He knew his wife well enough to know that if she interrupted herself from the luxury of one of her orgasmic rages, the subsequent news was going to be bad. Miriam's eyes glittered. "I hear that Betty Thompson has been performing abortions on women in this community!"

Mort shrugged, relieved that the information did not contain news of his last surreptitious visit to Molly. "So?" he said. "What am I to do about it?"

"What if she aborts one of our Jewish girls?"

"Then," said Mort, *"then* I would do something about it."

Miriam returned to her favorite subject. "You have to see Reuben. We can't have our old ways destroyed by that brazen hussy."

"Yes, dear." The rabbi was finished and out of the door. Lucky Reuben, he thought, as he walked down the dusty street toward the Gottsteins' shop. His wife's going away.

Once inside, he was greeted by the peace which lay between Ruth and her husband. The talk veered rapidly toward the trip to the new country out West.

"Ach," Joseph Gottstein was excited. "I'm already thinking of packing cases," he said.

Ruth smiled. "We are both imagining a new home, a place where there are acres of quiet, maybe even a bigger shop. And I'm going to make food and have a few tables to feed travelers as they pass by."

Mort smiled. "You go with my prayers," he said.

Ruth looked at the man who had circumcised her son when he was eight days old, the man who had officiated at her son's *bar mitzvah* when Danny turned thirteen. She remembered her boy's high-pitched, nervous voice reading his portion in Hebrew from the Torah. Ruth suddenly felt sorry for the rabbi. "Why aren't you coming with us?" she said. "There are so many Jews leaving the East. If we can't go to Jerusalem, at least we can live somewhere away from the anti-Semitism that arrived with the other immigrants. The new world is a sort of promised land. We can have acres of our own for a few dollars."

"Miriam won't go." Mort shook his head. "She says she's moved for the last time. I can't blame her. It's a dangerous journey through Indian territory. Then again, this isn't exactly something new for us. We lost our children to the soldiers back home."

"I know." Joseph put his hand on Mort's arm. "We all lost members of our families and all our belongings. We're moving for Danny's sake. Reuben feels the same. The children are young enough to move, and then we will find a place to raise them in safety. Betty Thompson wants to move too, I hear. She'll live with Mary and Vincent Cooper."

Mort finished his cup of tea and sighed. "I must be going. Mrs. Schwartz has had another baby."

When he left, Ruth looked at Joseph. "How sad,"

she said. "I'll miss him. He's a good man, in his own way.

"Talking of Reuben, he has been quiet lately, don't you think? We really must visit him."

CHAPTER 12

Reuben knew, without being told, that Middletown thought he was insane to allow his wife to visit New York with a strange Englishwoman. He felt he was insane to even think of it. He also knew his mother, who was arriving any minute now, would berate him all the way back to his house. But for the moment, he didn't care. The waves were high. The gulls sailed over his head, and the smell of the sea invigorated him. He could see the boat tossing its way to the dock. The sea slapped the timbers under him and sent rolling shocks up his spine.

He was going West. Little Reuben Braff from Russia was going to be a cowboy. In his secret dream of America as a young man, he had always imagined the moment when he would dismount from his sweating horse, walk across a dry gulch, and cook himself a mess of beans. For a second, Reuben smelled the dry, desert air; heard the crackle of a few sticks of burning piñon; and inhaled the warm, dark, treacle smell of the beans.

The ship gave a triumphant hoot, its long journey accomplished, and roused Reuben from his distant imaginings. The rails of the ship were lined with passengers. Reuben snapped back into the present. Eagerly he scanned the rails. Where was she? Had she made the journey safely? Was she sick? Jostling with the crowd, Reuben pushed his way to the front of the dock, and then he saw his mother.

Clutching her many bags, Rebecca Braff walked imperiously down the gangplank. Reuben held her close to him. "Mama, you look as if you've just come from the market."

Rebecca looked at her only son. "Um. It's been a long time getting here," she said.

Reuben suddenly realized how much he had missed the twinkle in her eye. He had had no one to confide in for so long. His feelings of failure as a husband to Lilla had been kept in a compartment in his heart as if locked away in a vault that even he did not enter. The last blow, Lilla's decision to go to New York without him, caught him so by surprise that he had not even thought about his right to object.

Lately, he and Lilla seemed to live in two different worlds. His was a serene farm life with the children, and hers was a world of lace and silk in the big house across the fields. When she came back from her frequent weekly visits to Amelia Witney-Hay, Lilla chatted like a magpie about meetings and places and rich people who sat about and discussed things which had nothing to do with everyday living.

Rebecca stood very still and held Reuben. Still the young, vulnerable Reuben, she thought, even if he is nearly forty. Still the boy who saved the wounded birds that had fallen from their nests, the funny little Jewish boy who had fallen in love with the stories he had heard about a gentile man named St. Francis.

Rebecca was glad to be in her new home with him. Leaving her beloved husband, Oscar, buried in the old homeland had been the hardest part. Theirs had been a good marriage, but Rebecca knew beyond a doubt that now her place was with her son.

Lilla, with all her pretty ways, had never fooled Rebecca, even years ago in Russia when Lilla was still a young woman. Rebecca knew from the start that Lilla was poor marriage material. She had also heard on the grapevine that Lilla had been fooling around with a rich boy from St. Petersburg, an artist. When Reuben and Lilla first met, Rebecca knew that Reuben, as usual, was rescuing another hurt bird, only this little bird caught her rescuer in her small silver claws and did not let go until the day they were man and wife.

Reuben smiled. "You look as young as the day I left you, Mama. Here, give me your bags."

Mother and son walked down the docks to where Reuben had his two horses waiting for him. "My." Rebecca was impressed. "What a fine pair of horses. And such a beautiful carriage."

Reuben glowed. "Wait till you see the farm, mother," he said. "You can even have a bath, and we have electricity."

Rebecca laughed. "How about the children? Can I see them, before I see the inventions, Reuben?"

"Of course!" Reuben laughed. He launched into his favorite subject, his plans for going out West. He talked himself hoarse.

The long drive necessitated a stay overnight at an inn. The luxury of a bed and a room of her own stunned Rebecca. The magnificence of the huge houses, the department stores and the trolleys whizzing past, silenced her until breakfast the next morning. All the way to the farm, she listened avidly to all that Reuben had to say—particularly to the news about Lilla's new friends and Lilla's impending visit to the big city. "Let her go, Reuben. Let her go. I'm here now, and I'll take care of the children. At my age, you are content. Anyway, that's what grandmothers are for. Lilla is still young enough to want to spread her wings a little."

"But why can't she go to New York with me?" Reuben stared at the horses' ears. "I'd take her to New York."

Rebecca sighed. "Reuben," she said. "Times are changing so fast. Maybe Lilla is confused. Let me talk to her first. We haven't seen each other since she married you. Let me find out for myself."

Lilla both welcomed and feared her mother-in-law's arrival. Rebecca's presence meant that Lilla could relieve herself of the burden of running the house. On the other hand, Lilla dreaded Rebecca's penetrating eyes. Not much escaped Rebecca's quick intelligence.

Deeply rooted in traditional Jewish life, Rebecca was amazed to see that her son did not wear a *yarmulke* all the time. When she saw Lilla—the hardness of the face and the coolness of the body—she recognized why her son was so sad a man.

Lilla knew it would only take a few weeks for Rebecca to catch up with Middletown gossip. Her attempted abortion, she knew, was safe with Betty Thompson, but Lilla dearly hoped that Rebecca would side with her on the question of going West.

Going West was a fever that seemed to grip half the East Coast. Almost daily, carts piled high with goods and chattels rolled past the farm. Sometimes, a cart would stop and a child would come up the path with a pail in his hand looking for water. Lilla gave the water gracefully. Nora, however, excited by her father's stories of how wonderful life in the West would be, apprehended the child and subjected him to a grilling. The answer was always the same: "We're going West to find gold," or "We're going West to buy land." Dreams of the West thrilled Nora, but all this talk made Lilla very nervous.

The five children all agreed that a grandmother was a definite asset. Five bright, welcoming faces were waiting on the porch. Rebecca didn't know if she could contain her excitement. A flurry of hugs greeted her and her bags were carried into the house by many happy arms. "Hello," Lilla said with little emotion as she stood before Rebecca.

"Hello, Lilla," Rebecca replied. Lilla walked forward and dutifully placed an obligatory kiss on Rebecca's cheek. Poor Reuben, Rebecca thought. But I'm now here.

It did not take long for Rebecca to find out about Lilla's extraordinary friends. Miriam dropped by within three days of Rebecca's arrival. Lilla was out visiting Amelia at the time, so Miriam seized the chance to unload her store of venom. Rebecca listened quietly. She steered the subject to the world both she and Miriam had left behind. Secretly she resolved to visit Mrs. Witney-Hay.

Even in the three days she had been living in her son's house, Rebecca sensed the tension between the various members of the family. Ben, in particular, worried her. He seemed to take violent exception to his mother's visits to the big house. His possessive, dark, anxious eyes followed Lilla's exits and entries with a look that broke Rebecca's heart. To meet, for the first time, her own five grandchildren alive and well, living in America, was such an intense joy that Rebecca knew she could not get too involved in Lilla's world. For Reuben's sake, however, she knew she must ask Lilla to take her to have tea with Amelia Witney-Hay.

A week after her arrival, she tackled Lilla at breakfast. "Lilla, dear," she said. "I would love to meet your English friend."

Lilla bent her head and played with the napkin on her lap. Reuben and the children stopped talking to listen. "Well . . ." Lilla's speech was slow and hesitant. "I don't think you would really enjoy a visit there."

"No? Why not, dear?"

"Well, I . . . Even I find it difficult to keep up. It's all talk about books and politics."

Rebecca smiled. "Don't worry," she said. "Women always find something to talk about. How about next Saturday? The English like a cup of tea around four o'clock. Am I right?"

Lilla looked across the table at her mother-in-law. "Very well," she said. "I'll ask Amelia." She was unnerved at the idea of sharing with Rebecca her secret and personal relationship with a woman who was not only her best friend but was also the one person she now found worth living for. Lilla felt instantly nauseated. Pushing back her chair and with her hand to her mouth, she said, "Excuse me. I feel ill."

Reuben was immediately concerned. Usually, Lilla had headaches when she was upset. She can't be pregnant, Reuben thought. We haven't had sex for a year. An awful longing gripped him as he watched Lilla run lightly up the stairs. If only they could go to New York alone, just the two of them. If only they could lie together, cast away on an island of love and passion. If only he could kiss the nape of her beautiful swan-like neck, hidden from the world by the weight of her waist-length, jet-black hair.

Ben coughed, interrupting his father's thoughts. He, too, longed to be held by his mother. He, too, as a very small boy and only child, had given his heart to this beautiful, bewitching woman, the mother who treated him like a little doll. "My darling prince," she used to call him, years ago, as she kissed his naked pink penis. "My little man," she used to coo as she held him to her breasts. For Ben, Lilla's small breasts were still beautiful. Even now, guilty with unwanted erections, Ben longed for his mother's nipples. These thoughts caused him anguish. They tormented him with guilt. But he kept his secret deep inside himself, and no one knew of his pain.

Nora, especially close to her older brother, saw the sorrow in his face. She got up from the table and hugged him. "Come on, Ben," she said. "Let's race Bea and Naomi upstairs. We'll be late for school if we don't hurry."

Naomi stretched a long, cat-like stretch. "I'm going to see Matthew Kearney," she said, "after school."

Rebecca looked across at her lovely blooming granddaughter. "Not without your sisters being there," she said firmly.

Naomi looked at her grandmother. "Mother doesn't believe in all that old-fashioned stuff," she said. "Women can look after themselves these days, you know."

"My dear Naomi." Rebecca walked back to the table. "Women civilize men. If they don't, men behave like wild animals. There are exceptions, of course, like your father. But very few. Come on, children, hurry up. Ben and Isaac, you see your sisters home from school, please. Your mother may be a thoroughly modern woman, but I'm not. Now shoo. Go. Quickly."

Reuben smiled at his mother. "I'm glad you're here," he said simply. "I'm so confused by all these different rules. I'm not at all happy that Matthew Kearney is seeing Naomi. He isn't Jewish. He's a nice enough boy, but his father is a drunk and violent. And the mother . . . Well, it's hard to say anything about her, except that she's always pregnant. But then, I can't really stop Naomi. The Kearney family will be traveling with us when we go out West. Big John might be a drunk, but he is tough and can fire a good gun. So can his boys. And we'll need all the help we can get."

Rebecca picked up some more plates. "You know," she said, "I'll go anywhere you go. But how does Lilla feel about this move?"

Reuben shook his head. "She's not keen. But maybe two weeks away will make her feel anxious to be back with us. We have never been apart, except in the early days when I had to travel to sell goods. I hated every minute of it."

Upstairs, in her safe refuge by the window in the room she now shared with the girls, Lilla could see the house across the fields. Even to watch the sun rise across the sky over her dearly beloved Amelia calmed her feeling of sickness. Her heart grew appalled at the mere thought of Rebecca in her peasant clothes sitting on a chair, boring Amelia with her idle, ceaseless chatter. How could she explain this dreadful intrusion to her friend? Well, she thought, I'd better go and get it over with.

She opened the girls' cupboard door. There, inconveniently squashed up against the girls' dresses, was her own ever-increasing wardrobe. Lilla loved to see the appreciation in her friend's eyes as she walked across the cool library in yet another new dress. "Buy silk," Amelia would urge her. "You sound so good in silk. A few more scarves for your neck. That's what we'll buy you."

Last week, after an emotional meeting when Lilla once again poured out her concern at Reuben's pleas to move, Amelia did more than just kiss Lilla a soft goodbye. Lilla now remembered the moment when Amelia opened a small box on her knee and said, "Here. Let me put this brooch on your dress." Lilla allowed herself to remember—as she had remembered and relived time and time again—the moment when Amelia's hand slid between the alabaster skin of Lilla's breast and the material that was to be pierced by the gold pin. The hand knew how to place a brooch without faltering. "There," Amelia said, giving the brooch a little pat. "That looks lovely."

The brooch glinted from the pin. Two red rubies matched the flush which suffused Lilla's face. "You're too good to me, Amelia. How will I be able to thank you?"

Lilla remembered Amelia's smile. "You will one day," Amelia said.

Lilla remembered Amelia's peculiar ability to remind her of an Egyptian statue. Her eyes, so full of life, could suddenly, without warning, go blank. Lilla realized this morning, as she carefully slid a silk visiting dress over her head, she very desperately wished to kiss those blank eyes back to life.

Saturday arrived with an inevitability that woke Lilla early. Amelia had been charming when Lilla had asked if Rebecca could join them for tea. "Of course, my dear," she said. "Anyone's mother-in-law is worth a visit. Thank goodness that has never been one of my problems."

Lilla still felt mortified. Rebecca had taken the acceptance of the offer to visit in her stride. The day passed slowly for Lilla. She busied herself with half-hearted efforts to dust the furniture and to sweep the kitchen floor, until at last she and Rebecca walked in silence up the long drive to Amelia Witney-Hay's grand house. Huge trees guarded the big house, and the lawn lay silent. Only the sound of the two women's shoes gave any indication that anything was alive. Rebecca felt the silence very intensely, but she resolved to keep her inmost thoughts to herself.

Susan showed the two women into the house and took their coats. Rebecca's faded, black flannel coat sat on an expensively embroidered coat hanger next to Lilla's blue *moiré* cloak. Susan silently walked the women across to the library where Amelia rose to greet them. "Ah, Lilla," she said, standing very tall and erect. "This is your mother-in-law."

Rebecca looked up into Amelia's eyes. Way, way back, Rebecca could see a young girl. But now, for many years, that young girl had made bad choices, choices against all that was nurturing and maternal.

Indeed, Rebecca felt the woman before her to be almost masculine. "Mrs. Witney-Hay," she said. "How pleasant to meet you at last."

"Do sit down. Both of you." Amelia returned to her usual chair. She put her cane to one side and leaned back. "How was your journey, Mrs. Braff?"

Sitting perched on her chair, Rebecca chatted brightly. Lilla soon began to relax. Rebecca was not going to be a social embarrassment after all. But, she wondered, could Rebecca see anything that might give her a clue to Lilla's unholy desires? So far, Lilla had kept her secret world away from Reuben and the children. So far, Lilla had kept her deep yearning to be with her friend so separate that when she was in her own house, she could live across the fields in her mind. She could do the mundane day-to-day house-keeping chores with a song on her lips. She could cope with the demands of her five children by think-ing of where Amelia would be and what she would be doing. But with Rebecca's intrusion, would the dream fade into an illusion?

"I gather," Rebecca said, "you will be taking Lilla with you to New York in two weeks?"

"Yes. Lilla is looking forward to seeing Mrs. Rubenstein's salon. The dear girl is so talented that she really must get exposure to great art. Verity Lampson is attending, and various other luminaries from across America will be there. So exciting, don't you think?"

Rebecca nodded. "Certainly. Women are taking great strides forward these days. But then, there are those of us who wish to remain in our traditional roles. As long as we all have a choice, and our roles as wives and mothers are not devalued, I'm happy."

Lilla shifted uncomfortably. Wifely and motherly duties were not the usual topics for conversation in Amelia's house. Amelia smiled sweetly. "Of course," she said. "Traditional women are the backbone of our country, but those of us who wish to be artists must be encouraged. And Lilla is such an artist. We all love her and wish to help encourage her talent. How is the painting going, Lilla? I had an idea yesterday. How about doing a painting of this house for me? I could give it to Mrs. Rubenstein as a present, and it will give the other ladies a chance to see your work."

Lilla clapped her hands. "I'd love to paint this house," she said. "I'll be here every day till we leave." Turning to Rebecca, she said, "Could you take care of Reuben and the children? Would you mind? I'll be back to cook supper."

Rebecca looked at her daughter-in-law. Inwardly she sighed. Lilla resembled a bride going to the altar. Lilla's eyes shone in a way they never had shone for Reuben. Her cheeks were on fire in a way they never were in Reuben's house. Here, in this expensive, grand place, Lilla glowed like a flame. Rebecca nodded. What will happen will happen and there is nothing I can do to prevent it, she said to herself. "I'll take care of the house, Lilla. You paint."

"Good." Amelia rang her silver bell for Susan. "Tea for everyone," she said. Her blue eyes locked for a moment with Lilla's eyes. For a split-second, Lilla felt she had been passionately embraced.

⮾ CHAPTER 13 ⮾

New York was cloaked in a deep mist blown in from the sea. The shroud hung heavily on the shoulders of the huge buildings. Lilla had not seen New York for many years. She was amazed to see how much had changed. Electric lights in shop windows enchanted her. There was electricity in some homes in Middletown but, overall, change was slow in her rural area. People were largely suspicious of it. For Lilla, however, change was oxygen in her life. She breathed in deeply the thrilling air of New York and felt more alive than she had felt for years.

With Amelia as her guide, she saw a New York she had never seen before. The wealth that surrounded her, the beauty of the buildings, all were parts of a world that she had seen only in her dreams. Lilla was hardly sure she wasn't dreaming now. Ever since her artist had told her of the glories of St. Petersburg, she had cherished fantasies of such a city. Now, for Lilla, this world became real. When Amelia guided her into the magnificent hotel on Fifth Avenue, Lilla's heart trembled with delight at the perfect elegance that surrounded her. At last she had found her freedom. At last she was where she belonged.

Sitting by Amelia in her first really expensive restaurant, she was as excited as if it were her birthday. Indeed she felt it was not only her birthday, but also Christmas, Thanksgiving, and Passover all rolled into one. Lilla tried to remember if she had ever sat in such a beautiful restaurant. No, she thought. Never as a child, nor ever as a married woman. This really is my first time, she realized. In an odd way, however, she felt natural, completely at home, among the wealth and the opulence.

The restaurant was in the hotel. The bags had been taken upstairs by a large cage that winched itself up to the unimaginable heights of the rest of the hotel. Trailing after Amelia, Lilla was conscious of the covert glances from various elegant men who had business to attend to at the hotel. Catching a glimpse of herself in the mirror that took up a great amount of room in the restaurant, Lilla could see why. Today she wore a pale gray outfit. A tight-fitting little hat perched on her head, and a small gray veil misted her sparkling brown eyes. Lilla needed no rouge on her cheeks, nor did her full red lips make contact with a lipbrush. Her small feet were shod in pale satin slippers as gray as the dress.

The contrast between her slim elegance and the large, formidable bulk of her companion could not be more complete. Amelia wore an austere brown tweed suit with a large satin blouse. On her feet was a sensible English pair of Oxford brogues. Now Lilla was aware that, as a couple, they attracted a considerable amount of attention.

"What would you like for lunch, dear?" Amelia enjoyed the innocent pleasure in Lilla's eyes. "Here. Take a look at the menu." Lilla nervously hoped she would not make a fool of herself. She, by now, had learned not to spear her meat with her fork and hack around the fork with her knife. Now she ate the European way after much practice late at night in the kitchen. To her dismay, the menu seemed to have been written by a drunken monkey. Amelia laughed. "It's in French, you little goose. Let me translate for you."

The contents of the menu sounded so exotic, Lilla was quite content to listen to the never-ending amounts and varieties of food and sauces for the rest of the afternoon. But Amelia's melodious voice came to an end. She put the menu down and smiled. "Hurry up," said Amelia. "We're to be at Mrs Rubenstein's by four. The way you're going, you will have just finished your pudding."

Lilla laughed. At least she knew that "pudding" was the English word for "dessert".

"I suggest," Amelia said, "you try the duck for the main course. Victor, the *maître d'*, always recommends it to me. I must say, it's very good."

"Really?" Lilla was surprised. "Our ducks taste awful. All stringy and tough."

"Ah, well, that's because they're not penned and fattened for the table, are they?"

Oh dear, Lilla thought, I mustn't tell Nora—she'd cry fit to bust. "Do you think I might have some shrimp for my first course?" Lilla said.

Amelia leaned across the table. "Prawns, dear," she said. "In Europe we say prawns. The Americans are so uncivilized as yet. Shrimp are very little and we put them in butter and sherry for one's toast at tea-time or, of course," she drew herself up, "one can have gentleman's relish." She caught a glimpse of a shadow in Lilla's eyes. "I'm not cross, dear," she said, putting her hand on Lilla's arm. "We'll make a lady out of you yet."

Lilla smiled. "An English lady at that."

"Of course." Amelia was in an amiable mood. "There are only two sorts of women: English women, and then there are *women*. Ah. Here's Victor."

Amelia beckoned with a wave of her hand, and

Victor crossed the floor. He bowed deeply from his waist. "Mrs. Witney-Hay. What a pleasure to have you back. Last time you were here, we were remodeling, were we not?"

Amelia nodded. "We were *both* remodeling, Victor dear."

"Yes, indeed," Victor agreed. "May I congratulate you on *yours?*"

"You may," Amelia said. "I must say, the restaurant looks marvelous. May I introduce you to my companion, *Miss* Lilla Braff." Lilla's eyebrows went up. Amelia shot a mischievous look in her direction.

Victor bowed again. *"Enchanté, mademoiselle,"* he said. "Now. You are ready to order?"

Amelia ordered the meal, and then a bottle of Châteauneuf-du-Pape. The duck was as pink, as moist, and as delicious as Amelia had promised. The crisp of the skin mingled with the wine-soaked mushrooms, and the small new potatoes contrasted gently with the bright green, fresh peas. For the next course, Lilla gave in to the offer of dark brown chocolate, tenderly embracing small balls of brittle caramel afloat in a sea of cream, splashed with Grand Marnier. Amelia noticed the flush of Lilla's cheeks. Lilla's white teeth sank delightfully into the profiteroles. Her delicate fingers wiped her soft, mobile mouth with a thick linen napkin. As usual, everything was going very well for Amelia Witney-Hay.

To Lilla's surprise, after lunch, she discovered they were to share one large room. A great deal larger than any room she had entered before, with the exception of the library at Amelia's home. Not only was the bedroom big, but the two beds were also enormous.

"You could fit our whole house into these rooms!" Lilla cried, opening yet another door which led to a drawing room. It was the bathroom, however, that really confounded her. Never before and never again, she was sure, would she ever see a bathroom so magnificent. She stood openmouthed in the doorway.

A vast tundra of white marble lay before her. Raised on a platform, sat a large square bath. Big enough for the whole family, Lilla thought, and then she saw the enameled lavatory. Next to it stood a very weird contraption. If that were not enough, there were mirrors everywhere. On the big brass radiators, huge piles of thick white towels sat waiting. Jars of bath oils, bottles of perfumed hair potions stood at the ready. Lilla, a little drunk on red wine, turned like a top and spun in the mirrors. "You like this life, don't you?" Amelia said.

"I love it, I love it, I love it! I'm in love with it." Lilla came to a stop. "And I'm so grateful to you, Amelia." She walked up to her friend. "You gave me my life back," she said. "Before I met you, I felt I had nothing to live for. Of course," she said quickly, "I miss Reuben and the children, but I must have more out of life than just that."

"Quite right." Amelia turned and moved back into the bedroom. "Come on, dear,' she said. "I must have a bath before we leave. Help me undo my stays. Susan tied them too tightly." Amelia unbuttoned her blouse.

"Of course," Lilla said. The white whale-bone stays were tied at the top with an inextricable knot. Lilla struggled, her face pink with embarrassment. She felt she was failing Amelia. Susan would have undone the knot in a moment, but Lilla had never worn stays. Slim as she was, she had no need. Amelia's huge breasts seemed to threaten to cascade from their moorings.

"Here." Amelia took pity on Lilla. "Let me show you." With a deft tug, the knot dissolved, and Amelia expertly unhooked herself and handed the stays, which looked much like a suit of fearsome armor, to Lilla. "There." Amelia heaved a sigh. "Thank goodness for that." She lifted her arms above her head and gave a huge yawn. "I hate stays, you know. Absolutely hate them. Do go ahead, Lilla, and run my bath. Lukewarm for me, please."

Lilla ran into the bathroom and turned the faucets on. A mass of steam spluttered and hissed its way into the bath. Lilla struggled with the recalcitrant taps and then watched the water reconcile itself with the cold sides of the marble bath. Turning around, she saw Amelia walking into the bathroom with her shift on her arm.

Lilla was startled. She had seen women naked before, but never had she imagined she would see Amelia without her clothes. Amelia smiled at Lilla. She bent over the bath and touched the water with her hand. "Excellent, dear," she said. "Not only will you become an Englishwoman; you are an excellent companion."

Lilla blushed. She felt the familiar red tide of embarrassment climbing into her face. Amelia was well-made. Her breasts were huge, melon-like mounds, but, unencumbered by childbirth, they were unlined. The nipples were a pink, soft, early strawberry color. Her pubic hair was fair and faint under her smooth belly. Surprisingly, Lilla felt at home with this woman who so casually slipped into the bath and reached for a flannel as if they had been intimate all their lives. "Do wash my back, dear," Amelia said. "I need a good scrub. New York is filthy."

Lilla took the flannel and the thick bar of white soap. The only soap Lilla had ever seen was the green carbolic used at home. This soap was a pure and sensual delight. The creamy bubbles popped softly on Amelia's thick white shoulders. Mesmerized, partly by the smell of the soap and partly by the rhythm of her hand encased in the soft flannel, Lilla found herself wishing that she, too, was in the tub with Amelia. One of the few warm memories Lilla had of her childhood was that of bathing with her older sister to save water. They both, she remembered, played for a while, and Lilla washed her sister's back, just as she was doing now.

"Please put out my black outfit, would you? And don't forget the picture that you painted." Amelia's voice broke Lilla's reverie. Reluctantly Lilla handed the flannel over to Amelia. "Thank you, dear." Amelia busied herself with the flannel below the bathwater. Hypnotized, Lilla watched the square, capable hand move in and out between Amelia's thighs. An almost unbearable feeling of exaltation carried Lilla out of the bathroom to pull Amelia's visiting dress out of her big, black hold-all.

While Amelia dried herself, Lilla changed as quickly as she could. She chose to wear a delicate white, silk blouse over a long, black skirt, and she put on a pair of neat black shoes with a big, brass buckle. Amelia, after applying a thorough amount of powder, climbed back into a black pair of stays. An enormous pair of *Directoire* knickers were hoisted over the stays, then a silk chemise, over which a black bombazine dress came to rest on Amelia's large frame.

"Before we go, dear," said Amelia, "let's have a look at some jewelry. Here you are." Amelia peered into the depths of her jewelry case. She pulled out a string of pearls. "Now, look carefully, dear. A girl has to know her pearls. By the way, did you notice how I divested you of your husband and your five children at lunch?"

"Yes, I did."

"How does it feel to be single again?"

"Wonderful," Lilla said. "Just wonderful."

Amelia took the pearls that glowed softly in the light of the room. "Here. Run your teeth across a pearl." She held the string up to Lilla's mouth. "Can you feel the roughness? If they aren't rough, they aren't real."

Lilla stood quietly. The pearl gritted against her teeth. Her nose absorbed the clean smell from her friend. Amelia's thick fingers touched her neck.

"They're for you," Amelia said. "They were my mother's."

There was such pain in Amelia's voice that Lilla gently kissed the hand that lay on her shoulder. "I'm sorry," Lilla said.

"Don't be," Amelia answered harshly. Lilla knew the door to Amelia's pain was shut.

CHAPTER 14

Lilla was ushered into the large salon, with Amelia leading the way, by a tall woman with coffee-colored skin, and a large diamond stud in her nose. Lilla's painting was promptly taken off her by a passing servant and carried over to Mrs. Rubenstein. Lilla was so fascinated by the diamond in the nose that, for a moment, she forget where she was. Amelia took Lilla's hand and gave it a sharp squeeze. "Manners, dear," Amelia whispered. "Manners. It isn't polite to stare."

"Oh, I'm sorry," Lilla whispered back.

"Don't be," Amelia laughed quickly. "There's a lot to see in this room." She turned, smiling widely to the black woman. "Julie," she said in a loud voice. "Julie, I'd like you to meet my friend, Lilla Braff. Lilla, this is Julie Youngblood. Julie and I have known each other for years."

Again, Lilla found herself staring as she shook the tall woman's hand. Julie, Lilla guessed, must be in her late thirties, but her eyes held a brilliant sparkle, a thrilling and youthful vitality, that matched the sparkle of the diamond in her nose.

"Delighted to meet you, Lilla," Julie said. Her rich voice was warm and smooth. "If you'll excuse me, I must circulate. But I hope I'll have a chance to get to know you better."

"I'd like that, too," Lilla said genuinely, quickly feeling at home in this kind woman's company.

Though Lilla did not notice, Amelia's face gave a small, jealous wince. "Come on," Amelia said, pulling

Lilla by the hand. "It's time you met our hostess." She steered Lilla through a jostling crowd of people, up to a throne-like chair upon which sat a very shrunken and very shriveled old lady. "Mrs. Rubenstein," Amelia announced. "May I introduce my companion, Miss Braff."

Lilla looked up into Mrs. Rubenstein's face. A peculiar smile appeared on the old woman's wrinkled lips. "A good choice, Mrs. Witney-Hay," she leered.

Lilla realized then that the woman had had a stroke and was partially paralyzed. Her eyes seemed to undress Lilla. "How do you do, Mrs. Rubenstein?" Lilla said nervously.

Mrs. Rubenstein put out a small, scaly hand. "I do very well." Mrs. Rubenstein's voice was rough and scratchy. She looked at Lilla. "And how do you do?" she asked archly.

"Very well, thank you."

Amelia smiled at her oldest mentor. "We must go," she said. "I have many people who want to meet my little artist. We have a picture of hers for you. You will remember my house, won't you?"

Mrs. Rubenstein inclined her head. "I'll always remember your house," she said.

While the two women talked, Lilla looked around the room. People were everywhere, some in silk suits with ties and shirts, some in long, clinging dresses. A few wore tight-fitting hats with chin straps. Some stood against the fireplace with cigarettes hanging from their languid fingers. Others smoked cigars. A very fat woman stood encircled by an adoring coterie of fans. Lilla could not quite put her finger on the mood in this very long room. Huge picture windows let light fall upon the paintings on the opposite wall, one of which was her own, she realized with great pride. Some people sat with their arms around each other. Maids in black uniforms with clean white aprons continually moved around, replenishing the champagne glasses with an amber liquid. Other maids passed heavy plates of tiny sandwiches and little chocolates topped with green and red berries. The room hummed with conversation. A fat lady's voice could be heard alone above the noise.

Then Lilla realized what was different. These people were all *women*. This party, she thought, must be for the new women. That fat lady must be Harriet Smythe-Jones, the very famous poet whose "Women in Chains" Lilla had read several years ago. Lilla turned to Amelia. "Amelia," she said, "there are no men here."

"Certainly not," Amelia agreed. "Men have their clubs to go to, and now we have ours."

"Is that Harriet Smythe-Jones?" Lilla asked.

"It is indeed. Come along. I'll introduce you."

Harriet was delighted to meet Lilla. "I do love artists," she said. "We need more women artists. Too many men painting nudes. Why don't you paint nudes, dear?"

Lilla was taken aback. "Well, I don't. But I'm sure I could try."

"Well, there's an excellent art school in New York. They're just now taking new students after a dreadful battle with the faculty professor. Woman hater, he is. Lizzie, hand me a smoke. Thank you." Harriet grinned, lighting her cheroot. "I blew smoke in the old buzzard's face. Anyway, just let me know if you want a place. Amelia, come over here and talk. What have you been doing in the country?" The two women forgot Lilla in a genial catching-up conversation.

Lilla moved away and wandered into the far end of the hall where a cadaverous woman, with a chalk-white face and huge nose, was reading aloud from a book. Drawn into the circle by a friendly young woman who took Lilla's elbow, Lilla began to listen to the poem that was being read. "Enslaved, betrayed, beaten, and despaired," the woman read, "our lot is to fight. Sisterhood is to share."

"Who is she?" Lilla whispered.

"That's Julianne Timpiece," the friendly young woman whispered back. "She's one of our best poets."

"Oh." Lilla was fascinated. "I've never heard a real poet read poetry."

"Yeah, well, Julianne's my lover, and I'm very proud of her."

Lilla's eyes widened. She restrained an urge to move away. There had been talk in Middletown five years ago about two men who behaved more like women, but the idea of a woman with another woman . . . Lilla wasn't quite sure what to think. She felt dizzy. For a moment she felt like bolting through the door and making for home. Home, where, by now, the evening meal would be prepared. Reuben, sitting at the head of the table, would say the *Motze,* the old familiar grace. The five children, with heads bowed, would follow him, and then there would be a rousing "Amen." She could see Ben's head the most clearly.

"Ah, daydreaming, dear?"

"No." Lilla jumped. "I'm just a little tired." Suddenly safe with Amelia in charge, the room lost its feeling of evil.

Amelia stopped a passing waitress. She picked up two champagne glasses. Lilla took a sip of hers. "Lovely," she said. "What is it?"

"Champagne cocktail. A small cube of sugar, a dash of Angostura bitters, good brandy, and the finest champagne. Best drink in the world."

Lilla decided that when she was a rich and famous artist she would drink only champagne cocktails.

"Lilla dear, do you smoke?" The diamond-studded woman reappeared, offering Lilla a purple cigarette.

"No, I'm afraid I don't."

"How about you, Amelia? Can I tempt you into another bad habit?"

"Julie, I have my own bad habits. I won't share yours."

Julie Youngblood laughed a deep-throated, warm, sensual laugh. "Amelia, I'll share *your* bad habits any day you care to ask." She touched Lilla on the shoulder. "You watch out," she said. "We don't call Amelia "The Fox" for nothing." Lilla looked perplexed. "Grow up, Sunshine, or the barn will be empty."

"What does she mean?" Lilla asked Amelia.

Amelia shook her head. "Don't worry. Nobody ever knows what Julie means. Look, Mrs. Rubenstein is going to judge the paintings."

An expectant hush fell over the room. Slowly, as the guests lined the room, Mrs. Rubenstein was pushed in her wheelchair down the wall studded with paintings. Lilla stood beside Amelia with her heart beating like a trapped lark. Clenching her hands until the nails hurt the palms, she willed herself to breathe slowly and quietly. Trying to calm herself, she remembered the happy hours she had spent standing on the drive to Amelia's house, her easel before her and her palette in hand, painting what she considered to be her finest work yet.

The wheelchair slowly passed the first ten paintings. Lilla's was number fifteen. As the wheelchair crept forward, Lilla felt she was going to faint. Her heart stopped beating altogether when Mrs Rubenstein raised her hand imperiously and stopped in front of Lilla's painting. Impatiently Mrs Rubenstein waved the same hand for a pair of lorgnettes which were carried by the second nurse. Casually, Mrs Rubenstein perused the picture of the big house. She made a signal and moved on. Three times more she stopped before different paintings. Then the nurse turned the chair back toward the dais.

It seemed like an eternity to Lilla before Mrs Rubenstein was settled back into her chair. Once seated, she raised her hand. Again, no one whispered or moved. "I have three choices," she said. "The first place is Diana Rosenbeck's portrait of Susan B. Anthony. Number two is Miss Lilla Braff's excellent painting of a private home. My third choice is . . ."

Lilla was overjoyed. "Never mind." Amelia put her arm around Lilla's shoulder. "You'll be number one next time."

"I don't mind. I don't mind at all," Lilla whispered. "I'm thrilled to win anything."

"Go on." Amelia shoved her toward the dais. "Go and say thank you to Mrs Rubenstein."

Lilla threaded her way up to the stage. I can't wait to tell that bitch, Miriam, she thought. Wait till they all hear I won a prize in New York. That'll shut them up.

By now she was directly in front of Mrs Rubenstein. "Well done, my dear." Mrs Rubenstein smiled.

Very broken and cracked teeth were exposed. "Here. Let me hang this little token of our esteem around your neck. Lean forward." Mrs Rubenstein's clawed hand touched Lilla's neck for a second as she wrapped round it a ribbon with a medal suspended from the end. A chill went down Lilla's back. Mrs Rubenstein's hand felt cold and dead, like that of a corpse.

"Thank you very much." Lilla gave a small curtsy. She turned and was suddenly aware of a whole room full of people clapping just for her. That elusive moment she had so long dreamed of was here. She was famous. Tears ran down her face. She lifted her arms and stretched them out to the other women. "Thank you. Thank you," she said. And then she ran through the crowd and threw herself into her mentor's arms.

Amelia held her close and kissed her gently on the side of the head. "It's all right, darling," she said. "I'm here."

೫ CHAPTER 15 ೫

Back at the hotel that evening, dinner was a huge celebration of amazing food and plentiful wine. Dining alone together, Amelia and Lilla shared plates of lobster thermidor, two bottles of Dom Perignon, and hours of congratulatory laughter. By the time they went to their suite, Lilla felt contentedly tired and more than a little unsteady on her feet thanks to the champagne.

While Amelia changed into her nightdress in the bathroom, Lilla lay on her bed staring at her medal. She could still only barely believe she had won. Second place or first place, it did not matter. She had won. New York loved her. New York appreciated her art, even if her own family did not. True, Reuben had built her the easel, and Ben was always quick to say he liked a painting or a sketch, but Lilla felt their interest in her work to be trivial. Everyone at home treated her art as if it were nothing more than a hobby, a woman's way to pass her time. But New York, *New York* recognized her as a genuine artist. How, she wondered, could she ever go back home, back to the drudgery of being merely the wife of a farmer who wanted nothing more than to travel to the godforsaken empty West?

"It's free," Amelia called, standing at the bedroom door in her long satin nightdress with a fringe of lace at the throat and cuffs.

"What?" Lilla, startled, half-jumped.

"It's free now. The bathroom's free. Get changed for bed then come and kiss me good night."

"All right," said Lilla. As she climbed off the bed, she noticed a slight spinning feeling in her head. Shaking her head to clear it, she walked into the white-tiled luxury of the bathroom. There she undressed, washed, and put on the magnolia-pink silk négligé that Amelia had once given her as a present. This was the first time she had worn it with its low neckline. She could never have worn such a thing in front of the girls, and if Reuben had ever seen her in it, she knew he would have been unable to control himself. The silk of the dress was smooth and cold against her skin. It's tight fit caressed her intimately around her breasts, down over her lips, and past her thighs.

Barefoot she returned to the bedroom and sat on the edge of Amelia's bed. Amelia lay beneath the covers, the blankets pulled up tight under her chin. "It's been the most wonderful day of my life," Lilla said. "Thank you, Amelia. I'll never forget today." She leaned forward, kissed Amelia on her soft cheek, then sat up straight.

"I'm very proud of you. I truly am." As she spoke, Amelia pulled back her bedclothes and took Lilla's face between her hands. Looking down between Amelia's outstretched arms, Lilla was surprised. She had seen her in her nightgown. But now, in bed, Amelia lay naked. Lilla felt the hands on either side of her head pulling her in close. Without resisting, she let herself be pulled until her head rested on Amelia's breast as if on a soft, down pillow. A rosy nipple pressed against her cheek, as pink as it had appeared in the bath. "Come," Amelia said quietly. "Lie beside me. Just for a little while." With one hand, Amelia held open the blankets to make room for Lilla's legs.

Lilla moved her legs up under the sheets and blankets. She snuggled into the bed until her silk-encased body rubbed against Amelia's bare skin. At first she felt unsure about lying so closely, so intimately, with Amelia, her friend, another woman. But the comfortable softness of the body beside her soothed her and overwhelmed all doubts. Lilla felt the sedating effect of the champagne calm her. With her face against Amelia's breast, she lay for what felt a very long time. Amelia remained motionless, except for one hand that gently stroked Lilla's hair and cheek. Through the cushioning breast, Lilla could hear a heartbeat, a steady lullabying pulse. Its gentle muffled rhythm rocked her, like a drowsy baby, nearly to sleep. Then she heard, "Lilla". Through the chest beside her ear the word resonated and stirred her. "Lilla," Amelia said a second time, and Lilla lifted her head.

Again Amelia took Lilla's head between her hands, but this time she pulled the face up beside her own. Amelia kissed her lightly, first on the cheek, next on the lips. Then Lilla felt a tongue push between her closed lips, as Reuben's tongue had done in the past, as her artist's tongue had done very long ago. Without thinking, Lilla responded, opening her mouth to receive it. She returned the kiss, and a warmth spread throughout her body.

Suddenly the power of thought pounced upon her. What on earth was she doing? This was *Amelia* she was kissing. Another woman! She pulled her head back in alarm and stared wide-eyed at her friend.

"Oh, don't be such a child," Amelia said with a smile, but her voice held a slight edge of harshness. "Don't act so surprised. We've both been waiting for this moment ever since we first met. You know it as well as I do. It's no use pretending to be surprised now."

"But, Amelia—" Lilla was genuinely shocked by what she found herself doing, what she discovered herself *feeling*. She was excited. Her body wanted to respond. At the same time she was frightened. The edge in Amelia's voice seemed almost menacing. But Amelia was right. Lilla could not say she was completely surprised, not after the bath earlier in the day.

"Shhh. Don't worry yourself." Amelia's voice softened. "This is how it's meant to be."

"But—"

"Quiet. Let yourself relax. Let us enjoy each other. There's nothing wrong with pleasure. There's no need to deprive yourself any longer." She lifted her head and kissed Lilla's mouth again, pressing deeper and deeper into its wetness.

And Lilla let herself be carried away. She pushed aside her doubts and yielded with increasing eagerness to the warmth of the body beside her and the heat that took over her own body. Their movements seemed to merge into a shapeless, timeless, rolling wave of touches and sensations. One moment Lilla found herself hungrily mouthing a nipple on a comforting breast, and the next she was pushing her fingers into a hot, wet fold of skin.

Lilla felt a rising energy in her body, a force that was nearing explosion, but just before she could burst, Amelia shook with a small shudder then lay back, breathing deeply.

Lilla lay quietly, still dressed in her négligé. She waited for Amelia to move again, to continue, to satisfy her as she had satisfied Amelia. Amelia made no motion. "Lovely, my dear," Amelia said at last. "Very lovely." She fell silent as her breathing steadied. Then she said, "Now isn't that far more satisfying than with a man?"

Lilla thought. Indeed, the absence of Reuben's rough beard and dogged thrusting was both noticeable and welcomed. With Amelia, everything was softer, more like herself, more diffuse yet more intense. "Yes," she replied. "It is nicer, I suppose." Mustering her last bit of determination to reach her own explosion, she added, "And I came very close to being satisfied."

"Oh really, Lilla," Amelia laughed. "There's more to making love than climaxes."

Lilla felt frustrated and slightly hurt. "But you did."

"Of course I did," said Amelia. "I do very easily. But we haven't started to keep a tally already, have we? Don't worry. Perhaps we shall see to your satisfaction another time. Perhaps not. It really doesn't matter. It's not the essential." She rolled away from Lilla and nestled into her pillow. "I will sleep wonderfully tonight," she sighed happily. "Good night. You can sleep beside me, if you wish. Please shut out the light."

Lilla reached for the light switch then lay back beside Amelia in the darkened room. A confusion flooded her as she heard Amelia's breathing soften into light snores. She had enjoyed the warmth of the body, the softness of the kisses, the delicacy of the touches. But did Amelia have no desire to pleasure her as well? Had she merely serviced Amelia?

No, she realized. She had found something in their lovemaking, even if the physical pleasure seemed to be one-sided and perhaps a bit selfish. She had found something she had been missing for most of her life: a strange sort of comfort, the singular solace of being embraced to the breast of an older woman. Amelia's right, she thought. It's not a matter of climax. The satisfaction she had found was deeper than that.

Besides, Amelia had brought her to a whole new world of art, fashion and wealth. She turned over on her side and shut her eyes. At last I've found my freedom, she thought. With those words singing in her head, she let the champagne lull her weary mind to sleep.

* * *

When Lilla took her courage into both hands and confronted Reuben with the fact that she had accepted a job as Amelia's companion, Reuben felt the blood drain from his face. His heart felt as dark as the night outside. "I don't believe you are doing this," he said. The Lilla that had left for New York was not the same Lilla that walked back into the house two weeks later.

"I am." Lilla's voice shook with intense anger. "I want to live with Amelia and go to art school. Reuben, you've got to believe me. Rebecca," she said, "tell him. Tell him I've got to go . . . Oh"—she shook her head in frustration—"I don't expect either of you to understand. I can't live like this. I can't go on pretending I like being a farmer's wife. I hate cows. I hate mud. I need beauty. I want all the things Amelia can give me. Look, Reuben." She put out her small, delicate foot. "See? Handmade shoes, just for me. In Butlin's shoe store, there is a wooden last of my feet. The only one like it in New York."

Rebecca said nothing. Her face was impassive. Go, you bitch, she thought. We'll be better off without you.

Reuben sighed. "I can give you handmade shoes, Lilla. You know I'll give you everything you want. That's why we're going West: to make my fortune. It's all for you. Everything I do, everything I have, is all for you. I don't ask for anything for myself, do I?"

Lilla knew what he meant. Days, nights, and years of abstinence had so eaten into Reuben's soul that he grew to leave Lilla alone. He ignored a deep, rich part of himself Lilla never appreciated. "It's not just possessions," she said, reminding herself she must remain strong. "It's a whole new way of life. You would never fit into it. You wouldn't even understand it."

"What about the children? Thank God they're all asleep upstairs. It would break their hearts to hear you talk like this." Reuben looked at Lilla. "But tell me. Are you really able to leave your children?"

Lilla moved across the kitchen to the stove. She poured herself a cup of coffee. The warm, familiar smell of the freshly ground beans, along with the slight bitterness of the liquid that quietly brewed all day, helped her to stay calm. "Don't think I haven't thought of that for many hours," she said at last. "Especially Ben. But then, you have your mother to go with you. Honestly," she looked at Reuben as if for the first time, "I honestly think they'll be better off without me. I never really wanted children. I know you did, so I had them. But as for me, I was never cut out to be a wife and mother. Look." Lilla pulled a ribbon out of her pocket. "See, Reuben? I won second prize for my painting of Amelia's house. I am an artist. I'm not just pretending, here in this house; I won this in *New York*."

Rebecca moved toward her son. "Let her go, Reuben," she said. "She always was a wild bird. Let her go."

Reuben stood, feeling as if he would die from the pain.

"I'll send a servant tomorrow for my things," Lilla said. She put her coffee cup down on the table and quickly kissed Reuben on the cheek. "I'm sorry," she said, looking at her mother-in-law. "I'm sorry." Her neat nervous steps ran into the hall. Reuben and Rebecca heard her shoes quickly rap the wooden floor.

* * *

Lilla was halfway out the door when she felt a hand on her shoulder. She turned around. "Oh, God," she said. "Ben."

"I heard you from upstairs," he whispered. "I know what's happening."

"Ben, I . . ." she started to explain.

"Take me with you," he said. "Please, mama, Don't leave me without you. Take me with you."

She opened her mouth but no words came out. She just stared at her eldest son. His dark brown eyes seemed to read her thoughts.

The twelve-year-old boy looked back at his mother. She looked as he had never seen her before. Her black hair glistened silver in the moonlight through the door. She appeared to him as a roped wild horse, dying to be set free. There was a remoteness in her eyes as if she were answering a call that was very far away. He looked at the face he loved so much, but now it was the face of a stranger, of a woman he hardly knew. "Goodbye, mother," he said quickly as Lilla still looked for words. He kissed her quickly on the cheek then ran upstairs as fast as he could so she would not see his tears. He had lost his mother forever.

From the kitchen Reuben and Rebecca heard the front door slam. Rebecca put her hand on the back of Reuben's neck. "I'll start getting her wardrobe together," she said but Reuben did not hear her.

BOOK TWO

Nora and Esther

1895

✥ CHAPTER 16 ✥

For Nora, only six years old at the time, the trip West became a nightmare. It began harmlessly enough. Reuben, after selling his farm, packed his mother and his five children into proper railway compartments, and some livestock and as many of the family's belongings as he could manage into the cargo carriages. The Braffs boarded the train in Newark, New Jersey, then transferred in Philadelphia to the *Santa Fe Express,* the train which would carry them to their dreamed-of destination. Everyone in the family was so busy seeing that they, and their belongings, changed trains safely in Philadelphia they hardly had a free moment to feel the excitement of the great city. Once the train pulled away from the station in Philadelphia, however, the family settled into what would be their home for the next two weeks.

Steadily the great, steam-powered engine pulled its many trailing carriages over the fertile farmland of Pennsylvania, stopping briefly in Pittsburg, then across the Ohio River, and on into the state of Ohio. As the passing fields grew wider and the horizon larger, a quietness took possession of the Braff family. No one talked about Lilla. The pain of her abandonment was still too fresh. Rebecca sat silently next to Reuben for many hours, knowing that only time could lessen his agony.

Ben withdrew nearly completely into himself. Since his mother had walked out, his world had become one of almost unendurable pain, as if some vital part of his body had been torn forcibly from him. His father and grandmother felt helpless as they watched him suffer. But what could they say to him? How could they explain a mother's abandonment of her son only months before his *bar mitzvah?* That occasion—what was supposed to be the highlight of any Jewish boy's young life as he moved into manhood—passed without much celebration. Mort had officiated at the event, but the mood of the day had seemed to him more funereal than celebratory.

The three middle children, however, adjusted with equanimity to Lilla's departure months ago. Isaac had understood from a very early age that his mother's affections were reserved exclusively for Ben. An independent child, Isaac had learned to get on with his own life. As the train rolled through Columbus, Ohio, the single thought dominating his mind was whether or not they would see any cowboys and Indians once they reached the Wild West he had read about.

Naomi and Bea also reconciled themselves to Lilla's absence. Lilla never did have much time for the two young girls. On the train they busied themselves playing with their dolls and running between the carriages, making their rounds of visits to all their neighbors from New Jersey who were making the great journey with them: Vincent and Mary Cooper, Betty Thompson, the Gottsteins and their teenage son

Danny, and, of course, the Kearneys. Naomi, in particular, was especially fond of visiting the Kearneys. For years her friendship with Matthew Kearney had grown. Now, as a chirpy eleven-year-old, she was even beginning to fancy him in adolescent earnest.

Spending time in the Kearneys' compartment was always an adventure. In their carriage, Irish anarchy prevailed. Big John was drinking as a rule, his wife Lizzie had a habit of nagging, one or other of the brothers was usually fighting, and the girls were cavorting with several handsome lads somewhere else on the train. In the middle of the commotion, Matthew and Naomi would sit, giggling.

But to Nora, Lilla's desertion had brought actual joy. Not having a mother meant no more being hit or screamed at. No longer did she have to watch her father desperately trying to please a woman who seemed to do nothing but complain. A bright and astute child, she had never thought it fair that her father should be bickered at by a bad-tempered woman, when she, Nora, found it so easy to please him. All she had to do was to smile at him and the warmth in her eyes put a smile on his face in return. As the train pulled itself over the endless flat fields of Indiana, Nora spent days sitting with her father and grandmother. She played on the floor, and her little jokes and cheerful smiles brought a light of innocent joy into Reuben's otherwise gloomy darkness. Someday, Nora hoped, she would marry a man as kind as her father. And, someday, she would cook as well as Grandma Rebecca cooked to keep him happy.

Even Ben seemed to brighten momentarily as the train stopped to fill its water tanks and to take on extra cars of coal in the huge maze of railway switchings called Chicago, the pulsating heart of America's iron-railed body. An unimaginable amount of trains could be seen in all directions. The squeaks and groans of the great machines filled the air as they grinded against each other to rehitch. Through the open windows of the carriage the smell of cattle wafted, as did the mournful lowing of the cows making their last stop before the slaughterhouses.

With a jerk and a blow of its whistle, the *Santa Fe Express* set off once again, carrying the Braffs over Missouri and into the wide expanses of Kansas. The air of Kansas seemed different to any the family had smelled before. The fields were as flat as Indiana, but there was something in the wind—a certain unleashed, untamed excitement—that told Reuben and his children they were entering the West. Then, in Kansas, the peaceful hours of the train's gentle rocking turned into days of horror.

No one on the train could be sure how it started. Perhaps, some conjectured, it was bad water they had taken on board in Topeka. Perhaps it was contamination picked up from the livestock in Chicago. These, however, were mere guesses. It didn't really matter. What did matter was that first one, then a second, then a third, passenger took ill as the train roared mightily across the open plains. A spiraling fever seized the suffering passengers. Their skin paled, then red spots appeared. Hair fell from their heads like fur off shedding animals. Nothing could be done to avert the fury of the disease. Typhoid fever swept through the carriages of the train, transforming the locomotive into a steam-powered epidemic.

Reuben was awakened one night by the sound of Bea crying. Fearfully, he ran to her berth. She lay shivering and sweating. Reuben felt the heat of her forehead: the fever had clutched his daughter. He stayed beside her all night, washing her with moistened cloths, desperately trying to wash away the disease as well. By morning she was no better, and Reuben was horrified to see that Isaac, too, awoke with the same symptoms. By that evening, hellishly red spots covered both children. For days, Rebecca and Reuben had no sleep. Together they nursed the children and prayed for their lives.

The crew and passengers of the train were helpless against the typhus. Soon, not illnesses but deaths were being counted. When the train approached the border to Oklahoma, the head engineer informed his passengers that carrying the infected dead bodies any further would only endanger all of their lives. In the middle of a windy plain, the train stopped and many rows of graves were dug beside the tracks. Into two of those graves, Reuben laid the bodies of Isaac and Bea. Rebecca held Nora back as the thin dirt was poured over the children's bodies.

Not even a headstone marked the graves of those men, women, and children, who paid such a high price for going West. From that day, Reuben's face acquired new lines. His fine head of black hair turned gray. Compounded by the abandonment of his beloved wife Lilla, he mourned the loss of his two children.

Vincent and Mary Cooper did what they could to comfort him, as did Joseph and Ruth Gottstein, but it was Big John Kearney who, in his own way, proved to be the most consolation. Big John's version of comfort consisted of several shots of whiskey, followed by beer chasers, and ramblingly philosophical sermons.

Late into the night, he sat with Reuben, expounding on his favorite subjects. The only good woman, he explained, was a pregnant woman, kept preferably on a lead that allowed her access to the bedroom or to the kitchen sink. "Like me own wife Lizzie," he bellowed.

When he saw that such talk seemed only to deepen Reuben's grief, he steered his speeches to a more theological bent. "We both share the same Bible you know, we Catholics and you Jews," he pointed out. "Well, at least the first part of it." Thus begun, his lectures then demonstrated that God, having gone through all the trouble of taking His children into the wilderness, didn't plan to just dump them there. "No," Big John assured Reuben, "there's a reason for it all. And surely there's a promised land waiting for us at the end of the ride."

Reuben listened with only half an ear. But there was a comfort to be found in the loud company of this enormous Irishman and a very strong solace in the whiskey that inevitably followed each speech, announced with the words, "Here. What do you say we have another little drink?"

When, at times, even the whiskey could not numb Reuben's pain, he found he wanted to fling himself off the train as it hurtled through the Oklahoma panhandle. No, he reminded himself. That would be too easy. He still had to care for what was left of his family. When whiskey failed, then duty kept him alive.

The train's crossing into New Mexico brought on a new and very immediate struggle. By now, most of the region's Indians had been settled by the government within the confines of reservations. There remained, however, a few wandering bands, Apaches in particular, who shirked the harness of reservation life and who continued to fight for their freedom against the government and against the trains full of white men who, the Indians believed, were nothing more than government emissaries. The threat of attack by Apaches was especially fear-inspiring to anyone, like the train's crewmen, who had traveled this territory before.

When the train left Oklahoma and entered New Mexico, a renegade band of Apaches sat on horseback on a hillside waiting to attack. Shrieking shrill cries, the warriors descended upon the train, firing rifles they had captured in previous raids. Again, Big John Kearney proved himself invaluable. Handy with a gun, he did much to secure the safety of the train. "Here," he said, handing Reuben a loaded rifle. "Take that bastard injun over there."

Shooting out of the carriage window at the brightly painted warriors, Reuben put all of his anger, all of his pain, into every shot. He imagined himself pumping bullets into Amelia Witney-Hay. As he shot bullets into the bleeding bodies of Indians, he found to his amazement that the will to live had not left him.

Big John understood.

The surviving Indians knew they were defeated. They disappeared as quickly as they had come, and the train continued on its way.

At last, after what seemed like years since it had left New Jersey, the *Santa Fe Express* chugged past Lamy, New Mexico, only fifteen miles outside Santa Fe.

The small village of Lamy vibrated with life. Reuben, Rebecca, and the three children stared out of the window. They were astonished at the variety of faces. The village was surrounded by the tents of Chinamen, the original builders of the railroad. Black cowboys, more numerous than they would have imagined, rode horses along the village's one street. These were the children of the freed slaves who had resettled out West.

As if physically exhausted by the long trip, the train climbed slowly up the last miles of the land seven thousand feet above sea level. Then, in the heart of Santa Fe, it jolted and hissed to a final stop. New Jerseyans no more but now New Mexicans, Reuben and the remnants of his family climbed off the train and looked around them. Low adobe buildings, the same color as the brick-red earth, were everywhere in sight. Spanish men rode past on horses while woman sat and children played in front of the houses. White men and women, too, could be seen walking in and out of the few shops along Guadalupe Street across from the train station. Above it all rose great blue mountains.

Reuben blinked in the brightness of the sunshine. He no longer had a wife, and two of his children lay buried somewhere nameless in Kansas. But now, surrounded by desert on one side and mountains on the other, Reuben stood in an oasis of a city that felt at peace with itself. Nora, standing beside her father, held his hand. "Well," he said with a tired sigh, squeezing the small hand in his own, "we're here." Will we ever call it home? he wondered.

❧ CHAPTER 17 ❧

From the sale of their store back in Middletown, Joseph and Ruth Gottstein had amassed a sizeable profit. Property and goods were so much less expensive in the West than on the East Coast that, after their move, the Gottsteins found themselves in a position of great wealth. The proceeds from the sale of their New Jersey business had enabled them to put Danny through Harvard Medical School. Furthermore, with a good amount of cash in hand, Joseph decided to open a bank in Santa Fe. Having suffered, along with Reuben and the rest of the Jewish, at the hands of anti-Semitic gentile bankers in New Jersey, Joseph now made it his bank's policy to be particularly helpful in lending money to other Jews who were establishing new lives on the Western frontier. Ruth Gottstein, retired from her years of hard work as a shopkeeper, enjoyed—for the first time—her life as matron of the comfortable house Joseph built for her on a hilltop overlooking Santa Fe, where Mary and Vincent Cooper lived nearby. Vincent, with Mary's help, opened a dry-goods store and it was now the Coopers' turn to serve as shopkeepers, servicing the community of friends transplanted from New Jersey to New Mexico.

Little Nora Braff never imagined she would fall passionately in love with the rich, successful, brilliant doctor Daniel Gottstein grew up to become. Nora had adored Danny when they were both children in New Jersey. Every time Lilla used to go to the Gottsteins' shop back in Middletown, Nora asked to go with her. Occasionally, if Ben didn't want to go, she could go in his place.

Nora was a very quiet child. Unlike her sisters, she did not have a range of idle chatter. While Bea and Naomi were pretty to look at, like their mother, and both girls elicited compliments from other shoppers, no one really noticed Nora, a shy presence whose only redeeming features were her warm, brown eyes. Those eyes shone especially warmly whenever she saw Danny, eight years older than herself.

For Danny, after the aggressive women who were beginning to make their presence felt in medical schools across America, Nora was a welcome relief. He watched over her while she grew from a little girl into a shy, gentle eighteen-year-old. At twenty-seven, he was ready for marriage. It was Nora Braff he asked to be his bride, and it was a very delighted Nora Braff who agreed, at the age of nineteen, to become Mrs. Daniel Gottstein.

Danny loved his job, but he adored his wife. He treated Nora as if she were made of spun glass. When he made love to her, it was with a reverence and gentleness which never ceased to amaze them both. Nora was amazed because Lilla had warned her as a young girl that sex was all a man wanted. Sex was the reason why a man married, and sex was an onerous burden on a wife. Even as a small girl, Nora knew, as did all her brothers and sisters, that Lilla didn't do "it". Walls were thin in the early days when they all lived in Middletown.

So Nora was especially delighted to put her pale, white arms about her husband's neck and sink into their private ecstasy. Unlike the other young married women of Santa Fe, Nora would say nothing about her private life with her husband to the other wives. Neither did she find clothes-shopping and gossiping to be an attractive way of life. Soon, as a young married woman in the fashionable capital city of New Mexico, Nora was quietly dropped by the other women. Nothing suited her better. She still had her sister Naomi who, despite the fact the Kearneys were not Jews and Naomi was not Irish, had been happily absorbed into the Kearney clan. Nora loved to visit the loquacious Irish family, as Big John expanded his business to include the local whorehouse and a liquor store.

"You are pregnant indeed." Dr. Paul smiled at Nora.

Nora, sitting in her shift on the end of the examining couch, looked shyly at this large, quiet man.

It was only at times like this Nora found herself wishing she had a mother, an older woman who could help her deal with the facts of her own womanhood. Nora loved her grandmother deeply, but Rebecca still retained too much old-worldly austerity for Nora to feel completely comfortable discussing everything with her. Reuben had worked hard to see his children through the last years of their growing up. With the money from the sale of his farm in New Jersey, he had bought a ranch outside Santa Fe. Reuben grew old and plump, watching over his children anxiously.

Every so often, as Nora had passed through her teenage years, news of Lilla's exploits was relayed from Middletown to Santa Fe via Miriam, still in Middletown and a copious letter writer. Lilla's escape from domesticity became an obsession to her. She culled from the grapevine all she could about Lilla's whereabouts, and her bits of information were carefully reported in her letters.

With time, Nora's feelings for Lilla had changed. Her gladness at no longer being mistreated had worn thin over the years. Her memories of Lilla had faded so that she could no longer be sure whether she missed her or not. On occasion, however, she was aware of a void in her life that she sensed could be filled only by a mother's love. Dressed and sitting in Dr. Paul's office at the age of twenty, Nora knew that now was such an occasion.

Dr. Paul looked at the quiet girl with the soft black hair sitting at his desk before him. "Mrs. Gottstein," he said. "You have been suffering a lot of nervous depression. Danny tells me you have periods of crying."

Nora nodded. "I do," she said. "I feel dreadfully anxious."

"What worries you?"

Nora sighed. "I suppose I miss living with my father. Danny and I have a nice house, but you know better than anyone how hard Danny works, since he's your partner."

Dr. Paul smiled. "In six months, you won't have time to worry your pretty little head about loneliness. You'll have a baby to keep you occupied."

Nora's eyes glowed. "That makes me glad," she said. Then she hesitated. "But there's Ben. He never really got over my mother leaving us. He was her favorite, you know."

"I do know." Dr. Paul sighed. "Such a dreadful thing to do, abandoning all the children."

"She's an artist," Nora said. "She felt she had to go. She had so much talent, we were holding her back."

Dr. Paul raised his eyebrows. He too read the New York newspapers. He too heard the gossip in Santa Fe. But he held his peace. Nora needed to defend herself from the knowledge that her mother had run away from her family to live with a woman whose public life had been scarred by one affair after another, mostly with other men's wives. "Do congratulate Danny for me, won't you?" Dr. Paul said as he opened the door of his office for Nora. "He's a fine doctor, and I know he'll make a wonderful father. And if you're worried about your brother Ben, I'll see what I can do."

"Thank you." Nora's eyes were wet. "I mustn't cry," she said firmly. "Crying upsets Danny."

Nora knew that when her time came to give birth, Betty Thompson, with her firm North-country bedside manner, would be there to deliver the baby. Meanwhile, Nora knitted little boots in white so as not to be mistaken or to anticipate the birth.

Naomi had married Matthew Kearney and they already had Sam, a big, bouncing baby. He was Reuben's particular joy, his first grandchild, with red hair and blue eyes. He was so dear to Big John's heart that even Lizzie, after her eight children, smiled to see the child astride his grandfather's shoulder as they went marching down the Old Santa Fe Trail toward Big John's business on Burro Alley.

Reuben had realized, with Sam's birth, that Lilla was not coming back. He treasured the newspaper cuttings of her in various settings. He passed news of the family to Miriam in the hope of a response. When Bea and Isaac died, he tried to find Lilla. He received a curt reply from Susan, the maid, that Lilla and

Amelia were away traveling. When Naomi got married, Reuben again tried to contact his wife. She was in Paris, and then in Rome. But when he held Sam, his grandson, in his arms and felt a new world growing under his feet, he finally faced the truth: Lilla would never come back.

Vincent Cooper, who by now had two of his sons join him from Ireland, said at Sam's circumcision (the Kearneys' gesture of respect to Naomi's religion), "You'd best forget her. She'd never survive a frontier town like Santa Fe."

Reuben knew his friend was telling the truth. All around him stood the people who had known Lilla for many years. Winter set into his heart, and he laid a grave on his ranch for his wife. He put a white picket fence around it, said *Kaddish* for her memory, and vowed never to speak her name again. He stopped writing to Miriam, who then switched post-boxes and sent her information directly to Nora.

Unlike Mort, the rabbi in Santa Fe was fiercely orthodox. He demanded that women shave their heads. He also demanded that Jewish families in Santa Fe leave the gentile community well alone. Long ago, Reuben and Rebecca had discussed the synagogue with the children. Because of the friendship, and now the marriage, between Naomi and Matthew Kearney, the rabbi resolutely barred the synagogue doors to all members of the Braff family.

Word of the Santa Fe rabbi's decision found its way two thousand miles northeast to Miriam's ears in Middletown. She received the news with glee. "Always knew they would come to a bad end," she chortled.

Mort made a face. If going to Santa Fe, New Mexico was how you ended up badly maybe he should join them. After all, he had not found a satisfactory replacement for Molly Parkington. The two remaining resident whores in town were crones, and Miriam only got fatter. By now Miriam had appointed herself chief sleuth on Lilla's trail. Mort was very bored. What women did with each other did not excite him. What excited him were a pair of skinny legs and a blonde muff, both of which were now missing in his life. No matter that little Nora Gottstein was pregnant with twins or that Reuben was well on the way to making his first million in the ranching business. Maybe Mort wasn't cut out to be a rabbi. The very thought shook him. His mother's life depended on his being a rabbi. Sometimes he wished that news from the new world never reached the old. He wondered what Reuben did for sex and thought again of Molly Parkington.

For a prostitute like Molly, Santa Fe was a dangerous place. The small town crouched, almost precariously, at the junction of the dry desert and the green piñon forests of the Sangre de Cristo mountain range—the beginning of the magnificent Rockies. The men rode into town from the surrounding coal and turquoise mines in the smaller towns of Cerrillos and Madrid and the railroad tent camps in Lamy. They arrived with money in their pockets and liquor in their bellies. Many of them lived dangerously. Stakes were high. To die by the gun or the knife was a daily risk, and if fighting didn't end your life, a rattlesnake would.

Even Nora knew that feelings between the Indian and the Hispanic communities were tense. The Catholic priests were mostly illiterate Spanish peasants who were sent to this most unruly of all the United States by the Franciscans in Italy. For many of the priests, to come to New Mexico was an act of faith, a willing martyrdom in the name of Jesus. The priests were expected to wean the Indians away from heathenism and encourage them to embrace the Catholic faith. Also, the priests fought against the Brotherhood, an ancient and secret order of men who lived in and around Santa Fe.

For centuries the Brothers ruled New Mexico with a rod of iron. The Hispanic people of New Mexico revered this ancient order, whose lives were dedicated to living as Jesus lived. At Holy Week, the Brotherhood walked from the far corners of New Mexico to join the pilgrims at the miracle church in Chimayo to the north of Santa Fe.

When Nora was four months pregnant, Dr Paul told her she was going to have twins. Danny was delighted when he heard the news.

The Easter lilies were in bloom at the time. Even though Danny and Nora were Jews, Nora very much wanted to go to the miracle church to pray. She had the latest clipping about her mother from Miriam in her purse when she set off to the little church of miracles in Chimayo.

It was hot; the Easter Sunday of 1909. The roads to Chimayo were lined on either side with pilgrims. Some came to pray, some to watch. Those on crutches hoped for miracles. The church was famous for them. Nora had several reasons to ask for miracles. One was for the safe birth of the twins. She was small, and they were larger than normal. Betty assured her she was fit and healthy but Nora still wanted the precaution of prayer. Her second desire for a miracle—and this was her secret wish—was that Lilla would come back. Nora wanted to present her mother with grandchildren, and maybe, somehow, the rift could be healed between herself and her mother.

A third wish was that Nora's brother, Ben, would reform his ways. His drinking and his gambling had become legendary in Santa Fe, but his womanizing was worse still. Rumors of numerous married women, entertaining Ben in their beds while their husbands were out of town, were legion. Only Nora could talk to Ben when, in his drunken soliloquies, he spoke of the loss of his mother. Only Nora could hold him quietly and lay her cheek on his black head as he cried. Probably only Nora, by now, understood his need to pursue women, any woman that would have him, in his need to look for the unobtainable: his mother's arms.

The road was dusty and barely visible from where Nora and Danny sat on the seat of the trap. The steps of thousands of feet flattened the earth. Groups of priests and nuns swished past singing in Latin. Families with babies tramped all day and sat and slept by fires at night. People prayed together and for each other. But Danny knew that Nora could never walk that far in her condition, though many other women did. Danny had a sleek gig, with two fine bay horses ready to take his wife on the drive, through the verdant valley of Pojaque, up into the hills, and then down through the Nambe valley, green with grass and alive with the sound of the Rio Grande river, overflowing from the melted snow of the mountains, running steadily over the brown stained stones. Large wooden crosses on craggy hillsides beckoned the travelers into the mysterious ways of the little church.

Vendors in the town sold holy pictures and rosaries. Food merchants sold *burritos* and fried bread. Here and there an Indian face, converted at last by a priest, stood out, the fierce long black hair tied in a pigtail to signify respect.

Nora looked at the people as they passed. She thanked God and her father for the chance to live among such a group. Middletown, with its strictly observed rules and regulations, would have stifled her. Only Danny knew that Nora spent her days in the houses of the sick and the dying. Reuben would have been appalled if he knew that his favorite daughter nursed those suffering from fever, especially if he knew she took her pony and trap and visited the Indian reservations. When the Medicine Man failed, Nora tried.

Tuberculosis was the scourge of the reservations. The white man had brought not only guns and whiskey to the Indians, not only his Western decadent ways, but also his diseases. Nora protected herself from these diseases with an ancient herbal treatment. Every morning, with a grimace, she swallowed a tablespoon of vinegar and garlic. She brewed the vinegar out of the apples that grew in her back garden. She bottled it and added ten plump cloves of garlic. The bottles sat in the larder for three months, and then the liquor was used to cure sick babies. Nora also washed herself and her hair after each visit to the reservations.

Now that she was pregnant, Nora gave up visiting and stayed home. With her extra energy, she cooked huge stews and soups and, above all, her famous chicken soup. If Danny had a patient that could not eat, he asked Nora for a bowl of her fresh chicken soup with a dash of red chilli to get the appetite to return. Gladly, Nora cooked.

Just as gladly now, she watched the never-ending stream of people approach the little church, fan out into the area around the churchyard, and then get on their knees to pray. Danny did not try to push her into the throng inside the church. They both sat in the trap where they could hear the priest praying aloud with the congregation. The little bell, paid for by the villagers, called sweetly across the valley, answered by the restless voices of the cows that were disturbed by so many strangers.

Near the church stood the *morada*, the home of the Brotherhood, out of bounds to all except the initiates and a few women who took vows never to tell what took place behind those walls. The village knew what took place. Everyone in Chimayo knew which man had been chosen to play the part of Christ to be hanged from the cross on Good Friday. Should the man not survive the night, his family would know of his immediate acceptance into heaven by his shoes alone that were returned to the family home the next morning. Nobody said anything, but the family so blessed sat in the front pew of the church when deep night enclosed the village for the final *penitente* ritual to put the old dead year away and to welcome the new.

Nora knew more about *Los Hermanos*, the Brothers, than did most people. She, unlike some other empty-headed housewives, spent her time in Santa Fe listening. Danny was called on one occasion when a Santa Fe Brother's self-inflicted wounds refused to heal.

But today, a joyous mood filled the crowd. They were here for all reasons. Above all, they were happy to have just survived the raw New Mexico winter of the old year. Nora looked at Danny. How did plain Nora Braff ever marry such a wonderful man? In turn Danny looked down at Nora. Her belly was tight as a drum. He put his hand on top of the huge mound and he laughed as his babies kicked vigorously. Many of Danny's patients came up to the gig to talk and wish Nora well. New babies were what New Mexico needed. At last, with the light beginning to fade, Danny and Nora left the singing throngs of pilgrims and made their way to an inn in the Nambe valley. After dinner, Danny cradled his tired wife in his arms and dreamed of his children to come.

❧ CHAPTER 18 ❧

Nora was very happy. She lay in bed feeling the contractions ebb and flow. The babies had been quiet for the last few days and Danny had been gently undemanding. For that she was always eternally grateful. Listening to the other women, she realized Danny was an unselfish sensitive man. Now he lay quietly asleep next to her. She watched with special tenderness as his dreams sailed across his face and caused his mouth to quiver. Soon, she thought, he'll be a father. She winced as a spasm tightened her belly. "Darling?" she said. "Danny, you'd better get Betty. I think I'm in labor."

Danny woke up with a start. "Really? Here, let me feel." He grinned as he felt the muscles taut under his hand. "You certainly are in labor. Let me get dressed. Lie still. Don't move." Danny was up, dressed and out of the door in a few minutes.

Once Nora heard the door slam, she swung her feet over the bed and stood up. Frowning slightly at the pain, she made her way slowly across the floor to the kitchen. In the kitchen she stood at the sink and gazed at the red copper basin in front of her. Real zinc, she thought. Then she looked out of the window shaded by a tall apple tree: apple sauce for the babies. She moved slowly out into the garden and stood with her hand on top of her stomach, gazing at the hen-house. Speckle, her favorite hen, was laying furiously, almost as though the little hen knew her eggs would be needed soon. "Thank you," Nora said as she bent over with difficulty. She slipped her hand under the hen and retrieved a warm, brown egg. Several nests later, Nora had collected sufficient eggs to return to the kitchen and make an omelette.

On the way back past her flourishing kitchen garden, she stopped to pinch out a few fresh strands of parsley and rosemary. In the year since her wedding, much of Nora's time was devoted to the growing of vegetables and fruits. Already her plums and her peaches were pickled in strong brandy provided by Big John Kearney.

Big John loved to visit Nora. Arms full of fancy foreign liquors he was a welcome visitor. He often sat in the kitchen, scented with pies and stews, and talked. His own wife was a pale, frail woman who whined a lot. Sometimes, Big John looked at his herd of children and wished he had not been quite so incontinent. When the world of barroom fights and wine and women (particularly women! His prostitutes were a quarrelsome lot) became too much for him, he retreated to Nora's house and sat in the peace and calm of her company until order was restored to his soul.

Today, Nora gazed at her row of pickled onions, white and hard as bullets sunk in a sea of apple cider vinegar. The huge wooden barrel sat in the barn near old Jack, the bull. Nora collected last year's apples for this year's crop of pickling vinegar. Certainly her cucumber relish was a big delight. Big John treasured Nora's relish nearly as much as he treasured her fresh tomato sauce. Smiling at the thought of the look on Big John's face when she produced a steaming turkey, Nora, now in her kitchen, cracked open the first egg. The yolk fell into the brown porcelain bowl with the round sound of a plop. Nora looked at the yolk, It was an intensely satisfying bright orange. The other yolks followed quickly.

Now in the fecund month of September, the apple tree hung heavy with fruit. The potato plants lay stranded on the thick sandy soil waving their ready-harvested roots, bare and abandoned. The light brown potatoes lay in the sand at the dark end of the barn. Nora was particularly pleased with this year's crop. The magic moments when the first potatoes left the boiling pot, when the butter, lightly salted, melted into the potato, when Nora took her first bite, and when the crunch, and the slightly nutty taste of the potato, filled her mouth, were well worth the hours she spent among the potato plants weeding and discouraging the grasshoppers and the weevils from consuming her plants.

Nora moved across to her icebox and took out a small chunk of frozen butter. Chipping off small pieces she remembered the smell of the fresh milk as she tipped it into the churn. She remembered the satisfaction she felt when she spooned the thick white butter out of the new churn. The milk for the butter was particularly sweet. Reuben's cows wandered his many acres and fed on the mesquite that grew everywhere. Reuben saw to it that his family had fresh milk and Barnabas, Reuben's favorite servant, spent each morning delivering milk and ice in his ice-cart to the close members of Reuben's clan. This clan was by now swollen out of all proportion by its merging with the Kearney family through Naomi's marriage to Matthew.

Now, looking out through her kitchen window, Nora could see Barnabas' smiling black face coming up the road. Lazily beating the eggs with a wire whisk, Nora felt the contractions renewing their grip. Barnabas, at the door, looked concerned. "It's your time now?" he inquired.

"Yes," Nora said. "I should have the babies soon."

Barnabas eyed Nora's stomach. "I'll fetch ice," he said quickly. Barnabas did not appreciate birthing. At his end of town, women could be heard screaming and wailing when giving birth. Barnabas' reaction to his wife giving birth was to leave for Big John's bar and to stay for as long as it took. In fact, Barnabas could not remember the first glimpse of any of his six children. "They're all pickaninnies, as far as I'm concerned," he would tell Nora. "All pickaninnies till they grow up. Then I can tell them apart."

Barnabas loved Nora with a special love. She had

saved his third son's life with her chicken soup. "Like a miracle," Barnabas was often heard to say. "One minute the boy was dying, and a spoonful later, he was alive." Barnabas also dug the vegetable garden for Nora, then he put in the flower beds so that Reuben could visit his daughter and sit among the roses and the alien trees he had imported from the new world of California. Roses loved the New Mexico soil. Cottonwoods also thrived when planted next to the great river, the Rio Grande, which trailed across New Mexico on its way down south.

Nora heard Danny drive up. She had learned every squeak and clunk of Danny's carriage. Often, when she could not sleep and Daniel was out, she lay and listened as one carriage after another pulled past the little house with the neat fence, built by Barnabas when she and Danny were first married. "That'll be all?" Barnabas asked.

"Yes. That'll be all," Nora said.

Danny waved to Barnabas and ran up the path. "Betty will be here in a minute," he said. "How are you feeling?"

"Fine." She smiled. "I'm fine. I'm making an omelette for breakfast, or do you want steak, dear?"

"You shouldn't be cooking now," he said with some concern. "Why don't you lie down?"

"It helps me relax," she said with a smile.

Danny looked fondly at his wife. "In that case I'll have an omelette, but I'm almost too excited to eat."

Nora poured the eggs into her favorite frying pan. It had belonged to Lilla. With the tightening in her abdomen becoming more frequent, Nora earnestly wished her mother were here. The last time she had thought about her mother was a few weeks ago. Yes-

terday, Miriam, with her cunning—almost psychic—
knowledge of Lilla's whereabouts, had sent a clipping
of a fashionable party. Inset in a corner of the newspaper was a small picture of Lilla. Her beautiful, thin
face was hidden by a fashionable lacy veil and surrounded by a small, black, satin hood. Nora looked at
her picture intently. Was her mother happy? From
the picture, no emotion could be seen through the
veil. The eyes were mere black shadow, blurred by
the inky newsprint and only the outline of a mouth
could be discerned, turning down. Nora, safe and
secure in her marriage and very much in love, hoped
her mother was happy.

The omelette began to firm. Nora decided that
today she was not going to think about her mother.
Thinking about Lilla made her miserable. Anyway,
thinking would not bring Lilla back. Even Reuben,
her father, was getting over the desertion, and Ben
. . . Well, Ben was Ben. "There you are, darling," she
said to Danny. Neatly dividing the omelette in two,
Nora slipped the eggs onto two blue tin plates.

Danny sat at the kitchen table with his fork in the
air. "I can't wait," he said.

"For the eggs or the birth?"

"Both!" Danny laughed.

"You know," Nora leaned heavily on the table,
"Naomi came by yesterday. She said women are
chained by men to the table and the bed." Nora sat
back in her chair and put her hand again on her
stomach. "For the life of me, I can't think what's
wrong with that."

Danny grinned. "They're your two favorite places,
aren't they?"

"Yes." Nora smiled back, a mischievous twinkle in

her eye. "Soon there will be more bed, once this is over."

Danny sighed. "Thank God I married a traditional wife. You know, Naomi better watch out. All this newfangled stuff about the new woman . . . Well, Matthew won't take kindly to any of it."

Nora shook her head. "Don't worry. Naomi was just repeating what her friend Gloria had said. Naomi won't even go to the meetings. She said they're all too ugly and all they do is drink tea and complain about the men they can't catch. In fact, most of the group are from the East Coast. They came down with other families as tutors and seamstresses. But the Hispanic women don't listen to all that rubbish."

"What rubbish?" Betty Thompson's voice floated across the kitchen.

"Oh, you know. All that new woman stuff."

Betty made a face. "I don't mind them being new women, or even being with other women if they must. But I do mind when they declare free love and then they come to me for help." Betty looked at Danny.

He nodded. "Yes," he said. "I'm the first one they ask for help with their unwanted pregnancies." Betty was Danny's right-hand in the community. She carried the burden of aborting these feckless young women so sure of their new religion. She risked her life to get rid of the unwanted babies. Or, if she possibly could, she persuaded the women to have the baby and find a family to adopt the fatherless child. But these new women rarely took the responsibility of carrying the fetus to term. They were a hard, angry, little group, hurt by the East Coast and rejected by the tight traditions of relationships between men and women in a frontier town. They were shown no mercy by the local men. If the new women claimed they needed no protection against men, then by God they would get none. The local men loved and left them. Betty knew this and said nothing.

But today was a good day. The sun was shining and the bluebirds flew overhead as she walked into the little house and prepared to birth Dr Daniel Gottstein's and Nora's baby. Babies, she reminded herself as she saw Nora's belly.

ᯓ CHAPTER 19 ᯓ

"I do think you would look less dowdy if you cut off some hair."

Lilla shrugged. This argument had been going on between Amelia and herself for several weeks. "It's against the Jewish tradition to cut off a woman's hair. My hair is my crowning glory." Lilla stood uncertainly in the doorway of Amelia's bedroom. Fortunately, Amelia liked her own bedroom. When she occasionally needed Lilla to lie by her massive body and satisfy her with long strokes of Lilla's slender fingers, Lilla was glad to return to the sanctuary of her own little room and climb into the small, childlike bed that had been Amelia's as a little girl.

On the whole, Lilla found that she was tolerably happy. Amelia could be a harsh critic and a severe judge, but Lilla was good at anticipating Amelia's needs. A book or a cushion or even a hug in the proper place kept away Amelia's wrath.

But this argument was certainly making Amelia angry. "Amelia," Lilla held firm, "I really do want to keep my hair." Her voice was shaking. "I'm not interested in being terribly fashionable. There are enough women in our circle who think of nothing other than their bodies and clothes. I'm an artist." Lilla's voice rose. "I left home to paint, not play models. I want to be remembered for my paintings. 'Lilla Braff: Artist.'" Lilla walked slowly toward Amelia's bed. "Please, Amelia," she said in a softer voice. "Please."

Amelia was sitting upright with a blue scarf over her shoulders. "Come here, dear," Amelia said, also in a calmer voice. "Sit beside me and let's finish this stupid argument." Lilla sat down. Amelia leaned toward her chosen companion. "Let me take your hair down." Amelia smiled. "Here. Let me take out the pins and I'll stroke your lovely long, black hair with my hairbrush." Amelia possessed a beautiful Victorian silver hairbrush. The family crest adorned it, and the softest pigs' bristles ran through Lilla's dark hair.

Lilla enjoyed having her hair brushed. As a child, there was never anyone there to brush her hair except her sister when she had the time. So having Amelia brush her hair was a sensuous luxury. Lilla sighed and let her eyelids drop with satisfaction. The brush slid slowly from the top of her head, down to her waist, and lingered on her buttocks. Amelia held the long tresses in one hand and brushed the side of Lilla's right temple.

Lilla was lost in a private sexual heaven of her own. This heaven was not shared by any other human on earth. From the first time she had lain with Amelia, it had been apparent that, as far as Amelia was concerned, Lilla was there to give, not to receive, pleasure. She expected Lilla to serve her needs with a childlike simplicity. Lilla, for the exciting, rewarding, endless rounds of parties and pleasure seeking, was more or less happy to oblige. The freedom her life-style offered was worth the sacrifice.

She learned to pleasure herself. Only Lilla could satisfy herself to orgasm, alone in her small bed. She did not even share herself with a fantasy of another human being. She merely imagined different situations, mostly her being accepted by the applause of a crowd of people and, above all, she recaptured the moment when the ribbon that sealed her fate forever was slipped over her head by Mrs Rubenstein. The orgasm that the public honor engendered was far superior to any fleshly attempts to seek sexual satisfaction.

All these thoughts ran like colored ribbons through Lilla's head. A sudden movement and a flash of silver woke her with a start. She looked quickly at Amelia, who was smiling. "Here," Amelia snorted. "That's an end to the argument." She threw a handful of tresses onto the floor. "See? Go and look for yourself. You look much better with a bob. Well, anyway, half a bob."

Lilla looked at her mentor. She put her hand behind her head. Half her hair indeed was missing. Amelia was holding a wickedly sharp pair of scissors. "Oh, Amelia! How could you?" Lilla ran to the big cheval glass that stood at the end of the bedroom. She looked at her shorn head and then turned herself to look at her face in profile. Something fragile, some precious part of Lilla, snapped. She felt as if her heart were made of glass and Amelia, by cutting her hair, had taken away the only soft part of her: the part of her capable of appreciating great beauty, the part of her that had loved Ben and thought of Nora from time to time, the part of her that still escaped occasionally from the hot whirl of women who lived without men in their lives. The heart lay shattered and splintered on the floor.

With it, in the hanks of what had been her hair, Lilla felt her freedom lay too. Everything she had ever done had been for freedom: loving her artist, marrying Reuben, leaving Russia, traveling to America, running away from her family. But Amelia, with her usual, selfish cruelty which showed itself more and more frequently, was behaving like Lilla's current captor. Was this the freedom she had always wanted, to be treated like a servile pet by some woman who, she knew, wasn't even faithful to her?

But it was too late. All of Lilla's life and future lay in the hands of a woman she both loved and feared. Amelia had shown Lilla a whole world. At the same time she kept her leashed within that world. And Lilla could not hope to shake that leash. Her acceptance in the world of chic women depended upon Amelia. Without Amelia, no one would even know her name. Without Amelia's money, Lilla would be nothing, a mere parasite clinging to the periphery of the circle of new women.

For now, Lilla resolved, she would have to pay the price and accept her life on whatever terms Amelia dictated, but only for now. Some day, she would see to it, all of Amelia's money would be hers and hers alone. She would have truly found her own freedom at last.

From this moment, Lilla thought, I will be like them. By admitting she had not been like them, Lilla had also admitted that Sapphic ecstasy had eluded her. Now, perhaps, it was the road to follow. Whatever she had to do to get there, to be like them, she would do. Looking at Amelia sitting triumphantly in her bed, Lilla decided she needed to make a move. "You're quite right," she said cheerfully. "Why don't you cut off some more? I want to look good for Harriet Smythe-Jones' party."

"You're a good child." Amelia was pleased. "Come and give your friend a kiss."

Lilla looked at Amelia's puckered mouth with sudden disgust. If she had to share a bed and please a body, it might as well be a slim body like Julie Youngblood's. Dutifully, she kissed Amelia and said, "I'll send Susan up to collect the hair. I must go now. I have to choose a new dress."

"Get anything you want, darling." Amelia waved a languid hand. "Don't spare any expense. Just charge it."

Lilla nodded. A good wardrobe was just what she needed, she thought. She looked forward to seeing Julie. Black, alive, exciting Julie. Julie with the diamond peering beguilingly from her nose and who, word had it, had her initial "J" picked out on her clitoris in tiny chip diamonds to match. Amelia insisted that was no rumor. Lilla, slightly shocked on first hearing the news, realized that Amelia, indeed, would know.

The crowd who shared Lilla's life had no secrets, no boundaries. The night's events were the day's concern. Endless whispering at breakfast, endless luncheons followed by endless tea, endless traveling from continent to continent . . . All was observed and all was shared. From now on, Lilla would play the women's games by the women's rules.

Africa was now the only place to go. Amelia had booked a safari for herself and her companion. Mrs Rubenstein was already there. Lilla decided Julie should join their party. After all the heavy politics in the movement were said and done, Sarah Harding and her lot remained dull in their hysterical need to hate men and reform the world. Lilla did not care if women voted or not. To see real lions and tigers, to paint in Africa as she had so far painted in France and in Italy, to see London and Paris—this was what Lilla wanted.

Occasionally, Lilla sold a painting, but overall the Sapphics were not much interested in art. They preferred the world of carnal knowledge—what could be tasted and felt, what could slide through fingers swollen with desire—neither sexual nor sensual; more of a perverse sense of delight at the unexpected. When Amelia was away some nights, Lilla so far asked no questions. But she knew, in the eyes of another woman when they met, that Amelia was as fickle in bed as she was in her moods. Amelia demanded—and got—what she wanted. In this world, so tightly knit that no strand could be completely unraveled, the knot which held the community together across the world was composed of dreadful secrets and hideous deeds. If a woman chose to leave that decadent world and to strike out on her own, her life was in peril. If she were unwise enough to tell what happened in Cairo or in Gibraltar, when the ambassador's wife was caught in bed with one of the sisters, the traitor could expect to be found in a river with a small neat dagger in her heart or an even smaller hole in her head. Lilla knew that for all a man might rage, the silent anger of her sisters, if incurred, could be deadly.

Today Lilla shopped with a new song in her heart. Let Amelia cut her hair. Lilla was going to have her own fun.

The chance came, in the safari in Africa one hot musky night, when Julie slipped from under Amelia's thick, white mosquito net and into Lilla's sweat-soaked sheets, Lilla was amazed to find herself responding with immeasurable passion to Julie's nimble fingers. For the first time in her life, she felt herself hurled into a private orbit of pure sensation. When she returned to the dark, African night and heard the crickets and the frogs celebrating the odd habits of their human visitors, Lilla looked at Julie wide-eyed. "Don't thank me," Julie smiled. "I can wank off anything."

"Does this mean I actually *am* a lesbian?" Lilla asked in amazement.

"No. There's no such thing as a lesbian, unless you're born that way. I've only met two of them—*true* lesbians, from birth—in my life. No. You're just like one of us, perverse. That's all." Julie lay back on the pillow. She reached for her familiar packet of Black Russian cigarettes. She lit her cigarette and exhaled a long thin stream of smoke that lazily fought its way through the mosquito net. Above the two women in the bed, the big bright moon glinted on the lips that lay in the patch of hair between Julie's legs. Suddenly Lilla felt very grateful to Julie. So far in her life, Lilla had never experienced sexual pleasure with another human being. Sex was a brutal transaction perpetuated on her by Reuben, then Amelia, and then one or two other women who sought to seduce such a virginal look off Lilla's face. Now Lilla knew what it was that held together all those people she knew: it was the search for shared ecstasy, physical ecstasy. Emotionally, Lilla felt nothing, but for the first time in her life, she felt her body drained of desire, drained of tension, and finally slaked. She felt she had been a dry river bed. Now she knew how to fill her banks, not just by herself, but with another person. Gently she bent her head and kissed Julie's lips, the first pair and then the second. "Thank you," she said.

Julie grinned. "Wait till Amelia finds out," she said.

❧ *CHAPTER 20* ❧

While Lilla's life took on a sharper intensity Nora, in Santa Fe, was unaware of her mother's predicament. Rebecca was in the kitchen, on hand if Betty needed help. True, as Nora pushed and heaved, she joked about Lilla. "Mother went through this five times," she gasped.

Betty, kind dear Betty, whose round cheerful face hung over Nora's laboring body, smiled back gently. "I was there for you," she said. "Little scrap of a thing, you were. Now, breathe in deeply. The baby is crowning. Pant. Go on. Short breaths. And don't push."

All of a sudden Nora could pant no more. With a convulsive shudder and a burst of energy, Esther shot into the world crying loudly. "The other one is still in there." Betty was busy cleaning the baby. She cut the cord and wrapped Esther in a cloth. "Rebecca!" she called. "Your greatgrandchild has arrived!"

Rebecca came from the kitchen and lifted Esther into her arms. *"Bubela,"* she crooned. "My great-granddaughter." She gently kissed the crying baby. "Hush, little one," she said. "Don't come crying into the world, or the world will give you plenty to cry for."

Betty, meanwhile, patted Nora's still-distended abdomen. "You can tell there's another baby," she said. "Feel. Your belly is still hard."

Nora smiled. "Well, it's taking its time."

Half an hour later, Etta slipped quietly into the world. By the time Danny arrived home for his dinner, prepared for him by a thrilled Rebecca, his wife sat proudly in bed, supported by two huge down pillows with a baby at each breast. "Let them suck," Betty said. "The milk will come quicker."

"Already I can see the difference," Nora said. "Look, Danny, the first one fusses like a terrier, and the other"—she shook her head—"What a fat, lazy baby. Look at her. She's calm and happy."

Betty planted the two placentas in the back garden under the rose bushes. "Good for the roses," she said. "I had a friend who nursed in Arabia. They always planted the placenta. Then you know your roots."

Tired as she was, Nora could not help laughing with the dear woman who had not only brought her into the world but had now delivered her own two daughters. This lovely, eccentric Englishwoman, far away from home.

Later that night, Nora lay beside Danny in their big, warm bed. "You know," she said, "I thought of my mother this morning. What she must have gone through for all of us. Maybe that was what made her so angry with me—I wasn't meant to be. Not like these little darlings."

The little darlings were snugly asleep, their hands firmly closed like soft flowers and their bodies relaxed. Two pairs of pink lips were shut firmly and blissfully. They slept in the safety of their parents' house. Danny put his arms around Nora. "Darling," he said. "I'm sure she loved you in her own way." He fell asleep before Nora.

Nora lay awake thinking about her mother. Finally, she slept a troubled sleep, dreaming of Lilla, dreaming of herself as a very small girl running down a long dark road after her slim, young mother, who always stayed one step ahead of her daughter's outstretched arms.

The next day was when the babies were to meet their grandparents for the first time. Joseph and Ruth were thrilled. They stood, Esther in Ruth's arms and Etta in Joseph's. At last, Joseph turned to his wife. "I've waited fifty-one years for this moment," he said. "At last I have grandchildren. We escaped the Czar's troops, came to America, and worked until there could be a new generation of Gottsteins in the New World. And now here they are."

Reuben was no less thrilled when he first saw his daughter's daughters. He leaned over the two wooden cribs and stared at Esther. Even in her second day of life, her wide, unfocused eyes seemed to show a determination, an impatience, to jump into the world. "She is going to look just like Lilla," he said. As he gave the baby back to Nora, he vowed he would make sure the forces that went into twisting his wife would not be allowed near his beloved Esther.

Picking up the younger twin, Reuben watched the plump baby sleep without a care. Etta, Reuben knew in his heart, would be like his cheerful, happy Bea who had died so tragically and so young during the long journey out West. Now, God had sent him two more little ones. As the patriarch of the family, he had a duty to guard them with his life.

⊛ CHAPTER 21 ⊛

When the First World War erupted in Europe and the American government sought out every recruit it could find in 1916, Nora's first reaction was one of relief: Danny was thirty-five, too old to be drafted. Daily she watched the young men of Santa Fe filling the platform of the train station, leaving for the first leg of the long journey which might take them to a gruesome death in Europe. She saw white young men, Hispanics, blacks, all waiting for their orders. But at least her husband was safe.

Danny had more difficulty in accepting his exemption. America had given him so much, he told his wife, he felt obliged to give back whatever he could. Surely he could be useful as a field doctor, treating the wounds of the thousands of men the newspapers reported to be suffering in the trenches. But Nora held firm. His first obligation, she insisted, was to his family. "I could not bear the thought," she told him, "of sending you off, not knowing if you'd ever come back."

In the end, Danny agreed. His conscience was soon calmed as trainloads of Santa Fe's young men returned wounded and mutilated. The hospital in Santa Fe quickly filled with the broken bodies of soldiers. Danny tended the wards daily. "The war is five thousand miles away," he told Nora sadly one night, "but for the soldiers I see, it will always be with them."

Nora, too, helped as much as she could. Leaving Esther and Etta in the care of their grandparents, she worked beside Danny in the hospital, dressing wounds and trying to comfort the young men for whom horror had become an unshakeable companion. And where was Lilla? Trapped in some European city with war thundering all around? No news arrived now from Miriam, and the papers were too full of reports from the front to waste their pages with social gossip from abroad.

Nora's concerns for her mother were in vain, for Lilla and Amelia were secure in the social circle of the Long Island wealthy, sitting out the war until it was safe once again to return to Europe.

At home, more immediate matters consumed the bulk of Nora's thoughts, providing her with merciful relief from her fears. In the first year of the war, Esther Gottstein, an intense and bright child at five years of age, was ready to attend the local school run by the Little Sisters. Nora was not exactly thrilled to send her daughter to a Catholic school but Santa Fe, at the time, offered virtually no alternative. Etta was definitely not ready for school at all. From the day she and Esther were born, Esther proved herself to be an

energetic and aggressive baby. Etta was quite content
to lie in Big John's arms and fascinate him. "My, she's
a beauty," Big John, an easy captive, would say.

"Oy," Reuben said after five years of Etta and Esther in his life. "What a handful."

Both Etta and Esther spent Friday evenings alter-
nating between the grandparents' houses. The Gottsteins were, at first, upset when they heard that their
granddaughters were to go to school with the *goyim.*
Reuben, however, convinced Joseph that nowadays a
good education was a necessary part of a woman's
life. Privately, Joseph doubted, as he remembered
Lilla's defection from her home and family, but he
was too fond of Reuben to argue.

Truly, there was not much to be said about the
synagogue or about the local rabbi in Santa Fe. He
still had not lifted the ban against the Braffs and the
Gottsteins. Anyway, Ruth thought, he was a danger-
ous-seeming man, giving off a strangely unwholesome
air, and the girls would probably be afraid of him.

Peace returned to Europe, and Santa Fe resumed its
sleepy life. Esther and Etta grew in a world of renewed prosperity. As the tranquil years slipped by in
the sunshine and the clear air, the girls delighted their
parents.

When Esther came home from school one day, at
the age of fifteen, and announced she was planning to
attend a university, the family all agreed that clever,
intelligent and ambitious Esther would probably be
the first girl in the family to get a degree.

"A degree in what?" Big John, by now an integral
part of the extended family, asked.

Esther was sitting on the ground on a big blanket.

She was a graceful figure dressed in white who had a
square brow and had inherited her grandmother
Lilla's small, well-proportioned nose. Beside her, as
always, lounged Etta. Etta, in sharp contrast to Esther's neat and dainty presence, still retained a round,
dimpled shape. Her rich mouth continually smiled at
the world, and her eyes danced with untold jokes. Big
John Kearney and Vincent Cooper had some mysterious work to do in the mountains, but on this lovely
summer's day, they both attended a large family picnic. Naomi and Nora sat apart with the older members of the combined families. A number of heads
were gray, and Reuben looked anxiously at Rebecca.
Time and the altitude—for Santa Fe was seven thousand feet above sea-level—had taken their toll. Rebecca was frail, but she so much hoped to see the two
girls married to suitable husbands. "I'm going to
study literature," Esther replied. Her dark eyes
burned with intensity. "Sister Angeline says I could
be a really great writer. I'm going to work hard and,
in just three more years, I'll have six women's colleges
to choose from."

"My, my." Rebecca caught Esther's conversation
with Big John. "A writer yet in the family. What
about you, Etta?"

Etta stretched. With a little cat-purr in her voice
she said, "I'm going to stay home and chase Tom
Harding all over town."

Nora looked across at her child. "Etta," she said
sharply. "You will do no such thing."

Etta turned to her grandfather Reuben. "Well, I'll
go and live with you then, and run your house. I don't
see why I have to have a career. What's wrong with
looking after Grandpa?"

Reuben was pleased. He loved soft, smiling Etta, even though she was always in trouble at school and local boys did always pay calls on Nora to ask Daniel if Etta could sit in the parlor with them: she had a particularly scented mouth . . . Nora, Reuben decided, should be pleased to have such fine girls.

Nora spent a lot of time worrying about Etta. Her report cards were dreadful. Etta only really lived to dance. Every Saturday, chaperoned by a very bored Nora, she went from 4.00 to 6.00 P.M. to dance at the La Fonda Hotel on the Santa Fe Plaza. For naturally shy Nora, the whole thing was a weekly ordeal. Young men, washed and cleaned and squeezed into unfamiliar fancy clothes, took Etta's round body in their arms and floated away. Nora was left sitting on one of the chairs lining the walls, wishing she were back in her kitchen. Nora, like the other women in the family, now had sufficient money to hire maids. Unlike the other women, however, she did not want outsiders in her family home, much to Esther's annoyance.

Etta was always amiable if asked to clear the table, but Nora was lucky if all the plates survived her vigorous onslaught. Etta's idea of washing the plates sounded like a personal vendetta. Esther would have none of such menial tasks. As soon as the plates were cleared, she brought out her books and spent the evening lost in the pages of her latest assignment. Nora felt a little helpless as the information in the books was way above her own comprehension.

Danny enjoyed Esther's fierce desire for knowledge. He also encouraged her ambitions. Etta, however, was the girl who rode with him across the miles of stubborn wastelands. She would also rise at night to help him tend a patient. Now Dr. Daniel Gottstein had a car, so they could bounce up the farm tracks to deliver babies. Properly trained nurses were arriving in Santa Fe, schooled in big cities like Chicago. But even Chicago did not know how to suck the bite of a rattlesnake or draw the poison from a black widow's wound. Here in the southwest, diseases like bubonic plague, spotted fever, and encephalitis carried by infected mosquitoes, were rampant. Etta knew how to nurse her patients, but refused even to consider attending a nursing college. "I'm lazy," she replied happily when Nora nagged. "Anyway, I'm never leaving home."

Nora sighed when she watched her daughter dressed in the latest fashion dip and sway on the dance floor. Life had been so much easier for her own generation: there had been no choices. A few independent women like Betty had careers, but most simply knew they were destined to raise families. Even Betty, in her own independent way, had contributed to the family life of her community. She lived surrounded by people, nearly a hundred of whom she had birthed as babies with her capable hands. In the community of Santa Fe, she was an honored and respected person. Betty Thompson, Rebecca Braff, Mary Cooper, and Ruth Gottstein—all were revered as senior members of Santa Fe. They were counted among the busy women, women who saw to it that the poor were fed and libraries were supplied with the latest books. They created the huge, successful charity balls for Jewish—and gentile—charity works. Here on the frontier, religious differences tended to merge in the all-out fight to live a better life. All the people in Nora's life who came with her family from Middletown had prospered, but none of them forgot the early days when they lived off the land and their wits in the cutthroat world of the Wild West.

Perhaps, Nora thought, Etta and Esther are the first in their generation not to know hardship. Both girls knew only of soft beds and gracious curtains. The floors of the house now had polished wood for a covering, and on top of that rested carpets from India and China. Nora loved her carpets.

Etta, soon back from her Saturday night dancing, threw herself down on a chair beside Nora at the magnificent La Fonda Hotel. "Let's go home and see what the bookworm is up to." Etta was flushed and smiling. "That," she said with a bead of sweat on her upper lip, "was Tom Harding."

Nora looked across at the legendary Tom Harding. "He looks dangerous, Etta," she said. Tom Harding was older than the other boys. He was twenty-one and a ranch owner's son. Word was out he was a ladies' man, just like his father. Tom, the mothers of Santa Fe all agreed, should not be encouraged. "Etta." Nora's voice was sharp. "He's not to call on you."

Etta shrugged. "Tom's not the calling type," she said.

Nora went home with a frown. Etta was definitely what was called a flirt. If only Esther would take her nose out of a book, the two girls could chaperon each other. Not that Esther ever needed a chaperon. She surrounded herself with gentile friends, and they seemed to move in a charmed circle of erudition. Sometimes, Nora noticed, they arrived like a flock of seven black ravens, their little polished heads bowed over various books, talking in low, muted tones of

Willa Cather, of the new writers breaking away from the old traditions, of the new painters in Paris. Above all, they talked of women writers and artists.

What Nora did not know was that when she announced at fifteen that she was to go away to college, Esther had made a vow to escape the immeasurable boredom of Santa Fe and to return to the East Coast. Emily Atkinson, her best friend, did likewise. Sister Angeline promised both girls she would make it possible for them to attend one of the New England sister colleges. Sister Angeline tended to lean toward Wellesley. It had been as a student at Wellesley College in Massachusetts that Sister Angeline had first been called by God. She left the college afire with the need to go West and spread the Good Word.

For Esther, Sister Angeline served as mentor and beloved teacher. Sister Angeline's stern figure and her eyes full of fire—a fire fueled by her desire to impart knowledge to her girls—delighted Esther. Esther spent days with the Sister, dissecting a poem by Edna St. Vincent Millay, or comparing the difference in style of a new writer to that of the great Russian romanticists. Esther preferred the new writers. Sister Angeline had a brother in Paris who sent her reviews of new novels, copies of the badly smudged literary magazines, and news of Sylvia Porter—an American woman who ran a magazine and was publishing a strange Irish writer called James Joyce.

Esther had an even deeper secret than her wish to escape. Her secret dream was to find her grandmother Lilla. Just before Miriam had died in a terrible epidemic of flu which wiped out so many of Mort's friends and congregants back in Middletown, she had sent Nora a fashionable magazine. It was in

French, but in it there was a picture of Lilla with another woman, sitting side by side next to a swimming pool. The other woman was brown and seemed ageless. She wore a diamond through her nose. She and Lilla were smiling at each other in profile. An ink-smudge on the page prevented Esther from seeing clearly the details of her grandmother's face. Behind them was a big, bulky woman staring straight at the camera. Beneath the picture read the caption, "Amelia Witney-Hay and her companions Lilla Braff and Julie Youngblood."

Esther stole glances at the magazine and she found the picture unbearably exciting. She felt the women were free—free of the tyranny of bed making, free from cooking for a man. Even Emily Atkinson, whose mother had servants, still resented her life surrounded by hedges of protection. Her brothers could do as they pleased, but Emily and Esther knew that the first hint of evening shadows was a call for the girls to return to their homes.

The phrases "good girls," "nice girls," "proper girls," ran continuously over their heads. "Don't worry your pretty little head," was an expression Reuben often used. It infuriated Esther. Etta was quite content to have her head patted and doors opened for her. Esther and Emily, however, both agreed it was too high a price for the slavery of the future: marriage and motherhood.

Each time her circle of gentile friends left Esther's house, she was left with her mother's endless conversations about cooking or her committee work. Etta chatted back like a magpie and counted the latest fashion magazines while Danny, tired after a hard day's work with his patients, was content to listen to sporting events on his much-prized radio. Esther thought she would go mad with boredom.

In her books, women were freeing themselves daily, having illicit affairs followed by even more illicit abortions, competing with men, winning in their battles. There was even talk of a book written by a woman who, it was whispered, was having an affair with another woman. The idea, however, was so shocking that the book was banned in America. The writer was English and rumors of a trial flitted across the schoolrooms of America.

Esther knew as she struggled her way through her teenage years, these were indeed stirring times for other young girls who lived in exciting places like Boston. There, Esther was told, Mrs Isabella Stewart Gardner drove in her magnificent cars, attended balls, bedecked with jewels, and all without her husband. When a ship docked in Boston Harbor, Mrs Gardner filled her house, fast becoming a museum, with paintings and statues from across the world. She could be heard at dinner to interrupt men. And, most scandalous of all, she *argued* with men from all walks of life. Her repartée was the stuff newspaper stories were made of.

Long after the event, the newspapers from the East Coast would arrive in Santa Fe. Nora and Etta read the fashion and recipe pages while Danny grabbed the sport. But Esther awaited a visit from Emily Atkinson, and together they would pore over the society pages. Esther always looked for news—for some mention—of Lilla.

Sometimes, in conversations with her great-granddaughter, Rebecca would supply titbits of Lilla's early life, but even Rebecca had forgotten a lot of what happened. She sat on the front porch of Reuben's ranch and rocked away the summers.

One autumn, the autumn of Esther's and Etta's eighteenth birthday, the autumn which should announce Esther's entrance to Wellesley College, Rebecca was to turn ninety-two. Both occasions, the young girl's announcement and the old woman's birthday, were to be celebrated. Esther was very curious that she should be one of the only Jews, if not the only Jewish girl, to attend Wellesley. This was a challenge Esther would enjoy.

Etta had decided that she would move into her grandfather Reuben's house for the summer to look after her great-grandmother, who was now frail as a bird but still amazingly alert. Nora was feeling the onset of winter even in the heat of the day. As August slipped into September, the chilly wind warned of the snow to come. Nora knew both her girls were ready to spread their wings, each in her own way. She also knew that, while there would be an emptiness in her heart and in her home, she could now have her beloved husband back again.

☙ CHAPTER 22 ❧

The news came on a Saturday morning. Both Emily Atkinson and Esther had passed into Wellesley. They were the first two women from the state of New Mexico to be accepted for that learned establishment.

Immediately they began to prepare for the departure in two weeks' time. Nora organized a tremendous party to be held the next Saturday at Reuben's ranch.

The local New Mexican newspapers had a banner headline, and all day long, upon receiving news of their acceptance, Reuben's house was full of family and friends. Even Emily's mother deigned to call. Reuben's overstuffed Jewish household, like Nora's, was an awkward contrast to Mrs Atkinson's home where the edges of the tables were sharp and the new, fashionable linear look held sway: sharper furniture, stark and simple, kept the back straight and thoughts from straying. Emily much preferred the soft, voluptuous sofas at the comfortable ranch house belonging to her friend's grandfather.

Rebecca took the news quietly. She was pleased for Esther. She was happy that her great-granddaughter's childhood dream had come true. All Rebecca had dreamed about when she was eighteen was to find a good husband and have his children. Her dream had been fulfilled. Today, in the soft light of the Tiffany lamps, she looked at Esther's face. How like Lilla, she thought. Esther, when she was excited, had the same flush to her cheeks, the same intensity in her eyes. Unlike Etta, whose smile embraced the world, Esther's was one of pure, unswerving ambition. She was on the brink of her great adventure.

The past, with its years of boredom, was gone. No need ever again to give those years of adolescence a second thought. Esther Gottstein was about to be free.

Rebecca looked at her beloved son, Reuben. The party to honor her ninety-second birthday, and Esther's entry into Wellesley, was held in the big generous dining room at Reuben's ranch. All the old crowd were there. Vincent Cooper looked frail and old, but Mary guided him gently to his chair. Rebecca herself could walk with a stick, but even with the help of spectacles her sight was failing. The huge table, piled high with food, beckoned the guests to eat. The room was vibrant with voices.

Only Esther sat quietly, oblivious to the hum. This was not real life. Real life was out there in the big cities. Real life was happening in Boston, Paris and London. Esther felt she had lived the last eighteen years like a caterpillar in a cocoon. Now she was free to wriggle out and dry her beautiful wings and fly. Where to, she had no idea, but in the rare ether where ideas are spun, there would be a beautiful, dangerous web. In that web, Esther would find her place.

Betty Thompson watched Esther from across the room. She made a mental note to tell the child about contraception for men. Etta, Betty hoped, would not be swept up in the new movement called "free love." Betty snorted at the very idea. Free love, as she well knew, put the whorehouses out of business and the men got it for free. Big John Kearney was already complaining. With an increasing amount of new women in Santa Fe urging for the bonds of matrimony to be broken, his business was suffering. They were the same women who bullied and rallied against liquor. Nobody in town believed in the idea of prohibition except for those fierce women. They were also attempting to stop the sale of tobacco. Was there no end to their ambitions? Big John thought not.

This afternoon, the meal nearly at an end, Big John felt keenly the death of his wife Lizzie. Pale and thin, but tougher, in her own way, than he, she had been his mainstay. For Big John, it always amazed him to see her surrounded by the exuberance of the children she bore him. She died more quietly than she had lived. Now, looking over at Rebecca, Big John, who knew death so intimately from the violent scenes at the saloon, saw death standing behind Rebecca. On Rebecca's face was the same resignation Lizzie had had before she died.

The last goodbye resonated on the big front porch. Betty had a chance to capture Esther in the hall. "I know all about that," Esther said impatiently. "You'd better lecture Etta. I'm going to get a degree, not a man." Her eyes swept the gracious silent hall hung with Reuben's carefully selected paintings. "I don't want to live in a prison like this. Etta can run a house for the rest of her life; I want to adventure."

Betty frowned. "Don't you want to marry—ever?"

"You never did." Esther's voice was sharp.

Betty smiled, seeing such an earnest look on a young girl's face. "Some of us didn't have a choice. I would love to have married, but I look on you all as my family, I really do. Especially your mother."

Esther's eyes, to her own surprise, filled quickly with worried, teenage tears. "You will look after my mother, won't you?"

Betty was relieved. At least the child had some feelings. "I will," she promised, and hugged the thin, uncompromising shoulders. "I really will."

Later that night, when the servants clattered off to bed, Barnabas put his face around the door. He and Reuben had been together for a long time. It was his habit to say goodnight to his master and see if there were any outstanding instructions. Barnabas' hair was now white and cropped close to his head. He no longer had to haul huge blocks of ice into his cart. He was retired and lived in a small cottage by the ranch house. He occupied himself by carpentering furniture for the family or for anyone else. His needs were few.

Tonight, he saw Rebecca in the chair by the fire. The piñon wood was still a bit green so it spluttered and smoked. Rebecca sat quietly, waiting for Reuben to say goodnight. Because her legs were troubling her, Reuben had had her bed brought downstairs and put in the room next door. It was Rebecca's habit to have a last cup of hot milk, made by her son, with a sprinkle of freshly ground chocolate. Quietly the two of them would sit by the fire and discuss the day's events. Rebecca, for the last few months, had known her days were drawing to a close. She was ready to go home to her God she served so faithfully; home to her husband, Oscar, who appeared in her dreams last night. Her only sadness was leaving Reuben. He had been all her life, after her husband died. Even her love for her grandchildren and great-grandchildren could not match the abiding passion she felt for her son. She had not been able to cook for him for some years. Now a Spanish woman ruled the kitchen but Etta was a match for any servant, and Rebecca felt better the day Etta moved into the house. Not for her own sake, but for Reuben's.

Now, tonight, she heard Reuben's soft footsteps down the hall. "Here's your milk," he smiled. The smell of the slightly sharp chocolate, freshly grated, filled Rebecca's nose. "Thank you," she said. "What a day, eh?"

"Yes." Reuben sat down opposite his mother. The big reading chair, his favorite, engulfed him.

"What a truly wonderful day. Esther on her way to college . . ." Reuben shook his head. "Lilla would have been very proud today to see her granddaughter going off to college."

Rebecca nodded. "Yes. She would have been. But I am ninety-two years old, and I don't for the life of me see what a college degree will do for Esther. Maybe she'll teach, like that Sister Angeline. That would be a good thing. I just hope for both girls they find a good man to love them."

Reuben nodded. "And they are both able to love a man back," he said softly.

Etta slipped into the room like a pale, white shadow. "I've come to kiss you good night. And you, grandpa. I'm tired. I could do with an early night." Etta leaned over and kissed Rebecca. "By the time we celebrate your hundredth birthday, I'll have a handsome husband and at least ten children. Think of that!"

The old lady looked into her great-granddaughter's brown eyes. Rebecca nodded and smiled. "I'm sure you will, *bubela,*" she said, and in her smile lay her last goodbye.

Tonight, even as Reuben bent to kiss her, she motioned him not to lift her from the chair. "I'll sit for a while," she said. "You go upstairs. I'll ring the bell when I'm ready to go to bed." She heard Reuben's steps on the stairs and she counted each step with love. Slowly, as she heard her son reach the landing, her life ebbed away. A few small gasps escaped her lips, and her eyes grew dim. Rebecca felt, as her life drained out of her body, she was in a bright tunnel. Her soul slipped out of the chair, up and away through the dusk of the night. Only an owl saw it pass and commented.

Reuben was asleep, too tired to keep his promise to listen for the bell. He found his mother the next morning when he entered the library. With a start he saw the back of her head leaning against the chair she had occupied the night before. Thinking she had fallen asleep, he put his hand on her cheek. The chill of her face told him she was dead. Reuben felt a gap in his heart he knew could not be filled.

The news of Rebecca's death was told by the bells of the Santa Fe churches. It was no matter that she was a Jew and the bells were gentile. Quietly, and without official public acknowledgment, Rebecca was much loved in the little community. Her wanderings around Kaune's Food Store every morning for the daily groceries (though leaning on Barnabas' arm in the last few years) were a legend. Strangers told her their troubles on street corners. Reuben had been forced to remove her checkbook, lest she bankrupt the family (and Joseph Gottstein's bank as well) with her generous heart. Deep in the pocket of her familiar black skirt, Rebecca always carried sweets for the gutter-urchins who danced after her down the dusky, newly paved streets of Santa Fe. If a child had a cut or a suspicious rash, it was liable to find itself kidnapped and driven to Danny Gottstein's office. A decayed tooth landed the child in the fearsome dentist's chair.

All of Santa Fe loved Rebecca, and as the bells cried out in their deep, native tongues, the people gathered outside the house to pay their last respects. Betty Thompson and Mary Cooper came at once. Together they bathed Rebecca for the last time. In a reverent silence they took her wedding gown from the cupboard where it hung, then took the white satin dress, with its pretty blue train, to the bedside. Gently dressing Rebecca, they settled her back on her pillow.

Rebecca lay in the dress that she was married in all those years ago. Her hair surrounded her face and she looked young again. Both women kissed their old friend and left the room.

Reuben was waiting outside in the hall. With a heavy heart, he entered his mother's bedroom to say goodbye. He could not bring himself to lay her in the wooden coffin placed on two wooden sawhorses by the bed. Barnabas had promised he would rest Rebecca on the satin pillow in the plain, pine box.

Reuben leaned over his mother and kissed her. He felt a hand on his shoulder. It was Etta who stood silently by him. In the doorway, the men of the family stood in a silent group. Etta took her grandfather's hand and led him, blinded by tears, to the drawing room, past the men who murmured their sympathy. There, Nora put her arms around her father. "We will sit *shiva* for seven days," she said. "Tomorrow we will bury her."

Esther kissed her grandfather, and suddenly Reuben wished that Esther's arms could have been Lilla's.

⚓ CHAPTER 23 ⚓

Esther could not wait for the train to leave the station. The faces of Reuben, Nora, Danny and Etta disappeared into the blur of the Lamy railway tracks. Reuben felt a twinge of loss. Esther's high spirits during the last two weeks had kept him from deep mourning for his mother. He knew much of Esther's character and her fierce energy came from Rebecca's love for the twins. "Come along, Nora," he said after the train turned a bend out of sight. "Dry your eyes. I'll take you all out to lunch."

The inn at Lamy served good food, and if the house next door was reported to be a whorehouse, well, Reuben would not tell his daughter. If Nora heard from Naomi that Ben made a point of frequenting the whorehouse, well, Nora was not about to tell her father.

Ben Braff's ever-increasing need for women and alcohol had driven him by now into a lonely, black space known only to a handful of other men, equally desperate. He had few friends, except among the outcasts of Santa Fe. When he was desperate for more money to buy moonshine, he crept into Barnabas' cottage and begged. When he needed to scrape the filth off his body, he visited his sisters, Naomi and Nora. Both girls agreed to keep his malodorous visits from their husbands. Big John Kearney and Vincent Cooper tried to help Ben but, finally, after Ben broke into Big John's private still in the mountains and drank too much, they realized that if they employed him, with his lack of discretion, the deputy sheriff would soon be on their necks.

The only woman who could calm him down fully was Molly Parkington. Molly, now past her years of whoring, could reason with Ben after yet another dreadful binge—a vast beast, with rolling eyes and blood-drenched teeth, carrying the drunken Ben whither it would. At first, Ben drank to keep the beast at bay. Now, all these years, and many gallons of whiskey later, Ben drank because, when sober, he feared the moment the beast stirred in his brain. He imagined it crouching in his head and at times he could see it, an animal with no name but with a mission, a pact with some devil to take his soul away to a very far place so that he would wander for the rest of eternity, a husk searching for himself. When Ben finally came to and found himself in a gutter or behind an inn searching for food, it was Molly Parkington he needed. Ben always knew he had a place in her heart and in her bed. A man, Molly knew, could cry for all sorts of things when, really, his tears were for his mother. Ben's soul lay captive in Lilla's arms, and Lilla had no idea.

Briefly, Esther thought of her Uncle Ben as the train left the station. Esther knew about Molly Parkington and, young as she was, Esther rejoiced that Ben had someone to love him.

Esther pulled her straw boater from her head and sat down. "These seats," she said. "They're divine."

Emily Atkinson lay her blonde head against the stuffed cushion and yawned. "I hate trains," she said.

Esther laughed. "Well, I've never been on one before. I'm going to enjoy every minute of it." Esther looked out of the window as she lay in the chair. The luggage rack contained her overnight case, in which lay a vast flannel nightgown. This object was a source of abysmal loathing to Esther. "Why, mother?" Esther had argued. "Why flannel? I'm eighteen."

Nora had fixed her daughter with a very fierce stare. "No one will see you in your nightgown. At least, I hope no one will see you in your nightgown. And flannel keeps away the cold."

"If anyone saw me in the horrid thing, they'd drop dead with horror."

Agreeing on a wardrobe had been no easy thing. The tension between Nora and Esther became so obvious that even Danny got involved. "I will not have a daughter of ours go off to college looking like a streetwalker," he had insisted. This attack arose over a blouse that Nora said was far too tight across the chest. She also felt the blouse needed a collar and an extra button to hide a glimpse of the cleavage between Esther's small bosoms.

"Don't be silly, mother," Esther retorted. "I'm going to college to get a degree. I'm not after a man. Anyway, there won't be any men at Wellesley. It's an all-girl college. You'll have nothing to worry about."

Now, sitting, listening to the clackety-clack of the rails, Esther felt a sense of sexual excitement. So far in her life, apart from a few heroes in the very literary novels that she enjoyed, she had given little thought to men. The cheerful youths that flocked to Nora's house to visit Etta had never interested Esther. She was drawn to a mixture of emotions in a man. Occasionally she imagined herself having a relationship with a professor. He would perhaps study Russian literature and wear a black, fur hat. The hat shaded, hopefully, glittering black eyes and a soft mouth containing even, white teeth. Their nights together would be spent in long, detailed, literary conversations. He could compare the works of the great Russian writers with those of the poets and writers on the American continent . . .

"Esther, stop dreaming." Emily pinched Esther's arm.

She smiled. She enjoyed the idea of sharing her berth with Esther. From New Mexico to Boston the ride was long and tedious. Not even a few handsome bandits were now likely to attack the train to give two girls some light relief. But Esther, with her eagerness to experience all that the journey had to offer, would lighten the burden of the days.

Dusk settled on the two girls' faces. Way back behind them, gentle lights sat in the carriages, pulled so energetically by the big, black, imperious engine. Smoke billowed out of the huge, relentless smokestack, and Esther imagined the sweating backs of the coalmen heaving the heavy shovels of coal into the bursting engine, the flames sucking and flickering greedily, absorbing the black shiny coal, and turning these solid lumps into steam—a transformation which was a miracle. Then she imagined the solid white heat tearing its way out of the train and settling into clouds above, to come back again in the form of rain that would sink deep into the ground, to recreate the coal waiting for the next millennia . . .

Esther looked across at Emily and said, "Let's go to bed. Tomorrow we'll be passing through farm country. I hear they grow corn there, only there's water. That'll make a change from New Mexico." Old Barnabas used to get down on his knees and pray for water all summer long.

Emily stretched and stood up to take down her bag. She giggled and wrinkled her delicate, up-turned nose.

"What?" Esther was curious.

"I have a present for you. Promise you won't tell?"

Esther made the sign they had shared for years. "I will die if I tell," she said, making a gesture of slitting her throat. "Quick! What is it?" Emily snapped open her overnight bag and withdrew a parcel wrapped in blue tissue paper and tied with a dark blue ribbon. "Oh my." Esther felt the parcel. It was soft.

Emily was giggling so hard she fell back on her seat. "Try it on," she said. "Go on." Esther carefully unwrapped the tissue paper. Before opening the parcel she rolled the blue ribbon into a little ball and slipped it into her purse. "Hurry up, you goose," Emily instructed. "For heaven's sake, hurry up!"

Esther looked at her friend and said, "You know, for me, now is the most exciting time. Now, when I don't know what it is."

"Don't philosophize, you idiot." Emily jumped up and tore the parcel from Esther's hands. "There you are. What do you think?"

From Emily's hands there dangled a sheer, black nightgown. Two tiny, delicate *diamanté* straps supported the two halves of the gown. Esther held her breath. The mere thought of touching the garment gave her goosebumps. The thought of putting it on summoned the look of fury on her mother's face. If she slept in it, God might strike her dead. "That's the wickedest thing I've ever seen," she gasped. "My goodness, Emily. Does your mother know?"

"Of course not, silly." Emily, now away from Santa Fe and from her mother's crisp, sensually arid household, reverted to the Emily that had visited the houses of rich relatives in New York and Boston. Ever since Emily had escaped—the summer she was thirteen—the clutches of her narrow-minded family in New Mexico, she lived for the summers away. Away with aunts who partied at the best parties. Away with uncles who flirted with her and took her to the theater. Away, above all, with her Uncle Eric, who took her to Jimmy Delgado's restaurant in the North End of Boston. Jimmy Delgado knew everybody in Boston and his magnificent presence was guarded by two huge, burly men, one black as velvet moonlight, and the other a Chinaman with half an ear missing and a slash across his face which gave him a permanently disfigured smile. No one knew Emily's secret yearning toward Jimmy, not even Uncle Eric, who made a habit of escorting his favorite niece to her favorite Italian restaurant in Boston, famous for its pasta and for the steaming pots of Italian tomato sauce prepared with red onions and huge cloves of garlic. Most of all, Jimmy Delgado's restaurant was famous for its pizza. As often as she could, Emily, who had developed into a beautiful rounded blonde with breasts which were a source of astonishment to her mother, sank her small white teeth into the risen, yielding pizza dough and sucked the red, thick, ambrosian sauce into her moist, waiting mouth. Through the jungle of her long, blonde eyelashes she would watch Jimmy Delgado and, for the last few summers, she thought she could see him watching her in return, this young girl, so fresh and so ripe . . .

Emily had plans for Esther which, fortunately, she had not yet shared with her friend. "Let's put on our nightgowns," she said.

Both girls modestly turned their backs on each other. When Esther was wearing only her shift, now called a petticoat by the fashionable few in Santa Fe, she took her toothbrush to the sink. Nora, disdaining modern ways, made her own toothpaste for the family and friends in round metal tins bought for a few cents. Nora made the paste out of baking soda and hydrogen peroxide. She flavored the mixture with fresh mint from her garden and claimed that the paste would scour even the most tobacco-stained teeth. Big John Kearney agreed and, as a proof, he grinned his cigar-filled grin with his big, square teeth as white as the doves that sailed the skies. "Not," as Nora had reminded Esther as she tucked six tins of the mixture into Esther's bag, "not that any child of mine will ever smoke."

Esther brushed her teeth and stared at herself in the small, dull-gray mirror. The yellow specks in the imperfect mirror gave Esther's face a mottled look. Esther watched herself solemnly. A sea-change is what I am, she thought. She imagined the wreck of a ship, an old ship, lying on the bottom of the sea. The ship had been there long enough for the sand to have covered all but a protruding mast. Barnacles and oysters clung to the mast, but just a foot or two away lay a shell. In the hollow of the upturned shell lay a gem. Fallen from a drowned person many years ago, the gem—a rare, multifaceted, blue sapphire—lay, waiting for someone with courage to dive deep into the water, reach down, pick it up and glide silently to the surface of life, risking themselves in the endless hazards which exist for people in the world excluded by Santa Fe, New Mexico. "Hurry up, Esther. Daydreaming again."

Esther turned her head. "It's not just a dream anymore, Emily. This is real life. We're free now."

Emily pulled Esther aside. "Come on. It's late. I'm tired."

Esther picked up her nightgown. Forgetting her

friend, and that they were in a train, the feel of the pure gossamer of the silk touched the raw nerve endings that had separated Esther from her family for so many years. For Nora and Danny, the flight from the East as children had been their parents' attempt to escape the booming, bustling, hustling economic race for money. Both of them had dreamed of the peace and quiet of a summer's evening. Etta was quite content to live and die in a town she knew and which knew her. For Etta, joy lay in a basket of fresh eggs, or the smell of fresh bread, or the moment her first ripe tomato exploded in her mouth. Etta's endlessly sunny nature always made Esther feel guilty. Why did she not love to gather the honey in the autumn with Danny? Esther hated the times when the family gathered the pails and went to the beehives. Wrapped in long veils, everyone except Esther laughed and joked. If the bees stung anyone, it was always Esther.

Now, Esther stood by her bunk. The lower one was hers. She raised her hands and her marble-white body, with a neat triangle of dark hair matched by neat black patches under her arms, embraced the gown as it slid, fold by gentle fold, over the young, untouched form which had so far been a girl who had felt apart all her life. Looking down at her small, round breasts and at her flat stomach encased in the black silk, Esther smiled. That's right, she thought. I've always been a black orchid among a field of very happy yucca plants. The yucca plants were sturdy and grew where the seeds fell. In the spring they produced huge, white, swollen flowers in profusion. Esther climbed into bed. "Goodnight, Emily," she called.

Emily, also wearing a matching black gown,

kneeled by the bottom bed. "Good night," she said, and for a moment her young, pink mouth held Esther's in an innocent embrace.

Had Lilla known her granddaughter was in a train hooting its way across America, she would have been surprised. But had she known Esther was going to stay with Marty Hollander, she would have been astonished. For years Lilla managed to keep thoughts of her life with Reuben and the children locked away. From time to time an irritating, newsy letter used to arrive from Miriam but, for a while now, Lilla had heard nothing. Occasionally, as she gazed into her own face in a newspaper or magazine, she wondered if Reuben or her children ever saw the new Lilla. Now, as she lay in bed beside a snoring Amelia, she looked at the ceiling and took stock of her life.

Certainly, since the African safari when Julie Youngblood had joined their *ménage* (and now, it was discreetly rumored, it was *à trois* instead of *à deux*), life had improved considerably. No longer did Amelia's titanic moods control Lilla's life. Julie, with a quick joke or a tart comment, could change Amelia's face from a thunderous frown to a cheerful chuckle. To Lilla's relief, Amelia often gave to Julie the burden of a night's sexual adventure in her bed. Julie, Amelia had said, reprovingly, to Lilla, was a great deal more innovative. Quite what Amelia's use of the word meant, Lilla declined to ask.

❧ *CHAPTER 24* ❧

"My God," said Esther in astonishment as she and
Emily stepped off the train in Boston's South Station.
The building itself was the largest Esther had ever
seen. Even inside, pigeons rode the brisk September
winds sweeping through the cavernous hall of gray
stone. The sights were nothing new to Emily who
assumed a blasé air toward the surrounding wonders.
But Esther felt as if she had stepped into a dream.
Marty's chauffeur was there to meet the girls. Offi-
ciously, he gave orders to the porters who removed
the trunks from the train, carried them out of the
building, and loaded them into the limousine parked
at the front.

Trying to appear as familiar to this luxury as
Emily, Esther waited for the chauffeur to hold the car
door open for her while she climbed into the back
seat. When the car moved away from the curb, Emily
began giving Esther a guided tour through Boston,
pointing out landmarks all the way. Esther, however,
heard not a word, so rapt was she in the sights and
smells around her.

As the car left the station, she first noticed the
ocean. She realized she had never seen it before in
real life, only in magazines. The smell of it surprised
her. The cool wind blowing in off Boston Harbor
carried with it a heavy odor of brine from the sea and
fish from the boats docked at the wharves. The bright
sunlight of early autumn glinted excitingly off the
water which Esther saw only in glimpses.

The car rode smoothly down streets, nameless as

yet. Congress Street, Esther noticed, as they passed a sign on a corner. The rows of high, red-brick buildings seemed to stretch on for eternity, putting to shame the low adobe structures Santa Fe called "warehouses".

Corners were turned and Esther found herself passing through the densest, busiest streets she could ever have imagined. ". . . downtown . . ." she caught from Emily's flurry of words. More corners and streets went by, full of fashionably dressed working men—and women—and the car steered its way carefully through old narrow streets of what she would learn was called Beacon Hill. To Esther, the streets of bricked sidewalks—red, to match the stately houses—the proud gas lamps, the trees now beginning to loose their leaves, seemed the most elegant streets on earth.

The car rolled downhill, past a gargantuan building crowned with a golden dome. Then it drove alongside a park with grass of vibrant, intense green, then turned into the widest boulevard imaginable, with huge townhouses along both sides and a row of tall trees standing in a strip of grass, right down the middle. The limousine glided to a half before a grand mansion with stone stairs leading up to an ornate façade. Esther heard only the tail of Emily's monologue. "This," she heard Emily explain, "is Commonwealth Avenue. And this," Emily continued, stepping down from the car, "is my aunt Marty's house."

Esther floated up the front stairs, unaware of all physical sensation. Her senses were overwhelmed by the extraordinary beauty and glamor in every direction. Her eyes could hardly focus. Inside there was too much to take in. She saw only, in the sea of shapeless beauty, a woman standing in the front hall with her hand outstretched to greet her. "You must be Esther," said the tall woman with gorgeously styled red hair as she shook her hand. "I'm Marty Hollander. Please, call me Marty."

"Very nice to meet you," were the words Esther heard coming from her own mouth. Years of her mother's training in manners now served her well.

"Emily!" Marty hugged her niece. "How lovely to see you again, darling."

Esther felt numb as she let herself be guided through her first hours in the mansion. The introductory conversation was completed, she was given tea with Emily and Marty in the drawing room, and she found her mind flooded by a tide of new information: museums she must visit, concerts she must attend, people to whom she would be introduced, Marty's husband, Ashley, whom she would meet another time (he was away, she picked up, on business) . . . "But there'll be time for all that later," smiled Marty, surely the most sophisticated woman Esther had ever met. "You must be tired. Have a good rest here for a few days, get your bearings, and then there's Wellesley! I'll have my chauffeur drive you out, and I know you'll be very busy settling in."

All that Esther knew was that she felt very much the peasant in the queen's palace. If a private house seemed so awesome, what would Wellesley College be like? Would she fit in? However much she had to change herself, she vowed, she would make it her business to see that she did fit in. For this was definitely her world. Real life had begun at last.

Standing in the great hall lined with dark oak paneling, Emily and Esther stood silently, watching the other girls flit to and fro. Emily, Esther realized, belonged here. The girls were a splendid group of the new American élite. Most of them had shorn their locks and wore the "new" look. Esther hadn't ever seen so much bare flesh in her life. Giggles, and the tearing sound of whispered information, sliced through the still, somber air. Esther stood sentinel outside a world completely foreign to her. She felt she wanted to take a giant step into this incomprehension. Her family laughed, hugged and shrieked; these girls shook hands. There were no hugs, but a complicit relationship existed in which everything was made known by a look, or turn of a graceful hand. This, Esther realized, as if for the first time in her life, was the world of the *goyim*. This was what Rebecca meant when she railed against a world that was so foreign to her that she and her family might as well have lived a million light years from their own planet. If this is what it takes, Esther said to herself on the first day of attending Wellesley College, then I'll do it.

After three days of recuperation from the journey, in Marty Hollander's vast mansion, Esther had no second thoughts about shedding her Jewish background, like the skin of a dull snake, and rearing up again, newly fashioned. She thought again of her black orchid, or maybe a diamond-backed rattlesnake. What she needed to do now was to get to work. "Come on, Emily," she said. "We're in the dormitory on the left. Tower Court. Let's go."

The first few months passed in a blur. There was so much for Esther to learn and to unlearn. First there was the question of table manners. Esther quickly noticed that beverage drinking was not the musical occasion it was in her family. The girls here sipped their drinks quietly. Then she watched the graceful cutting of the meat. Mouths chewed food with both lips clamped together. Etta, Esther realized, would never have survived Wellesley. Etta, with her loose, relaxed manners and her habit of bursting into peals of loud laughter . . . nobody in Esther's family would be welcomed at "The Vill," as she soon found Wellesley was called by its students (because of its English-village-like appearance). Indeed, even Reuben—shy, quiet, Reuben with his old felt black hat—would be out of place. Even his million gold dollars, if poured into the lap of the president of Wellesley College, would not give Esther or her family the right to live and breathe in such refined air. Esther learned that the hard way.

Every so often she made a mistake. She learned to guard her tongue. Too many words and the girls looked at her with surprise. Emily, kind Emily Atkinson, was her guide and mentor. "Don't talk so much," Emily warned. "It's not like your house, where everybody talks all the time." So Esther learned to keep her thoughts to herself. She learned to observe, a silent presence. She also learned the value of a nod or a wink. She learned to walk slowly and to rub her thighs together in a languourous gait which drew attention to her small slim figure.

It was her walk which first attracted Jimmy Delgado. As much as Jimmy enjoyed Emily's blonde shining hair and her eager eyes, it was her dark serious friend who caught his attention in the early days of December. Both girls were on their way back to New Mexico. Emily, at her home, would celebrate Christmas; Esther would celebrate Chanukah. Both girls were concealing a feeling of dread. Not that they did not love their families. It was just that, as Emily said so succinctly, "There goes our freedom."

Tonight, their last bit of freedom until the New Year, was celebrated with a meal by themselves at Emilio's in the Italian North End of Boston. There was no brother, uncle, or father to interfere, just two young girls with flushed cheeks and flashing eyes, sitting amiably at a table in a crowded restaurant. Boston's North End looked very like everything Esther had ever read about Italy. Even Emilio's, filled with smoke and gesticulating Italians, felt very like Reuben's big family house when the whole clan were together. That part of Esther immediately felt at home. For nearly four months now, Esther had suffered a surfeit of controlled emotions. Not only had she had to control her feelings, but she had also had to bite her tongue and, recently, she had run a box of henna through her hair to try to heighten the dead blackness of her tresses. After several painful appliances of wax, her legs were free of the offending black hair. She was still plagued by recalcitrant eyebrows. Wrestling with a pair of eyebrow tweezers before dinner, Esther had envied Emily's blonde hair which left no traces on her legs and arms. "Ouch," Esther had complained. "There are two long ones by your nose," Emily had said.

Now, sitting opposite Emily with the taste of warm ravioli in her mouth, Esther smiled. Her eyebrows, tamed by the tweezers, were perfect arches over her shining, dark eyes. Her smooth, alabaster skin reflected her happiness. And then she saw Jimmy.

His kingly manner spoke of proprietorship. "Is that Emilio?" Esther asked, sipping her chianti.

"There is no Emilio," Emily answered, biting a crisp breadstick. "That's Jimmy Delgado. He's the man I've been telling you about. He owns this place."

"Then why did he call it 'Emilio's'?"

"Well, my uncle Eric says he didn't think 'Jimmy's' would sound Italian enough."

"But that doesn't make any sense."

"Maybe not to you or me, but it's *very* Italian logic."

Jimmy had been watching Esther from the moment she walked into the restaurant. Lewis, his black bodyguard, noticed Jimmy noticing Esther. Lewis shot a look at Chi. Chi's permanently scarred smile moved slightly. Another girl to chase, Chi thought. He hoped she didn't have a furious father, or indeed uncles, armed to the teeth. Even if the Boston women had liberated themselves, men had not. Many times, Lewis and Chi had to pull guns to subdue irate husbands or fathers. The last time Jimmy gave chase, Chi got a splinter in his back. Chi did not like being shot at, particularly not whilst parked outside some millionaire's mansion with Lewis, awaiting Jimmy's descent by drainpipe. "There must be better ways to die, boss," he said. "I don't want to be remembered dying in a shootout over your chasing pussy." Jimmy just laughed.

Now Jimmy was smiling. Jimmy knew that the blonde one would be good in bed, warm, loving and kind. But the little dark one had ice in her fire, and it was the battle to melt the ice that excited him. The whole of the Boston rich and famous lay physically and metaphorically at Jimmy's feet, as unlicensed and lascivious as the Sapphists, but relying on husbands to keep them in the gold and jeweled lifestyle. If not a husband, then a rich lover. So the "Hets" worked hard at being women, real women, with a hint of sensual delights in their smiles because, under all the gilt and chatter, behind all the female luncheons and teas, women knew if they failed to catch a man they were doomed to a life of servitude. If they were lucky, they became maiden aunts, or were dismissively called "spinsters," who looked after nieces and nephews and mopped their married sisters' brows. They cooked, and tended the poor, and they prayed alone at night in their rooms for the advent of a husband. If they were not lucky, they became companions to widows or teachers. Now, thanks to the suffrage movement, they were also able to get paid jobs as clerks in banking offices and, slowly, to take menial positions in offices. It was the fear of a secretarial position which drove Esther to work her hardest to get her degree. Unlike sunny, easygoing Etta, Esther did not see marriage as her ultimate goal. Unlike Etta, who for years collected items for her future home, Esther had no hope chest. Esther saw herself on a podium giving lectures on "Early Renaissance Literature" or on the meaning of the first stanza of Dante's version of *The Inferno*.

Perhaps, she thought, sitting demurely, perhaps she could recite verses from Edna St Vincent Millay's lovely poem "A Few Figs from Thistles" to a vast sea of white, upturned faces . . . "You're dreaming again," Emily sighed.

Esther's ability to get lost in her head frightened Emily sometimes. "But if you don't dream, Emily," said Esther seriously, "why are you getting a degree?"

"Because I told you, you silly goose. I need an education to catch a rich man and run a good house.

You can't sit next to the Ambassador of Bavaria and not know where Bavaria is.

"These days, rich men are able to get 'it' whenever they want 'it.' When a man is ready to marry, he doesn't marry a girl who is used meat." Emily leaned forward, her fork upright in her hand. "Nowadays, decent husbands do what they've always done: they marry dear little unused virgins. Only when I meet my rich husband, I'll be more than just a virgin. I'll be a well-educated virgin." Emily leaned back and smiled a complicit, sensual smile. "Until then," she said, "I'll just fancy men . . . Don't look now, but you can see Jimmy over there looking at us?" Indeed, Esther found it difficult not to stare at the very dark man with the jet black hair and soft mournful eyes. Esther had been avoiding those spaniel-like eyes all evening. Emily looked mischievously at Esther. *"He's* the man I fancy." She ran her tongue across her lips. "Fancying Jimmy will keep me busy all over Christmas. I'll be so bored back in Santa Fe, but then," she laughed, "now that I have an indecent obsession, I can at least be busy in my head."

Esther smiled. "I'm taking home a mass of books to read. I'll keep myself busy. Come on, Emily. We have to go back to the Vill or we'll get locked out." Esther was very aware of Jimmy's hot, appreciative gaze between her shoulders. In fact, for a moment, she let his hot, melting, brown eyes penetrate her skin. She felt an unaccustomed heat rising in the depth of her stomach. The heat rose from between her legs then ran down to her knees. "Come on, Emily," she said firmly. "Let's go," and she hurriedly swung the door of the crowded restaurant open, and was refreshed by the icy, Boston winter wind.

~❂ *CHAPTER 25* ❂~

"I'm in *lurve*." Etta lay strewn across Esther's bed.

Esther looked at her twin sister. "In 'lurve'?" she asked. "With whom?"

A warm smile appeared on Etta's lips. "It's for me to know and you to wonder."

Esther frowned. "Really, Etta. I have more to do in my life than wonder about whether or not you are in love. I have about a hundred books to read, and I have to write a paper for my social psychology class."

Etta put her round, plump arms in the air and slowly laced her fingers. She had spent the summer at Reuben's ranch and had remained with him for the early months of the autumn to help him as he grieved his mother's death. Toward the end of autumn she had moved back in with her parents. Late autumn had been such a joy for Etta. Now, with the New Mexican winter wind blowing around the house, she remembered Tom Harding, the boy—now a man— who had haunted her childhood and then her adolescence. Tom Harding. All summer long he worked on his parents' ranch which adjoined the Gottsteins' property. In the harvest months of October and November, he stood, waiting for Etta to divert him from family cares behind the barn. Etta, too, waited for the moment when she fell into his arms and they sneaked into the barn to lie pressed tightly together in the hay.

Now, with a light lacing of snow on the windows, meetings were far harder for Etta and Tom. They arranged secret trysts during synchronized trips to town, but kissing was impossible in such a small place.

Etta knew that her father would not consent to an engagement between herself and her loved one. Unlike gentle, easygoing Reuben, Danny insisted that both girls marry good Jewish boys. That way Danny and Nora could be sure that the family would not shatter. The old traditions that bound family life day by day, week by week, from one High Holiday to another, remained inextricably woven in the matrix that was the Jewish family. No *shegitz* son-in-law would capture Danny's beloved daughter's heart and gallop off into the wilds of New Mexico to practice the barbaric new way of life adopted by the race of blonde-haired blue-eyed people who invaded the quiet city of Santa Fe and scandalized good families, such as the Gottsteins. Danny did not even approve of Emily Atkinson as a friend for Esther, but he had no solution. These two girls were the only girls from Santa Fe to go away to college that year.

Etta was far too young, in Danny's eyes, to even think about a serious boyfriend. "Let her meet Tom Harding on the dance floor once a week," Danny maintained, but he knew young love was fickle. Etta prattled like a child about this young man, but Nora was always quick to add that Joshua Finkelstein also paid court to Etta. Now *there* was a match. Joshua Finkelstein was working for his father, who ran a big attorney's office in Santa Fe. Nora and Danny spent nights imagining their Etta on the arm of Joshua Finkelstein. A good match, indeed.

Tonight, though, Esther was not in the mood to discuss anything with her sister. Esther was busy remembering the look, and the heat of the look, that drove her out of the restaurant into the Boston night. A small shiver crossed her skull. That was dangerous.

That was not the happy, joyous look that lay on her twin sister's face.

Hair strewn across the pillow, Etta smiled at her sister, her brown eyes glowing warmly. "I've missed you, Esther. I've really missed you. It seems like you've been away for years and years. It was awful when you left. I felt something had been amputated. A whole part of me went missing." Etta raised herself on one elbow and looked earnestly at Esther. "Did it feel like that for you?"

Esther nodded. "I did miss you at first," she said, "but, quite honestly, we're kept so busy I don't have that much time to think about home."

Etta sank back on the bed. "It's a funny thing about being a twin. You really share the same womb, then birth, and then each other for so long. Actually, Esther, I've been waiting to ask you this for some time— ever since you've been back. You're rather bored with us, aren't you?"

Esther looked at Etta in surprise. "It doesn't show that much. Does it?"

Etta shook her head. "Don't worry. I pick it up because I know you well. Not the others. Last night you were magnificent at Mary's house. She really has aged since Vincent died in October." Etta let out a long sob of a sigh. "Oh, I *hope* I can be that happily married. We're so different, Esther, even if we are twins. All I want is Tom, a little house with a garden, and six children. I can see them all now. Three boys, and three girls, and me cooking by the stove in an apron, and watching my garden grow, just like Mother."

"I'd die," Esther said. "I'd die of boredom. Or I'd kill my husband. Oh, but just try imagining my life at

Wellesley . . ." Then Esther looked across at her sister. "I always was different." She walked across the polished floor and sat down on her little, white bedside carpet. "Do you have any idea how many years I've dreamed of getting away from here? Not that I don't love you all very much," she said quickly. "But, Etta, I've got to have a career. I don't want to be like those big-bellied women who live in a maternity dress. I really don't want to spend my life living with a man who farts and burps in my bed and then snores like father. Why do Jewish men huck and spit? The men I meet at Emily's aunt's house in Boston, they never do that. And they don't flush the lavatory loudly so everybody knows they've been. No, those men up there are gentlemen. Any man I get involved with would have to eat properly. Eating at our house is rather like a visit to the zoo at feeding time."

Etta sat up. The warm, comfortable room seemed to be lit by her joy, something Etta had radiated ever since she was a baby. Around Esther, however, there always seemed to hover a dark shadow. Etta resembled a large, blousy, multicolored pansy, whereas Esther's slim, composed self brought to mind a darker image. Sometimes Etta saw a black ring around her sister, an aura which boded ill-will for her future. Tonight, Etta could see the aura. "Esther," she said. "Why do you feel so restless? You'll be gone in a few weeks. Can't you just be patient?"

"No," Esther said, shaking her head. "I've been patient for too many years. Only my books kept me alive. You know, Etta, I've been studying the work of a woman poet called Edna St Vincent Millay. I saw her once at a party in Boston. I looked at her surrounded by adoring fans, and I thought I'd like to be her, to have the whole of Boston and New York at my feet. I'd like to be a poet. After all, our grandmother is an artist so it runs in the family. Imagine, Etta—imagine a stage with the lights down. I go onto the stage, only me. No one else on the stage. I walk across the bare boards with my feet encased in the finest leather. I'm wearing a simple white linen shift. And I walk up to the lectern with my poem written in long-hand on thick, milk-colored sheets of paper." Esther rose to her feet and walked slowly over to the window.

Steadily staring out the window, Esther began to recite.

"The years fall away from my face, as I embrace
from the ageless age of childhood
to the welcome withering of the chains
that slip from my arms
that bound me for years to the rocks
and the dry sands of the West,
where they lie like rattlesnakes,
coiled to embrace another fugitive.

But I, far-sighted and furious in my defection, am free now."

Etta watched, entranced. Esther lifted her pale arms to the skies and continued in a pure hard voice.

"I will always be free
to follow the pathless path
that ends at the endless end
and is only for those who dare."

Esther lowered her arms and on the window pane, in the blackness of the night, saw her face mirrored in the moonlight.

"Gosh," Etta said. "I'm really impressed. Did that lady poet write that?"

"No," Esther laughed. "I wrote it yesterday."

"Golly." Etta got off the bed and ran over to the window. She wrapped her arms around her twin sister and her. "You really are good," she said.

Esther looked into her sister's fresh eyes. "But so are hundreds and thousands of other poets," she said bleakly.

"Come on, Esther," Etta was ready for a change of mood. "Let's go and see if any of the Kearneys are home." Tom Harding was sometimes a visitor at the Kearney's house. Maybe, Etta hoped, a touch of the hand or a quick peck on the cheek could be arranged. Esther relented. At least an evening at the Kearneys' house was entertaining enough to hurry the hours of another day, bringing close the freedom Esther so desperately missed.

Emily missed her college nearly as much as Esther. But then, Esther knew, as they met in various Santa Fe cafés for yet more coffee or chocolate, Emily had no need to be ashamed of her family. Wealthy and well-connected, the Atkinsons smelled rich. Esther decided a long time ago the rich had a special smell. It was not just the shine on their huge cars or the smart chauffeur. Even standing alone in sackcloth and ashes, the really rich looked immediately and recognizably different. It didn't matter how rich Reuben was (or her father, for that matter), theirs was still new money. New money had not had time to bear the dull patina of old gold. So, too, the girls from families with old money, like Emily, shone with a simple expectation that all their needs would be met automatically, as if by divine intervention. So Emily, unlike Esther, wasted little time in idle thoughts for her future.

Emily knew that, after she graduated college, her mother would choose a rather dull, vacant-faced Harvard man, or maybe a Yaley, but pick she would, and Emily from then onwards would become the wife of a man who hopefully would love her until the day she died and would supply her with a big house, servants, numerous cars, a string of children, and as much money as she could spend. "And what," Emily argued with Esther, "is wrong with that?"

"Nothing," Esther said as the train mercifully pulled her away from the old Lamy station. "Nothing at all. But maybe every family has to have a black sheep. Like my uncle Ben." She sighed. "I never like the color of all those white sheep, all looking alike. I don't want to be protected by a man all my life. I want to make my own decisions, open my own doors in life. Really, Emily. If I were confined by a man in a big house like you describe, I'd probably go mad."

Emily laughed. "Anyway, this time next week we'll be back at the Vill. Till then we'll stay with my aunt Marty."

Esther grinned. The more she saw of Marty, the more she liked her. Marty was not only a new woman in voice—she practiced what she preached. Marty wore outrageous hats on her fine red hair and smoked cigarettes in a long cigarette-holder. Marty also had parties, lots of parties, to which everyone came. Everyone in Boston knew about Marty Hollander's parties. Even the Astors and the Vanderbilts took the train to Boston just to party with her. And Esther was looking forward to the next party immensely.

"Darling." Marty was in one of her bossy moods. "You really must do something about your luggage."

Esther nodded miserably. "I know," she said. Her two heavy carpetbag suitcases stood squat and mute on the South Station platform. Emily owned a perfectly splendid, shiny, traveling trunk. Esther envied Emily her trunk more than anything else in her life. First, there was the musty smell of mothballs when the massive lock released its grasp and the dark green baize lining lay in anticipation of Emily's lovely clothes. On one side of the trunk, beautiful, thick, wooden hangers clutched a sliding rail and awaited the dresses, the middy blouses and the skirts which uniformed the very fashionable Emily. On the other side, deep, lined drawers with cupped brass handles awaited the jerseys and the neatly folded underwear. The very top drawer was divided, one side for the rouge and the face powder, and the other side for the jewels in their black velvet boxes from Garrards and Asprey's. The final drawer housed the shoes: flat, sensible shoes like Oxford walking shoes, or the shiny, pointed dancing shoes which clicked so sharply on the polished floor of Marty's massive Boston mansion on Commonwealth Avenue, between Arlington and Berkeley Streets. These shoes, as the huge Packard nosed its way to the head of the queue of passengers, lay vaulted, wrapped in gray-blue flannel.

Indeed, Esther minded her own suitcases most dreadfully, as much as she minded her maroon velvet skirt and her white middy blouse. Emily, of course, wore only the silkiest of suits. Her generous breasts strained contentedly against a warm, silk blouse tucked neatly into a pencil-striped skirt. Over her shoulders hung a black cashmere coat with small, elegant, black pearl buttons, shining dully in the weak rays of the watery January city sun which seemed to envelope Emily with welcoming arms.

"Esther," Nora had said sharply when Esther had begged for a similar cashmere coat, "my dear child. What would we want with spending such money on a coat? Your father could pay the electricity bill for the whole year with that kind of money. Anyway, your cloak is thick and warm. I checked it myself when I bought the roll of material." Esther sighed. Nora would never understand. However much money Danny Gottstein made, Nora was still poor. Etta cheerfully wore anything her mother's industrious, sewing hands produced. Only recently had Danny bought himself a store-bought suit, and that was only because Nora was having trouble with her eyes. Years of minute cross-stitching and making clothes for her beloved family were as much happiness as she could bear. At night, sitting on the porch in her rocker, or beside the fire on a cold day, she sewed as she talked. The first time Esther demanded a dress from Witfields in Santa Fe, Nora had been devastated.

Now, standing on the railway platform, Esther wished she could sink through the concrete and never return. Marty at least was honest and open, but everywhere she and Emily traveled, Esther dreaded unpacking. She remembered her first arrival at Marty Hollander's house when, through her overawed numbness, she had felt nothing but embarrassment at her own lack of style. At first, Esther had tried to unpack for herself. The maid, however, was so hurt that Esther, in the end, decided to let her unpack the suitcases which had followed her wherever she went. Not only did they look like two hideous, embroidered toads, but when they spewed their contents, all Esther could do was to retire to the pretty pink bathroom which was hers alone, and wait.

Presently, after the beautiful drive to Boston's Back Bay, the door to her bedroom shut quietly and Esther was alone.

For this trip Nora, fearing starvation possibly stalking her slim, petite daughter, had surpassed herself. In among the neatly folded clothes lay jars of jam, fresh from the last summer harvest. A big square tin carried a pound cake. A wide-mouthed pickling jar was filled with white mucus in which a very large pair of *gefilte* fish were laid to rest. The maid put these culinary items to sit on the sixteenth-century tallboy. Esther was again mortified. No doubt the maid was giggling downstairs. Esther took the offending objects and put them once more into one of the portmanteaux now tucked away in her pink-lined changing room. The first gong sounded. Time to change for dinner.

Dinner was served in the chandeliered magnificence of Marty's dining room. Ashley—Marty's affable, lovable teddy bear of a husband—sat at the far end of the table. He was large and genial, and he genuinely liked to see both the girls at his table. Pretty girls were to be liked far more than many of the sharp, pointed friends of Marty's who invaded his house and drank away his money. Pretty girls were getting harder to find these days, as more and more young women cut off their lovely long hair and took to the streets. These days, Ashley Hollander—known as "Ash" to his friends—reflected, one was rather startled to see pictures in perfectly reliable newspapers, such as the *Boston Post,* filled with photographs of very ugly women throwing things at people and screaming. For a moment, Ash sighed. He thought of the day when he became forty, twenty years ago. He was so depressed at the years rushing by him, at the weight of the responsibility of his mansion and his yacht tied at the Boston wharves. He thought of all the people who needed him to produce more and more money just to keep them afloat on the rough sea of life.

Ash returned from a walk in Boston Public Gardens and joined Marty and the girls for an after dinner brandy. As he sat in his palatial sitting room, Ash wished he felt less invisible in his own house. He liked Emily well enough, but he liked Esther very much indeed. There was a brilliant shine to her dark eyes, a willingness to learn, to learn everything and to understand everything. Ash wondered if she needed a job next summer. His business was beginning to employ women stenographers, and he could use a good head. Tomorrow night, Marty's Sapphic friends were coming into town. On those nights, Ash stayed at his club and snorted with horror. "What is the world coming to when a man is driven from his own house by a bunch of women?" he would ask on those nights, exiled from his home. "What, indeed?" several of his cronies would agree. Tomorrow night would be such a night.

❧ CHAPTER 26 ❧

Esther watched Harriet Smythe-Jones whisper into Mary Osborne's ear. From the wicked smile on Harriet's face and the twitch of her long nose, Esther imagined it must be one of the Sapphic poems she was recounting. Esther had a small, green edition of the love poems hidden under her mattress. Her pillow would not do because of the maid. The thick green covers with the shaded design of two women's faces gave her a curious thrill, as did the heavily scented, sexually explicit love poems. But now, armed with Marty Hollander's running comments and a new list of who was living, sleeping, or about to change beds with whom, Esther looked across the great dining room and she felt as if scales had dropped from her eyes forever.

While Emily floated over this crowd of hungry, ambitious women, her eyes adream with thoughts of marriage and Jimmy Delgado, Esther wanted to know—everything and all about life, with a capital "L."

"Esther," Marty's voice broke into the moment of silence that surrounded Esther. "Come, dear. Don't dream. Come and meet Julie Youngblood."

Esther jumped from her private moment into the present. "Of course," she said and put her hand into the warm, aging hands of an attractive, elderly woman. "I'm Esther Gottstein."

Julie smiled a warm, wide smile. A tall and still attractive woman, Julie had startlingly European features smoothed over by dark skin. Her eyes were whirlpools of laughter. So, Julie thought, this is little Lilla Braff's granddaughter. My, how like her grandmother she is. There were no secrets of identity in Julie Youngblood's world. "How do you do, Esther? Here. Let's take a glass of champagne together. I'm told that Marty always serves the finest champagne in Boston."

Esther felt little silken threads, a merciless undertow of tension between the women in the room, a tension that she never felt in her family gatherings back in Santa Fe. She walked beside Julie, who frequently stopped and talked to other elderly women. She obviously knew everybody. "This," Julie said, putting her arm around Esther, "is Esther Gottstein." Every time Julie introduced her, Esther felt as if there were a secret which excluded her. Every time her name was mentioned, another piece of thread seemed to attach itself to her person. By the time she arrived at the table, she was seriously perturbed. Various heads were nodding in her direction. Various mouths were whispering through red, pouted lips. White teeth gleamed and Julie was laughing. Still strong and healthy, not much had touched Julie. "Here, darling." Julie handed Esther a glass of yellow heaven. "Don't drink too fast."

Esther sipped her drink. "Ahh," she sighed. "I love champagne."

Julie looked down at the earnest young woman. "You'll have plenty of champagne if you want it, Little Love. It depends how you live your life."

"What do you mean?" Esther demanded.

Julie smiled. "Well, dear, you can either live like this"—she waved her hand at the packed room of exotic women—"or you can get married, have children, and keep ducks."

Esther paused. "Why can't I be a lawyer or a doctor?"

"You can, dear. Indeed you can. But all this is so much fun! Think of the years you'll spend being stuck at college while the rest of us are all off traveling. Are you doing the Grand Tour this summer?"

Esther shook her head. "I don't know if my mother would let me. I know Emily can go if she finds a suitable chaperon. We both very much want to travel. No one from Santa Fe travels to Europe. I feel I would die to be able to sit in a café in Paris. Have you ever been there?"

"Many times," Julie said. "Paris is one of my favorite places."

Esther finished her first glass of champagne. The mere thought of Paris made her heart beat even faster. "All the best writers live there," Esther said, taking another glass off a passing tray. "Emily and I want to be writers. We want to be where writers are, not locked away in boring college." The champagne had caused her cheeks, covered by a thin dew of perspiration, to flush.

So intense, Julie remarked to herself. So like dear Lilla. "If you like," Julie said, "I'll ask Marty if you two girls can accompany me. I shall be leaving for Rome and Paris and possibly London in August. Would you like me to ask?"

"*Like* you to ask? That would be marvelous!" Esther's voice shook with emotion. "I don't know when I've been more excited." Suddenly the room spun. Esther felt that she was being sucked into a vortex. The champagne was her last thought.

Expertly Julie caught her before she fainted. Julie removed the glass from her hand and carried the slight figure out of the crowded hot room. "Oh dear," Marty said, passing by like a Victorian sailing boat.

"Oh dear, indeed," said Julie. "Too much champagne on an empty stomach. I'll put her to bed. Don't you worry. Is Lilla coming?"

"No," Marty shook her head. "They're both in town at Amelia's town house. But I hear that Amelia is very ill indeed. Lilla is with her."

"Just as well she's not here. Poor Lilla couldn't cope with the thought of a granddaughter in town. She does so hate to age." As Julie stood beside the staircase she looked down at the young, white face of the child in her arms. She remembered Lilla's face when they were both young and briefly lovers. Since they had first met, money and time—thirty-three years—had treated Julie well. But for Lilla, time had etched hard, bitter lines between her eyebrows. Long, corrosive lines ran from her mouth to her chin. Rage against Amelia's tyranny lay fenced in a chest which was now subject to bouts of chronic bronchitis. Struggling for breath, Lilla tried to serve her companion, whose demands increased as age withered her bones and twisted her feet until bed was Amelia's only refuge. Lying there, the large commanding figure rang her bell relentlessly. Coughing, Lilla did her best. Most of their friends were now dead or dying. Some were attended by a new lover, some by old. And some were agonizing alone. They all did their best to keep up appearances. But for Lilla, only allowed to spend money for Amelia and not for herself, life had turned out to be very hard. Lilla hated being in her sixties. The best part of her life, she believed, was long since over.

Julie reflected on all of this as she took the mahogany lift up to the bedrooms. Gently, she put the girl down on the big, fluffy pillows and expertly she took off her clothes. When Esther lay naked, Julie looked at the pale, frail limbs. She ran a single finger over the white mound of the girl's belly. Her eyes feasted on the flesh so young and innocent. From under Esther's pillow, Julie pulled a nightdress. She smiled. The girl was definitely Reuben's granddaughter: the night-dress was made of soft, white flannel with a sentinel of buttons from neck to toe.

Having dressed and enfolded Esther in the downy sheets, Julie bent her head and kissed the dreaming mouth. Esther was in deep sleep, but she felt the soft mouth and she stirred. Julie stood up and, as an afterthought, she put her hand under the mattress and pulled out the hidden book of poems. Julie held the book in her hands. "Never," she promised out loud, "do I want to be that age again." She put the book on the bedside table. "All those decisions. All that pain," she murmured to herself as she left the room. The room settled into the black of the night, aroused only by the quiet breathing of the sleeping girl.

Julie felt tired. She arrived back on the ground floor and walked toward the other women. Reassuring Emily that her friend was all right, she went to find Marty. "Fast asleep, little angel," she said.

Marty raised her eyebrows. "Pretty little thing, isn't she?"

"Yes," Julie nodded. "She is. Poor child is desperate to get abroad. What do you say I take Emily with her to Paris in August?"

Marty, though not of Sapphic persuasion, looked amused. "Is this to be an educational trip or for pleasure?"

Julie shook her head. "I'm not one of your wrinkled old ladies after luscious young things." She sighed. "I've decided that chastity is my fairly permanent condition. The young these days have no respect. Besides, they don't read anymore. I really do think I would enjoy the company of the two girls. And anyway, who better than I to show them Paris?"

"All right." Marty was tired. The evening was drawing to a close. "We'll talk again." Women were leaving. Elegant minks and chinchillas, were being draped onto elegant bodies. Hands brushed, filled with insolent desire for bodies not theirs for the having. Deceits, naked lust, and women leaving. Kissing cries of endearment, longing, sighing.

On the street outside, Ashley Hollander saw them leaving. He pulled into his garage and yawned. "Can't see what she sees in them," he said aloud. Suddenly, he could not wait until he lay beside his wife, warm in his winter pajamas and covered by a large, bearskin rug. "Happy, darling?" he said later that evening, an hour after they made love.

"Yes," Marty said with a deep sigh. "Of course I'm happy, darling." She fell asleep, vaguely discontent. She dreamed of Lilla in the old days, and she dreamed of ships that sailed across the skies, crowded with people having a party.

Upstairs, Esther slept quietly. Back in her secure apartment, Julie put out the light. "I'll take her to Paris," she muttered after she said her Catholic prayers. Julie fell asleep dreaming of Lilla long ago.

✑ CHAPTER 27 ✑

The cat sat, a black shadow on the long wooden plank which stretched along the width of the haybarn. Glinting in the late afternoon shadows, its yellow eyes watched for mice, but also watched Etta lying in Tom Harding's arms, Tom Harding's forbidden arms. More interested by the prospect of mice, the cat turned its head and let the young lovers carry on with their loving.

Since Esther had first left for Wellesley, Etta felt such a loneliness she thought she would be unable to recover her lost self. Esther's presence, energetic and forceful, had always swallowed Etta, dragged her about in the wake of its energy. Without her twin Esther, Etta felt inert.

True, Nora Gottstein had more time to spend with Etta, and Danny loved his warm, generous daughter But for Etta, the days were long and the nights even longer. Her girlfriends came and went like moths in the night, but they were not a twin. Twins, having left their shared womb, are referred to as "them" by others and "we" by themselves. There is no "I." Esther's absence meant that, for the first time in her life, Etta was forced to experience the loss of "we" and the painful emergence of "I."

With a fierce, physically palpable feeling of loss, she now lay in the one part of the world that seemed to offer genuine comfort: Tom Harding's arms. They were very different arms from her sister's pale white ones. These arms were fierce, the muscles huge from farming, the chest she lay against was broad, and the face above hers, fixed in its intensity. "We shouldn't be doing this," Etta whispered.

"I know." Tom's voice was low. "But that's never stopped us before." His fingers between her plump thighs moved convulsively. There was a smell of sensual sex intertwined with that of the damp hay.

Shutting her eyes, Etta gave herself over to the thrill of electrifying sensations. Her rounded young body lay naked, from the soles of her pink feet up to the top of her warm, black hair. From beneath, the hay teased every inch of her flesh and from above, the early summer breeze blew over her, making her skin tingle with its coolness. All around she was embraced by the rubbing of Tom's strong, smooth nudity. His mouth, warm and hungry, kissed its way from her ear, along her neck, down to her bare soft armpit, and finally all over the silky fullness of her naked breasts. With each of its movements his mouth brought Etta a new shiver of pleasure.

In her own hand, Etta held that which she had come to love. Eagerly, as with a joy of its own, it never failed to respond to her touch. Persuaded by the inducements of Tom's fingers in the slippery wetness between her thighs, Etta parted her legs and her hand guided Tom until, with a moan, he slipped inside her.

Between the bursts of ecstasy each of his undulations gave her, Etta caught flashes of her mother's face. The face looked sad. Etta sighed. She and Tom had been lovers since the beginning of February and now it was June. Today, she knew, as her mind wandered from the pleasure of the present, she must tell Tom about her fear, the fear that she mostly managed to push aside. She had missed her time of the month since March, only weeks after they first had delighted each other completely with the gift of their young bodies.

From their first time together, Etta had loved golden-haired, gray-eyed Tom Harding with an unwavering certainty. She loved the misty gray of his eyes and the gentleness in the curve of his full sensual mouth. She loved the maleness of his thick, scarred farming hands, hands that gently cupped her white breasts, hands that were capable of birthing lambs, of ploughing fields and of giving life to the land.

Now, he had created life in her. Part of Etta was exultant, the deep, womanly part of her nature. Her body was ready and willing to swell and then burst triumphantly in motherhood, eager to bear the child of the man she loved. Another part of her feared the danger from other people. And pain would come, inevitably, from her family. But her love for Tom, she knew, could endure any resistance her parents might offer. Her love for Tom knew no bounds.

With a great and growing strength, Tom pressed her more quickly, more urgently. For now, briefly, all fear was abandoned in Etta's mind to the passion of the moment, the passion distilled with first-found love. Her movements rolling with his, she rode her pleasure to its highest as he too burst forth within her.

Panting, he lay his tired head against her shoulder. Etta opened her eyes and beheld the glowing gold of his hair. She stroked it with her hand and kissed it with small kisses. "Hmm," he breathed, nuzzling his face into her breast.

"My baby," she said, kissing him again on the crown of his head. He answered with a contented sigh. "You know," she said, laying her head back against the straw and letting out a little laugh, "my mother says you're dangerous."

"Me?" he said with mock hurt in his voice, still facing downward at her breast. "Never. She must be thinking of someone else."

"No," Etta said with more light laughter. "She says that all the parents in town lock up their daughters when they see you coming down the street."

Tom lifted his head and gave her nipple a brief kiss. "I'd never be dangerous to you." He looked into her eyes and smiled.

"But what about other girls? It's no secret that you've known a few."

"Etta," he said, his gray eyes staring seriously. "Not since I've been with you. I love you. And I'll never love another girl again."

"Oh, Tom." She breathed out a happy relieved laugh, but he could see she was worried.

"What is it, Etta?" he asked with concern. "Tell me, please. What's wrong?"

"Tom," Etta hesitated, then lifted her head and looked directly at him. "I think I'm pregnant."

Tom Harding felt ice running down his chest. He fought an urge to clutch his groin. Suddenly he no longer felt as masculinely confident as he had half a minute ago. But, he told himself, he must remain calm. He loved Etta, and she needed him. Now more than ever. "Oh," he said, trying not to let his voice crack. "I see."

Etta sat up and shook her head. "I suppose I rather thought it would never happen to me."

Tom put warm arms around Etta and pulled her close. "Well," he said, feeling a resolve growing in his mind, "there's only one thing to do. We'll get married." He liked the sound of the words. Indeed, lately he had begun to imagine how nice the rest of his life would be if it were always shared with Etta. True, he had not thought of marrying so soon, but why not? Yes. Why not?

Etta pulled away. "Do you really want to marry me, Tom?"

He smiled a wide smile. "I've always wanted to marry you, from the day I met you, Etta." He grew more certain by the second.

"But what about your parents?" Etta frowned. Mr and Mrs Harding, though neighbors, were not known for their neighborly behavior. When Tom took Etta to tea at his house, Mrs Harding, in particular, had been less than welcoming. "She does like you," Tom had patiently explained. "She's always like that to any girl she meets." Etta had said nothing, but now she felt unsure. "What if your parents say no?"

Tom pulled Etta back into his safe arms. "They can't say no, silly. I'm of legal age. The captain of my own life. I'll tell them I'm going to marry you and that will be that." Yes, he thought. I'll *tell* them.

Etta lay against Tom's chest. "If only," she said, "time could stand still forever." Both of them, tired, lay content in the curl of the hay piled on either side.

The cry of the old, red barn rooster reached Etta's ears. "I have to go," Tom said suddenly. "I have to feed the hens." He scrambled to his feet. "I'll come by later and tell you what they said. After supper. Then we'll tell your folks."

Etta smiled and jumped to her feet. "Okay. I'd better get home or mother will worry." She plucked straw from her hair, and stood, hesitant. Quickly they picked up their clothes from the hay and dressed themselves. "Are you afraid to tell your parents?"

Tom made a face and then shrugged. "I love you, Etta. I want to marry you. I've done nothing I'm ashamed of." He put his hand on Etta's still flat belly. "That's my child." His eyes glowed softly. "I'm a father now." He hugged Etta hard. "Don't worry," he said. "I'll leave first and you follow in a few minutes." He heard his own words and laughed. "What am I talking about?" he said. "We're going to be man and wife, and here we are sneaking around like a couple of naughty kids." He kissed her on the cheek. "Don't worry. It won't be long. Once we're married, we won't have to hide anything from anybody." He hugged her tightly. "Goodbye," he said, and he ran off full of youthful vigor and love.

Etta walked out of the barn into the gray stillness of the evening. The first star of the night shone above her as she made her way across the fields to her home.

After a largely silent supper, Nora smiled at Etta. "Are you going to see Tom Harding tonight, darling?"

Etta was unusually subdued. "Yes," she said. "I am."

Nora looked at her daughter. "How serious is he?" she asked.

Dr Daniel Gottstein snorted. "He's not old enough to get serious. Anyway, he's not a Jew."

Etta turned sharply. "But we're all Americans."

Danny frowned. "Let Reuben say what he wants, but a good Jew is a good husband."

Etta squirmed in her chair. Time ticked by, minute after minute. When, oh when, was dinner to end? At last, Danny rose to his feet. He pulled a cigar out of his pocket and he joined Nora in the kitchen. How would she ever tell them? First, she thought, let Tom tell his parents. Then we can deal with mine.

Etta waited. She wandered out to the porch and sat on the swing. The swing had been there all her life. As a baby she had lain in her mother's arms on that swing. As a toddler she'd sat on her father's knee. Both parents had been full of marriage plans for their daughters. "A double wedding yet," Nora used to joke. "Two handsome sons-in-law to make a fuss of me . . ."

Etta heard Tom's footsteps crunch up the drive. She looked eagerly into the darkness. Tom ran up the narrow path leading to the porch and threw himself down beside Etta, his head on her lap. For a moment he lay still. Then he raised his white face to hers. He looked horrifyingly pale. Oh no, thought Etta. He's not going to marry me. His parents have said no. "Tom?" she asked anxiously.

"Well," he said, managing a smile. "It could have been worse. No," he said, shaking his head and forcing a cough of a laugh. "On second thoughts, maybe it couldn't have."

"I guess your parents weren't too pleased." Etta tried to sound as relaxed as possible.

"That's putting it mildly," he said, again with a nervous laugh.

"Tell me. What happened?"

"Well, when I told my parents over dinner that I wanted to marry you, my mother—you know how calmly she takes everything—she fainted. Right there in the middle of dinner. Passed out. Dead on the floor."

"Oh, Tom——"

"And my father, he was so busy yelling at me "Look what you've done to your mother" on the one hand and trying to haul her up on her feet on the other, I guess I never really got around to mentioning you were pregnant."

Fear and disappointment seized Etta. The man who had left her in the barn, it seemed, had returned to being a frightened boy. "Tom," she said sternly. "Does this mean . . ."

"Wait," he said. "It gets better." Color began to return to his cheeks, as even he could see the black humor of the ordeal he had just suffered. "When my father got my mother back into her seat, I told them both I was very sorry to make my mother faint, but my mind was made up. "I'm still going to marry Etta Gottstein,' I said. So my father smashes the table with his fist and says, "If you marry that girl against our wishes, then you'll never get another penny from us as long as we're alive!' " Etta listened with confused interest. " 'Come to think of it,' he says, 'you'll never get another penny from us even after we're dead. And you need never darken our doorstep again.' So you know what I said right back to him?"

"What?" Etta did not know whether to feel disappointed or thrilled.

"I said, 'That's fine by me.' "

"Oh, Tom!" She threw her arms around his neck and squeezed him tight. "Then you do want to marry me!"

"Of course I do. I told you that back in the barn. Did you really think I'd let my parents stop me?"

"No." She was embarrassed to have doubted him. "No, I knew you meant what you said." At that moment, she felt more love for him than she remembered ever having felt for anyone in the world. Her eyes filled with emotion. "I guess you really must love me," she said in a small voice.

"I do love you, Etta. I always will." He pulled her close and kissed her on the mouth, deeply and for a long time. She responded with joy. When he withdrew his mouth from hers, he lowered his head and let his hands fall in his lap. "You know," he said. His voice was serious. "It's not going to be easy for us this way, what with me having no money and all." He looked up at her. "But I've got it all worked out. My uncle owns a ranch up in Chama. My father's brother, you know. He's always told me how much he wants me to help him out up there, seeing as how he's never had a son of his own. Anyway, if I go and work on his ranch, then I can begin to get some money together. And then I'll buy a few acres of the land off my uncle, and I can build a house on it for the two of us to live in once we're married. You'll like it in Chama. It's beautiful. And even if my parents get on to him and tell him not to sell me any of his land— which isn't likely to happen, because he hasn't listened to anything my father's said for years—but even if that happens, well, I'll just take the money I earn and buy some land someplace else. So you see? It's all worked out."

"You mean you're going to leave me here alone?"

"Only for a little while, Etta. Just until I get enough money to get us set up. I wouldn't feel right having a wife when I couldn't even support her. Really, I promise. Just for a couple of months. Then I'll come back, and we'll get married, and I'll take you to live with me forever."

"But the baby. It'll be coming in six months or so. And what would people say if it's born so close to our wedding?"

Tom was silent. Then he said, "That's tough. But look at it this way, if I'm willing to get thrown out by my parents, then I guess I shouldn't care too much for what other people think."

Etta shook her head fiercely. "Marry me now, Tom. No, please. Right away. It'll be better this way. Then we'll be safe together and so will the baby."

"I just wouldn't feel right, not being able to support you yet. And besides, what would your parents say? I mean, in a way, this has been on the cards with my parents for years. We've never really got on smooth. I always knew I'd have to walk out some day. But with your folks, it's different. They love you, Etta, and you love them. And I don't want to tear you away from them all of a sudden. It's going to take some time for them to get used to the idea."

"But . . ." Etta fell silent. She knew he was right. If Danny and Nora were ever to accept the idea of her marrying Tom, it would surely take time. Tom knew her well. He knew that she would have to give them that time. She couldn't just run out on her family. She loved them too much. "I suppose you're right." She hugged him and lay her head against his chest. "But I'm so afraid. If you go away now, how do I know you'll come back?"

"You don't have to worry about that." His voice was soothing. "I'll come back. And in just a couple of months. That's all. In the meantime, I'll write to you every week. And when you think the time's right, tell your parents. Easy at first, to let them get used to it."

Etta hung her head. "When will you go?"

"Tonight. I figure the sooner I get working, the sooner we can get married. All my stuff's hiding outside the barn. I climbed back in my bedroom window, after my father threw me out, and packed up everything. I'm all ready to go."

They hugged each other and kissed as if for the last time. "Goodbye, Etta," said Tom, and Etta sat on the swing, weeping silently, as she watched him run into the darkness.

❧ CHAPTER 28 ❧

Lilla knew Amelia was dying.

They missed Marty's publicized parties—even the gossip columns made comment. The absence of Amelia's huge, commanding figure was noticeable, as she no longer held court in the center of drawing rooms across the world.

In the middle of the hot June when Tom left his Etta, Lilla decided to take Amelia back to New Jersey, back to the house they had regularly returned to over the thirty-odd years which bound them together. Amelia agreed with a weak nod of her head. Her large family and rich relations were tentatively enquiring, from a distance, about her health. Reggie, her long-lost husband, still immersed in his gambling lifestyle, wrote with ill-concealed impatience. Lilla kept all letters away from Amelia. She tried to interest her. She tried to keep her abreast of the latest news, but deep down inside herself, she knew Amelia was going to die.

Preparing herself for what seemed to be the inevitable, Lilla wondered how she would feel when her friend died. She had not found the freedom she had hoped to gain by leaving her family in favor of Amelia. For years she had been bound to Amelia, restrained from traveling on her own to see the world and to seek out her own friendships. On the other hand, Lilla reasoned, she could not deny the luxury of the life she shared with Amelia. To be sure, there was an ugliness in the shrewd manipulations and cruel gossip of the sisters, but even this ugliness was masked by a perpetual veil of monied beauty, aesthetically pleasing surroundings, and new titillations to the senses. Perhaps, Lilla recognized in a retrospection which spanned many years, Amelia had been her liberator as much as her captor. Or perhaps she had merely moved her from one trap to another. But imprisonment with Reuben had meant grim peasantry—at least Amelia had provided a well-appointed cell.

What would she do with her life when Amelia died? Lilla did not exactly know. Her time, however, would be her own. For once, she would be answerable to no other person. And with the money she was certain she would inherit from Amelia, she could spend her time doing anything and going anywhere she pleased. Would she miss Amelia? Perhaps. Perhaps not. Their years together had created a familiarity between them. Whether it was a familiarity of animosity, tolerance or fondness, Lilla could no longer be sure.

When they arrived at the big house near Middletown, a new maid opened the door. As Amelia was carried in on a stretcher, Lilla smiled at the memory of her young self all those years ago, standing nervously on the same stone porch. Far away across the fields, a new generation of larks spiraled in the blue sky. A new generation of people farmed her farm. The big house enveloped her in its arms, and she walked up the steps to oversee Amelia being settled into her bedroom.

Amelia ate little these days. Lilla held her gray head, sometimes gently and sometimes impatiently, persuading her to sip homemade soups through a feeding bowl. Amelia was slow and Lilla found herself tired, but Amelia insisted that she wanted only Lilla's hands around her, so Lilla did her best to meet her friend's needs.

Once Amelia was asleep, and Lilla had checked the doors of the big house were locked, Lilla went to her own familiar room. The same bed lay silent, awaiting her. The same dressing table mirror reflected a very different Lilla from the nervous young woman. All the years now sat in lines on Lilla's face. The good years gave her narrow shoulders authority. The harsh quarrels and humiliations gave her creases of weariness. But, over all, Lilla refused to consider her age. She scorned mirrors. She ate like a sparrow and she dreaded the onset of senility. To fend off old age, she dropped ten years mentally off the true total of her life. She adopted several mannerisms—a girlish laugh and a youthful style of dressing—that deceived most people into believing that she was a spritely woman in her early fifties.

Amelia made no such attempt. She wore down over the years like an old grandfather clock. The fierce tick in her life became the tock of a mechanism that was damaged years ago in childhood. While Amelia was young and hearty, she thrived in her monied, solipsistic universe. Now, her generation gone forever, the "new" and the "different" in the younger generation disgusted her. The need for the younger generation to prate and rave dismayed her. She expected them to sit at her feet and listen to her wisdom as she, in her turn, had listened. But these young things did nothing of the sort. The women all wore gobs of makeup and short skirts. They flaunted their flat chests and talked of politics. They talked in hushed tones of workers and predictions of a great depression. They discussed abstract art and free love. Amelia always knew the joy of love. Sometimes, the emotional price was high. In her later years, the financial pressure was often higher than the pleasure of a fresh, young body with sensuous breasts and a tight pair of buttocks.

But Amelia knew she had Lilla at her beck and call: Lilla, with her apparently dog-like devotion, always ready to serve. No matter that young people were more inclined to throw out their parents' carefully collected antiques or well-preserved art collections. Gone were the beautiful Spode teapots, the hard-earned Oriental rugs, the hevy carved Chinese screens. In their place stood bare rooms and shelves full of books about politics.

In Lilla's opinion, it was no surprise that Amelia withdrew into her own, rich, Victorian world, a world of luxury, literature, and wonder. When Amelia was too weary to talk, Lilla read to her, while Amelia sipped her way, cup after cup, through a steaming pot of tea, taken English-style with milk and sugar. Rarely would Amelia like to hear anything written in the 1900s. A woman who never really made the transition from the nineteenth century into the sharp, uncaring twentieth, Amelia had Lilla read the works of writers who died before, as she saw it, the world became a vast hurdy-gurdy.

Christina Rossetti was her favorite poet. "When I am dead, my dearest, Sing no sad songs for me" from Rossetti's *Song* was a verse that brought tears of sadness to Amelia's dim eyes. Lilla made efforts to keep Amelia's spirits high but, on reading these lines, she was surprised to find herself choking on the words. Try as she might, she knew that every one of these last days counted.

Those days in the great house were long and largely quiet. When Lilla was not tending to Amelia, she had hours to herself to do nothing but listen to the echoing silence and sit with her memories of their years together.

Lilla knew the ordinary people of the world never even came close to understanding their life together. Their money had set them apart, preserved them as if in a bubble, protecting them from everyday cares. Other people, if they noticed the two women at all, regarded them with a detached sort of incomprehension. Little children had always tended to like Amelia for her fat laugh and for her deep pockets which invariably carried a fat, striped humbug. Lilla was made of sterner stuff. She was shy and apt to retire from the full-blooded arguments which could so swiftly erupt between Amelia and her many friends.

Now, however, the stillness of the house seemed to reflect the demise of those more intense years. The two gardeners outside bent over the summer garden.

The maid worked at her chores, quit and watchful. The days slid past. The curtains remained drawn. Lilla watched and waited.

All business usually done by Amelia now slid onto the mat and was passed over to the awesome attorney who attended the family affairs. Amelia aways considered herself an excellent businesswoman. Lilla agreed but she was privately worried about the huge pile of bills which sat in monstrous heaps in the apartment in Boston and in the various houses they inhabited in their peripatetic lifestyle. Amelia always carried quantities of small gold coins which jingled in her capacious pockets. If her mood was excellent and a child was captivating, the child was just as likely to get a gold dollar as a candy humbug. If, by chance, a desperate shoemaker was lucky and presented a bill in person, he was liable to get not only full payment but a humbug as well.

In nearby Middletown, the people had come to honor the women's privacy. If any of them gossiped, then the gossip was idle. Amelia and Lilla lived their lives in respectable solitude.

The relationship which grew over their thirty-three shared years was an alliance which bore no name. It was a mystery to most people, deemed "unnatural" by some, but never had sex become the essential binding force between the two women. Sexual pleasure had been a small force in their early lives together, but later it was their companionship which provided them both with what was, perhaps, the simple solace of not being alone in the world. Their physical intimacy was more in their early years of student and mentor. How odd, Lilla sometimes thought, that now it was Amelia who seemed to need her. So very green had Lilla been at first, such a dependent puppy. But now, Amelia was the one who so badly needed someone to look after her.

As Lilla sat in the cavernous house, she looked around at all the booty the two women had acquired. Lilla always loved to shop as much as she loved to collect, and the big house was a repository of treasures from all the worlds they explored together. The lion that lay magnificently on the floor of Amelia's bedroom was shot by Amelia all those years ago in Africa. Hidden away in the bottom of the cupboard in Lilla's room lay a bath towel from the big bathroom in New York when she had shared her first night in a hotel with Amelia.

For all the possessions, however, only two seemed irreplaceable to Lilla. One was a trinket from a life long ago, even before she had known Amelia or, for that matter, Reuben. Around her neck Amelia still wore her cherished piece—the golden locket with her own baby hair inside, the locket which had been her mother's. The other was the ribbon, the second place prize that her painting had won in New York when she was young, a monument to her once great artistic talent which had been buried over by years of other *divertissements*. She kept this ribbon in the drawer of the table beside her bed. It was the locket and the prize that seemed to Lilla the only things on earth that were truly her own.

Amelia, during these last trying weeks and days, knew the end was near. She talked with frankness about her death. She wanted, she said, to see that adequate preparations were arranged. She called her attorney, Mr. Treadnought to her side a month after she and

Lilla had returned from Boston. Lilla was there when Amelia made an attempt to organize her affairs, but Amelia had left it too late, and Mr. Treadnought's long-winded explanations exhausted the small bit of energy Amelia had left, making her face go ashen. "Don't dear. Don't," Amelia said to the attorney. "I'm sure everything is all right."

Lilla gently stopped the interview and saw the pompous Mr. Treadnought to the door. "I assure you," Mr. Treadnought intoned, "I have been the Witney-Hay family lawyer all my life. We shall see that you will be remunerated for your service as companion to Mrs. Witney-Hay." Lilla shut the door on him with a decisive bang and hurried back to Amelia.

"Amelia," she said boldly at first, then softened her voice, feeling more awkward than modest. "Amelia," she said again. "Have you . . . I mean, will I really be provided for?"

Tired by the lawyer's visit, Amelia was in poor humor. "I told you yesterday," she insisted sharply. "Mr. Treadnought will make all the arrangements. What's the matter? Do you think your time with me won't pay off?" A fierce hardness quickly captured Amelia's face. She stared at Lilla with an intense accusation in her eyes. "That's it, isn't it?"

"That's what?" Lilla asked, frightened that Amelia might be in one of her tempers which seemed to rise as quickly and as unforeseeably as a sea squall.

"That's the reason you've stayed with me. That's why you ever came to live with me in the first place, isn't it? It's my money you're after. I've been nothing but a bank to you, haven't I?"

Lilla exhaled deeply to calm herself. "Look, Amelia. You're obviously not in the mood to discuss this right now. It was wrong of me to mention it. Please, forget I said a thing. Now let's just drop it and we can talk about it another time."

"Don't you dare condescend to me!" Amelia rasped, her voice hoarse. "I'll talk about anything I want any time I please! Who do you think I am, that you speak to me that way? Do you think I'm some senile old biddy who doesn't know the time of day? Is that what you think?"

"No, I . . ." But there was no stopping Amelia, Lilla knew. Her anger was in full swing.

"And who do you think you are to talk down to me? Why, you were nobody when I took you on! Just a little nobody."

"That's not true!" Lilla returned, hurt past being able to stop herself. She knew it probably would not do her any good, but she had to try to offer some defense. "I was an artist. A very talented artist."

"A very talented artist, indeed!" Amelia spat with a malicious laugh. "Where is your artwork then? Why aren't the walls hung with your masterpieces? Where were your great exhibits? When were your art shows? Or am I too old and senile to remember such things?"

"You know I never had time to work on my art. You know we've been too busy together."

"Time. That's a poor excuse. A great artist *makes* time if she can't find it. No, it was never time you lacked. It was talent."

"But I did have talent. You know that. I won second prize at Mrs Rubenstein's salon. You remember—I did a painting of this house, and Mrs Rubenstein gave me second prize."

"You fool!" A horrid look of contemptuous triumph spread over Amelia's face. "You stupid, ignorant, childish fool. You actually believed you won that prize? Why, Mrs Rubenstein and I had it all agreed before she so much as set her eyes upon your painting. And you thought you actually *won* a prize for that second-rate, worthless piece of what you call art?"

Lilla stood speechless. She felt as if a great force had punched her hard and squarely in the face. "Oh, Amelia," she managed to say weakly. "You can't be telling the truth . . ."

"Of course I'm telling the truth! I thought you knew all along. How could you have been so foolish?"

"I don't know." She shook her head. "I don't know why I ever believed any of it." She lowered her head, hardly finding the strength to stand. Her one last dream—her vision of herself as an artist—had been annihilated. What did she have left? Heavy tears poured over her eyelids and rolled smoothly down her cheeks as she stood silently.

The silence became long and powerful. Even Amelia felt herself suddenly fall quiet. As her rage began to drain from her head, Amelia knew she had hurt her friend deeply, more deeply than ever before. Then, without another word, Lilla lifted her face and stared straight into Amelia's eyes. Through the clouds of tears on Lilla's face, Amelia beheld in those eyes a look she had never seen before. It was a look of utter defeat, of emptiness, of lifelessness. Yet there was an emotion in the look which frightened Amelia with its might, for it was past caring, beyond hatred. This time, Amelia knew, she had gone too far. She felt very afraid and very alone in the silent room. "Oh, Lilla," she said gently, shaking her head as if to rouse herself from a dream. "I'm sorry. Forgive me. I didn't know what I was saying." She laughed. "I'm the fool. I *am* just a silly old woman." She smiled and held out her arms. "Please, Lilla. Please forgive me."

Through the watery swirl of her tears, Lilla saw the woman with outstretched arms. Her life, she felt, had been torn from her, but still she wanted comfort from those arms. There were no other arms in the world left to hold her. She walked to Amelia's bed, sat down and hugged the large warm body, her face nuzzled between the old breasts.

The body began to tremble, then shake hugely. Amelia was crying, hugging Lilla's head tightly. "Don't leave me," Amelia cried. "Please. Don't let me die alone. You mustn't ever leave me."

The voice which a moment ago had cruelly wounded Lilla now sobbed like a frightened child. Lilla listened to the cries and let her head be hugged. A confusion took possession of her troubled thoughts. She was embracing the murderer of her soul but this woman, she realized, was her entire world. And soon it would all be over. For a moment, Lilla felt she would not want to live after Amelia died. Then she remembered the money which would at last open the gates to her freedom. Freedom. Lilla's numb mind was no longer sure she even knew what the world meant.

Lilla lay with Amelia for many minutes, until the cries subsided and the breathing quietened, then rumbled softly in small snores. Lilla removed the heavy arms from around her head and stood up. Her dry tears felt cool and taut on her cheeks. She walked from Amelia's bedroom to her own little room. She went to her bedside table and removed from the drawer the now worthless medal she had won, or not won, she reminded herself.

Refusing to think, she walked out of her room, down the spreading stairway, through the kitchen, and down the narrow dark stairs that led to the basement. There, in the oppressive heat of the furnace room, she opened the iron door, the mouth of the great inferno which always burned, even in summer, to keep the water hot. Hesitating only for a moment, she threw her prize into the flames. Shutting the door, she sat down in an old, wrought iron chair, across the fevered room. The heat choked her breathing and her chest began to shake with coughs, as it had done so often recently. The coughs became sobs, and it was Lilla's turn, alone, to be the frightened, weeping child.

A week later, on a Thursday morning, Amelia suffered a stroke. Lilla, upon entering the bedroom, saw that Amelia had fallen out of bed and was lying twisted on the floor. "Oh, God!" Lilla gasped. "Here. Let me help you." Amelia was weak, and one side of her face was still. With Lilla's help, she struggled back onto the bed. Her breathing was light and shallow. Her lips were blue. Lilla could feel Amelia's heart beating wildly and irregularly. She telephoned for the maid. "Get Doctor Johnson," she said. "Quickly."

She smoothed Amelia's brow. "Don't worry," she whispered and bent down to kiss the wide brow. "Only an accident. You'll be all right."

Amelia tried to smile. A brave, broken smile forced its way to her lips. The right corner of her mouth refused to cooperate. It slumped down chinwards and compelled her right eye to drop, as if in disagreement with the other side of her face.

The doctor was heard hurrying up the hall. He had

grown up with Amelia and cared deeply about her. A bachelor himself, he had tended both women as his patients. When they were sturdy and healthy, he saw them only socially, except to prescribe the odd medicine for Lilla's chest or for Amelia's blood pressure. Now he rushed into the room. "Dear, dear, Amelia," he said. "Had a little tumble, have we?" Quickly, he examined her chest. "A slight stroke, dear," he said. "Here. Let me see if you can squeeze my hand." Amelia's hand lay limp and white as did her right leg. "Never mind," the doctor said. "Only temporary, my dear. Miss Braff, come along with me and we'll devise a menu and organize some pills." He turned to Amelia and smiled. "You'll be well in no time." Expertly he shot a tranquilizer injection into Amelia's arm and then waited until her left eye closed in blessed sleep.

The doctor sighed. "I'm afraid we don't have long to go," he said.

Lilla stared at Dr Johnson. "I know," she said. "I've been waiting now for months. She lost the will to live, you know."

Dr Johnson sighed again. "I do," he said. "For many of us, the brave new world, and all it stands for, has very little to offer . . . But I'll give you a little cocktail of medicine. It contains a very strong opiate. If she is in pain or uncomfortable, let her sip it when she needs to. I'll give you a fair-sized bottle, but only a sip at a time."

Lilla took the bottle from his hand. She noticed the warning on the label. A skull with empty socket eyes stared. Two thighbones stood dutifully behind the skull. "Thank you," Lilla said. "I'll do my best for her. I really will."

The doctor patted Lilla's hand. "I know you will,"

he said, in a voice deep with compassion. "I care for my older sister who lives with me. I just pray that when the time comes, she goes quickly."

"Quickly," Lilla echoed. "Quickly."

The next three days passed as if in a dream for Lilla, like a dark and deadly nightmare. She knew that, even if Amelia was now speechless, Lilla alone must attend to her friend's private needs. For Amelia to be seen by the servants in an undressed state was unthinkable. So Lilla struggled to clean and bathe her. Ever since the stroke, she put a small cot in the room and slept beside her. She slept uneasily beside Amelia's drugged body, with an ear always open for any unusual breath.

On the third night, after she tucked the sheet under Amelia's chin, she saw her friend's eyes full of tears. Wiping them away, she found herself smiling. Amelia struggled to speak—a series of little grunts. "Don't," Lilla said, putting a finger to Amelia's mouth. "You don't need to say a thing." Lilla leaned forward and kissed her softly on her misshapen lips.

Later, in the early hours of the dawn, when the room was gray, before a ray of sun was in the sky, Amelia whispered in her sleep. Lilla was on her feet and bent low. Amelia's shallow breath pressed by her ear. A slight struggle. A few gasps for air. Lilla held her companion in her arms. Her black hair streaked with gray mingled with Amelia's pure white hair. Her tears of relief, of sorrow, of loneliness fell on the dying woman. "Goodbye," Lilla said. With a final groan, Amelia died.

Lilla lay across Amelia's body. After half an hour had passed, she climbed into the bed. She held the body and felt the warmth stealthily leave as the cold ice of death chilled the bones and the flesh.

At six-thirty the next morning, an hour before the maid was due to serve breakfast, Lilla got up. Amelia's sleeping face was as strong in death as it had been in life. For the last time, Amelia put her hand on the cold cheek and touched the closed blue eyes with a kiss on each lid. "Goodbye, Amelia," she said. "Goodbye."

❧ *CHAPTER 29* ❧

Mr Treadnought, the attorney, informed Lilla that the Will would be read after the funeral. He stood in the hall with large shadows from the skylight falling across his portentous face, his lips loose and flabby, his teeth of horse-like dimensions, stained yellow. He wore a green cravat. Lilla hated the vulgar diamond pin in it. She was too frightened of Mr Treadnought to dare to hate the man himself. "Mrs Witney-Hay's erstwhile lost husband will be at the train station within two hours. See that he is met."

Lilla twisted a white handkerchief—a gift from Amelia—and bit her lip. "I'll see that it's done," she said. "We don't have a chauffeur at the moment." The hurt of the word "we" hung in the air. "I mean, Amelia was ill for so long . . . I'll ask Jim, the gardener, to collect Mr Witney-Hay from the station."

"Good." The attorney smiled. "You'll see the family are well looked after. Mrs Witney-Hay was estranged from them all for so long. Brothers, sisters, cousins, nieces, nephews . . . such a shame." He sighed. "These family feuds are so wearing." He raised his eyes as if to inspect the ceiling above him. "I'd have thought Mr Witney-Hay will sell this house. I'd imagine it's much too large for a widower to run."

"But, I thought—" Lilla began. What did he mean that the house would be the widower's to sell? Amelia had always said the house and her fortune should go to Lilla. Indeed, Lilla knew there had been a Will to that effect. She was present when the Will was written and witnessed by Susan, the maid. But that was years ago. And now the attorney seemed to speak of a different plan. Had there been another, more recent, Will drawn up since then? Had Amelia made different arrangements with Mr Treadnought? Lilla could only wait to find out.

"Don't you worry," Mr Treadnought reassured her. "I've made provision for you in your old age. I know Mrs Witney-Hay was very grateful for you. You have been an excellent companion. Very faithful. And I know the family will be grateful. You can now retire in reasonable comfort for the rest of your life. Unless, of course, Mr Witney-Hay wants to hire you himself."

"I don't think so." Lilla looked down at the floor. The red persian carpet she'd always hated glared back at her. "I must go," she said. "I have to get dinner ready. We have no cook."

Mr Treadnought beamed. "You are a little treasure," he said. "Good servants are so hard to find."

Upon his departure, the door slammed. The sound reverberated around the house. For Lilla, the sound of the door heralded the full and final death of her former life. Not only had she lost the woman who had been her only mainstay in the world but, she thought with terror, was she to lose the house as well? In a horrified flash, she imagined Amelia, in her own careless way, had left her unprovided for—not out of malice, but in keeping with the way she always lived, from day to day, moment to moment.

Frozen with horror, Lilla sat on the third step of the stairway. She looked up at the walls covered with valuable paintings. The beautiful Bohemian glass chandelier glimmered softly. The stately white, marble fireplace looked compassionately upon Lilla's forlorn figure. Where could she go? she wondered. Who could she turn to? She had nothing of her own except Amelia's presents over the years. The women had given each other little things, tokens of affection. Lilla owned many handkerchiefs, like the one in her hand. Tears fell on it now.

She had a neat row of first editions. She gave Amelia books by Dornford Yates or Christina Rossetti. Amelia gave her collected children's books, long lost stories which meant nothing to anyone but themselves. Late at night, after sharing a bedtime cocoa, Amelia and Lilla would lie side by side while Amelia read in her deep, sonorous voice. Lilla's favorite ran, "Quietly, quietly went the mouse, into his well-remembered house—" The safe, secure words brought home the peace of the night, the warmth of Amelia's body, and the security of her magisterial presence. Amelia, when not in a temper, was as safe and secure Lilla could ever imagine a woman to be.

Now, in a blue dress, her white hair framing her lost face, she lay upstairs in a mahogany coffin, the deep red tones of the wood contrasting sharply with the gray-white of the dead face and hands. All day the people of Middletown had trooped past Lilla to pay their respects. Lilla didn't see them. She was insulated in that space where pain was suspended, lest the force be so great it catapults the sufferer, in an excess of agony, into the universe. The pain of loneliness, she knew, lurked and waited, dripping with pleasure at the thought of tormenting her. But Lilla held the demon at bay.

Quickly drying her eyes, she went to arrange for a car to meet Reginald Witney-Hay and then walked to the kitchen to prepare food. Tomorrow was the funeral. She had a lot to do and she was grateful for that distraction.

Much later, when she finished clearing up the debris of the family meal, she gave herself an allotted time to think about her predicament. One thing was certain: Amelia's friends would not be welcome at the funeral. To be sure, calls came in as news of Amelia's death reached the ears of her friends around the world.

"Amelia seemed to know rather a lot of people, didn't she, Reggie?" a cousin asked Mr Witney-Hay over dinner.

Reggie looked across the dinner table. Lilla was helping the maid serve the family. "Yes, indeed," Reggie agreed. He looked again at Lilla. "Life won't be the same without her."

Suddenly, Lilla felt afraid. All those years, like long corridors, stretched between them. Had she, in her young, innocent days, hurt this man? Had she been the final straw? She could barely remember. It was all rolled into the mists of time. Her life before Amelia was blank. Lilla could and did blot out anything she did not like. She took fastidiousness to an extreme.

Fortunately, Reggie had to entertain the Witney-Hay family. As they had no butler, it was Lilla who had to organize brandy for the men and liqueurs for the women. She put the delicious little truffles into bonbon dishes and remembered how often Amelia would trail behind her talking and gossiping after a good dinner. Tonight, no doubt, Reggie would sit in the chair which belonged to Amelia and sip the brandy which had been supplied by Amelia's personal vintner. The bottles, Lilla saw, were still cobwebbed from the cellar where they had lain beside the calvados for at least eighty years so that upon their opening library would be suddenly suffused with the smell of grapes and summer apples, and noses would wrinkle at the onslaught of the aged alcohol . . . Lilla pulled the curtains and felt very tired.

On her way to bed, she heard Reggie, drunk as always, chattering cheerfully with the rest of Amelia's family. The family were the usual inarticulate, over-educated bores Amelia hated. Amelia had never gone into the details of her past life. Occasionally, Amelia and Lilla would see pictures in the newspaper of the Witney-Hays on Reggie's side of the family or of Amelia's various nieces and nephews. Money insulated both families from any pressures of life. Divorce, death and birth were the only occasions to be formally celebrated. The results of such insulation were to be seen in the people gathering in the library. Even if the money is old, the rich can never be rich enough.

How unlike Amelia they are, Lilla thought, as she hurried her step to where Amelia lay so peacefully.

The room was bright in moonlight. Lilla kissed her friend on the forehead, still looking for comfort from her fears, and slipped a sprig of rosemary between the small Bible and the hands. Hastily, she turned, ran out of the room and across the hall to the safety of her bed. Finally, when she was too exhausted to worry any more, she slept and dreamed she was drowned, alone on the seabed, with hands stretched out for help.

The next day inevitably and inexorably dawned. Lilla was not there when the lid of the coffin was screwed down. The thought of the once expressive face suddenly darkened forever was more than she could bear. The guests in the house (whose house? she wondered. Hers? Reggie's?) wandered about like a gaggle of appraisers. Reggie, confident as if because of some secret certainty, carried a glass of champagne at all times.

After breakfast, he summoned Lilla to the study, Amelia's favorite room. Here the books hugged the walls. Here the carpets embraced the polished wooden floor. High above Lilla's head, naked, fat cupids flew around a woman who lay voluptuously pink and lovely, her eyes beaming, her breasts swelling, a bunch of white, bursting grapes in one hand. Reggie sat in the chair where Amelia had dictated her letters to Lilla. He appeared small and wizened. He had two glasses in front of him and filled them both. "Taittinger '21," he said. "Only champagne to drink in the morning." He gestured for Lilla to sit down. "Well, my dear. The party's over, don't you think?"

Lilla hesitated. "No doubt my life will change, if that's what you mean."

Reggie laughed. Lilla could hear the malice in the laugh. She realized now that she had been far more than just the last straw. Her clinging to Amelia had driven Reggie away. The other women came and went, but Lilla alone had arrived and stayed. "You know," Reggie began, "a man can cope with another man in his wife's life. An affair is an affair. But another woman . . ." He spoke tonelessly. "A fellow can't have that."

"But you didn't love her."

"And you did?"

Lilla was furious. "You were only there for the money."

Reggie looked at Lilla and laughed, shaking his head. "You always were a silly little thing," he said. His face hardened humorlessly. "Now you have nothing. Only what I choose to give you."

"There's a Will," Lilla protested. "I saw it. And Amelia left everything to me." Lilla's voice surprised her. It was harsh and grating.

"Oh yes. That little matter. Well, I'm afraid there is only your word for it." Reggie looked at the fireplace. Lilla followed his gaze. There, in the perfectly clean fireplace, lay the cold ashes of what was once Lilla's passport, her insurance against old age. Reggie stood up. "Let's drink a toast, my dear. To Amelia."

A coldness froze Lilla's soul. She knew she was defeated, with no hope. "It was never a war, Mr. Witney-Hay," she said with lowered voice. "You might find this hard to believe, but yes, in our own way, we did love each other. And now she's gone." The finality of her own words chilled her even more. She sniffed and raised her head bravely. "May I ask for—for one small favor?"

Reggie inclined his head. "Do ask."

"There is a little Sargent painting of Amelia in my room. I would like to have it."

"Oh, very well. He's that portrait fellow, all the rage these days. Have it." The sound of the cars pulling up in the front drive interrupted their conversation. "Come along, dear." Reggie shepherded Lilla out of the study. "You're in the last car."

Lilla smiled. She refused to give him the satisfaction of seeing her cry. The telephone rang as she walked through the front hall. "I'll get that," Lilla said, keeping her voice even, and she watched Reggie lead the family through the front doors.

Good, she thought, as she climbed into the last car beside the maid and the two gardeners. She did not want to be in a car with any of Amelia's beastly relatives. As far as Lilla was concerned, they could all go straight to hell, with Reggie leading the way.

The funeral was long and boring. The townspeople, in their best clothes, fidgeted and sweated in the June heat. These were not the people who used to visit the big house. They were dispassionate, dull and dreary. The children were clean and well-mannered. Where were the birds of paradise? Where were the gem-studded, bird-hatted women? Not there.

It was Julie Youngblood who had telephoned just before Lilla left the house. "I'll ring again this evening, when you have more time," she had said very firmly, upon hearing the situation. "I'm off to Paris with two girls. I think you need a break. You should meet us there."

"Thank you," Lilla said.

Standing by the open grave, watching the beloved

body sink into the pit, Lilla restrained herself from wild sobbing. She remembered the lines of poetry Amelia had loved to read:

> "When I am dead, my dearest,
> Sing no sad songs for me.
> Plant there no roses at my head . . ."

Lilla saw the two gardeners carrying six rose bushes from the back of the car to be planted around the grave once the hole had been filled. She gave a low moan and fell, senseless, to the ground.

⌘ *CHAPTER 30* ⌘

Esther was vaguely worried about Etta. When she telephoned home to tell her mother she had been offered a job by Ashley Hollander and Marty had suggested she spend the few months before her trip to Europe in their house, it was Etta who first answered the phone. She sounded very subdued. "Are you okay, Etta?"

"I'm all right," Etta said. "When are you coming home?"

"I'm not," Esther said. "I'm having such a marvelous time in Boston, what is there to come home for? Ashley asked me to do some clerking in his office, and Emily's uncle Eric is going to paint Boston red with both of us before we leave for Europe. Etta, I'm so happy I could die."

"Oh. So I won't see you this summer?"

"Certainly not! The idea of a hot Santa Fe summer with nothing to do except swing on the porch doesn't appeal at all."

"Okay, well . . ." Etta knew that Nora, desperate to hear from her clever daughter, would be hovering, listening. "Well, I must get off the phone and let mom talk." Etta forced a laugh and put down the phone. She left the house, suddenly anxious to breathe fresh air outside.

So far, letters were arriving for Etta almost daily. Work was going well in Chama, Tom reported. The cattle were selling steadily at market, and his uncle was letting him keep a commission on all the livestock that he helped to sell. He was saving the money so that in two months, at the most, he'd have enough to marry her and set up a home. No, he wrote, his parents still hadn't given an inch. Yes, he assured her, he still loved her and was true to her. Had she told her parents yet about the wedding and the baby?

July was a hot month. Etta helped her mother run the house and the garden. The ducks and chickens loved Etta. She had graceful, gentle hands which tended and lifted the plants with reverence. She liked to take the rose petals off their stems and steep them, red and pale ivory, in mineral water to make perfume, rose-scented and delightful, for presents at Chanukah for her family and friends. Soon she would pick the fresh English lavender to weave into bunches to lay between the thick white sheets, scenting the air of the guest bedroom. A bright patch of mint in flower, besieged by many-colored butterflies caught her attention. As she wandered across the lawn, she felt the kick of the baby in her womb. Next month it would be five months old. She counted again. Five months, and though her stomach remained mostly flat, she had had to move the button of her skirt twice. She had to tell someone. She couldn't keep the baby a secret much longer. She would have to tell her parents, but how?

The idea of telling Nora was unendurable. Her father, she knew, would be horrified at the idea of his daughter marrying outside of the faith. How she wished she could tell Esther, but somehow, as Esther was so pleased with her new life, Etta did not want to ruin her trip to Europe. Of course, Etta believed if she did tell her sister the news, Esther would immediately cancel her trip and come home. She could not do that to Esther.

Etta stood in the sun-filled garden and felt all alone in the world which spun around her at a seemingly frantic pace. In the house Nora was preparing the evening meal. Around Etta, the hens were scratching and clucking. They had their order. They knew their place. In the office, Dr Daniel Gottstein was listening to yet another tubercular chest. Reuben and his ranch-hands were living another day on the ranch. Naomi, Nora's sister, had gone to live with her husband Matthew Kearney and their children in Florida . . . Everyone settled, everyone permanent.

Maybe, Etta thought, she could tell her uncle Ben and let him break the news to her parents. Surely Ben would be sympathetic. But then he was the town drunk; he could be trusted to understand, but not to refrain from repeating in his cups the information to anyone who cared to listen. No, Etta really was alone.

Her mornings of nausea had passed. Still, she felt discomfort a lot of the time. Her once small nipples were a swelling reminder of the event which would inevitably make her the talk of Sante Fe and the downfall of her family's reputation.

With a sigh, Etta went back into the house. Nora was off the phone. "I'm a little tired, mother," she said. "I think I'll lie down."

Nora frowned. "Etta," she said, "lately you've been tired a lot. What is it?"

"It's nothing. Just the heat."

Nora gave Etta a look which let her know she was not believed. "Go lie down." Concern remained in her voice. "I'll get your father to give you a tonic when he gets home . . ." She wrinkled her brow. "You really don't look well. Are you sure there isn't something I should know about?"

"No, mom. It's just me. I'm disappointed, that's all. I wanted Esther to come home for the summer."

"*Oy,*" Nora laughed. "Your sister's found her wings. Now there's no catching her." Then she stopped her laughter, sensing she had been steered intentionally off-course. "Etta," she said, serious again. "Here. Sit down. You have that look on your face you had ever since you were a little girl, any time you were trying to keep a secret. Tell me. What is it?"

"I told you, it's nothing!" Etta said with irritation, plonking herself into a chair at the kitchen table.

Nora stared silently. "It's that boy," she said at last. "Isn't it? That Harding boy." Etta started to shake her head. "Now, listen to me. A mother knows her own daughter. Tell me the truth."

Etta exhaled loudly. Well, she reasoned, she had to tell her some time, and it never would be any easier than right now. She might as well get it over with.

"Yes," she said as calmly as she could. "He—he wants to marry me."

"*What?*" Nora's voice came out louder than she had wanted.

"Tom Harding has asked me to marry him."

"I heard what you said the first time. But you told him no, of course."

Etta felt every muscle tighten in her face. "No. As a matter of fact, I told him I'd love to marry him."

"You can't be serious." Nora struggled to restrain herself. "You know how your father feels about mixed marriages. You *can't* marry a *shegitz.*"

"I can and I *will*." Etta felt her own anger rising. She had never openly disobeyed her parents before, and she had always taken pains never to hurt either of them. But now she had no choice. "I'm nineteen years old, and you can't tell me how to live my life. It's all decided. Tom's in Chama, working for his uncle. He's saving up money to make a home for me."

"Oh, this is ridiculous!" Nora cried.

Danny Gottstein was just walking up the path to the kitchen door when he heard his wife's and daughter's voices raised. He entered the door, put his doctor's bag down on the counter, and kissed his wife on the top of her head. "What's the problem?" he asked.

"Danny! Thank God you're here." Nora steadied herself then spoke. "Etta tells me that Tom Harding has asked her to marry him. And she told him yes!"

"I see," said Danny, pulling up a chair at the table. He turned to his daughter. "Do you love him?"

"Yes," she said, relieved to think her father understood. "Very very much."

"Well," he said, his face expressionless. "That's a

shame. That'll only make it harder to get over him. But you can't marry him."

"But Daddy—" Etta wailed.

Danny shut his eyes, turned his head sideways, and raised his hands. Stop, his motion said. Etta stopped. He opened his eyes and leaned forward on the table. "Now, listen to me," he said measuredly. "You know I have never approved of Jews marrying gentiles. Your mother and I"—he turned toward his wife— "have talked about this many times. Mixed marriages break up a family. It's a fact. Now, your sister's gone off with that gentile girl to that gentile college, but don't get me wrong. We're both very proud of her." Etta rolled her eyes. "No, listen," he continued. "It's a good thing. I went away to Harvard, and it did me good. It's good to see the world and meet different people. But as for marriage? That's different. Take a look at your aunt Naomi. Now, for all that we've loved Big John and Matthew, I never thought the marriage was a good idea. What do a Jewish woman and an Irish man have in common? Nothing. And look. Now they've moved off to Florida, and your mother doesn't even know when she'll see her sister again—"

"You can't be serious," Etta interrupted. "I mean, you can't seriously tell me they've moved to Florida because Matthew isn't Jewish."

"Don't tell me what I think!" Danny retorted. "I'm telling you what I think." His voice was firm. "That's only one example of a mixed marriage breaking up a family. And there's been enough breaking up in the family already. Your grandmother Lilla left your grandfather Reuben—"

"But they were both Jewish," Etta pleaded.

"That's got nothing to do with it!" Danny spoke loudly.

"Listen to you!" Etta's voice rose to match her father's. "You're not even making sense now!"

"I'm a very sensible man," he maintained. "And if you'd listen to me, you'd see I'm telling you what I've always told you: a good Jew makes a good husband. And if you want a good husband and a good marriage which will last for as long as you live and keep your family together, you will marry yourself a good Jew like Joshua Finkelstein and forget all about Tom Harding. And that's that: period," he said, rapping the table with his knuckles. "Decided." He rapped again, punctuating his words. "Finished."

"No!" Etta said with bitter hoarseness as she stood up. "It's not finished! It's not that easy!"

"And why not? I've told you what to do."

"Because I'm pregnant, that's why not!" She sat back down, sobbing.

"Etta?" Nora was shocked. "Pregnant?" She put her hand across the table to touch her daughter's arm. "How can this be?"

Etta jerked her arm away. "How do you think?"

Danny felt a dagger had been plunged into his heart. "Don't talk to your mother that way!" he yelled and hit the table hard. Then he tried to calm himself down. "How do you know you're pregnant?" He reminded himself he was a doctor and tried to assume a professional composure. "I mean, how pregnant are you?"

"Nearly five months." Etta cried quietly.

"My God," said Danny, holding his head.

"Do Tom's parents know?" Nora asked.

"Not about the baby," Etta shook her head. "But

he told them we'd be getting married, and they told him they never wanted to see him again. That's why he's gone to Chama."

"When was this?" Danny questioned. "When did all this go on, and nobody even bothered to tell us?"

"We decided a month ago." Etta sniffed. "That's when he told them."

"A whole month ago?" Danny felt his anger rise quickly. "This has been going on, in my own house, for a whole month, and nobody mentions it until now? Why didn't you tell us earlier? Why didn't the Hardings come over and discuss it? They only live next door!"

"I knew you'd be upset!" Etta cried.

"Danny," Nora said, patting her husband's hand in an effort to calm him. "The Hardings are probably as upset as we are. And we've never really socialized with them—"

"Who's talking socialize?" Danny screamed. "I'm talking about their son raping our daughter then wanting to marry her!"

"He didn't rape me!" Etta cried, but both parents ignored her words.

"And they probably don't know what to do about it any more than we do," Nora continued.

"If they were Jews," he announced, with a decisive pound on the table, "they would have done the right thing! They would have come and talked to us!"

"I knew you wouldn't understand!" Etta shrieked, and she ran from the table up to her bedroom.

Danny sat beside his wife and held his head. "Danny," she said, with a misery in her voice he could not remember hearing before. "What are we going to do?"

His anger ebbed to sadness. He put his arms around her and hugged her tightly. "I wish I knew." He sat back. Both of them stared at the table.

"We've got to do something. I mean, she's nearly five months pregnant, and soon she'll have a baby." She raised her eyebrows. "Maybe they should hurry up and get marr—"

"Don't say it." Danny shook his head. "Please, Nora. Don't say it. We need some time to think about everything."

"But we don't have much time."

"I know," he said, holding up his hands in the "Stop" gesture once again. "I know. But we just have to take our time. Please. Give me a little time. Then we'll decide."

In the weeks that followed, a silence fell between the Gottsteins and their daughter which neither side dared break.

CHAPTER 31

Emily's uncle Eric was true to his word. Never had Esther had such a good time. All day she worked silently and efficiently in Ashley Hollander's office. She spent the money he lavishly gave her in the Newbury Street dress shops on the way back to Marty's mansion. Soon, she had the beginnings of an excellent wardrobe. Above all, her first and favorite purchases were a sea trunk with a matching suitcase and hatbox. Esther Gottstein was going to tour Europe in style. Passing off a slight feeling of guilt at abandoning her twin sister for the summer, Esther reasoned that she was now earning her own living and, after a hard year's work at Wellesley, she deserved some time just to herself.

Esther and Emily Atkinson had had long talks this last semester about free love. Emily stood against the feminists in the Vill who claimed they had as much right as their brothers to experience the heady raptures of sexual encounters. The acknowledged "fast" set at Wellesley were definitely the most popular girls at the proms. Esther stood back and watched.

No callow youth for her first experience, she decided. Furthermore, she convinced herself, the time for that first experience was at hand. Emily's endless mooning about marriage bored Esther—so did her own virginity. She had had nineteen years of virginity. Now she felt ready to try the alternative. She had read, in poetry and novels, the thrilling throes of sexual love, but the heroines of the poems and the characters of the novels all seemed to share a knowing complicity that firmly excluded Esther. If her life was to have any depth, she told herself, and if her own poems were someday to reveal any worldly sophistication, then she must experience the mystery of physical intimacy first hand and with it all the attendant emotional nuances of passion.

So far, Esther was unacquainted with any of these necessary muses, but Uncle Eric was there to see to all that. Esther had recently bought herself an incredibly sheer set of underwear and a red garter to wear under her now fashionably short skirt to remind herself that her maidenhood was there for the having by a man whose experience would make the night of several thousand memories last for the rest of her life. What Esther had not expected was that Jimmy Delgado—whom she had seen only from across the restaurant with his two brutal body-guards—would be precisely the man to rampage full-storm into her well-protected life in reality, not mere fantasy.

Uncle Eric knew everyone worth knowing in all continents of the world. He had known Julie Young-blood from childhood. Eric Atkinson lived in a well-appointed flat on Boston's fashionable Joy Street. He was a tall, ectomorphically attractive man. His hair was slicked to the side of his charming head. His nose was beakily aristocratic, underscored by a small, neat moustache, and his blue eyes were shaded by lazy eyelids which drooped suggestively. Hanging from a black, silk ribbon at his slender waist was a gold-rimmed monocle used to watch a pretty leg pass by. Eric found his niece Emily a dull pudding, but Esther was enchanting.

"Who's the broad I've seen you around town with?" Jimmy Delgado was impatient. "Not the blonde, the dark one."

Eric winced. "Jimmy, dear," he said, leaning back in his chair at the Paradiso Bar on Hanover Street in Boston's Italian North End. "That is not a 'broad'; that is my tender little charge. The blonde, as you so crudely put it, and as you already know, is my niece. The dark girl is her friend."

Jimmy grinned. Eric always cracked him up. When Eric first set foot in one of Jimmy's many bars, he thought of Eric as yet another rich, young fool come slumming. But after three games of poker in which

Jimmy soundly trounced Eric, the two men began a friendship that was to last a lifetime.

Black Lewis frowned at Chi. "Oh, brother," he said. "He's hot for the little cat." Chi's mouth twisted. They sat behind Eric and Jimmy. A huge mirror over the bar gave them a panoramic view of the large room filled with men and a few women. Most of the women were whores. A few of the New Age women sat together, chattering nervously. Black Lewis' hands butterflied around the handles of his two ostentatious pistols. Chi's lethal hands lay on his huge muscled thighs. He needed no weapons. His hands, trained to crush concrete, moved faster than an eye-glance. A sharp blow and the assailant slipped into oblivion. A good kick, and the enemy's face needed a transplant.

"She's not for you, Jimmy," Eric explained. "She's young and inexperienced."

Jimmy leaned forward. "Let me tell you something, Eric my friend. That girl is dying to give it away. If I don't take it, someone else will. And you know that as well as I do."

Eric sighed. A man of the world and something of a connoisseur of women himself, he knew Jimmy had a point. Though Emily did nothing but rattle on about husbands and marriage, Esther asked Eric questions. Questions about art exhibitions in Paris, about wine suitable for drinking. Champagne? "Taittinger in the morning," was Eric's reply. Poetry? "The imagists or, if possible, the vorticists." Jewelry? "Pearls when young. Rubies look best with age and experience on the face. Always a diamond. A flawless carat is better than three cheap carats. Never marry a man if he doesn't know his diamonds." Eric remembered Esther's laugh. "What happens if I don't want marriage, Eric?"

Eric looked now at Jimmy. "Well," he said, "you may be right. But if you upset her, my sister Marty will kill me. She's staying with Marty and her husband Ash for the summer."

"Good." Jimmy tossed back the last of his whiskey. "You'll introduce me." Eric nodded. "What's her name?"

"Esther. Esther Gottstein."

"Okay." Jimmy stood up. He felt alive and happy. Good virgins always excited him, and they were getting hard to find. "Okay," he said to his two bodyguards. "Let's go." Then he turned back to Eric. "What about Saturday night? My place?"

Eric raised his eyebrows. "So fast?" he said.

Jimmy laughed. "Speed's the thing. You know what I mean?"

Eric put his monocle to his eye and looked at his friend. "Well, she's got to start somewhere, I suppose. But leave Emily alone."

"Sure. You'll be there anyway. So long, guy. I've got to cruise my other joints." With a careless wave of his hand, he was gone, both bodyguards behind him.

"Nice work, Boss," Black Lewis remarked. Chi opened the door.

"She's young, true," Jimmy said philosophically. "But I guess a woman's heart was made to be broken."

"Yeah," Black Lewis laughed.

Chi kept smiling. He just wanted his boss to make it safely to the car. There were enough people in Boston who wanted Jimmy dead.

Esther and Emily were both thrilled at Jimmy's invitation. At six o'clock on Saturday evening, standing side by side in Emily's beautiful, blue marble bathroom, Emily raised her arms above her head and looked into the French rococo gold and white mirror. Before her lay her mahogany traveling case full of a symphony of crystal bottles with hooded silver tops, of perfumes and potions, eye-gloss, lip-gloss, a sunburst of eyeshadows. Like fillets of anchovies in exquisite order lay scissors, eyebrow tweezers, nailfiles, and a defunct button hook. "How exciting! Can you imagine dinner with Jimmy Delgado? Mother would die if she knew."

Esther smiled. She watched the practiced pout bloom in the mirror. "What my mom doesn't know won't hurt her. Marty doesn't seem to mind."

"I know." Emily leaned closer to the mirror. Her plump breasts swung in the loose petticoat prettily frogged in Venetian lace. Her breath covered the mirror in a fine mist.

Esther took her long, slender middle finger and gently rubbed a clear hole. Her eyes, black and impenetrable, stared back. I'll do it, Esther thought. This time, I won't just imagine doing it. For nights now, Esther had lain hot in her bed. Electric thrills had run up and down her body, her nipples had been tense and erect. She had a fever, a fever which would only be satisfied by the harsh arms of Jimmy Delgado, the fierce, urgent desire of him . . . Something in Eric's manner of invitation had suggested to Esther an implicit agreement, an understanding, a licence. A look of quiet amusement had lit Eric's eyes.

Esther ran the tip of her pink tongue around her lips which felt they would burst into flames if they were not promised a wetness of their own. "We'll have fun," she said and looked at Emily briefly in the mirror.

Emily smiled back at Esther's reflection. "Wow," she said. "You look sexy." Esther lowered her eyes and grinned. Emily shrieked and pushed Esther across the room. "You'll get raped!" she screamed.

Esther giggled and fell on the floor. "With any luck," she said. "I'm off to get dressed."

Saturday afternoon was hot in Santa Fe. As Etta stood in the kitchen garden and walked between the rows of plants, she was pleased to see the intense July sun's rays begin to throw pink light onto the ground, the trees and the side of her parents' house. With the rosing of the light came a slight cooling of the air and the first, refreshed breeze of approaching evening blew across Etta's face. She sighed.

The past weeks with her parents had been far from easy. No one showed any temper. The silence, however, that had fallen over the family remained strong. She spoke to her parents politely and civilly, but she stayed no longer than necessary in the same room with them. Meals were strained, as no one raised the subject of Etta's pregnancy or plans to marry. Her father had made it clear that he needed time to think, but time was running out. The baby inside her was in its six month and it would not be long before Tom was ready to send for her. His recent letters were encouraging. He was saving more money by the day. She had received no letter for the past five days but, she knew from the usually regular frequency of his correspondence, the next could not take long to follow.

Etta walked toward the house and felt her heart grow heavier. She did not feel up to facing another evening being uncomfortable in her parents' awkward company. With a dread of inevitability, she pushed open the kitchen door, ready to help her mother prepare the dinner. At least that would give them both something to do, if not to say. "Do you want me to make the salad?" she offered as she walked into the kitchen.

Both her parents sat at the table. "Thanks, sweetheart," Nora said. Her voice was relaxed. "But that can wait a minute. Here, come sit down first." She pulled back a chair.

Etta looked at her father. His face revealed no emotion. Warily, Etta sat down.

"Etta," Nora began. She smiled. "Your father has something he wants to say."

"That's all right," Danny said. "You can tell her for me."

"Oh, Danny. Don't be so silly. She needs to hear it from you."

Danny exhaled loudly. Etta held her breath. "Etta," he said. "You love this Tom Harding, don't you?"

"Yes." She felt her heart beat faster.

"And he loves you?"

"Yes."

"And you've been carrying his child for the last six months?"

"That's right."

"So," Danny raised his eyebrows. "What's to say? Marry him."

"Do you mean it?" Her voice was exuberant. "Really? You'll give us your consent?"

Danny shrugged and half nodded. "Yes." Nora laughed. "That's what he means." She reached across to her daughter and put her hand on top of Etta's arm. "Of course. We'll give our consent."

"Oh, mom, dad. Thank you. I'm so happy. I can't tell you how happy you've made me. I love Tom so much and now we can get married." She jumped from her seat, ran around the table to behind Danny's chair and hugged him from behind, kissing the top of his head. "And I love you both."

Danny blushed and felt himself loosen to laughter. "As long as you're happy." He laughed and lifted his hands to loosen his daughter's arms squeezing him enthusiastically around his neck. *"Mazel tov,"* he said.

"Then you'll give us your blessing, too?" Etta asked.

"I don't know what kind of blessing to give," Danny said. "Does he understand Hebrew?"

"Oh, Danny." Nora gave his elbow a playful slap. "Don't be terrible."

"What?" Danny laughed. "You want consent and a blessing both the same day? These things take time. You have the consent today and the blessing we can worry about later."

Etta laughed, released her father, walked to hug her mother, then sat down in her own chair. "Oh," she said, "I wish Tom's uncle had a phone up in Chama. I wish I could tell him right now."

"Well," Danny said, straightening his hair back down with his palm. "I tell you what. I'll give Mr and Mrs Harding a ring. Maybe I can straighten things out between them and their son. We're going to be in-laws, after all. Anyway, it's worth a shot. I'll let you know how it goes." He stood and walked down the hall to his study, shutting the door behind him.

Mother and daughter stayed in the kitchen and began to make the first wedding plans.

* * *

The drive from Commonwealth Avenue to Prince Street went as smoothly as a slide down a velvet hill. Eric drove an English Rolls-Royce—a grey Silver Phantom—through the dark streets of Boston. The chauffeur had been dismissed for the night. Esther sat beside Eric, and Emily chattered from the back seat. One day, Esther thought, I'll own a Rolls like this. She glanced up at Eric's serene face. They talked of this and that, the trip to London and to Paris. "Do see more than just the inside of the hotel," Eric commanded. "Don't let old Julie drag you round a series of salons. You can always hear all the gossip in Marty's house. Same gossip in Paris, Rome, or Florence. No. Get yourself a young man to take you to the *Folies Bergère* in Paris or the Café Royal in London. Chelsea's fun, and see if you can get in a couple of plays." Eric drove elegantly, unlike his sister Marty who swooped around the streets in a bright red sportscar. Esther realized, as she kept the conversation light and flowing, that she was nervous. Well, she reasoned, I don't *have* to do anything I don't want to do.

They pulled into a long drive. Black Lewis and Chi anticipated their arrival. They were to be the only guests. The door, large and black, was opened by the hall porter. Ahead of the guests stretched a long, gracious hall, leading to a staircase carved from red cherry wood. On the bottom of the steps stood Jimmy, his hands spread out in an ebullient welcome. "Ah, Eric and the young ladies!" he called. Esther thought the walk toward her host would take forever.

Emily reached Jimmy's hand first. Eric introduced his niece. "Emily Atkinson," he said.

Jimmy enveloped Emily in a warm brown Italian

smile. "How wonderful," he said. "I always wanted to know who that beautiful blonde was eating with her friend in my restaurant."

Emily blushed and giggled. "Mr Delgado," she said, "this is Esther Gottstein."

Eric put Esther's frightened white hand into Jimmy's big brown hand. Esther stared at the black hairs that lay on the hand's muscle. Both hands gripped hers. Was she dreaming, or did those hands give an intimate squeeze to hers, so willingly trapped? She looked into Jimmy's eyes. There was no doubt as to his intentions. His eyes were hot. They absorbed Esther in a preliminary embrace. Esther looked down at her shoes and saw suddenly a vision of both of them without clothes, merging, his legs bare against hers . . . She caught herself and smiled. "What a lovely house you have," she said.

"Tonight," Jimmy inclined his head, "my house is all yours." He bowed and spread an arm in the direction of the drawing room.

Black olives, glazed with rich, aromatic olive oil, lay in green Chinese rice bowls. Anchovies curled intimately on slivers of marinated fish. Red and pink slices of parma, and other, hams lay supported on neatly manicured biscuits beside sliced eggs, truffles, small artichokes. The table was a feast for an army, but then the room was a love affair with life. Jimmy spent much of his money and his time on this house. Illegal deeds and muffled gunshots through the years had bought Jimmy a great deal of respect in the community and a greater deal of money. Respect came from the Italians who had always done their business their own way. Money came from the others who had no choice.

Esther stood in the deep, wine-red carpet and gazed at the marble pillars which surrounded the room. Good artists had painted Italian gardens between the pillars, and the effect was to make Esther feel as she imagined she would feel standing in a garden in Rome, loud with bees. Emily, used to such magnificence, had her mouth full of food. Eric picked at the ham. Jimmy offered Esther a bowl of olives and he watched her sharp, white teeth sink slowly into the purple sun-stretched skin. "Umm." Esther smiled. "These are delicious." She took another olive from the bowl and put it to her lips. Jimmy smiled. Everything was going to be all right. He could tell.

Nora and Etta were sharing a relaxed laugh when they heard the study door open and Danny's footsteps walk up the hall. But when they saw the ashen grayness of his face as he stood in the doorway to the kitchen, their laughter quickly stopped. "Well?" Nora said, concerned by her husband's expression.

Without saying a word, Danny walked to his chair, sat and leaned forward on his elbows, his hands holding up his face. "I just spoke with Mr Harding."

"I didn't think you'd have much luck with him." Etta shook her head, still feeling happy. "Tom says he's never known his father to budge an inch."

"Etta," Danny said, but he stopped himself. "Etta, it's not that."

"What is it?" she asked. Her father looked so very serious. "What's the matter?"

"Etta, I don't know how to tell you this."

Etta felt her body slump into the chair. She lowered her head. "Oh, no. Tom's changed his mind. Maybe that's why he hasn't written yet this week."

"Etta." Danny shook his head. "That's not right." Etta looked up at him, a question in her eyes. "Oh, Etta. This isn't easy." How was he to tell her? He reminded himself, as was his habit, that he was a doctor. Speak to her, he told himself, honestly and professionally, as if she were a patient. "Etta," he said at last. "There was an accident. Up in Chama. Tom was killed."

"My God," said Nora.

Etta felt her stomach tighten. Her heart felt like it stopped. A knife-stab could not have been more painful. "When?" she said simply. "When did he—die?"

"Two days ago," Danny answered. "On Thursday. The funeral was this morning in Chama. That's where the Hardings are originally from. And Tom's been buried in the family plot. Mr and Mrs Harding just got back, just before I called."

"How did it happen?" Danny said. Nora put her arms silently around her daughter's shoulders.

"Etta." Danny shook his head. "The details aren't important. It doesn't really matter how he died. What matters is . . ."

"It matters to me." The tears pushing from within seemed so powerful that they threatened to overwhelm and destroy her. Etta kept herself calm by talking, asking questions, finding out. Her soul was in agony. "Tell me," she said. "Please. I have to know."

Danny spread his hands. "Well," he started. "It seems the ranch up there is a very big ranch. Lots of land, lots of different fields. Anyway, Tom went out by himself with the tractor and the plow to one of the farther fields. It seems he was supposed to plow it up to start getting it ready for planting the winter crops. Apparently, his uncle stayed behind, doing some work in the barn. Well, Tom was out there, ploughing up the field, miles away from the barn. And . . . Nobody's exactly sure what happened. But the best they can figure it, it looks like the plow got stuck on a rock or something. So Tom got down from the tractor to work it loose, but the machinery hadn't been switched off . . ." Danny cleared his throat. "His arm must have got stuck in the works. One of the blades"—he cleared his throat again—"severed his arm."

"My God," Nora said again.

"He was alone in the field, and there was no one around to help." Danny wrinkled his face, disciplining himself to maintain his professional composure. "Apparently, he bled to death. And when they found him a few hours later, it looked like he had started to walk back toward the barn." He stopped and looked up at his daughter. There was no color at all in her cheeks. "Now"—he wanted to comfort her—"I know that sounds terrible, but as a doctor, listen to me. There probably wasn't much pain involved. When the body's traumatized, it goes into shock and most of the pain isn't felt. It's nature's way of—"

"Don't," Etta insisted. "Please. Don't say another word." She fell silent. Never in her life had she felt such emotional pain. Her stomach knotted harder. That her happy dreams of a whole life together with Tom should be decimated so quickly and thoroughly left her aching to the deepest level. She felt she would die from the pain. Then she felt her pain transform itself to anger. "It's your fault," she suddenly exploded. "Both of you! It's your fault he died! We should have been married by now, and I would have been with him, and this never would have happened.

But we waited instead. Tom said we had to give you time to get used to the idea." She began to cry. "So I wasn't with him and he's dead." Her weeping became loud sobbing.

"Etta," Nora tried to comfort her. "That isn't true. You mustn't say that. It's not our fau—"

"And you're glad," she stared furiously at her father. "You're glad he's dead! You never wanted us to get married in the first place."

"Sweetheart," he pleaded. "I'm not glad at all. This is just terrible. I'm not glad at all."

"You wouldn't give us your blessing!" she accused.

"Oh, honey," Danny shook his head. "That was just a little joke. You knew that. I was just having a little fun with you, that's all."

Etta sobbed while both her parents hugged her and apologized and said "Shh," and "It will be all right." Then, suddenly and with astounding force, a sharp, physical pain burst into her emotional suffering. Her stomach felt as if it were being torn in two. This new pain hit so hard and so quickly that Etta felt wretchedly frightened. The pangs of her soul were pushed aside for the moment, overwhelmed by this intense, urgent excruciation. She blinked. She heard her mouth gasp. Something, she knew, was wrong. Horribly wrong.

The sharp twinge eased momentarily and Etta, terrified, caught her breath. She had to be alone. She had to deal with this alone. She had to get her parents out of the way, quickly, and get herself alone.

She sat up straight and pushed Nora and Danny off her. Calming herself she wiped her eyes. "Etta?" Nora asked.

"It's all right," she sniffed. "I'll be all right. I'm just

upset, that's all." She shook her head. "I'm sorry," she said, "about what I said. I know it's not your fault. Forgive me." She rubbed her cheek in agitation.

Danny sighed.

"Look," she said quickly. "I really think you should go and see Mr and Mrs Harding. I mean, I know they had thrown Tom out and everything, but he's still their son. They must be heartbroken. Why don't you go over and spend an hour or two with them?"

"Etta," Danny protested. "We can't leave you alone now."

"No," she held firm. "Please. I want to be alone. I really do. I just want to be by myself. I'll be all right." She felt her stomach tighten forcefully. She knew the pain was about to return. She ran from the room and up the stairs, and threw herself across her bed.

In the kitchen, Danny raised his hands and let them fall to his sides.

"Well," Nora answered his silent question, "I don't know what else we can say to her. There's nothing we can do to make it hurt any less. Maybe she's right. Maybe she needs to be alone to think for a while."

Danny shrugged miserably. "I'll get our coats."

"Here you are." Jimmy pulled a large chair out from the huge dining table. "Tonight, we are only four," he said. "We huddle at one end." Esther smiled. The dining room was plump and overstuffed and the gigantic table could accommodate an Italian village. "My mother's furniture," Jimmy explained, waving a hand at the ornate collection. "My mother's cooking," he said, "is the best Italian food in Boston. Every Sunday I go home to Mama's cooking."

Eric laughed. "That's why you won't get married,

isn't it, Jimmy? You can't find a wife to match your mother's cooking."

Jimmy held the chair for Esther and motioned to Eric and Emily to join them. "My mother's pizza," he continued, "is a dream." Silently, a procession of waiters walked across the floor to the table. "A little fettucini?" Jimmy murmured to Esther who sat on his right. "A little sauce."

A little this and a little that soon filled Esther's plate. Emily twirled spirals of spaghetti around her fork. Eric and Jimmy talked business in the city, and Esther watched Jimmy's mouth and hands expertly consume a large amount of pasta. In her hand she held a glass of excellent chianti. It was young and full of the taste of grapes plucked from the sunburnt soil.

Alone in her bed, Etta lay helplessly while the pain increased. She had changed into her nightgown. Already it was soaked through with sweat. She knew with a frightening certainty that something was wrong, and she knew it was to do with the baby. She remembered Tom's cow. One year, the cow had her calf too early. Etta was afraid that was happening now. I must go outside, she thought. I have to get some air.

She rose to her feet and pulled on her dressing gown. Supporting herself against the banister she walked down the steps, then staggered out of the house and across the garden, heading for the looming comfort of the barn. Once inside, she took off her dressing gown and lay down on the hay where she and Tom had made love six months ago. As she labored, she remembered the strength and gentleness of his arms. The same black cat sat on a rafter and watched the woman writhe in torment. The cat contemplated its own swollen belly. Etta was crying softly. Her cries of "Tom, Tom," became "Mom, Mom," as she lay and waited for the agony to end.

"Stay," Jimmy said to Esther, "for a little while longer, and we can get to know each other. I'm sure Eric won't mind." He raised his eyebrows in a question. Esther's head spun with the wine. She felt dizzy and happy and in no mood to protest.

"I don't mind," Eric said, while Jimmy helped him on with his coat in the front hall. "But my sister would be furious if—"

"Don't worry," Jimmy smiled, and he opened the big front door. "She'll be safely back home before the morning. Your sister Marty has nothing to worry about. Emily," he directed her out with his arm. "How lovely to have spent the evening with you. A great pleasure."

"Thank you," Emily said nervously. She stepped out the door, turned and gave a quick wave to Esther over Jimmy's shoulder. Emily smiled widely. Then, as an afterthought, she called out, "Do you have your keys with you?" Esther nodded and waved with her fingers.

"Good night then, Esther," Eric said with a wink. He walked through the door and Jimmy closed it securely.

Jimmy looked at Esther and laughed. He walked to her and took her into his arms, hugging her tightly. She put her hands around his waist and hugged him back. Well, she said to herself, here goes. Without a word, Jimmy stood back and raised his arm, pointing toward the stairs. Esther lowered her eyes, then raised them, a smile on her lips, just as she had rehearsed in the mirror. She turned and walked up the stairs ahead of Jimmy, his hand on her shoulder to steer her.

They arrived at his bedroom and Esther saw the biggest bed she had ever imagined. Spread over it was a furry wolf-skin. She paused at the door, then walked her well-practiced, Wellesley hip-swinging walk to the bed and sat down. "You," Jimmy said courteously, "may undress here. I will go into my dressing room and join you shortly." He went into a room at the side and shut the door.

Esther slipped off her shoes and removed her dress. She lay back against the soft fur. Suddenly she felt very young and very afraid.

Etta lay groaning but the end was near. The contractions were coming close after each other, and now she could feel the pressure to push, to push hard. She lay on her back and spread her legs. The baby slid into a silent world. The afterbirth behind its body lay attached to the swollen cord. Etta, empty, forced herself to sit up. She took the small body in her arms and washed it in a bucket of water beside her. She gazed at a lifeless baby girl. The eyes were closed but the long eyelashes unmistakably belonged to Tom. Tom, who was also gone from her forever.

The perfect little form lay motionless. Etta kissed the tiny flower-like hands. She sobbed as she sat all alone in the barn.

She took off her blood-stained nightdress, put on her dressing gown, and wrapped the baby together with the afterbirth in the nightdress. Against the wall leaned a shovel. Deep into the earth, under the hay, she dug a hole.

Nora and Danny walked in darkness toward their home. Through the dusty window of the barn, silhouetted by the light from inside, they could see their daughter's form. "No, wait," Nora said, stopping her husband. "You go inside. I'll talk to her. We'll be in soon." Danny kissed Nora on the forehead and entered his house.

"Etta?" Nora said, standing in the doorway of the barn. But no explanation was needed. One look at the hole and the small body lying on the bloody nightgown, and Nora understood all that had happened. She ran to her daughter and hugged her.

"Oh, mom," Etta cried into her mother's shoulder. "I want Tom to be alive so badly. But now he's never going to come back. And . . ." She wept. "Our baby . . ." She shook with the force of her sobbing. "I was so angry at daddy and you," she said. "I'm sorry. I know . . ."

"Shhh," Nora held her tight, crying herself. "It's our baby, too," she said. "She's our grandchild."

Together the two women lay the baby deep into the ground and covered it over with the earth. Then, side by side, they recited the *Kaddish*, the ancient prayer for the dead.

"I'll have your father give you something to help you sleep," Nora said as they walked together from the barn to the house. "Let me put you to bed."

"My dear," Jimmy said as he emerged from his dressing room, wearing only his boxer shorts. He lay down on the bed next to her and touched her cheek with his hand. "I see you are modest. How very touching. Please," he said, rising, "allow me to help."

Esther nervously remained lying down as Jimmy stood beside the bed. Passively, she lay and let Jimmy lift up her right leg. He slid his hand along her black silk stocking until his fingers reached the clasps. These he undid, and expertly rolled the stocking down her thigh, over her knee, and past her ankle. With a final, playful tug, he flipped the rolled stocking off, leaving her naked foot in his hand. Tenderly he kissed her foot in the soft middle of her rosy sole. Esther let out a small whimper, as excitement shot through her body.

Then, turning his attention to her left leg, Jimmy reached high up her smooth, white thigh for the clasps. He laughed when he saw the red garter, and Esther felt herself blush. "Charming," Jimmy said. "Absolutely charming." He slipped the garter down over her left leg and rolled the left stocking as he had done the right. This time, when he had finished, he planted a delicate kiss on the very tip of each pink toe. Esther giggled softly.

He lowered her feet to the ground, sat beside her and pulled her up gently. He kissed her first on the forehead, next on the cheek, and moved to her neck. While his mouth lightly touched her neck and his tongue stole the occasional, quick touch, he slipped the straps of her petticoat from her shoulders. Where the straps had touched the soft skin of each shoulder, he placed a lingering kiss. Esther relaxed and gave herself over to the thrill of each new kiss, each touch, each stirring sensation. Silently, she let herself be adored.

Quickly, Jimmy reached beneath her to find the

end of her petticoat. This he found, and with a friendly "whoopah!" he raised her arms and lifted the ivory silk slip over her head. Holding one arm still above her head, he lowered his mouth and kissed her wetly in the sweet hollow of her armpit. His hand behind her back, he unclasped her brassière, then, pausing to admire the soft red beauty of each nipple and the unblemished purity of each round breast, he lowered his mouth and kissed them deeply, long and lovingly.

Esther, though briefly embarrassed to have her breasts exposed for the first time ever to a man, was so quickly overwhelmed by the warmth of his mouth and the waves of heightened feeling it sent through her entire body that, when he reached beneath her and clutched the material of her sheer panties, she raised her knees gladly, making it easier for him to slide off both them and her garter belt, the last pieces of material to hide her body. Finally, she lay completely naked, and every nerve in her skin tingled as if she had never been naked before.

"Beautiful," Jimmy said with a throaty gasp, and quickly he removed his own shorts. He lay next to her on the wolf-skin and kissed her on the mouth—deep, urgent, thrilling kisses, and his hands moved their way over her smooth skin.

When at last he moved his body closer, pressing to come inside, Esther with a shock of fear, noticed that her lower lips, as if through their own will, would not allow him to enter. Jimmy, sensitive to the tightening he felt in her body, was gracious. "Shhhh . . ." he said. "This is not a problem. I will help you. Sealed, it might be. But let us make it sealed with a kiss." Taking his time, he moved his mouth down her neck, her breasts, her belly. He stopped for a moment and touched her round, generous navel with a playful kiss. Lowering his mouth, he arrived where she felt a fire beginning to burn. With each of his movements, his kisses, his lovings, she felt the fire grow warmer and more intense.

Esther wriggled, pleasured almost unbearably by every touch. She felt herself relax, moisten, respond. When she felt she was about to explode, Jimmy suddenly slid up beside her, entered her, and rocked, his hands on her hips. The pain of his entering was soon overtaken by the boundless pleasure. Passive no longer, she moved with him, rocking herself in time to his rhythm. Her body more alive than she had ever dreamed possible, she joined him as, together, they soared over the zenith of ecstasy.

"You, my dear," he said when he had found his breath, "are an exquisitely beautiful child." He gave her a last long kiss on the mouth then stood. "Come," he said. "It is time to part."

"I don't want to leave," she said honestly, now proud for him to look down on the fullness of her nudity.

"Ah," he said with a deep smile, "but your friend? And Marty? It's only proper," he said. She took his outstretched hand and sat up. "But be comforted," he reassured. "A beauty such as yours demands many more opportunities for appreciation."

"We'll be with each other again?" She smiled, happy to have found his approval.

"There is no question," he said. He walked to his dressing room and returned wearing his slippers and a robe. "I'll wait for you downstairs. Black Lewis will drive Queen Esther back to her palace." He left and closed the bedroom door behind him.

Esther dressed quickly and borrowed a brush for her hair in his bathroom. She felt like she was leaving paradise but a paradisical glow still filled her thoughts and her body. When she walked down the stairs, she saw three faces looking up at her: Jimmy's, Chi's, and Black Lewis'. She knew they *all* knew what she had been doing, but she felt proud. Now, she thought, I am a woman. She held her head high as she descended the stairs and when she reached the bottom steps, she saw Black Lewis open the front door. Confidently, womanly, triumphantly, she walked the long hall to the door, and she turned her face to Jimmy before she walked out. She smiled at him and kissed him lightly on the cheek. "Goodbye, my love," he said. She walked down the front steps in the warm night and heard the door close behind her.

"Sweet kid," Chi said to Jimmy.

"Ah, yes." Jimmy nodded. "Very, very sweet."

"You'll see her again?"

"My dear Chi," Jimmy laughed as he walked with his hired friend toward the bar. "You know how it is. A woman is like a bottle of champagne. Once she's been uncorked for the first time, she loses all her bubbles." He laughed, then—thinking himself immensely funny—laughed louder.

Danny sat in a chair at the foot of Etta's bed until her weeping stopped and the sedative took effect. When her breathing slowed and became even, he stood and kissed her on the top of her sleeping head.

Lying in his own bed beside his wife, Danny knew that he would find no sleep tonight. A deep guilt allowed him no rest. The accident, he knew, had not been his fault, but he could not forget the vehemence of Etta's words to him. He had to admit it *had* been his stubbornness that kept his daughter and her true love apart. Never, Danny swore, never again would he allow his religious beliefs to cause either of his daughters such pain.

Staring at the darkened ceiling, Danny lay awake and prayed for forgiveness. His daughter seemed to be close to forgiving him already. But, he wondered, would he ever forgive himself?

All the way back to the Hollander house, Esther sat quietly in Jimmy's Dusenberg. Black Lewis said nothing but when he held the car door open for her, he said a particularly gentle "good night." After all, he reasoned with himself on the way back, the poor girl didn't know Jimmy like he did.

Esther let herself in quietly to the Commonwealth Avenue mansion with the key Marty had given her. She tiptoed up the stairs, undressed in her room and climbed into bed. She fell asleep with an unaccustomed pain between her legs but a new and wonderful feeling of love filling her heart. She dreamed of her love, Jimmy Delgado. They were leaving for London together on a huge ship, and Emily was waving goodbye from the docks.

❧ CHAPTER 32 ❧

Esther waited for a call from Jimmy. She was supposed to be putting the finishing touches to her packing. By her bed in the Hollander household sat her shiny new steamer trunk. Esther could not concentrate. She was in love.

Eating with the Hollander family was a chore. Try as she might, her stomach clamped and knotted. Even the most expensive food—oysters, smoked salmon, or a light dish of quenelles—refused to go down. General conversation between Marty and Ash made her want to scream. The only time she was happy was when she pinned Emily down in some private part of the house and talked about her absolutely all-consuming passion: Jimmy Delgado. Emily was at first intrigued but then, as the days rolled past, she was bored.

Still Jimmy did not phone. Esther did not sleep, and if she did manage an hour or two, her dreams were of her lover. The phone by her bed lay mute and still. She telephoned Etta, but was unable to say anything because Nora always listened avidly. Anyway, Etta seemed completely removed from the trip to London. For Etta, the distance seemed too great to share with Esther the total depths of her despair. Instead, she simply informed Esther she had been engaged to Tom, he had died and she had lost his baby. But don't worry, Etta assured. She was all right and, though upset, she would get over it. Esther was sympathetic, but found herself unable to partake fully in her sister's pain. Too much was happening in her own life and the dramas unfolding in Santa Fe felt a million miles away. Esther offered what condolences she could long distance, then chattered endlessly: about school, about the Hollanders, about Boston, about anything. She talked just to relieve the internal pressure of the dialogue she continually rehearsed should Jimmy telephone.

Every morning she waited impatiently for the post to arrive. Eagerly she scanned the letters laid out on the hall table. Nothing for her. Every time the doorbell rang or a phone anywhere jangled, she jumped. An invisible electric wire fused her skeleton.

At the office, on the last day before she left for London, Esther gave up waiting and telephoned herself.

"This is the Delgado residence." Black Lewis smiled into the mouthpiece. "Can I help you?"

"Yes. This is Miss Esther Gottstein. I wish to speak to Mr Delgado."

This one held out longer than most, Black Lewis thought. "I'm afraid, Miss Gottstein, Mr Delgado has left his residence."

"Oh." Even to hear Jimmy's name on the lips of a man who knew him was exciting. "Do you know when he'll be back?"

"We expect Mr Delgado on Friday."

"Well, could you tell Mr Delgado that I will be leaving for London tomorrow? We will be staying at the Savoy for two weeks, then we leave for Paris. We'll be at the George V. Do you have a pencil?"

Black Lewis sighed. "Yes, I do. Please continue."

"Then I'll be in Rome for two weeks at the Hotel Fortune . . . Well, maybe he can write to me. I'll write to him."

"Okay." Black Lewis looked across the hall. Jimmy stood in the door of the dining room. "I'll pass your message on. I am sure Mr D wishes you a good trip."

"Thank you. Oh, thank you! And thank him for his good wishes."

Esther put the phone back on its cradle. She wrapped her arms around herself in a big hug. She so much wished that they were Jimmy's arms, but now that he knew where she would be, she felt comforted.

Black Lewis smiled a watermelon smile. Jimmy laughed. "Have a beer, Lewis," he said. "One less virgin in the world. How's Delilah cooking?"

"Very nicely, Boss. I like mine older than you do."

Jimmy opened a beer. The cold foam reached his lips. "A good pizza and a cold beer win over women any day," he remarked. "When I'm ready, I'll marry a good Italian virgin from back home. These American women are disgusting. Too aggressive, too independent."

Black Lewis nodded. "I'll get me a good black woman who can cook and holler. I'll have a whole posse of kids, all named after me, and a good daughter to do me proud."

Both men stood companionably by the big bar. "Tonight," Jimmy said, "we have to move the goods from the pier." Soon both men were buried in business plans to move their laundered money on to Chicago.

Leaving her family in Santa Fe so many months ago had been an excitement. Leaving Jimmy somewhere in America was the hardest thing Esther had ever done in her life. On impulse, just before the great liner left Boston Harbor, Esther dropped a postcard into the ship's postbox for her uncle Ben. She and her uncle, she thought, were both outcasts in their family. Grandfather Reuben would die if he knew his granddaughter was no longer a virgin. As for her mother, the event, if discovered, would be unimaginable. From her talks with Etta, she knew her parents had the hardest time coming to terms with all that Etta went through. For them to deal with Esther's love affair as well would be too much to ask. Esther secretly felt proud of herself and when she took elegant, expensive Jimmy Delgado back to Santa Fe, Nora need never know of the prenuptial night, and Reuben and her father Danny would all like Jimmy enormously, Esther was sure of it. Jimmy was so warm and friendly.

As the boat pulled from the Boston shoreline with a mini-flotilla of tugs pushing and shoving, Esther leaned on the thick wooden rail, her chin cupped in her hands looking out over the harbor to see if she could catch a last glimpse of Jimmy Delgado's house on Prince Street. Long after the other passengers had left the rails to dress for dinner, Esther stood, smiling a soft dreamy smile. "Hey, Miss." The English chief purser touched her on her shoulder. "You should be dressing for dinner. There's drinks in the captain's suite tonight. The gong goes at six." The chief purser looked into Esther's pretty little face. "Left someone behind?"

"Yes." Esther blushed. "I have."

"Well, forget him and enjoy the trip." The chief purser's job was to see that all the passengers had a good time. "Plenty of handsome young men on board this ship," he said. "Can't have a pretty little girl like you with a broken heart."

"Esther." Julie Youngblood was cross. "Where have you been? Emily is already out of the bath and dressed. We've been scouring the boat looking for you."

Esther frowned. "I'm so sorry," she said. "I forgot the time. I'll change now and meet you in the Captain's suite." Esther hurried off.

The purser looked at Julie. "That one's got it bad."

Julie nodded. "Happens to us all," she said. "She'll get over it."

"Did you find her?" Emily came up close behind Julie Youngblood.

"Yes. It's all right. She's gone off to change."

Emily, in a flimsy chiffon dress with her mother's black pearl necklace, laughed. Her blonde hair was touched pink by the rays of the sun setting over the ocean. "Oh dear—poor Esther. I hope she isn't going to mope all the way through the trip."

The purser consulted his watch. "I must get going," he said. "Very nice to meet you, ladies. My name's Brown. Anything you need, just ask me. My office is on this deck by the gangway." He shook hands with Julie and then with Emily and was gone.

"Do you think Esther will hear from Jimmy?" Emily linked arms with her mentor. Both girls felt they could talk to Julie, who was a mature and relaxed woman in her sixties. No longer did the diamond glint in her nose. The other diamonds were her secret.

She looked fondly at Emily and said, "Men are all too predictable. Oh, I know new theories about them will go in and out of fashion, but most men have never changed and never will: they rarely want a woman once they get what they think a woman owes them. I don't know if Jimmy will contact Esther. I hope for her sake he doesn't. When Jimmy marries, he will marry a young virgin from his village. That's how it's done in good Italian families. His mother would not tolerate anyone else for a daughter-in-law."

"You never married, did you, Julie?" Emily sauntered beside this exotic, coffee-colored woman. "Why not?"

"Well . . ." Julie paused. "I suppose in my early days I was against marriage, and I thought men chained you to the bed and the kitchen. But now, years later, I think I had such a remarkable father. He was an ambassador to Rome representing Abyssinia. I never found another man to replace him." She suddenly had a vision of Amelia and Lilla, the three of them in Amalfi. "I have known love," she said. "I really have." Lilla's stricken white face stood before her eyes. "We will be meeting a woman who played a large part in my early life when we reach Paris. We are attending a French soirée for poets and painters of the new wave."

Emily's eyes widened. "Esther will be thrilled. You know how much she wants to write."

Just then the gong sounded for drinks. "Come." Julie took Emily's hand. "Esther said she'd meet us there."

Esther had attended many functions in her life. Marty probably threw the most extravagant parties in Boston, but Esther was unprepared for the curious formality of the English guests and crew. Captain Phillips was exceedingly formidable. His cap and his coat were decorated with gold. A variety of impressive medals hung from his chest. "Good day, my dear," he said when he was introduced to Esther. "This is your first trip?" Esther nodded, too intimidated to reply. "I've put all the pretty ladies on my table. Can't spend the trip with lords and ladies. All too old anyway."

Julie grinned. "We'll keep you amused," she said.

Brown, the chief purser, rolled his eyes. "Can't imagine the rearrangements," he said. "I had to bump Lady Clarring and her two sisters to make room at his table."

Emily looked across the room. There, talking to an elderly woman the size of a midget and smothered in emeralds, stood a young man of medium height with brown eyes which stared back at the young—and very radiant—blonde, blue-eyed girl. Muttering excuses, he took a glass of champagne from a passing tray and made his way carefully through the crowd. "For you, mademoiselle," he said, putting the glass into Emily's astonished hand, and he smiled as he watched the telltale flush spread over her cheeks. "Is this your first trip to Europe?" Emily nodded. "Ah. May I present myself? My name is Gaston. Gaston St. Honoré. I am returning to Paris to my studies. And you are . . .?"

"Well, my name is Emily, Emily Atkinson. I'm a student at Wellesley College. I'm on my first trip to Europe. We're going to London, then to Paris, then to Rome." She was furiously aware that she was talking too fast. "This is Esther," she said, pointing to her friend, "and this is Julie Youngblood, our chaperon."

Julie looked at Gaston. "Very nice to know you," she said. They shook hands.

Esther and Emily immediately wished they could acquire European manners. All around them was a quiet, discreet hum of etiquette, disturbed only by a loud American couple by the door. To Esther's embarrassment, the couple were joined by a huge, fat man wearing a pair of spectacularly awful trousers topped by a revolting shirt screaming with palm trees. The three of them were loudly discussing the value of the dollar versus the pound. Esther decided to make it her business to develop an English accent. Emily decided she would make it her business to get to know Gaston. Julie decided she was hungry.

"Come along," Julie said. "Let's go to eat." She saw the shy look on Emily's face. "Perhaps you would like to have a drink after dinner?"

Gaston smiled. "Even better," he said in flawless, slightly accented English. "I checked. We—that is, my grandmother, the Baroness Haute-de-Ville and myself—are at the Captain's table with you."

"Oh good." Julie was pleased. Now Emily would be well occupied on this trip. All she had to do was find a romance for Esther.

✤ CHAPTER 33 ✤

But Esther wasn't to be distracted. True, their first class suite was delightful and she could stand on the deck in the morning watching the dolphins jump and leap in the air, and the flying fish soar over the bow of the ship. She could hear the gong sounding for lunch, heralding an untold delight of crayfish, swordfish, anchovies, and pink-as-dawn prawns. After lunch came a nap or shuffleboard, perhaps a swim with Emily, who now drenched the silence in a torrent of information, all of which centered on Gaston if he were absent, or to Gaston if he were present.

Gazing at her own, rapidly browning body while dressing for dinner, Esther felt Jimmy's absence like a physical pain. During dinner she made automatic chitchat with other guests and then escaped to the back of the great ship where she would watch as the sharks stalked in the rush of water. Big, oily, gray bodies waited for the moment the deck hands raised the sluices and the effluence of the day flooded the sea. Esther found a strange comfort in the direct fervency of the sharks as they fought for food. Somehow their primeval lives matched what she felt about Jimmy. Here, danger was not hidden. Here, living was primal, death immediate. Back in the dining room, danger crept, hidden behind façades. Clothes, manners, tradition . . . Esther preferred her violence naked. She appreciated danger in a man's world. She wanted to reach out and take the power, so carefully held by the men in her world, and cram it into her body. Esther felt she had spent nineteen years on a diving board waiting for the chance to dive into life. With Jimmy, she felt she had at last plunged deep into an ocean filled with dark and dangerous things. Now, on this trip, she was awash on a beach with other opportunities but none of them sufficiently dangerous to excite her. The boys and the men on the ship treated her with respect, but none of them interested her in the slightest.

Only the Baroness Haute-de-Ville, Gaston's grandmother, seemed to know some of how she felt. "Little one is in love," she said, putting a long bejeweled finger on Esther's breast. "The man is not *comme il faut.*" She smiled, revealing half a century of promiscuous affairs in her smile. "Call me *La Reine, ma chérie.* I have the experience."

When the ship docked in Liverpool, Esther was relieved. "Please God," she said in her now frequent prayers. "Please can there be a letter from Jimmy at the hotel?"

The train journey from Liverpool docks was a depressing journey. All of the north of England seemed crammed into small, shadowy houses, clinging grimly to the dark earth shrouded in soot. "Don't worry, child." Julie Youngblood was worried about both girls. Emily moaned incessantly about how much she missed Gaston already, despite the fact that she would see him and his grandmother in Paris. Both parties arranged to meet at the hotel.

Finally, the train pulled into Charing Cross Station and a limousine stood waiting to be loaded with their luggage. The car pulled away and Esther felt, for the first time, a glimmer of interest. "Look, Emily. Look at that." Prostitutes, their pimps and poodles, jostled the streets lined with barrels of food. Flower sellers sang loudly. Evening was falling and, on its heels, young men in black-tie with fashionable London ladies were arriving to decant themselves into the elegant restaurants and theatres just above Trafalgar Square.

"Now!" Emily said, putting aside for the moment her longing for Gaston. "I think we'll like London," she continued, as the limousine turned off the Square and up the Strand toward the Savoy.

When they pulled into the private entrance that protected the Savoy from ordinary intruders into the lives of the very rich, Esther sighed, happily embraced by the luxury. Across from the hotel door stood the Savoy Theater, the marquee of which advertised that evening's D'Oyly Carte production of *Trial by Jury*. They had tickets to see the show after dinner.

A doorman opened the door of the limousine. "Fred, dear," said Julie. "How nice to see you again."

Fred's friendly face had seen Julie regularly over the last forty years. He, a doorman and she, the daughter of an ambassador, had developed a mutual respect. "All right then, madam?" he said.

"Quite all right. This time." She smiled. "Still the same *maître d'* in the River Room?" Fred nodded proudly. "Ah, good. That is all right then. Girls, you'll have the best-served food in England."

Both girls were busy collecting their things. "There must be a letter," Esther whispered to herself as if the wish would give birth to a fact. Once upstairs in the drawing room of their suite, Esther saw an enormous bunch of flowers with a card. Her heart leaped, and she shook so hard Emily had to open the letter. "It's from Gaston," Emily said, her eyes alight with pleasure. "He sends you his love. So does *La Reine.*" Esther turned and walked into the white-tiled bathroom. She splashed her face with icy water from the taps to rouse herself from the disappointment.

After she regained control, she washed her face in the generous washbasin. Maybe there'll be something in Paris, she thought. Maybe he got delayed and didn't get home in time to get something off. Anyway, American men don't send flowers. It's a European habit . . . She stamped on the memory of her father's face beaming from behind one bouquet or another for his wife. "Boring," Esther said crossly and left the bathroom.

For dinner, in defiance of disappointment, she wore a long, beaded gown of mauve and purple sequins with a small cap which sat tightly on her cropped head and buttoned under the chin. Emily wore a dreamy cream silk dress, and Julie looked magnificently secure in a slender red voile. The three women, like glittering jewels, walked into the dining room. There the *maître d'* met Julie with open arms. "Ah, madame," he said. "We have your table ready."

Julie was pleased. In a capital city full of modern Englishmen, the *maître d'* was an old-fashioned, European gentleman. The great English middle-classes—unlike the workers of England whose quiet good-humor Julie much appreciated—often possessed a general boorish attitude, a smug arrogance, which made Julie angry. Too many dreadful dinner parties in too many freezing houses with insufficient bathrooms convinced Julie that many Englishmen were not only impervious to cold, but also addicted to inedible food and were dirty round the edges. Instead of the usual English disregard for cleanliness, Julie believed, one of the many joys of the Savoy were the huge tubs and the showers. And as for the rest of the British, Julie knew they could be pleasant, civil and charming, but they lacked that certain Continental flair, that titillating edge, that sophisticated appreciation of the perverse, which Julie so relished. Never mind, she thought, as she walked through the restaurant full of the English. Soon, we'll be in Paris.

The entry of the three women caused a stir, but the two girls had no eyes for men. Each felt suspended. Julie looked around and saw none of her cronies. They must all be in Paris, she thought. Her "set" seldom stayed long in London, for it lacked the European warmth and glamor, the very French or Italian way of waving an expressive finger, or drooping an eyelid. The English contingent was inclined to stride about in Oxford soles and baggy tweed skirts, and they rushed to discuss gardening instead of sex. Still, Julie was content this night to have dinner and share a bottle of Pouilly Fuissé with the girls.

Later that night, after the Gilbert and Sullivan, she saw both girls—now tired—to bed. Sitting by herself, she sipped a late-night glass of brandy and watched the great river, silver in the moonlight, slide by. In her hand she had a letter from Lilla. The letter awaited her arrival and was undated. The return address was the Hotel de Voulage, Paris. Lilla wrote to say she would meet Julie at Madame Rosenthal's salon. Julie wondered if Lilla would announce herself to her granddaughter. Knowing Lilla as she did, she doubted it. Lilla had not prospered or become the great artist she had hoped. Amelia's death closed the door on life for Lilla. Most of their friends were now settled and elderly. Julie had no financial problems to wear her out with worry. Her father had left her well-protected. But Lilla?

The rest of the fortnight in London flew by. The flag was flying at Buckingham Palace letting the world know the King and Queen were in residence. The House of Commons was a visit not to be forgotten. Lunch with a real lord in the House of Lords, tea at the Maid of Honor in Kew after a visit to the Gardens, Syon House and a British public house, were all kaleidoscoped into a whirl of memories.

The ferry from Dover and the train to Paris magically swept the three women to the George V. No letter from Jimmy Delgado, but Gaston and *La Reine* were at the hotel to welcome them.

La Reine kissed them all. Her little, bird-like eyes were alight with a secret. Gaston, serious, held Emily tenderly in his arms. "I have a question for you," he whispered in Emily's ear. Emily, her blue eyes drowned in a mist of emotion, clung to him.

La Reine, overhearing her grandson's whisper, smiled. "But not until after dinner," she said. "Come, Julie. We must discuss this matter privately between ourselves. Children, go out for a walk."

"All right, *grandmère*," Gaston laughed. "I'll let you talk women's business. We'll be back for supper."

"Exactly at six, *chéri*. I need my first sip of champagne at exactly six."

"I know, I know. We'll be there."

La Reine sighed. "Such a happy day," she said.

"Now, Gaston, you can begin." The five of them, pleasantly sated from dinner, were in the luxurious presidential suite at the hotel. *La Reine* had planned for this moment ever since she saw her beloved grandson fall immediately and eternally in love with Emily. A few discreet inquiries, much thumbing of family references on both sides of the Atlantic, a long conversation with Emily's mother, an "Oh, why the hell not?" from Emily's father, and permission was granted. "Here, Gaston, is your grandfather's diamond ring." Slowly *La Reine* slipped the huge family heirloom off her finger and put it into Gaston's waiting hand.

"*Merci, grandmère*," Gaston said. He stood up and bent down to kiss the old lady's brow. "Emily," he said nervously. "We have asked your mother and father, and they have agreed, if you wish, that you may be engaged to me and we can marry after I finish my medical studies and your college is complete. You have their permission." He put his hand out and took Emily from the table to the window which opened out onto all of Paris. "My dear," he said, "will you marry me?"

Emily could barely nod. She felt paralyzed with joy. "I would love to marry you," she whispered, finally.

Gaston pulled his fiancée into his arms and kissed her tenderly on the mouth. Then he took her left hand and pushed the magnificent diamond ring onto her finger. Behind them Julie and *La Reine* smiled at each other. "My daughter, bless her dear departed soul, would be so happy tonight," the old lady said.

As Esther sat looking at Emily, she felt utterly and totally alone.

☙ *CHAPTER 34* ❧

At the Hotel de Voulage, Lilla Braff dressed with great care on the night of Madame Rosenthal's salon. She knew she would be meeting her own grand-daughter for the first time. The loss of Amelia, and the bulk of Amelia's estate, had left her emaciated, strained, and in failing health. She coughed now al-most incessantly. Her chest wheezed with pain. Before leaving for the salon, she took several sips from the large bottle of morphine she kept by the bed in the room she had always shared with Amelia when they were in Paris. Now Amelia's bed lay empty.

Lilla took the locket from her neck. Slowly, she opened the little golden heart. Taking a pair of scissors from the drawer of her dressing table, she cut a small lock of her gray hair. Carefully she laid it in the locket beside the downy hair that had been hers as a baby. Very methodically, she slipped the locket into an addressed envelope, and on her way to the party, she posted the package.

Lilla first saw Julie in the throng which chattered like a flock of birds. Then she saw Esther. Her first thought was how alike they were. She saw the same, quiet determination in Esther's face, the same slim steel-like carriage of her body. Without even knowing the child, she could see the fluttering of wings determined to fly above the mundane landscape of the day.

Julie pushed past the hordes of welcoming friends and brought the two girls to stand beside Lilla. "This is an old, old friend of mine," Julie said, without further introduction.

Lilla took Esther's hand in hers. "How very lovely to meet you," she said.

Esther smiled at this gaunt, coughing woman. "Thank you so much," she said quietly. Emily also extended her hand.

Lilla looked at the ring on Emily's finger. "Engaged," she said, "so young?"

Emily blushed with pride. "I'm going to get married," she said.

"And you?" Lilla looked back at Esther.

"I'm not sure. I'm studying at Wellesley now, and

maybe I'll become a writer," she said, bitter with the gall of Jimmy's absence.

"Wellesley," she said. "That's very, very good. And a writer, you say?" Lilla shook her head. "That's a long, lonely road for a woman."

Esther looked startled. "How do you know?"

Lilla smiled sadly. "I've tried it, as an artist." She paused and quietly remembered the vision of her cherished medal burning in the furnace of Amelia's house. "But maybe you'll have more luck than I did." Lilla stood and stared at Esther. The stare stretched into a very long moment of silence. As Lilla stared, she found the urge to reveal her identity almost overpowering. No, she thought. I have broken my ties with my family. They must remain broken for now. Esther stared back, feeling strangely unsettled in the company of this woman. There was something familiar in the woman's eyes. Lilla restrained her feelings with great effort. Suddenly she felt weary and faint. "I must go," she said quickly. Holding out her hand to Esther, she said, "I'm very glad to have met you."

Esther returned the handshake politely. But inside herself she felt a deep impression had been left by the brief meeting with this unknown woman.

Julie took Lilla's arm and helped her to find a cab. "Goodbye," Lilla." Julie waved. "I'll see you for dinner before we leave Paris." Lilla, in a spasm of coughing, said nothing.

Quietly, like a wraith, Lilla slipped into the Hotel de Voulage and up to her room. Quietly and meticulously she sat on Amelia's bed and drank the rest of the bottle of morphine. Carefully she lay upon her friend's pillow and slipped into death with a smile on her lips. Meeting her granddaughter had made some part of Lilla complete. Now she could greet death calmly. Death was a friend, a way out of the unbearable pain of being without Amelia, of being alone.

News of Lilla's death swept the salons of Europe. The shock sent waves of horror into Paris and London. Several days later, they had reached Florence and then Rome. Rome, the heart of the dark sisterhood, whispered. Everywhere the delinquent and deviant met, they shook their heads. Poets, musicians, painters, all felt the fear which stalked and haunted those who were different, set apart: people whose feelings shivered like an exposed nerve, all those who feared death or dying. And death by suicide was felt to be even more horrible. Suicide, the edge, the abyss that, for all its horror, had a special magnetism to those with the souls of artists.

By now, Julie and the girls had moved on to their suite at the Hotel Fortune overlooking the ancient Forum in Rome. One afternoon, when the Italian late summer was burning its hottest and highest, the three women sat at their table, lunching at the hotel's rooftop restaurant. Beneath them stood the ruins of the Forum. Just up the road stood the austere and monstrous Colosseum, the many-eyed walls which, thousands of years before, had signified amusement to prominent Romans and death to the unlucky slaves. As Julie, Esther and Emily looked down on all this from their table, the stones of ancient Rome quavered in the white heat waves of the scorching day.

A waiter interrupted the women's quiet homage to the city. Leaning over, he whispered in Julie's ear that a telephone call waited for her at the *maître d*'s station. Julie excused herself from the table and walked into the roof entrance of the hotel.

A quarter of an hour passed and Esther and Emily waited for Julie to return. After another quarter of an hour, the girls decided there must be something wrong. Esther signed the bill for lunch and quickly they returned to their suite. There, on the bed, Esther and Emily found Julie crying. "I should have known. I should have known," Julie repeated ceaselessly.

"Should have known what?" asked Esther as she sat down and put her hand on Julie's trembling shoulder.

"That woman—the one you met in Paris. I should have known." Julie covered her face with her hands. At last she lifted her face. Her mocha skin was sickly gray. "She's dead," said Julie, staring wanly at Esther. "She killed herself."

Emily's eyes widened, aghast. "That nice lady? I thought she looked like Esther."

Esther felt a knot seize her stomach. "Who was she?" asked Esther without expression.

Julie stared for a moment then shook her head. "If she had wanted you to know, she would have told you herself."

"Who was she?" Esther repeated, her voice insistent.

Julie hesitated for a moment. "She was your grandmother, Lilla Braff."

Ever since her earliest memory, Esther had been given only obscure hints of her missing grandmother by her parents and grandfather. It had been implied that the shadowy figure had lost her senses and abandoned the family in shame. Then, as Esther grew older, she knew of Lilla's lifestyle as an artist. She had read the newspaper stories tracking the movements of her grandmother, but the newspapers had shown only unclear pictures. Never before had she seen the face. For all of Esther's life, her grandmother had remained a mystery, a haunting specter. Now, Esther had to know all there was to know. "Tell me about her, Julie," said Esther. "Please."

Slowly, as the tears dried on her cheeks, Julie recounted everything about Lilla's past that discretion would allow. She described Lilla's devotion to Amelia, leaving out only the extent of the intimacy between the two women. She told how she, too, had loved Lilla in her own way. She talked of Lilla's artwork, of her failed hopes to succeed as an artist. She talked of Lilla's past beauty, her vitality.

At last the women sat in silence. An emptiness possessed Esther, a desperate feeling of loss. She had come so close to knowing her grandmother, had stood before her and taken her hand. But the lost link had not been forged. All that Esther was doing now— her travels, the beauty of Rome—all seemed frivolous and vain. She longed to be back where the buildings were familiar. She wanted to feel loved by someone until the emptiness in her was filled. "Let's go home." Esther looked at Julie.

Julie looked at Emily. "Yes, let's go home."

Emily agreed. After all, Gaston was studying for exams.

Esther nodded. "I want to get back to Boston."

Julie sighed.

Plans were made to abort the remainder of the tour. As quickly as possible, the women traveled to the port of Marseilles. The same ship which bore them to Europe was ready to leave France in the next few days with them aboard. In the hold lay Lilla in a zinc-lined casket. Julie, in good conscience, could not allow the body to be interred in the foreign soil of Europe. Instead, as a final gesture of friendship, she made the arrangements for Lilla to lie in the only place in the world which seemed fitting: beside Amelia's body.

The ship docked in New York City. The passengers disembarked and Lilla's body was loaded aboard a train to Middletown, New Jersey. Julie and the two girls traveled with the body until it was laid to rest beside Amelia's grave. Autumn winds blew angry, gray clouds over the cemetery. It became apparent to the small funeral party that the residents of Middletown were not about to honor Lilla's burial with their presence. Amelia, to some degree, had been loved in Middletown. Lilla, however, was evidently still considered the town's disgrace. While the Middletonians all remained tucked safely in their warm houses on that stormy day, only Emily, a benumbed Esther, a weeping Julie and the two local gravediggers stood to say goodbye at the deep hole, dug to receive Lilla's resting body.

"Never did seem right to me," said one gravedigger to the other as the women drove away from the graveyard, leaving them to lower and bury the coffin. "Two women sleeping together. Damned perverts."

"No wonder nobody showed up," said the other, and both men went to their work determinedly, eager to return to the warmth of their homes.

After returning to New York by the next train, Julie Youngblood, a paler and more disheartened version of the woman who, only a few weeks before, had set sail from Boston with her two protégées, said her goodbyes to the young women. Emily and Esther had

to return to Boston to begin their second year at
Wellesley College, and Julie had the usual round of
social appointments to attend in New York City.
Each in their own way, the three women were anxious to get back to their own lives, to some form of
normality. Esther could not wait to get back to
Jimmy.

By the second week of September at the Hollanders'
house, Emily had stacked up a huge pile of letters and
enough love poems to fill a book. Esther's heart was
broken. Jimmy Delgado proved to be as elusive as the
businesses he ran. Phone calls to his residence were
met with a polite answer. "Mr. D. is out/away/in a
meeting/abroad." Visits to his restaurant proved fruit-
less. Politely, either Chi or Black Lewis turned her
away.

Finally, a week before Esther was due to return to
Wellesley, Chi took pity on the small, determined
figure. "Don't look for Mr. Delgado, missy. He don't
want nothing more to do with you."

Esther looked shocked. "But he—" She was too
embarrassed to continue.

"I know. I know. He only wants virgins." Chi was
sympathetic. "You go home and marry a nice man.
You're a good girl. Stay away from Jimmy. Do yourself a favor."

Esther felt an overwhelming tide of disgust roll over
her body. Everything she had ever done or experienced seemed worse than useless to her: Jimmy, Boston, Paris, Rome, even Wellesley. Thinking about
any part of it served only to hurt her more and more
deeply. She had to leave. She could not bear to spend
another moment in the same city, even the same

state, as Jimmy Delgado. She wanted to put the whole, wretched business far behind her.

On the way to the Hollanders' house she sat in the cab with her fist clenched. When she got there, she telephoned her mother. In a tense voice, white with rage, she told her mother she was packing to come home.

The packing, the goodbyes, and the journey to Santa Fe were a blur. Emily's sad face at Boston's South Station, the endless train trip out of New England, through the Midwest, her arrival at Lamy, New Mexico, and her father's warm embrace did not deter the iron rage Esther felt. Something precious to her, beautiful and generously given, had been fouled. In Esther's mind, no blame for the contamination rested with herself.

When she got home, her mother put a small package in her hand. "This was delivered while you were away," Nora said. "It's for you."

Esther opened the package. In her hand lay a small, gold, heart-shaped locket. Inside was her grandmother's hair and the soft hair of a baby. Esther looked up at her mother. "It's Lilla's," Esther said simply.

Nora stood beside her daughter and stared at the locket. She had seen it before. Barely within reach of distant memory, a picture stood in Nora's mind, a picture of her own young mother with the locket around her neck. With the memory, a very deep pain arose from many years ago, the pain of a small child abandoned by its mother. "What . . .?" Nora could hardly find words. "How do you—Yes. It's hers. My mother's. But how do you know?"

Esther held her mother's hand and explained how

she had met her, how she had died. She told Nora everything Julie had said.

"You mean," Nora asked incredulously when Esther had finished, "her artwork . . . I mean, after everything, after leaving us all . . . She failed?"

"Yes," said Esther sadly. "She failed as an artist."

Nora hung her head. "And she failed as my mother." She wiped her eyes and a peace settled over her. Her mother's abandonment had left a hole. She knew now that the hole would never be filled. But her own daughter had met her mother and, in an inexplicable way, the circle felt complete. The last note of the scale had been played. The hole inside her would hurt no more. "I'll say *Kaddish* for her tonight. That will lay her to rest. For good."

"No," Esther said. She felt an anger rise within her. "That isn't good enough. It doesn't matter that she failed. What counts is that she tried." She shook her head. "I don't know. Maybe the world wasn't ready for a woman with dreams. But that just isn't good enough."

At that moment, all of Esther's confusion, heartache, despair, loneliness, and disappointment crystallized into a rock-hard certainty: Esther knew she wanted revenge, revenge on the man who cheated her and revenge on the world of men—the world which, she believed, had reduced her grandmother to a coughing, weeping wreck of suicide. It was men's fault. Men made no room in their world for an artist like Lilla, and men—Jimmy, a man, *men*—had betrayed her.

Her own life felt a ruin. She had sampled the world and it had failed her. She hardly felt the will to take on the world again. She had been so hurt that she no longer felt the strength to fight for herself. Lilla had fought and Lilla had been beaten. The struggle to finish her degree, to become a writer herself, to take the world head-on, seemed beyond Esther's might. But she sensed a different power inside herself, the power to create another life as the instrument of her revenge. Someday, Esther decided, she would have a daughter. She, Esther, would wield a sword at the terrible world which had betrayed her and her daughter would be that sword. Her sword would fight, if not for the enemies who had killed her grandmother, then for the future of all women who wanted power. Someday her daughter, she vowed, would make the world change. Esther made her pact.

Slowly, Esther put the locket to her lips. "I promise," she whispered to herself "even if the pact is with the Devil himself."

BOOK THREE

Jenny
1931

⤳ CHAPTER 35 ⤳

Three years passed so slowly Esther thought she would die of boredom. Reuben, after hearing of Lilla's death, died a year after. He left the ranch to Etta, feeling this beloved granddaughter might never marry.

Since Tom's death and the loss of her baby, Etta had suffered a marked withdrawal from life. It was not that she turned from all things living; no, it was from her own life, her own future she withdrew. Once given totally to a man, as it had been given to Tom, her heart could never belong to any other man. Though a young woman in her early twenties, Etta lived already as a stately spinster. She took to running Reuben's ranch with great dedication. She tended the garden with special care and found a quiet sort of solace in the regular recreation of life among the growing plants. "I know how hard it's been for you," Esther tried to reassure her. "But someday the pain will fade. Someday you'll love another man, get married and have children, and be very happy."

Etta smiled, her baby's face close to her heart and never forgotten. "No," she said. It was a moth-filled summer's night at Reuben's ranch. He was buried on

his own property, under a huge cottonwood and beside a deep well. Horses cropped the grass, and Esther
sat on the swing which Reuben had made all those
years ago. Beside her, Etta lay on the lawn. "No,"
Etta repeated. "You're the one who will get married.
And when you have children, I'll be very happy to be
their maiden aunt."

"Me, get married? That'll be the day!" She
laughed.

Both girls had celebrated their twenty-first birthday
the year before and both had attended Emily Atkinson's wedding to Gaston. Etta had felt uncomfortable
in the antiquity of the Santa Fe Cathedral, but Esther
fell in love with the richness and the smell of incense,
the reds and the gold, the intricate details of the
vestments, the supplication and the obeisance of the
priest's back. All of it reminded her of the splendor
she had seen in the cathedrals of Europe. Watching
Emily stand so still, so pure, and so virginal beside
Gaston, so somber and handsome, Esther had felt a
renewed bitterness toward Jimmy Delgado. He
should have been the groom, and Esther should have
been the bride. When Gaston lifted his bride's veil to
kiss her deeply and with reverence on her mouth,
Esther winced.

"Do you remember how beautiful Emily looked
coming down the aisle?" Etta was in the mood to
reminisce. "I'll never forget the look she gave Gaston.
That's what real love is."

Esther said, "Huh. She'll soon find out what real
love is." She shrugged. "Being hurt. That's what
loving a man means. Being hurt by a man who
doesn't love you back. And why Emily threw her
bouquet to me, I'll never know. You should be the

one. Marriage and maternity would suit you. Not me."

Etta smiled. "You'll get married, Esther." Then she laughed a laugh which betrayed what remnants of girlishness she had left in her. "George Jensen's mad for you."

Esther snorted. "Georgey Porgey, pudding and pie, kissed the girls and made them cry. Not this girl though. Uncle Ben is right—"

"Have you seen Uncle Ben lately?" Etta interrupted. She was still very fond of her recalcitrant uncle.

"Yeah. I had lunch with him in Lamy last week, then we went over to the general store and saw George." She made a face. "I wish George'd lose weight. I hate being pressed to his fat stomach. He's not at all like the men I saw in Europe. They're so sophisticated. But George—he's just a loud-mouthed, bad-mannered Texan. And he sweats so."

Etta sat up and put her arms around her knees. "If you really loved him, Esther, you wouldn't care how he looked. Emily would have married Gaston whichever way . . . That's why I'll never marry. I can't imagine life without Tom, and any man I married, I'd always compare him."

Esther felt an irritation growing within her. All this talk of marriage seemed so calm, so mundane, so predictable. Night-time, with its warm, sensuous calls and smells, quickened her blood. The howl of a coyote in the distance reminded her of the more dangerous, more exciting, side of life. She had known it once, briefly, with Jimmy. Would she ever, she wondered, stop missing that promise of excitement Jimmy had held for her?

In her sister's silence, Etta could sense a change of mood. "Come, Esther." She stood up and ran her hands down her skirt, chasing away the grass and the burrs. "Let's fix some dinner."

"I'll be with you in a moment," Esther said. "You go ahead. I have some thinking to do."

Etta walked through the trees to the house and Esther began to swing. George Jensen was a problem. At one of the family enclaves in the early spring, the subject of George Jensen had come up after dinner. Esther had been seen, with her parents' permission, on innocent dates with George at local restaurants. Word was out in the small town of Santa Fe that George was smitten by the wealthy doctor's daughter. Danny Gottstein, always mindful of his vow never to let issues of religion hurt either of his daughters again, disciplined his mind to overlook the fact that George was not Jewish. After that springtime dinner, Danny remarked that the Great Depression had not harmed George's business any more than it had hindered doctoring. "A fine, handsome boy," Danny said to his daughter with a friendly twinkle. The whole family laughed and Esther blushed a deep red.

At the memory of the moment, Esther began to swing in earnest. A life robbed of sexual ecstasy had to find its fulfillment elsewhere. Unlike Etta, who put her entire wounded heart and soul into running the ranch, Esther had no interest in housewifery. Neither did she have any interest in the boringly hairy, smelly, radical feminists who haunted the cafés of Santa Fe.

As she swung backwards and forwards, she imagined the wind rushing by the stars, huge prisms of light encouraged by her flight. She handed herself over to a dark and dreamy fantasy, filling the nightsky with her unfulfilled longing for passion. She allowed her thoughts to turn to memories of her night with Jimmy as she flew in the swing, remembering and re-experiencing the thrilling sensations she had shared with him.

Then, slaked and sensuous, Esther slowly rejoined the earth. The swing stopped. Esther's feet dropped to the ground and she sat very still. Where was she? she wondered. Santa Fe, going nowhere. Her life was on hold. All her excitement lay in the past and she was doing nothing—*nothing*—to secure any excitement for herself in the future. No, she decided. She could not wait forever. She knew what she wanted: a daughter to change the world of men, a lifestyle that would give her excitement. Well then, she thought, if that's what I want, then I'll have to do something about it. And even if getting what she wanted meant taking some undesirable steps along the way, then she would have to be willing to pay that price.

"Esther!" Etta called from the house. "Dinner!"

Esther got down off the swing. She had made her decision. She walked toward the house.

"I'm going to marry George," she announced to a startled Etta. "I've decided." Later, after sharing her parents' and grandparents' pleasure, she lay alone in the New Mexican moonlight. She contemplated her new life. First, she thought, I'll take Catholic lessons. And second, I'll be very, very rich. Being married might be boring but in the end I'll get my own kind of fun. On that cheerful note she fell asleep.

George was thrilled his beloved Esther intended to be his bride. Within the week, Esther sported a huge diamond ring. Within the month, George transported her back to Texas to show off his bride to his father, a withered, dried-up old man. Esther took an instant dislike to him. "Done any storekeeping?" the old man questioned. "Don't look as if those hands ever lifted a bale of hay."

"I'm not marrying her so she can do any storekeeping, Daddy. I'm marrying Esther so she'll never lift a finger again. Not like Momma, dead from overwork before her time." George grinned at Esther. "She's my little jewel." He put a huge arm around her diminutive shoulders and squeezed her tight. "Come on, honey. We've got folk to see."

Esther grimaced. George's folk were all dirt-farmers with bonneted wives who cackled like hens over dreadful amounts of food, mostly beans. This was Texan chilli country and Esther felt if she had any more beans pushed down her throat, or saw another tortilla, she would faint. Even worse were the dreadful orange pumpkin pies. To her horror, she learned her husband-to-be made no attempt to control his wind, any more than the rest of his family, who all talked at the top of their voices in between horrendous rumblings and grumblings. To make matters worse, the men interrupted themselves regularly with huge brown streams of tobacco-stained saliva which splattered the floor.

George soon learned he was forbidden to spit or chew tobacco, on the grounds that Esther was unable to kiss him because the smell made her sick. George very much wanted to kiss his pretty bride, even if her kiss resembled only the peck of a small sparrow. But George knew, once married, there would be passion locked in those little white thighs. Then he could drink deep in her arms and lie with her head on his chest. All George had accumulated in the twenty-four years of his life, he lay at Esther's feet.

Esther awaited impatiently George's triumphant return to Santa Fe with her, she to arrange her wedding and George to buy her a house on the expensive north side of town. "I can only live on the north side," she said firmly. "I couldn't possibly live in Lamy. I can't abide the smell of the poor."

George understood. Emily and Gaston lived on the north side. *La Reine,* in her will, had left Gaston a huge fortune. Gaston discussed with George the French need to celebrate the gray, dry lives of the proletariat. Worried that his priceless Rubens and Vermeers might be slashed, and sensing the germ of war brewing—a war he was sure would decimate all of Europe—Gaston decided to make their home in Santa Fe. Despite the few politicos of the left who sat on the Plaza and plotted their dreary revolution, Gaston felt America and Americans were too independent a people ever to endure a totalitarian state. Men like George Jensen, a venture capitalist, were more the mold and the energy of this huge land. Gaston liked George, but with his fine Gallic understanding of women, he wished he could warn him Etta was a far better bet than Esther, both as a woman and as a wife. But Gaston also understood men and George, he knew, was in love. When a man gives his heart truly to a woman, he never quite takes it back. What George did not realize was that the exchange was one-sided. Esther's heart was with dangerous, dark-souled Jimmy Delgado, but now she had made her commitment to George, Gaston decided to keep silent. Love had come so happily and gladly into Gaston's life, he hoped that years of marriage and love would bring happiness to Esther.

For now, Emily and Gaston were content to let Esther move from Nora and Danny's house and live with them until the wedding. Nora and Esther were having a difficult time. "I'm getting married in the cathedral," Esther said, her face white and tense. Nora was appalled, but she held her tongue. She, too, would not risk harming her daughter for religious reasons. Shortly afterwards, Nora received another blow. "I'm having my reception at Emily's house," Esther informed her mother. This was more than Nora could bear.

"But no good daughter has her wedding catered by a company."

Esther stood defiantly. "Times have changed, mother," she said tensely. "I'm not little Esther Gottstein any more. I'm going to marry one of the richest men in New Mexico, and I want everything to be right. You and daddy don't live on the north side, and you don't live in style." She gave a short half-laugh. "Please, please, buy yourself a decent dress for the wedding. I don't want my family to look as if they just left the *shtetel* back in Russia."

Nora was too hurt even to reply. Later, when Esther packed her belongings and left, Nora cried in Danny's arms. "My girls have gone for good," she cried. "Etta has her own ranch, and Esther doesn't even want me to give her a wedding. I know they've come and gone before but this time it really is for good."

"There, there." Danny was solicitous. "The young things are headstrong these days," he said to his wife. "So many new ideas. Esther was always headstrong, and she tells me George is taking her on a ship to Africa for their honeymoon. All that way. It'll take six months." Danny hugged Nora. "Maybe she'll come back pregnant. Then you'll have a grandchild to fuss over."

Nora laughed through her drying tears. "Trust you, Danny," she said, "to think of sex."

Danny pulled Nora out of her chair. "Come on," he said. "Now the mice are gone, let the pussycats play." For Danny, his wife asleep at his side, the sound of silence in his house was heaven.

✑ CHAPTER 36 ✑

The wedding drifted by for Esther like a fragrant white cloud of fluffy cottonwool sprinkled with colored spangles. The reception floated away in the gush and bubbles of champagne bottles. Faces, family, and friends swam in and out of Esther's vision. So many hands to shake, so many faces with puckered mouths. Nora—stiffly, uncomfortably, and fashionably dressed—cried. The sun shone, fierce and hot. The New Mexican band bellowed music. The Spanish dancers clicked and sang wild songs of love and passion. Emily watched calmly, her belly just beginning to bulge with new life, a child for Gaston.

Esther was about to leave for their honeymoon. Changed from her pale cream silk and satin bridal dress into a neat maroon going-away outfit, she stood before her friend. "Goodbye, Emily," she said. "I'll be back in six months with tales of Africa—you'll be about due to have the baby then."

"I hope so." Emily smiled. "Have a wonderful time, darling."

Esther looked seriously at Emily. "Keep in touch with Julie, all right?"

Emily made a face. "Esther, you're married to George now."

Esther sighed. "I know," she said.

"Forever," Emily reminded her.

"I know . . . It should all have been very different."

Emily watched Esther's small, determined back recede and saw her face light up as she laughed, getting into George's big Dusenberg. She watched her lean out of the window and wave at the crowd as the car pulled away. A rain shower of rice splattered on the roof and the car rattled on the ground, bumbling, rumbling along as the newly married young couple left for a honeymoon the talk of Santa Fe.

The boat in the bay of San Francisco hooted loudly. George and Esther Jensen were busy unpacking in the stateroom. "Oh, look," Esther said, pointing at the car as it hung suspended high above the ship in the grip of the derricks.

Sex with George had not been as unpleasant as she had expected. She knew she had put up a sufficiently passionate act to fool George into thinking he was the best lover in the world. To tell the truth, she did not much enjoy touching his penis but maybe, with time, things would change. Quite why men needed sex so much was a mystery to Esther. George's idea that they spend most of the trip in bed was not Esther's plan. Esther loved to dance. George did not.

After the first few days, the ship's doctor danced

most evenings with Esther, while George sat at the bar and watched his pretty wife.

Most nights, flushed with exercise, Esther fell asleep halfway through their lovemaking. Or George, having swallowed too much whiskey, found himself impotent. But the sun and the sea, the Panama Canal, the change in scenery, the food were such diversions that nothing mattered. Two young people off to Africa without a care in the world. If Esther was perhaps a bit less responsive than he had hoped for, George consoled himself with his belief that she was a virgin, and all day long he followed her adoringly.

Mrs George Jensen was the talk of the boat. Mrs George Jensen's wardrobe was the talk of the laundry room: fresh silk camisoles, knickers. And her size four AAA shoes stood neatly outside the stateroom door next to George's huge, out-of-place Western boots. "So in love," the passengers sighed.

The ship's doctor knew better. He could feel the flutter of desire unslaked in Esther's featherweight body. He could tell that a secret lay behind the small, tight breasts—a golden locket glinting between them—which pushed so eagerly at his chest as they dipped and swayed. He also knew he would keep his hands to himself. This woman was trouble, and as ship's doctor he had plenty of opportunity to take advantage of the other graceful young women who called him to their cabins and stretched out their perfumed arms. This lady was not for him.

George and Esther finally reached the Gambia on a dark, stormy day. George, who had lived with the Texas lightning, lay beside Esther in the deck chairs which lined the promenade. The ship rode at anchor and was pulled by tugs to the docking area. Esther watched the smaller boats juggle their way to the ship. Little boys, naked and black, swarmed up the rigging. The crew dashed about trying to catch them. "Buckshee! Buckshee!" the boys yelled, holding out hands and dancing away from the crew with an insolent wiggle of their naked bottoms. George and Esther took tea then were ready to disembark.

Esther's eyes shone. This was a real adventure. All of Europe paled into gray insignificance. This was Africa. This was the smell—half of flowers, with a whiff of corruption. Huge black men with careless muscles pulled the trucks loaded with luggage into the Customs sheds. Fat ladies with baskets of vivid, voluptuous fruit wandered by, their wraps brightly colored, their heavy bodies moving effortlessly in and out of the crowds of people who surrounded the boat.

Later, much later, as George lay sleeping, Esther felt she had found a home. The sweet, sticky smell of the jungle which enveloped the hotel, the glottal croak of the frogs sitting like massive green puddles outside their room, the creaking of the crickets, lulled her to sleep. For the first time since her wedding, Esther felt excited.

The weeks slid by as George and Esther traveled from one government rest home to another. The English there amused Esther. The men wore huge white shorts and seemed in a permanent state of sunburn. But they did their jobs well. The food was, unfortunately, modeled on the kitchens of the middle class nurseries but the large, clean bedrooms with their chicks and white, welcoming mosquito nets pleased Esther. The humidity made George sweat even more than usual, but the hot days and the driving made him tire, so sex was neither nightly nor such a chore.

The days were brilliant with color and sound: a huge snake pulling its way across the road, a puma's cough at night, the shrill mad giggle of a hyena, all made Esther's blood race.

At last they found the hotel built in the trees—Treetops—in Kenya. The first night there at the end of the long trip, Esther stood beside George in the stars of the night when the African sky was ablaze as if all the heavenly lights joined hands and sang for joy. Esther saw a big, black puma walk slowly out of the jungle. The magnificent beast stood, its head raised in the moonlight. The huge bulk of his body rippled with bloated muscle. A silence fell among the chattering tourists. The warthogs pulled away from the watering hole. The gazelles shook their heads and went skitting and skatting into the jungle. The puma, aware of himself as the undisputed monarch of the jungle, moved down to the water. Just before he bent his noble head, he looked straight up at Esther. His great, golden eyes stared. The glistening yellow drew Esther's soul out of her body and she merged into the huge beast. "Jimmy," she whispered. "Jimmy."

Beside her, George was clicking his camera furiously. "Man oh man," George said. "He sure is a big one."

Esther smiled. "Yes, he is," she mumbled distractedly, forgetting for a moment that she was married to the large, perspiring person beside her.

That was to be her most treasured memory of Africa. Here in the jungle, thousands of miles away, she had found her Jimmy. I'll always think of him that way, she promised herself.

* * *

The six months honeymoon was over. Now the trunks were packed not only with her clothes but also with African face-masks, African bark paintings, and African memories. For Esther, these were her days of glory. Young, rich and beautiful, she and George had been entertained across the African continent: shooting, polo matches, dinner parties, tiger hunts. They had been made welcome by the settlers who loved visitors, even if the mention of New Mexico often brought a frown of misunderstanding. "No," Esther always explained with a laugh. "New Mexico is an American colony."

George, by the end, was ready to go home. He loved Africa but New Mexico was his home. He missed the desert. He missed the more gentle, less dramatic, sunsets of Santa Fe. He missed the moment at three o'clock in the afternoon when the sun turned the earth the palest, most delicate pastel pink and then the ground sank into its nightly sensual ecstasy as the pink intensified until the sky was streaked in deep, passionate reds and purples, finally exploding into the blackest of black nights, pin-pricked with diamond stars.

Esther never wanted to leave Africa. She wanted to live on the edge of tiger screams, of death in the roars of lions, of the pull and stretch of the great rivers, of the rattles and hisses of the nights, of the long furry legs of the spiders. Esther knew she would miss Africa. Africa was a woman deep in dark secrets. The drums telling all to the villages, the intense, consistent throb, the fiery heart of the she-bitch, the smell of the English gin, the crack of the ice, and the sexual intensity of Africa—she knew she would miss it all. From now on, real, boring married life would begin in earnest.

Well, she would make a promise to the great bitch goddess Africa: when she had a daughter, she would see her daughter would do better than simply become a wife.

As the boat pulled away bound for San Francisco, Esther leaned over the back of the ship and threw a handful of frangipani leaves into the water. "For my daughter," she said softly. "For my daughter."

❧ *CHAPTER 37* ❧

When the boat docked in San Francisco, George felt like kissing the American ground. Esther beheld the tranquil bay with distaste. She begged George to stay in San Francisco for at least a few days but, for once, George was adamant. "No, honey," he said. "I have to get back to the store." He could not communicate the fierce longing he felt for the Sangre de Cristo mountains or the need to see the Jemez, the mother mountain since the death of his own mother. His eyes often turned to her when he was hurt or upset. "It's different for a man, honey," he explained, miserable at Esther's white face being cross with him for declaring his own mind.

All the way back, past the Grand Canyon and through the Painted Desert, Esther sat silent. Never in the hotels did she allow George to touch her. George, she decided, was merely a management problem. Over the six months of their marriage, she recognized one controlling factor in their relationship: George could bear anything but to see her upset or for Esther to refuse his affection. Sex he could do without, though less than happily. A headache or a pain in her back and he was all solicitous. But the withdrawal of affection left him deeply, deeply insecure. Now she was practicing withdrawal.

By the time they reached Santa Fe, Esther decided to warm a little. She smiled gently and glanced up at George. "Tonight we'll be in our own home," she said, dropping her voice and lowering her eyelashes.

George felt a familiar sexual tug of hope. "That's right," he said. "All by ourselves."

"Let's stop and get a bottle of champagne for the bath."

George was elated. She had forgiven him. Staying angry any longer would outlive its original purpose: to teach George a lesson. George, Esther decided, had learned some humility indeed, and he would think twice about imposing his will over hers again. Besides, more immediate plans were at hand, like settling firmly and quickly into the upper echelon of Santa Fe society.

The house, designed by Esther and based on the big houses in Boston, cost George a fortune. Esther had left instructions with the builder to rip out the inside of a magnificent old adobe in Tesuque, a lush valley just to the north of Santa Fe, and to install rooms of palatial proportions and elegance. The master bedroom and bathroom were an extravaganza. The rest of the house was just as lavishly decorated. The windows were enlarged and the pool area was a delight. Esther's house was one of a kind, and she was ready to take her place as Queen of Santa Fe, with George as her consort.

* * *

After four months, Africa was a fabulous dream. Esther carefully placed the masks on the library wall. The painted heads with black empty eyes stared down at the group of women who flocked to Mandalay, as she had decided to name her mansion. The library was stocked with English classics and French poetry. Italian Renaissance paintings hung on the walls.

Ensconced in her new home, Esther began her deliberate measures to dominate the social world of Santa Fe. Within six months, she was chairman of the Santa Fe Choir, the Santa Fe Opera, the Public Library on Washington Avenue and the Photographic Society. She was a leading member of the Republican Party and all fund-raising events took place at her house. Her cook was Malayan and Esther's food became the talk of Santa Fe. Every Sunday, the cook prepared a reistaffel of between sixteen and twenty-five different curries from Malaya and Sumatra. On the table lay plates of plump prawns in a sauce so perfumed that, even if the Santa Feans had never left New Mexico, the dishes gave a hint of the hot, humid Far East. People fought to get to Esther's house.

She grew famous for her hospitality, and she was learning in a way that George never would. "All this politics," George would complain. "All they do is eat my food and talk politics. Hell, women shouldn't talk politics. Women should have babies."

The last remark never failed to hurt Esther deeply. Making love to George was a chore but inescapable if she wanted a daughter. So she grimly set about achieving her ambition. On special days of the month she doubled her efforts and a delighted George willingly complied.

Lamy, the small town fifteen miles east of Santa Fe and the home of George's business, grew over the early years of marriage, and George soon decided to sell out. Santa Fe, the Europe of America, was beginning to expand. George talked with Esther, and Esther said she would like him to buy real estate. A real estate owner, Esther felt, fitted her image. "Let Etta manage the office," she said. "She could do with a job."

Danny and Ruth Gottstein agreed wholeheartedly. Not only would it do Etta good to socialize (and maybe, God willing, meet a husband), but the Gottsteins—including Etta and Esther—had capital, all well-provided for by Reuben's will. A consortium was formed, and Esther enjoyed buying crumbling, old adobe structures and making them rise like a phoenix from their ashes. The consortium was called the Phoenix Company. George applied all his business acumen to it. Soon, it grew to deal with investments of all sorts. Esther was appointed a director and ever after refused to be called a housewife. "I am," she would say coldly to her many house guests, "a company director, not a mere housewife." Though she rarely, if ever, set foot in the office. Young women of her age at home were careful of Esther's sharp tongue.

Children were not encouraged to visit Mandalay. They might wipe their sticky fingers on the brocades or wet the carpets or even worse. Esther was convinced children should be seen and not heard, in the English fashion. As she grew older, she modeled herself more and more on her memories of England. She ordered her teasets from Harrods and gave English teas at four o'clock in the afternoon.

Her friendship with Emily St Honoré was not as strong now. Emily always arrived with babies clamped happily to her side. Slowly, as Esther's child-less years dragged on, Esther began to feel bitter.

Then it happened, after all the false starts, all the alarms and tearful disappointments. It was nearly eight years after their wedding—in the February of 1939, a month which clutched the country to her frozen bosom, when Esther was twenty-nine, when her favor-ite English poet, Auden, arrived in New York and the Hudson River had frozen over (according to the local *New Mexican* newspaper)—that Esther heard from her doctor she was finally and indisputably pregnant. She walked to her car in a daze. Carefully she sat in the driver's seat and then she went to the Phoenix Com-pany's head office. "George," she said, entering the spacious office, "I'm going to have a baby."

George lifted her up and swung her in his arms. "How wonderful!" he said. Then he realized he might hurt her and his child, so he settled her softly to the ground. "Gee! This calls for the biggest celebra-tion."

"No." Esther smiled. "It's unlucky to celebrate until after three months. I've got to be very careful." She lowered her eyes. "This means," she said, "no sex." She looked at George and saw the disappoint-ment obvious in his eyes. "The doctor says so," she added quickly.

"Oh." George felt something inside him wilt slightly but he scolded himself. How could he think so selfishly when he had his wife—and now a child—to think of first? He put on a smile. "Of course, honey. Anything you say. I'll take you out tonight. How about that?"

"That'll be lovely." Esther smiled. "I'll go home and lie down for a while." She had a huge list of women to telephone. Her barren years had not gone unremarked. Several catty women would now learn that not only was Esther Queen of Santa Fe, but she was also fertile. And Esther planned to spend the evening getting George to agree to a floor-length Russian sable.

As she dressed for dinner, she stood by the wall of mirrors which lined the bathroom. George was in his dressing room, loudly singing hillbilly songs. Behind her was a large, framed photograph which George had taken in Africa. She stood quietly, her white silk dress cut low to reveal the golden locket and just the right amount of cleavage. Her hair was in a neat bun behind her small, white ears. For a moment she felt the hot, yellow eyes from the picture rest on the nape of her unprotected neck. She heard the rasping breath of the puma all those years ago in Africa, and she thought of Jimmy between her thighs. She wished, oh how she wished, she was carrying his baby now.

From time to time the national news on her radio occasionally gave a few passing mentions to Jimmy Delgado and his empire. Even more occasionally, when Black Lewis and Chi had seen to some bit of business or other, a photograph appeared in a newspaper. Unbeknown to George, Esther kept the cuttings under their mattress. In moments of great boredom, she would take the cuttings out and pour over Jimmy's dark, Italian profile.

As much as George loved her, he bored her. He was a large puppy dog. Successful at business, popular in Santa Fe and with a beautiful wife, he was much admired. He knew everyone in town. Esther deplored the way he drank with the riff-raff, the Indian traders, the drunks and even her uncle Ben. She knew Ben was dying. The alcohol had got his liver. He grew thinner and thinner, and lay in the Plaza with a bottle in his hand. What she did not know was that the only image that man held in his now-rotted brain was a picture of Lilla, his mother. Esther did not know either that George, against her orders, saw to it Ben had all the money he needed. "If a man's got to go," George secretly instructed Etta, "at least he can go fast and happy. See that he gets what he wants." George was a man of compassion. He was known to have a soft heart. Whatever hurt Ben was so deep George felt he could not interfere. The Temperance Society which harried the men in the town was nothing more than a bunch of interfering manless women. If a man had a wife like Esther, George was sure, he'd be glad to rush home after work. Etta kept silent and Ben knew he could always take refuge at the ranch. But the pain kept him crazy, and the whiskey kept him quiet. So he rambled and ambled about Santa Fe, much to Esther's embarrassment.

The next seven months, Esther knew, were to be filled with appointments, and she wasted no time in beginning the preparations for the birth of what she was certain would be a daughter. A private nursing home was chosen, and baby clothes from Italy. Julie Youngblood, old now but a link to Jimmy, was asked to act as godmother. The Governor's wife, Marquita, was to be the second godmother and Senator Roberto de Chavez was the godfather. Senator de Chavez was the most influential politician in New Mexico. He represented the state in Washington, DC, the nation's capital.

Julie said she was too old to attend the christening. The flights on the clippers were long and arduous. She was in retirement in a palazzo in Venice. She sent a pile of exquisite lace dresses for she never doubted that, with a will like Esther's, the child would be a girl. The Daniel Neils store in London forwarded a Silver Cross pram and English flannel nightdresses. And Nanny, good, gray-coated, pudding-hatted, sensible-shoed Nanny, arrived in August, a little bewildered by all this modern travel.

Nanny was unaware the Victorian era had come to an end. For her and her charges, life was, and would remain, fixed like the English cream tea. However vulgar she felt Mandalay to be, she had no complaints about her accommodation. Her mistress was now seven months pregnant but still bustling around, organizing her committees. Nanny took over the nursery wing with pleasure. The nursery wing at Mandalay, with its softly carpeted, large white rooms and its cheerfully covered chairs, was a dream. Once informed that she was not quite alone in Santa Fe, and that two other English nannies would visit with their charges, Nanny settled in.

Maria, Esther's personal maid, thought it was all crazy. *"Loco,"* she complained to the cook.

Ah Ling grinned. There were many Malaysians and Chinese on the West Coast. The Tong fraternity had moved into San Francisco. They operated their opium dens and ran restaurants. Many other Orientals had remained in the Western states after the great railroads were built. Ah Ling was young and ambitious, and had no intention of spending the rest of his life cooking for Esther. He hated Esther. He thought of her as the stupid white bitch who swept through the kitchen every morning, issuing orders, carrying lists of the various dishes she expected him to prepare for her large crowd of other spoiled women. Ah Ling grieved for his wife and children still in Kuala Lumpur. He wrote when he could but Esther left him little time. Ah Ling learned over the years to hide his hatred. What was a thirty-year old woman doing giving orders to a man of twenty-five? These white women had no caste. In Malaya, no woman would dare give a man orders, nor would they be seen on the streets with bare legs and bare arms. The brothers of the family would see to that.

Esther was oblivious to Ah Ling's feelings. She was in the last stages of pregnancy and felt like a very cumbersome cow, only she had no intention of spoiling her breasts with milk for the baby. The bottles, sterilizer and milk powder all waited in the nursery. Nanny's bed was installed by the cot especially carved by George, who could whittle anything out of wood. George's father had died quietly when Esther was five months pregnant and had had an excuse not to attend the funeral. George had attended alone. "If it's a boy, I'll teach him to whittle just like you taught me," he had promised the old man as the coffin had sunk into the ground and the green trees had celebrated summer.

Jennifer Jensen entered the world in September 1939. Santa Fe was still green. The summer had been hot and dry. But now the days were less airless. The aspens up on the Sangre de Cristo mountains would soon turn from silver to gold. The town relaxed in the sure promise of cooler days to come, but for Esther the birth of her baby was not an easy event. The child was large and Esther labored and labored in her bed in the small nursing home. Finally, after two days, her doctor consulted Danny, who agreed his daughter must have a Caesarean section. Her pelvis was too small.

The baby was delivered at six o'clock that night. George heard her thin scream of protest as he paced the hall for the third day. "Is my wife all right?" he anxiously asked the nurse who left the delivery room with the baby in her arms.

"Yes. She's fine. She'll be out for a day or two. She had a bad time but here you are." She put the baby into George's arms. "It's a girl, and a beauty at that."

Jennifer had inherited George's white skin and her mother's black hair, mixed with a remarkable amount of auburn. She was not at all wrinkled, but seemed to be perfectly formed. Her long eyelashes rested on her cheeks and she searched her father's face with her newborn, blurred eyes. It was as if some exquisite flower had been plucked from Esther's womb and handed to George. He could barely breathe. How could anyone so big and clumsy have created such a delicate little thing? he wondered. At that moment, George fell in love with his daughter for life. "Anything you want you can have," he whispered, and Jennifer wriggled with delight before letting out a yell of hunger.

It took Esther two days to recover from the chloroform. It would take many years and plastic surgery to get over the scar on her stomach. Her breasts were sore from the bandages which bound them tightly so that the milk would not engorge and scar them. Her stomach, too, was sore and her mood terrible when she woke from her drugged sleep.

She pressed a button beside her bed and heard the bell ring in the nursing home's hallway. Half a minute later, a neatly uniformed nurse appeared in the door. "Bring me my baby," she said, still irritable from the drowsy effects of the chloroform. The nurse returned with the child in her arms and lay the blanketed bundle across Esther's chest. "Thank you," said Esther simply. "You can go now."

Alone in the room with her baby, she opened the blanket. "You *are* a girl," she said to Jennifer. "I knew you would be." She stared at the new life in her arms and remembered her vow. This would be the child to do what she could not do. This would be the child to take a stand in the world of men. This child would use men as men had used Esther. This child would move among men but not need them. This child, Esther smiled, would have power over men. This was Esther's daughter, her second chance, the repository of her dreams.

For many moments, Esther gazed at the small sleeping form. She adjusted its position in her arms. She held it with its head in the crook of her elbow. No, that wasn't comfortable. She moved it again, sitting it up away from her own body, holding the head in her hand. No, that didn't seem quite right. She turned it around again so the face lay against her bandaged left breast. She could feel her heart beat against the head and wondered if the baby could hear the rhythmic thumps.

Esther felt as if she were holding a doll. A memory arose of a young Esther—very young, before she had learned even to read—holding a borrowed baby-doll of Etta's in her arms. As a child, Esther had never had much time for dolls but now, she thought, she might grow to enjoy this one.

Just then, Esther's doll (her daughter, she reminded herself) decided, in its half-sleep, it was hungry. Perhaps it was the smell of the milk through the bandages which stirred the baby's senses. Instinctively, the child turned its head and rooted around, trying to attach its toothless gums to Esther's nightdress. Esther found herself strangely surprised and almost frightened. The baby, she noticed, had a life and a will of its own. It wanted milk from her, whatever her own plans might be. "No," Esther said, with a light laugh at first. "You have a bottle for that."

Jennifer evidently did not listen. Determined to be fed at once, she waved her hands and arms. One arm hit Esther directly against a sore nipple. "Oh," Esther gasped. With her hand she clutched both the baby's arms. "No," she repeated, more firmly. There was no reasoning with the infant. Still intent to have its feed, it wriggled and kicked its legs within the wrapped blanket. Though the newborn was no larger than a doll, its movements were strong enough to give Esther genuine pain when the kicking struck her freshly stitched abdomen. "Ouch!" she cried. "Stop that! Don't do that! I told you to stop!" Irritably she took the swaddling blanket and pulled it tighter to make the wriggling stop.

The baby began to cry. Esther squeezed it tightly in one arm and reached for the call-button with the other. "Here," Esther said, holding Jennifer out at arm's length when the nurse arrived. "I think she needs to be fed or something."

The nurse knew that not all mothers bonded immediately with their babies. "It will take time before you get to know each other," the nurse said and quickly left the room with the child.

Disgruntled, Esther turned into her pillow and waited to slip back into the last traces of her chloroform sleep.

Every afternoon, the nurses brought Jennifer to her. Part of her was still thrilled to have a daughter, but another part of her was deeply frightened. Not all aspects of the child appealed to her fastidious nature. Sometimes, when the baby had settled, Esther's nostrils would be struck by sudden distasteful odors. She would quickly hand the baby over to a nurse with the words, "Take care of this, please." Overall, Esther found herself noticing how very visceral the small creature was. At times it appeared to be a single collection of bodily functions. "Still," Esther would whisper in the moments when Jennifer lay silent in her arms, "you're my daughter. And we have a long life ahead of us. Together." The thought reassured Esther, but it also brought with it a fear: How would she manage when she got home? Nanny would be there. That's right. She could hand the baby to Nanny whenever it became too demanding.

❧ CHAPTER 38 ❧

Within fourteen days, mother and baby returned to Mandalay. George, during the rare moments he was home, hung over his daughter's cot, a look of wonder shining in his eyes. The birth had been a great strain on Esther's body, and it took many months for her to recover. For weeks on end she lay in bed, bored.

George's work at the office of the Phoenix Company kept him busy every weekday. He volunteered his hours away from the office in aid of the war effort.

News of the war reached Esther's ears but had little effect. The fate of European Jews was still a mystery to America, and Esther no longer felt herself to be Jewish. Her main concern was for the fate of the European cities she had visited what felt a very long time ago. Some day, she hoped, she would visit London again, and Paris, and Rome. Her daughter too, upon coming of age, would visit the great capitals of culture, or what would be left of them. To Esther, Europe felt light-years away. What was real to her was monotony, day after day of bedridden boredom.

Her only relief came from her talks with Jennifer (a good name for a woman of substance, Esther had decided). She sat in her bed and talked to the infant in the baby-cot. The cot, Esther had soon realized, was the best solution. Jennifer could lie there and her gurglings and wrigglings would not disturb her mother.

Every morning Nanny brought Jennifer to Esther's bedroom and put her in the white lace cot at the side of Esther's bed. For hours, Esther lay back against her pillows and talked, assuming that Jennifer was listening. She talked of Wellesley, Boston, her travels in Europe. Whenever she reached the part of her history about Jimmy, she paused. "Yes," Esther said, as if the baby had asked a question. "Yes, there was a man." She would give a small laugh. "I loved him. I thought he loved me. But you know how men are, at least the ones you can love. Exciting men just don't . . . I don't know. They just don't love you back. That's why I married your father." Her talking would then take a different turn. "Oh, but the plans I have for you, my little girl!" And an intensity would burn in Esther's eyes. "The plans I have. You know your godfather is a senator. And one of your godmothers is the Governor's wife. Maybe you'll be a Governor someday. What do you think of that? Jennifer Jensen, the first lady Governor of New Mexico. Wouldn't that be something?"

Months of such talk, instead of lullabies, floated over the baby's cot. Jennifer was more interested in sleeping. When she was not sleeping, she was demanding. If the baby cried or needed changing or feeding, Nanny heeded the electric bell and came running. "Poor little thing," Nanny said, cuddling Jennifer to her soft breasts. Privately, Nanny was disgusted by Esther's behavior. How could a mother not hug a baby? How could she resist the warmth of a baby's smell? But Nanny wasn't paid to have opinions, so she kept them to herself.

Over the weeks and months some days were punctuated by the arrival of guests arriving to admire the baby and to lavish clothes, silver feeding spoons and forks, baby dishes, rattles and soft toys. Emily and Gaston were thrilled for Esther and Esther felt a certain fondness for Emily in return. Gaston was now the director of the Santa Fe Museum of Art. Devastated by the thought of France being overrun by a madman from Germany, he put his priceless paintings from Europe at the disposal of the people of Santa Fe, so that not all the treasures of Europe should be lost to the public forever. Emily now had five children, all of them boys, and she envied Esther her daughter. "Boys go," she said once when she paid a visit. "A daughter stays for life."

"I know," Esther said proudly.

The new year passed, bringing with it a new decade, and Esther only ever discussed news of the war with Emily for, to both women, Europe remained a treasured place, a sanctified time in their lives. Both Esther and Emily were worried about Julie. How was she faring amid the fires burning across Europe? The January snow lay on the ground and a thin high voice from London promised victory down the radio.

Jennifer grew to be four months old, a happy baby. Though she slept passively in her cot while her mother talked, she loved being thrown into the air, tickled and teased by her big, energetic father. Nanny, however, was the true light of her life. Jennifer sat enthusiastically upright and dribbled on the nursery floor. She loved Maria and Ah Ling who, to his own astonishment, took the little white girl into his lonely Malayan heart. For her, he cooked tiny delicacies and when he served Nanny her food, he popped homemade sweets into Jennifer's mouth when Nanny wasn't looking.

By the time Jennifer was five months old, Esther deemed herself recuperated from the birth and she began to resume her active involvement in Santa Fe's social world. She swept through the town's stores with Nanny pushing Jennifer in the pram behind her. In one shop then the next, she bought clothes for Jenny, dresses and coats, and more toys than the nursery could hold. Everything was signed for on charge accounts then delivered by a procession of young boys from the shops. Esther recommenced giving dinners and cocktail parties. At these, Jennifer was always dressed up by Nanny and presented to the guests at an appointed hour then sent off to bed.

To the staff, Jennifer seemed an emotional orphan. More things were bought for her than she could use, but the essential—that special nurturing between a mother and her child—was missing. For all Esther doted and fussed over Jennifer she seemed incapable of giving simple, warm, peaceful love. And George, though he loved Jennifer wholeheartedly, was so busy working at the office to keep up with Esther's spending, and squeezing in his voluntary service when he could, his moments with his daughter became more and more rare.

At home, Esther took to swimming frequently in the indoor pool. When she was not entertaining, she would instruct Nanny to bring Jennifer to the poolside. There, Nanny sat watching while Esther would hold the baby on the water's surface and whizz her around as if making her fly. Jennifer, not feeling safe in her mother's hands, would begin to cry after a few turns and would be handed back to Nanny whose head developed the habit of shaking most of the time.

The pool was also a great focus for socializing. Esther's friends often sat around it, their children left at home with Spanish maids. It became the center of Esther's life as she fought to get back the taut tummy forfeited by the pregnancy. At the end of the poolroom there was a gymnasium and round the pool grew orange trees and exotic, tall palms, a memory of Africa. By the huge windows grew bougainvillaea and hibiscus trees. The sensuous, pink hibiscus flowers stirred memories in Esther. They bloomed overnight.

Sometimes, after the shock of the birth began to wear off, Esther lay in her bathing suit alone at night when George was working and Jenny had been put to bed. She was a small, pale shadow in the huge rattan chair which guarded the pool, blue and purple in the dimness. Alone, with a drink in her hand, she imagined herself and Jimmy making love in the water. George knew that sex between them was rare at best, particularly since her "illness", as she chose to call her recovery from childbirth. Occasionally, feeling she had to keep him happy if her charge accounts were to remain unlimited, Esther would let him find his pleasure, but she herself felt nothing. The only true sexual pleasure she sought was in savage fantasy.

The other comparable pleasure was when she was about to acquire something new, particularly shoes. She recognized her addiction: the point when the money breathlessly changed hands and the shoes, with their sharp stiletto heels, were wrapped in white tissue paper, put in a box, taken home, and unwrapped to allow the wonderful smell of leather to fill Esther's nostrils. The new shoes were then added to the immaculate row in the big, white dressing room. Maria's job was to see that the row remained precise.

Esther's routine grew fixed. Breakfast in bed with only one cup of coffee because coffee can stain the skin. Read the newspapers, write letters, a bath. Then, right on schedule, Nanny would bring Jennifer in for her continued daily talks with Esther. When Esther had finished saying all she had to say to the baby, Nanny would be summoned and given instructions to read to Jennifer for at least an hour. Esther then left her room to visit the kitchen to see Ah Ling, issue commands to several indoor servants and then to the gardener. Lunch was followed by a nap and a committee meeting, perhaps. She would return, have her swim and, if there was time, Jenny would participate too. Goodnight to the baby, and then out for the evening, with or without George.

Interspersed with all this activity were visits to try on clothes, furs, jewels and, of course, the beauty parlor. Esther decided to learn to paint, though she never really found time to pursue it with anything other than occasional dabblings. Her young ambitions for a literary career had been abandoned long ago. Life was too busy to write the great novel or the perfect poem. But an easel in the pool room with a large palette of water-colors could be attended to when necessary. And whether she actually painted or not, the mere thought of it provided infinite opportunity for fantasy. Perhaps in a year's time, a show in a Santa Fe gallery and then, who knows? Fame . . . An exhibition at the Boston Museum of Fine Arts . . . Invitations to all those patrons . . . Dinners at . . . The possibilities were endless.

America was now engaged in a war, both in the Pacific and in Europe, that seemed to drain it of its manpower even more than the First World War had done. Danny Gottstein again assumed the sad role of doctor to the wounded returning to Santa Fe. George, however, felt impotent. He was thirty-four years old and he now had not only a wife but also a daughter to support. Helping the country abroad was out of the question. Nevertheless, George felt he had to do something. He could not simply sit and watch as trainload after trainload of Santa Fe's younger men went off to fight for their country. After much deliberation, George volunteered to do paperwork at the Santa Fe train station. The west-bound trains arrived from the East and the Midwest, en route to the California ports where their burden would be unloaded and moved to the ships, then on to the Pacific Theater. Full of supplies and men and munition, the trains moved on from Santa Fe, and everything had to be accounted for. George helped with the daily chores of inventory. Sitting in an atmosphere that felt more like Mexico than America, Santa Fe remained a strange way station, a queer crossroads on the roof of the world, one thousand miles away from the nearest ocean, oddly removed from the horrors shaking the rest of the earth. Well, George told himself guiltily, at least I'm pitching in.

CHAPTER 39

Jenny was three when she first realized her mother did not love her. The thought was not conscious until one day when Esther returned from a luncheon. Jenny was standing by her mother's chair. Esther looked tired and harassed. Jenny was due to take her afternoon nap but she whined and pulled at Esther's fingers. "Don't do that, Jennifer." Esther frowned.

"No by-by-by's?" Jennifer continued to whine. Exasperated because Jenny was trying to climb onto her lap, Esther pushed off the child. Jenny fell to the floor and howled.

Nanny was there in a minute. She gathered Jenny into her arms and carried the shrieking child back to the nursery. "That woman." The words escaped from Nanny's mouth as she hurried down the hall. "Don't cry, darling. Nanny will rock you."

Jenny fell silent, feeling the warmth and safety of her Nanny's arms. But before she fell into a deep sleep, she knew in her young mind that being held by her mother never felt the same as being cuddled comfortably and lovingly by Nanny, or by her grandmother Nora, or her grandfather Danny. There was something different, missing, in her mother's arms, and Jenny had her first, faint inkling that something, therefore, was missing in her own life, however many toys and clothes her mother bought her.

George adored his daughter. When he had time they played together. Nevertheless, he could not make up for what was missing in her mother. From then on, Jenny stopped her frantic efforts to attract Esther's attention, much to Esther's relief. Esther still believed Jennifer to be the eventual fulfillment of her dreams, her ambitions. In moments of reflection, she still imagined the wonderful things Jennifer would achieve: renown, strength, power. But in her mind remained her first image of Jennifer as a little doll in her arms and she could not reconcile it with the fact that Jennifer seemed determined to have a will and a life of her own. So many times, Jennifer seemed too demanding, too inconvenient. In the end, Esther decided there was nothing wrong in letting Nanny meet the bulk of the child's apparently endless demands. "Nanny," Esther remarked, "you're doing wonders." Nanny, with all her English stiff upper lip, said nothing. She was wise enough to know that any criticism of Esther and she would have to go.

Etta was quite a different kettle of fish. Often, when Jenny needed an outing, Nanny packed a picnic lunch, and the chauffeur, driving an English Rolls, took her to the ranch. Etta was now only working part-time in the Phoenix Company. Money and real estate were at an all-time high, for the war undoubtedly improved the nation's economy. With less time needed at the Phoenix Company, Etta was free to devote herself fully to life on the ranch.

Why, Nanny wondered silently, during her outings with Jenny at Etta's, wasn't Esther more like Etta? Indeed, everything Esther lacked by way of nurturing, Etta possessed in abundance. Etta seemed to delight genuinely in the child's company, and she was thrilled to spend many peaceful hours tending the kitchen garden while Jennifer invented games and amusements among the growing vegetable plants. Her body having spread to generous proportions, Etta took every opportunity to hug Jennifer. While she busied herself around the kitchen, her "little helper," as she came to call Jenny, followed closely behind. Why, Nanny thought, couldn't Jenny have Etta for a mother?

Three years became five, and then primary school at six. Jenny clung to Nanny. She did not want to leave the warm world of Nanny, Maria, and Ah Ling. She knew some of the children but she never felt the school to be a sanctuary or refuge. At home, there were magnificent paintings to stare at, huge Victorian oils of ships lost at sea.

Esther now ran an English salon. Writers, poets

and artists stayed for months in the guest houses which sat like fat, brown mushrooms in the grounds of Mandalay. Sometimes the artists were very wild and threw parties which did not include George.

One night, when Jenny had first started school, she stood at the window of her bedroom and watched her father lean out of the master bedroom window and bellow, "Where are you, Esther? You're *my* wife! Get back in here!"

The door of a guest house opened, and Jennifer saw her mother, dressed in her favorite white gown, glide swiftly across the lawn. She noticed her mother's tiny, shoeless, white feet.

Nanny, who no longer slept with her charge, snapped on the light. "Go to bed, darling," she said, with a funny look on her face. "Go to sleep. You'll forget by morning."

Jennifer did not forget. She thought of the guest houses as evil places, like oak mushrooms which sat, sinister and slimy, under the trees.

At ten, Jennifer felt herself living a double life. Part of her had an insatiable desire for warmth which she sought avidly, as a person half-frozen to death sits beside a fire, wanting to take all the hearth's heat into her own body. The glowing flames in her life were her father, her grandparents, her aunt Etta and the servants. But she kept largely secret this yearning to be heated. Too much else was expected of her. At too many dinner parties and social functions had she heard her parents' friends say to Esther, with a congratulatory wink in their eyes, "She's her mother's daughter."

The thin, intense child, whose dark hair held a glowing flame of auburn, moved through the ordinary world as a stranger, a visiting dignitary from a distant country. She had few friends at school, for most of the other children all seemed too happy to giggle in class, to argue flirtatiously with each other, to whisper within their exclusive, closed circles. Jenny knew she could not join them. She lived by some strict code of protocol: she was always to be on her best behavior. She was to behave as if on show at one of her mother's cocktail parties. She was different from the rest, set apart, "better," as her mother told her frequently. She was to be the sort of girl the adult members of Santa Fe's fashionable and prominent set could admire for her manners. She was to be at all times, as her mother never stopped reminding her, "a lady."

School, Esther informed her, was a place to learn, not to socialize. With marked doggedness, Jenny devoted herself to her studies. She learned that only the best grades would bring a "well done" from her mother. If a grade in any subject fell even to a B+, Esther would immediately storm into the expensive private school, take Jennifer by the hand, march into the headmaster's office, insist upon a conference with the teacher in question and demand an explanation of why that teacher was apparently unable to teach Jenny properly, to "bring out the full potential of such an obviously gifted child." The school's teachers soon recognized that there was no arguing with Mrs. Esther Jensen. After all, she had placed herself prominently on the school board. The teachers would placate. At first Jennifer was embarrassed to see them so humiliated. But after years of this treatment, she began to regard them with distaste for the weakness of their cowering to her mother's strength. Strength,

Jenny gradually learned by Esther's tuition, was what made you get ahead in the world.

So let the children giggle, Jennifer decided when she was eleven. Let them wear their relatively casual clothes in poor taste, while she wore only the perfectly cut European dresses and fancy shoes Esther brought back to her after the increasingly regular shopping jaunts abroad. ("I'll take you with me when you're older," Esther always explained when saying good-bye, off on yet another long trip overseas, unaccompanied by her daughter or her husband. With each passing year, the excursions became longer and more frequent and Esther always returned with clothes to exhibit on her daughter and works of art to show on her mansion walls.) Let the other children, Jennifer decided, leave me alone.

Jennifer's world was inhabited by grown-ups. At eleven, she was expected to hold her own in the conversations at her mother's parties. She found, in the midst of these fashionable adults, a confidence, an acceptance. They treated her with an amused admiration ("She's so grown-up for her age. A proper little lady!") and it was with the adults she felt most comfortable. Anyway, Jenny thought, it wasn't her fault if other children mistook her shyness in their young company to be snobbishness.

She also found a greater confidence, an adult awareness, in the guest houses of Mandalay. As Jenny matured, she found that the guest houses' air of foreboding changed to an atmosphere of excitement. Spending some afternoon hours there, surrounded by the artists and painters her mother seemed to collect, Jenny grew familiar with their flirtations. She learned to laugh at the titillation of their very grown-up jokes.

These were the liberated, free-thinking, unencumbered Bohemians who were not afraid to experience all of life's pleasures. She watched as, after teasing and joking, they embraced each other, and held each other's hands with knowing looks in their eyes. And when she joined in the laughter, teasing and tickling by some of the more friendly male artists, she also learned hints of the complicity they all seemed to share.

It was only occasionally, when her mother was away and she could spend a weekend or a holiday at her aunt Etta's ranch, that Jenny felt she was a child. Only at Etta's could she take off her fancy clothes and throw on an old pair of overalls. Only with Etta could she laugh and not be self-conscious. Only at Etta's could she enjoy thoroughly good food without having to mind her table manners. When her body began to change, it was Etta, not Esther, who told the young girl of the beauty of entering womanhood and explained how to handle the monthly proof of that maturity.

This friendly, womanly world, however, Jennifer knew she had to confine to secrecy. She did not discuss her body with her mother, nor could she tell Esther how much she loved the rough feel of the overalls against her skin, the softness of the mulched earth beneath her bare feet in Etta's garden. Moments at Etta's ranch might have their own relaxed rules of freedom, but Jennifer knew these rules were to be left at the ranch's front gates whenever the Rolls-Royce came to collect her to return her to life in Mandalay.

Never did Jenny question or break the rules of Esther's world. Some deep instinct inside the young girl sensed that—however much Esther might effer-vesce warmly in public, however much concern and attention she might demonstrate about the propriety of Jenny's upbringing—Esther's wrath was not to be risked. Beneath the beauty of Esther's face, behind the often excited glow of the eyes, Jenny detected an impervious strength, a dangerous hardness, as solid and unyielding as granite. No physical force was nec-essary, nor any raising of the melodious voice. Jenny had only to see a sudden and sharp accusation in her mother's eyes and any word uttered out of place, any socially unacceptable movement, was immediately corrected.

George, when he was home, could be funny, affec-tionate and lovable but Jenny knew who sat upon the single throne in Esther's world.

❧ *CHAPTER 40* ❧

Impossible, Esther thought when she first learned she was pregnant again. Unbelievable. How could this be?

She hardly thought her forty-one-year-old body capable of pregnancy anymore, and the great infre-quency of intimacy with George made the idea of conception virtually unthinkable. Damn him, Esther thought bitterly. I let him use me once too often.

"Really?" George said when he heard the news. "Pregnant?" He sat behind his large desk at the Phoenix Company, amazed at what he had heard from Esther's high, hysterical voice down the telephone. Then he began to think about what it all meant: maybe he would have a son. Certainly there would be a new addition to the family, whatever the sex. A new baby to hold and kiss. And if it *were* a son (of course, he did not care whether it was a boy or a girl, just as long as it was healthy), but if it *were* a son, then just think of that. George Jensen, father of his own son. "How wonderful!" George said at last, realizing how long his mouth had remained silent beside the telephone's mouthpiece. "Honey, I'm—I'm thrilled!"

"Well, I'm not," Esther snapped. "Do you really know what this means? I mean, we'll have to start raising a child all over again. I don't want to. Do you? I mean, really, George. We're too old to go through the early years all over again."

"Yes, but honey—" George was anxious to calm down his wife. "Nanny would be happy to look after another kid and who knows? This one might be a boy."

"I don't want a boy." Esther began to cry. "I don't want another baby. Look, it's taken us eleven years to get Jenny's life into the right kind of shape. And now she's a proper young lady. There's her future to think about. We can't have the burden of raising another child. Jenny will be a teenager soon and we'll have our hands full seeing she does it all properly."

"Yes, but . . ."

"And there's *my* life to think about, George," Esther continued. Her tears turned to anger. "Not that you ever think about that. I've just started to enjoy life. I'm traveling now. At last. But, God knows, not enough. And there's all my committee work . . . Why, don't you see, George? I can't just give it all up."

"You won't have to," George reassured her. With every year that had passed, George had found himself missing his wife more and more. But how could he stop her? How could he cage the beautiful creature he loved so much? And now, there was no point in taking away any of her freedom. She would only hold it against him and he couldn't have that. "Listen, once the baby's born, you can travel as much as you like. Even more than you have been, if that's what you want. Nanny can look after the baby. And so will I. It doesn't have to slow you down."

"That'd better be a promise, George."

"It is," he said, relieved to hear her voice relax a bit. "I promise. All right? I love you, honey."

Esther put down the telephone without replying. She sat on her bed and looked over to the photograph of the puma hanging on the wall. She sighed. However distraught she felt, she had to admit to a feeling of relief. Fine, she decided. This can be George's child. I'll carry it for nine months, have it delivered, then it's George's problem. And after that?

Esther lay back and thought. A trip to Europe. That's what she needed. A trip to Europe and time spent with some real Europeans. The American artists in the guest houses were becoming tiresome. They lacked the worldliness of the painters and writers in Europe. I'll send them away, Esther said to herself. All of them. And maybe I can bring back some real artists, from Europe.

Esther made her plans. Once the baby was born, she would give herself the trip. And she would visit Julie Youngblood. Julie was now in her nineties and Esther had crossed paths with her without managing to arrange a visit on past trips. This time, she would go to Venice and stay with Julie. Maybe, Esther thought, with a sadness at the idea of seeing part of her youth leave, maybe for the last time.

Ringing the bell for Maria to bring her a cup of tea, Esther felt reassured. She dreaded the pregnancy, but then her life would begin again.

The months passed slowly. Esther decided the only way to deal with the time was to consign herself to bed. Why not pamper herself? Her committee meetings and parties could wait until she got back from Italy, and she could use the time to catch up on her letter writing. After all, there were the arrangements with Julie to be made. Besides, taking to illness would keep George off her, at least for the next nine months, and then she would be gone. Esther spent the time controlling her impatience like a prisoner enduring his last months of captivity.

Jenny experienced a strange sense of respite. True, she visited her mother in the master bedroom every day and had to give a full account of how she was doing in each of her classes and yes, she had to be especially careful not to make any noise in the house lest she disturb her resting mother. But she enjoyed the relief of knowing she could get on with her life in Mandalay without always feeling her mother over her shoulder. She could sit in the library and read without having to listen for the sharp clack of her mother's high heels on the tiled hallway. She was free to lean against the kitchen counter and talk with Ah Ling while he cooked, safe in the knowledge that her mother would not appear suddenly in the doorway and look at her accusingly for fraternizing with the servants. She could eat dinner with her father alone

(Esther had all her meals served to her in bed) and enjoy his good-humored company.

When Jenny was twelve years old, her mother gave birth to Maxwell Jensen. This time, Esther had decided resolutely in advance, there would be no suffering the agonizing pangs of labor. At the first sign of a contraction, she had George drive her to the nursing home and, according to previous arrangement, was put to sleep under general anaesthetic. She had been warned of the risk of tearing open her old Caesarean scar if she tried to deliver naturally. So, also by arrangement, she was wheeled into the operating room, the doctors cut through the remnants of her scar, and the baby boy was painlessly removed from her body. In the waiting room George was overjoyed to learn that he had a son but Esther slept on through the news.

When she woke, her main concern was that she be given enough painkillers to numb the incision. The nursing-home staff, having spent hours in preparation for the birth after listening to Esther's careful instructions that they were to ensure she suffered no pain or else she would see they were not paid, provided more than adequate medication. She returned home by private ambulance, and lay in her bed, drowsy from the drugs, for two weeks until she was confident she could get up without pain.

From time to time, as she drifted between sleep and wakefulness in what could not be discerned as night or day, she heard George's footsteps going to the nursery and caught fragments of his proud conversations with Nanny. Occasionally, she was aware of Jenny's face peering through the door to check on her. Jenny was pleased to have a brother but part of her was frightened she might have lost a certain exclusivity with her mother. Sometimes she stared at the baby, and didn't know what to think. She felt an odd loneliness as the guest houses, even though they had been filled by people of dubious principles, were emptied, according to Esther's instructions.

"Mother?" Jenny asked tentatively one day, when she could see Esther's eyes half-open. "There's something I'd like to ask you."

"Not now, Jennifer," Esther said wearily. "I'm too tired."

Jenny watched her mother's eyes close. She shut the door behind her.

Ten days after the operation, Esther took no more medication. Mercifully, her incision did not hurt. A doctor came to remove the stitches. Still, she decided to give herself another four days in bed to sleep off the last effects of the painkillers. Her breasts were swollen, but those, too, would soon return to normal. Without discussion, Nanny had known to prepare a row of sterilized bottles in the nursery, even before Esther had entered the hospital.

Her fortnight of recuperation over, Esther arose from her bed one morning feeling oddly refreshed and summoned Maria to pack for her. Jennifer knocked on the door when Esther was seeing the last pairs of shoes tucked neatly into the trunk. "Yes?" said Esther.

"Mother," Jenny began with hesitation. "I wanted to ask you . . . I've been reading about Italy and looking through the art books downstairs. Do you think I . . . Could I go with you?"

"Jennifer," Esther said with a harshness in her voice. "I've just given birth. Stop thinking about yourself for a change and think about me. I'm still recovering and I need some time to myself." Then, seeing the disappointment on her daughter's face, she softened. How could she explain how eager she was to be alone in Europe again, to feel the exhilaration of being free from all responsibility, all care? "Don't worry," she said sweetly. She kissed Jennifer on the forehead. "When you're older, maybe eighteen or nineteen, I'll take you to Europe for your grand tour. That's when I did my grand tour, you know. That's the proper time for a young lady to see Europe, when you're old enough to appreciate it fully."

"All right," Jenny said, lowering her head. She left her mother to pack.

The next morning was a Saturday morning, so George was home from work. He stood with Max in his arms and Jenny beside him, watching Esther get into the limousine. Secretly, George felt astonished that Esther could remain so true to her word. She really didn't have anything to do with their son. How could she not notice her own baby? George wondered for a moment then he stopped the thought. He could not allow himself to think so disloyally of his beautiful wife. He picked up the baby's hand and made the little arm wave. "Bye bye," George said in a baby voice as Esther waved through the Rolls-Royce's closed window.

Standing next to her father, Jenny watched the car roll away. When it disappeared at the end of the driveway, she felt she had no mother at all.

❧ CHAPTER 41 ❧

A sprightliness still sparked in Julie's eyes, but Esther was concerned to see that, for the first time in her life, Julie looked her age. "You look wonderful," Esther laughed. "I never would have believed you to be in your nineties. Why, you could pass for a woman in her sixties. You look as young as when we first met."

"And you," Julie said, "are a good liar." She laughed. "Just my luck," she said. "Live till I'm bloody hundred-and-ten. Then you'll have to finish me off." Esther laughed back. She always liked the hard cutting edge of this woman who knew her so well. It felt so good to be in her company again.

All day they reminisced about the people they knew, about the tedium Esther felt married life to be. "I think I've found a remedy for you," said Julie. Her face lit up. "Maybe you'll finally forget Delgado. First love, always tricky." Her voice softened. "I'll never forget Lilla. Or Amelia. When I lie here and hear the tide rush in over the cobbles and the gondolas glide by, I think of our times together. And your grandmother and I, and Amelia, all laughing and chattering about the people we knew . . . Just like we're doing now."

Esther nodded. "I wish I'd been born earlier. I don't feel I'm part of this new generation." She looked out the window to the canals of Venice. "I love Italy. I love the fashion here. It can't be found in America. Everything there is too new. But here—look at this jacket. I got it yesterday. The Italians can make suede look like silk, and silk look like suede. Isn't it beautiful?"

"Let an old letch like me watch you take it off." Julie smiled. "I may be old, but I can still appreciate a lovely woman's body."

Esther, understanding, nodded. She had always anticipated sharing secrets and intimacy with Julie. In her own way, she had been waiting for it since she was the young teenager first meeting this worldly woman.

She took off the jacket, unbuttoned her shirt and undid her belt. Her skirt fell to the floor and she dropped her shirt slowly to join it, lying like a stain on the white marble floor.

Slowly, she turned her back to the bed and walked to the great shutters, drawn against the sun which normally flooded the room. Today, the sky was overcast. Gulls called and reeled in the sky. Esther removed her camisole and then her small black lace brassière. These she dropped to the floor. She turned slowly, clad only in a brief pair of delicate black panties. Outlined against the great Venetian sky, she walked slowly down the room with its huge colonnade to the Roman four-poster bed. Set against the white marble, Esther looked like a perfect miniature porcelain figure.

Age had not yet brushed her body with a dry wrinkled finger. Two breasts untramelled by breastfeeding and nipples still flat, unsucked, neck tall and swan-like, waist taut, and skin even. Her thighs were still superb (a credit to all the exercise), and the hair she now allowed to fall to her waist was thick and shiny. Julie smiled to see the golden locket hang between the firm breasts. "Tsk, tsk," she said when she saw the still-healing scar on Esther's belly.

"Children," Esther replied with a shrug, and covered the scar with her hand. "Another bit of plastic surgery and you'll hardly be able to see it."

"Never mind." Julie smiled. "Still beautiful," she said. "But untouched."

Esther grinned. "Well, one can't exactly say George has much to offer. So straight, that man is. Not a perverse bone in his body." She walked back to the window to collect her clothes.

Without warning, the bedroom door opened. "Is this a party for two, or can anyone join?" Esther stood rooted to the spot. "Really!" A man, who struck Esther as youngish and very handsome, bounced up to the enormous bed. "Really, Julie! At your age!" He turned and looked intently. "Turn," he said to Esther. "And again." She obeyed. "Very good," he said. "Ever considered being an artist's model?" His accent, whatever it was, sounded wonderfully European.

"No." Esther was nonplussed.

"Well, you should," he said, and threw himself on Julie's bed.

Esther felt a hot flame burn in her thighs. She felt as if the tip of a knife had been inserted into the most secret part of her universe. Never, since Boston, had all her passionate feelings, carefully packed away, been opened. This man, this satyr, must be hers.

By the end of dinner, the three of them were entranced, drowned in soft candlelight. Julie, in bed with her plate in her lap and a glass of champagne on the bedside table, said, "Well, you two, here's to a betrothal." She lifted her glass, gently fluted. "I bequeath my friend Orlando Machado to my friend Esther Jensen. May you have better luck with him than most women."

Esther did not hear the last sentence. She and Orlando were gazing at each other through their glasses. The champagne bubbles rose and hissed as they exploded.

Orlando, slightly drunk, left in the middle of the dark night. Esther saw him to the door. Julie had long been asleep and Orlando and Esther talked. For Esther, years fell away as they giggled and whispered. When they got to the door of the palazzo, they stood still. Orlando pulled Esther to him and kissed her, a shy question or maybe a confusion in the kiss. Esther was surprised, sleepy and confused. "I'll come round tomorrow," he promised. "For breakfast."

"He's one of us," Julie announced the next morning. She was sitting up, bright and chirpy. Matchmaking was Julie's forte. Now, after all these years, she still felt slightly guilty about not trying hard enough to protect Esther from Jimmy Delgado. Now was her chance to square things. Jimmy Delgado might have been a disaster but even if Orlando did have his quirks, Esther would discover them and be able to handle them in good time. Besides, Julie decided, Esther certainly needed a distraction, tucked away in Santa Fe. Orlando Machado was distraction enough for any woman. He was free of his last lover, a particularly burly gondolier. He was free to travel.

Esther sat at the table by Julie's bed and put her head in her hands. Do I really want to get involved? She thought. Last night's champagne still bubbled through her veins. She looked up at Julie. "Should I?" she said.

Julie shrugged. "That's not for me to say. But if you get bored enough, you'll get wrinkles. Boredom is so aging and you're still so young. Why, you're barely past forty and you've hardly lived at all. Stuck away in Santa Fe with a man you've never loved."

Esther nodded. "I need some fun," she said. "It's been a long time. The Santa Fe artists are such phonies. Only Downey can really paint and he's happily married. At least I've seen one happy marriage, so I know it can happen." She sighed. A knock heralded the maid. She carried a large tray which she put down before Esther. "Ah, Venetian chocolate." Esther was grateful for the warm smell that cleared her head. A plate of fresh plump golden croissants sat beside the chocolate pot. Feather by feather, flake by moist flake, they sat on the thick, white linen napkin.

Julie never ate breakfast but she smoked a villainous cheroot. She had switched from the Black Russians to the cheroots. This was her new habit. "Too old to die of cancer," she explained to anyone who asked. The telephone by her bed shrilled. She smiled as she nodded into the mouthpiece. "Yes," she said into the phone, "he came by last night, and he met my friend Esther." Then she rolled her eyes, covered the mouthpiece with her hand and whispered to Esther, "My friend Dixon doesn't approve of men of Orlando's habits."

Esther blinked. Such sexually rich descriptions, once heard so commonly during her Boston days, struck her with a sense of novelty and strangeness. The exciting pique of Julie's worlds reminded her how isolated her life was in Santa Fe. She was glad to be back in the titillating swing of European life. To Esther, Orlando offered a refreshing attraction.

Within minutes of Orlando's noisy arrival that morning into Julie's bedroom, Esther was genuinely besotted. She found his zest and decadence irresistible. All day, the two of them roamed the canals, Orlando's arm resting lightly on hers. That evening they excused themselves from Julie's dinner party and wandered hand in hand until they reached the Bridge of Sighs. There, like so many lovers before them, they gazed down at the muddy malodorous waters which seethed and tumbled under the bridge.

Side by side they stood, and Orlando slipped his arm around Esther's slim waist as if they had been intimate for years. Esther breathed in deeply. She liked the way Orlando smelled. His smell was clean, young, and indescribably European. She exhaled her breath with a happy sigh. "Esther," Orlando hesitated, his eyes remaining fixed on the water below. "Esther," he said, looking into her eyes. She smiled at him. The radiance of her face offered an invitation. "You know, Esther," Orlando began again. "You are the kind of woman I would want to love."

Esther's heart beat fast. Old feelings, like living diamonds, had been unearthed from deep within her. She felt young. She felt as if she had her Jimmy back. She looked up at Orlando. The curls of his dark hair blew softly in the evening breeze. His eyes glowed with a warmth which Esther had waited many years to see. "And?" She smiled coquettishly.

He smiled back. "And—"

"Shhh," she silenced him and, putting her hand behind his head, she drew his lips to her own. They were soft, she noticed, but they remained closed. Maybe, she thought, he isn't as bold as he seems. She found this shyness endearing. He's young, she reminded herself. I'll show him how.

She moved her mouth to kiss him first on the top lip then on the bottom. Then she let her tongue softly touch the fullness of his lower lip. Hesitatingly, he parted his lips, allowing her warm, wet tongue to slip inside. His mouth, she found, tasted sweet. When her tongue touched his, he pulled back.

He turned and leaned once again on the railing of the bridge. "Ah, my Esther," he said, shaking his head. "My dear Esther. How can I tell you?"

"Tell me what?" She was hardly sure if this was some flirtatious form of a joke. But his eyes were serious.

"I can't make love to you," Orlando said after a long silence.

"Orlando," she said with real affection in her voice. "If it's my husband you're worried about, he doesn't have to find out. I mean, I've never done this before. But then, I've never met a man like you before." An image of Jimmy flashed before her but she knew there was no reason to tell Orlando about him now. That would wait until its own good time. "A man who makes me feel so alive," she continued, "so young again. A man I can feel so comfortable with—"

"No." He shut his eyes and shook his head. "It is not your husband."

"Then what is it?"

"It is that I . . . Oh, Esther." She could hear the genuine sadness in his little laugh. "Why am I telling you all this?" He shrugged. "Maybe I also feel comfortable with you. Here, let me explain. I would like to make love to you."

"But?"

"But . . . I can't?"

"Why not?"

He hung his head. "I simply can't make love. To any woman, I mean."

"Oh," she said. Disappointment settled quickly

over her. "I see." I should have known, she thought.
I should have recognized it the minute I saw him. I
never should have got my hopes up. She cleared her
throat. "Forgive me," she said. "I didn't mean to
offend you. I feel silly for asking."

He smiled. "You are not silly," he said. "I am the
one with the problem."

"Then you've—" Frustrated hope still urged with
Esther. "I mean, you've been with men?"

"Yes." He nodded. "With men, no problem."

"Then how do you know? Maybe with women, the
right woman—"

"How can I explain? Believe me," he said. "I have
tried, and it never works. It feels like a sin, if that
makes sense."

"Not really." Esther raised her head and looked at
the darkened sky. Passion, she realized, and desire
and excitement and fulfillment, all would have to be
pushed back within the grave to which she had rele-
gated her deepest longings years ago. Maybe she had
been foolish, she thought, to think the ecstasy she had
known once could ever be resurrected. No, life would
go back to usual. Boring predictable usual. Or maybe
not, she thought, her mind turning. Maybe excitement can be found in other ways. "Well," she said
with a sudden decisive smile. "Ours can be a pure
love."

He smiled back, comforted, and nodded as if in a
small bow.

"For as long as it lasts," she added.

"For as long as it lasts," he said.

She laughed. "And at least this way George won't
have anything to complain about."

Orlando laughed with her. "And how long," he

asked, "do you think it will last?" She cocked her
eyebrows. "Ah," he scolded himself out loud. "Such
a silly question. You have your family, your husband
and children and house to go back to. I mustn't ask.
Of course." He paused, his mind working quickly.
"Listen," he said, the mischievous sparkle returned
fully to his eyes. "Before you go, why don't we take a
week motoring around? Amalfi is beautiful in the
spring. Then we can go on up to Portofino. I have an
English Jaguar. Huge red animal, it is. You'd love it.
What do you say?"

Esther, for the moment, had forgotten her family in
Santa Fe. Adventure beckoned, and Esther had to go.
"I'd love to," she said, and she reached forward and
gave Orlando a great hug. Her feet left the ground as
he swung her in his arms. To anyone floating by on
the dusky river in a lazy unhurried gondola, the two
embracing people on the bridge would have appeared very much in love.

❧ CHAPTER 42 ❧

The sign to Amalfi thrilled Esther. When she traveled
it was usually with a woman friend. This time she felt
marvelously illicit and wonderfully single. The first
sight of the little town nestled in the bay delighted her.
Here, in Italy, she always felt young and alive again.
She looked up at Orlando from under her wide-
brimmed sun hat. "Have you been here before?" she
asked.

"Yes, often," he screamed over the roar of the Jaguar's engine. "It's a well-known place where two men can be together and no questions asked." He grinned. "We'll have dinner at Ravello's fish restaurant. That'll surprise them! Me with a woman!"

Esther grinned. Life had not been this exciting since Africa.

"I'll take a double room." Orlando did not need to explain. The manager of La Rimina Hotel knew him well. Both men stood silent. Giovanni grinned. *"Benissimo,"* he said wryly.

Orlando nodded. "She's rich. I'm going to get to America! She doesn't know it yet but just watch me!" This was said in staccato Italian.

Giovanni laughed and slapped Orlando on the back. "Okay," he said with a heavily accented English in deference to the American woman. "I'll take you up myself."

Esther followed, feeling helpless. She had expected separate rooms. She was a little taken aback—but secretly delighted—that they were to share a small suite with a double bed in a pretty bedroom, and a sitting room which offered magnificent views of the harbor. "Let's take a bath before we have dinner," said Orlando, unbuttoning his shirt.

"I must ring George."

"Tomorrow," Orlando insisted. "Tomorrow. Always make a husband wait. He'll find you more attractive." Orlando unpacked quickly. When his clothes lay neatly folded in the drawers, he waited impatiently while Esther undressed to join him.

Orlando, sitting at the opposite end of the bath, was busily struggling with a bottle of iced champagne. Esther lay back in the massive, black marble bath. A loud pop echoed off the tiled walls. "Here you are. A toast." Orlando stood up. "Get up," he said. "You can't drink a toast on your back." Esther obediently stood up. Orlando lifted his glass. "A toast to Mrs Jensen, and a toast to Orlando Machado. Poets and artists." He lifted his glass, delicately etched with flowers, and solemnly placed it with a slight chink against Esther's.

Esther sat down, pleased to be back in the warm water. Orlando, she observed, had such a beautiful body. Smooth, no horrid bulging muscles, no patches of hair which attracted sweat. She couldn't imagine him sweating, or farting, or clearing his sinuses. He looked like a Michelangelo portrait—escaped, perhaps, from a Florentine museum. Then she decided, even if he had escaped, she was going to capture him. "Orlando," she said, "how about your coming back to Santa Fe to paint me?"

Orlando raised an eyebrow. "Your husband?" he inquired.

Esther smiled and looked at him through the tangle of her black eyelashes. "My dear boy, American men do as they're told. They're famous for it."

"I'll think about it," Orlando said. "But first let's have dinner."

Dinner was at the Ravello Restaurant at the end of a boardwalk which stretched out to the sea. The evening was chilly but the trees flowered in the spring air. The same air which blew from the sea tonight promised a hot, heavy, sensual summer. The usual horde of tourists were not yet in for the season so the restaurant was still only half-filled with Italian families. Contented babies blinked owlishly at Esther, so fashionable in her slacks and cashmere sweater. Esther looked at the women and frowned. Most of them wore cheerful, bright clothes and many were fat. She grimaced. "Goodness," she said. "What a sight."

Orlando pulled out a chair for her. "They are good women," he said. "I know them. They love their husbands and their children. Not all this modern rubbish."

Esther was surprised. "Don't you think women have rights?"

Orlando shrugged. "No. In Europe, a woman waits to get married. When she is married, her duty is to the family. You Americans don't fit in here in Italia, or in Portugal, where I come from. I know I have only to telephone and my mother makes my special dinner and opens the wine." He leaned forward. "And that, my little chicken, is why I am a happy man . . . Ay!" He snapped his fingers. "Ay, Angelo! Over here!"

Angelo Ravello, the restaurant's owner, grinned hugely, threw his arms around his friend and kissed him on both cheeks. "Where have you been, you son of a bitch?" he bellowed. "I looked for you."

"I've been busy," Orlando said. "Angelo, this is Esther Jensen. And I"—he smiled hugely at Esther—"I am going to America!" he announced to the company in general. "Here." He gave Angelo a wad of lire. "Chianti on me for everyone! Hey! Hey!"

"Then you've decided!" Esther heard herself cry out. "How wonderful!" Orlando's enthusiasm for life excited Esther. He was so different from George. He paid attention to what Esther thought or felt and he was thrilling in his own right. She was living life through him . . .

Orlando was now doing the cakewalk up and down

the center of the room. He had a cigar jutting out of his mouth and both thumbs under his armpits. All the families laughed and cheered. Esther was ravenous when Angelo arrived with two thick dinner plates of fish stew. He poured a glass of chianti into Esther's glass and smiled at the pretty lady in front of him. "Madame," he said, looking at her wedding ring. "Take care. Orlando is a heart-breaker." He left the table and Esther.

Could she afford not to risk having her heart broken? Life so far had consisted of three stages: Boston, Africa and marriage. Boring, mundane marriage. But now, hopefully, Orlando. Terminal boredom causes cancer anyway, she decided. She ate the hot, garlic-smelling seafood stew. She gazed at the clams, open and available. I'm a clam, she thought. I've been a clam on the seabed of life far too long. I want some fun.

And anyway Esther knew the secret which rarely occurred to men—real men, that is. Esther used the technique for years: if an affair of the heart happened only in the head, the woman kept the power. The fantasy of ecstasy was so much more potent an aphrodisiac than the often unsatisfactory consummation. Jimmy was her bitter, tear-stained lesson. The vow she made extended to all men. Several men in Santa Fe were now her swains for life. All it took were a few jungle-hot looks, a slight moistening of the lips, and sighs. Orlando would be fun. A few remnants of disappointment lingered but, in their nonconsummation, she had to admit there was a certain safety: she would never be hurt as Jimmy had hurt her. And there was more than a safety; there was a definite strength. No physical union would spoil the intensity between them, and through it all *she* would remain in control.

Orlando came back to the table, puffing and blowing from his strenuous parading around. "Oh," he said, "I'm out of shape. Okay, now you can tell me everything about America. What's it like?"

Esther explained America to Orlando over dinner.

Both of them were tired when they got into the hotel and got into bed together in a haze of alcohol and good food. Esther lay in her satin nightdress staring dreamily at the ceiling. Orlando got into bed beside her. "Did you have a good day?" he asked.

"Fabulous," Esther said. "Really great."

"Good." Orlando kissed her chastely on the forehead and fell asleep. Esther soon joined him. What would Etta say? was her last thought.

After a perfect and riotous trip through Italian villages and cities, it was time to go home. George sounded bereft on the telephone and Esther felt guilty. "I'm leaving now for New York," she said down the overseas telephone wires, "and I'm bringing that painter I wrote to you about. He wants to paint me."

"Why, that's a good idea." George was genuinely pleased. "I want a painting for the office so I can look at you all day long. I've missed you, honey. So has Jenny. And Max . . ." Then George remembered his promise. Esther, he knew, was not interested in Max. "Well," he said. "Max is fine. Bring Jenny back something nice, will you?"

Esther made a face. "I can't," she said. "I don't have time to shop. Tell Nanny to go out and get something for me. I really don't know what to get a twelve-year-old."

"All right, darling. Do you want me to book a table for dinner your first night back?"

Esther paused. Dinner with George was so boring. "No, sweetheart," she said. "Let's just have a night at home. You and me by ourselves."

"Okay." George's voice was ebullient. "I'll get fresh lobsters and Ah Ling can do them the way you like."

"And get me some wine to go with it."

"What sort of wine?" he said warily. (Try as he might, George could not drink wine. "Tastes like horse piss," he always said. So he stuck to beer.)

"See if the liquor store has chianti," Esther answered.

"Chianti?" George sounded aggrieved. "Never heard of it. Anyway, we don't need to talk about this now. Just get yourself back here."

"Please, George. Please get me some chianti."

"Are you sure it ain't some foreign Eyetie drink?"

"Yes, it is. But Italy exports her wine."

"Okay then," George said. "I'll get a case for you, even if I have to get it flown in from Boston. There're lots of Eyeties up there."

Esther shut her eyes. "Yes, I believe there are," she said. Sometimes, she thought, George can be a truly incredible boor. "I've got to get going now."

Orlando stood behind her, massaging her shoulders. "Come on," he whispered. "We have to catch the boat." He gently kissed her ear. Esther put the phone down, her goodbyes still hanging in the air. "Don't look so guilty, little donkey." Orlando grinned at her. "We're not doing anything wrong, are we? You're as chaste as a nun. So why do you frown?"

"I don't want to go back, Orlando. I really don't

want to go back. I want to live in London . . . You could paint and I could write poetry, and paint as well. I don't have to be married to George. I have money in my own right."

Orlando put his arms round her. "Come," he said. "We'll have lunch. You'll think better on a full stomach."

During lunch, before catching the boat, Esther tried to explain her confused thoughts to Orlando. "I feel guilty because I don't love George. I never did. And I didn't really want Max, either. But Jennifer, I promised myself, would have a different life. I want her to have a career, something that will give her respect for herself and for me as her mother. I don't want Jennifer to have a mother who spent all her life doing boring, household things. It's all right for George liked the look of Orlando very much indeed but he had ordered only two lobsters. Nestled in George's arms in the bedroom for an obligatory matrimonial cuddle after so long an absence, Esther whispered in his ear, "We can't let him have dinner on his own on his first night here. We're his hosts. It would be dreadfully rude, George. Really." She put her little pink tongue into his mouth.

George, besotted, agreed. "I'll get Ah Ling to run and get another lobster," George said. "Jenny is waiting for you in the library."

Orlando met Jenny before Esther did. Having unpacked in his spectacular guesthouse, Orlando walked across the green lawn into the open library doors. For a while, he amused himself looking at the rows of books. Having met and shaken hands with George only briefly, and still curious to find out about the sort of husband Esther was married to, Orlando realized that if you knew a man's books, you knew the man. On the shelves before him, Orlando found adventure stories—Neville Shute, the English writer, Dos Passos, a shelf of Hemingway, hunting books. He bent over to open the bottom cupboard. That's where a man keeps the books he does not want the guests to see, Orlando figured. "What are you looking for?" a polite voice asked from behind.

Orlando jumped. "Oh," he said. "You must be Jennifer."

The girl of twelve looked amused. Her dark hair burned with auburn and her face showed a precocious intelligence. "I am Jennifer," she said. She stood up and put out her hand. "Did you have a good trip with my mother?" She said it in such a way that Orlando knew he was not the first man to become an interest in Esther's life. The child knew. She had a look in her eyes which was not only eternally womanly but showed a carnal knowledge. Also she was beautiful.

Now that Orlando had seen Jennifer's Titian beauty, he knew he had to paint both mother and daughter together. The mere thought of the aesthetic tension between such a sensual, radiant child and the somber sexual power of the mother made Orlando's fingers twitch to hold a brush. With his brush he could feel both bodies, both breasts and groins, the fall of the velvet dresses. The very folds yielding to the hairs of his brush gave him orgasmic pleasure. He must do it. His eyes stared at her unwaveringly.

Seeing the look on his face, Jenny blushed. "What?" she asked, a little nervously.

"What what?" he laughed.

Jenny giggled. "Why are you staring at me that way?"

"Because you're so beautiful," he said. "Has anyone ever told you that before?"

Jenny laughed. "J. J. Lipstone. When we grow up, he wants to marry me." She looked at Orlando. "Do you think I should get married or go to college like mommy says I must? My mother wants me to be the Governor of this state. Senator de Chavez is my godfather, and Marquita is my godmother. She's the Governor's wife." Jenny made a face. "But the Governor's Mansion isn't nearly as nice as ours."

"You can always build a mansion of your own, you know." Orlando was intrigued. Obviously it had never crossed this child's mind that she should not speak openly with an adult or that she shouldn't be the first woman to inhabit the Governor's Mansion. He had to give Esther credit. She'd done her job well. Jenny, he could see, had the powerful business drive of her father and ruthlessness from her mother. Still, there was a further quality in her which gave Orlando the feeling that under the exterior, there was a genuinely nice, warm little woman. Hopefully, Orlando thought, some man would love her enough to find it for her. Orlando knew many young girls old before their time . . .

"There you are, Jennifer. I've been looking everywhere for you." Esther felt flushed and guilty. A quick trip to find Nanny, and she carried a long flat box in her arms. "I've just been checking on the baby. Here," she said, handing over the box. "I bought you this in Venice, darling."

Jenny opened the box eagerly and then a familiar pain shot through her heart. The obviously expensive, but definitely sensible, dress was just the sort of thing Nanny would choose. Her pretty and elegant mother would never dream of buying such a thing. "Thank you, mother," she said. "It's very nice."

"I'm so glad you like it. Come and give me a kiss. My, you're taller. I must talk to Nanny about a diet, dear."

"I don't want to diet."

Esther's manicured eyebrows flew up like startled blackbirds. "Darling," she said. "You'll have to diet all your life. All women diet. Don't they, Orlando?"

Orlando, used to finding a diplomatic middle ground between his mother and his grandmother, agreed. "But then," he said, giving a compassionate glance at the girl, "she is perfect now . . . and if she doesn't put on another single pound ever again— maybe a curve here and a curve there—then she'll be the exception." He smiled sweetly at Esther. "Really," he said. "You are to be congratulated, Esther. You really have produced a lovely daughter, and I want to paint you both together. So not only I will have the pleasure of your creation, but the whole world will share it with me."

Esther looked bemused. There goes hours alone with him, she thought. But the idea of a mother-daughter portrait . . . She could see it. The Tate Gallery maybe. The Musée des Beaux Arts in Paris. For once, Boston did not cross her mind. "All right," she said. "Come along, Orlando. There is time for a quick tour of my gallery. I hang the paintings myself. Run along, Jennifer. Nanny's waiting for dinner in the nursery."

"Can't I have dinner with you tonight? I haven't seen you for ages."

"Don't be silly, dear. It's my first night back. I need some grown-up time."

Jenny watched her mother's proud back leave the room with Orlando trailing behind her. Locked away in her heart, Jenny felt a terrible power stirring. She knew all about what adults did. From time to time, she had allowed some of the less drunken artists in the guesthouse to run their fingers through her legs. And then, once she realized she had the power not only to tell but also to have the men jailed by the police (and what if her father ever found out? Why, he'd go positively berserk), she recognized that she was in possession of a great and powerful secret. She liked Orlando very much. He was amusing and handsome.

To her father, Jenny was more precious than the diamonds he had given her mother. He treated Jenny like a princess. When Esther was away, George's business friends crowded into the house. Things that were not allowed in Esther's reign happened then: chewing tobacco, spitting into the virgin spitoons and playing pool and poker for money. "Don't tell your mother, will you, darlin'?" George said. Jenny loved those rough New Mexican men. They were the salt of the hard earth and they had endured years of effort. Now these men were rich enough to wear the best turquoise and the biggest gold rings, studded with gems. Their womenfolk stayed home. "Men's talk," George would say, patting Jenny on the head.

Even old Widow Joe (so named because he was alone and meaner than any widow that climbed the walls looking for a place to lay her spider's eggs), who owned the nextdoor cattle ranch, made eyes at Nanny, who giggled and turned red. "One of these days," Widow Joe would say, "I'm going to take my horsewhip, put you over my saddle, and take you home for my wife."

"Not till Jenny is old enough to do without me," Nanny would retort.

Jenny sighed. Now, with Esther back, the tone must change. George's friends felt uncomfortable with Esther's formal entertaining. They knew that when Esther was home and giving a party, they could not drink their usual beer. Only George was allowed to drink beer at Esther's gatherings, for he always embarrassed her if she tried to force him to drink anything else. Esther's idea of entertaining consisted of elaborate dances and dinner parties. Jenny loved jazz but she had to confine the sound to her room. Esther had so far permitted only classical dancing. Jenny was allowed to pass the drinks with the servants and to sit in on the dinners to hear the politics for her eventual career. Then she had to curtsy goodnight to each guest, kiss her mother on the cheek, say goodnight to her father and leave.

With her mother back, Jenny knew she would have to take on again the role of Good Jenny: Esther's polite, poised, well-bred daughter. But a deeper feeling arose in her. Still the child hurt by her mother's inability to love her warmly, she knew that Esther, for all her attentiveness to Jenny's education and etiquette, could never really love her as she longed to be loved. Too much distance had grown between them. There was the new baby in the family. There were Esther's trips abroad. And now there was a man. Jenny, however, wanted something for herself.

Standing by herself in the library, she made a decision. She would fight her mother and win. Before her mother's eyes she would remain the perfect Jenny; in her secret world she would get what she wanted. She would not let her mother have Orlando. The attention of this new man was the something she wanted. Orlando was going to be hers to love.

⚬ৡ *CHAPTER 43* ৡ⚬

Nanny must go. Esther decided she wanted the house to herself. Maria, Ah Ling, and the other servants might gossip behind their hands but they were just servants. Nanny was a cut above all that and if she saw Orlando and Esther together too much, there was a danger that she would object on Jenny's behalf. For months before the last pregnancy, whenever the noise in the dining room wafted upstairs outside Nanny's window, she would march downstairs, resplendent in her thick English dressing gown with her gray hair streaming behind her head and grab Jenny's arm. "Time for little ladies to be in bed," she would say. Sniffing loudly, she frog-marched a reluctant Jenny out of the room.

Jenny, Esther knew, would make a fuss when Nanny was got rid of. Send Jennifer off to Etta's for a few weeks, Esther reckoned. That'll stop the row. By the time Jenny comes back, the blood-letting will be over. Anyway, thought Esther, Maria will still be here to take care of Max. The baby's sad, shrill cries never brought sympathy to Esther's heart. They sent only icy shivers of irritation up her spine.

Jenny was thrilled to hear she was to spend two weeks with her Aunt Etta. She loved her aunt with a passion and her love was returned in a singular fashion. Alone with the secret agony of her own loneliness, Etta, over the years, had gradually closed the gaping wound left by the deaths of Tom and her child. She had filled it with the love she felt for her niece. On the day Jenny was born, Etta always remembered, she had held the baby in her arms and looked into Jenny's face and promised the child her undying love. When Jenny was sad, she went to Etta. Nora and Danny spoiled her dreadfully but Etta really understood Jenny. Underneath the precociously adult little girl, Etta had recognized from very early on, there was the real Jenny: quiet, shy, and rather withdrawn. Jenny was so close to her heart that Etta had only to look at her face and she knew at once what was troubling her.

In her own way, Etta was aware of Jenny's double life, of how different life was at Mandalay and at the ranch. But Etta paid a largely silent tribute to this awareness. She knew life with Esther was not easy for the girl. Still, she hoped, if she could give Jenny her own love and caring, then perhaps she would grow to know what real love was.

This visit took place in the heat of the summer, the bark-scorching and earth-blistering heat of New Mexico. The mountains stared at the town until the aspens turned yellow on the slopes. The frowning mountains softened in the autumn, waiting for a cooling mantle of snow but, for now, there was no compromise from the heat except, it seemed to Jenny, in Etta's garden. Etta had one great weakness. She took plants from anywhere she could. While Jenny was used to the formal loveliness of her own gardens, she was entranced by Etta's vision.

As the car pulled into the drive of Etta's ranch, Jenny leaned forward and opened the window. The smell of roses gave her such delight she fell back into the deep leather seats with a sigh. All around the white framed porch, Etta had planted hollyhocks. They stood tall and poised, serene in their great beauty. Jenny threw herself into Etta's warm, plump arms. "Hello, darling," Etta hugged her niece. She also hugged the secret of Nanny's departure to her heart. Let the child have a good time for the next few weeks, she thought. "Come in. Grandma and Grandpa are here waiting for you."

Jenny felt herself relax in the tranquility of the ranch. Her thoughts of Orlando—troubling thoughts which came to her at night when she tried to sleep—could wait. For now, she was free to enjoy innocence again, the innocence of her life with Etta. What pleased Jenny most was the calm order of the house. Everything had a place, and there was a place for everything in the universe. Here, unlike her home—where Esther's whims dictated life—a settled routine began and ended the day. Here, the candles were still lit on a Friday night. Etta, unlike Esther, still considered herself a Jew. In fact the Jensen family, except for George, no longer even attended mass at the cathedral. But to arrive today, on a Friday, Jenny knew what to expect.

She ran into the house and made for the kitchen. There, Grandma Nora stood at the stove basting a succulent, freshly plucked chicken. Grandpa Danny was teasing Nora. "I'll buy you a fresh chicken from Kaune's next time. All day you've been plucking."

Nora released Jenny from her embrace and pushed the child toward her grandfather. "Doesn't taste the same, does it, Jenny? You tell him about your grandmother's chicken."

Jenny laughed. "It's the best chicken in the world, Grandpa. Even better than Ah Ling's, and he's the best cook in Santa Fe, the world and the universe." Laughter, humor and love surrounded the Gottsteins and their beloved girl all through the Sabbath dinner.

The meal over, the moon high in the sky, safe in Reuben's dressing room in a little, white four-poster bed, Jenny could hear Etta's comforting voice downstairs. She fell asleep. Here with her aunt, Jenny felt safe in a way she was never safe with her mother. Her mother did not love her like Aunt Etta did. For her mother, she was a doll to be fretted, scolded, and put away. Later in life, her mother had plans for her which included attending Wellesley and graduating *summa cum laude*. Then, of course, there would come her political future.

But for the next two weeks, there was applepicking, gardening. Jenny's favorite occupation, apart from reading, was picking the evening salad. The next day, clasping a big brown bowl made of thick, cream ceramic, she wandered into the vegetable garden. This was the first day of magic with her aunt. All day they talked. Etta walked her niece all over the flower garden. "Look," she said. "I got that cutting from the beds around the Capitol Building."

"Auntie," Jenny protested, "you'll get arrested if you're not careful."

Etta looked down fondly at Jenny. "No judge in Santa Fe is going to put a forty-two-year-old woman in jail for digging up a flower. Anyway, all the judges know me. I'll confess my sin and then do it again." She paused. The thought of sin and confession always reminded her of uncle Ben. In the thick of the winter, he had died alone in an alley, clutching an empty bottle.

The shadow left her face after a time and she smiled again. "Look, Jenny. See over there? That's my new dovecot. I have six young fantails up there. Here." She put her hands into her apron pocket. "Give them some corn."

With a cartwheel and a clap of wings, three of the doves alighted upon Jenny's arms and shoulders. Jenny stood still, awed by their presence. Etta looked at the child and hoped she could protect her from life's more dangerous moments.

"Let's go, darling," she said.

Now, dreaming in the gasp of the hottest day of summer, Jenny stood by the lettuce bed. The iceberg lettuce, swollen, tumescent and green, disturbed Jenny. The heavy fragrance of the garden air, the constant droning of the bees and the cicadas, the heat of the day that made her shirt stick to her armpits, all churned an uneasiness within Jenny. She was becoming, she knew, a woman. The onset of her periods, as Etta had explained, had signaled her body's growing up. Dealing monthly with her womanhood, as Etta had instructed her, had felt odd, almost a pretense, a child's game of playing grown-up. But now her mind, too, was calling her to follow the path to maturity, upon which her body was already set.

Jenny breathed deeply. Mixed with the smell of the garden, she smelled her own sweat from under her arms, no longer the odorless sweat of a child. And Jenny was surprised to find herself thinking of Orlando. Inexplicably, she wanted to be held by him, to be loved.

Well, she told herself with a young girl's sigh, that would have to wait. More immediate matters were at hand. The evening's salad had to be picked.

Another day gone, another night fled and tomorrow was safely predictable. The two weeks passed by like an oasis in Jenny's life. Aunt Etta was her oasis in a life which seemed turbulent and out of control.

When Jenny ran to find Nanny, upon her return, the world felt completely out of control. "Where is she?" she screamed at her mother, distraught to the point of forgetting her usual restraint. "Where is she?"

"Calm down, Jennifer. Do calm down." Esther frowned. "You're much too old to have a Nanny anyway."

"Has she gone back to England?"

Another frown crossed Esther's brow. Jenny realized that there must have been a scene. Esther rarely frowned because she believed frowning created wrinkles. "No," Esther said. "Nanny did not want to go back to England. She went to stay with that awful man they call Widow Joe." She pursed her lips. "She says she's going to marry him. Did you ever think of anything so absurd? Nanny left you a note and says you can visit her whenever you want . . ."

"Today?" Jenny said eagerly.

"Don't be silly, child. You're always so extreme."

Jenny hung her head and looked sideways at Orlando. He, lolling on the sofa in the drawing room, caught her eye and winked. The loss of Nanny stabbed Jennifer straight to the heart but she knew the futility of arguing any further with her mother. At least Orlando was still there. And from Orlando, Jennifer believed, would come comfort.

Slowly, with a sensual roll of her hips, Jennifer walked out of the library. Why, Esther thought, do I feel as if I just lost an argument? "Let's play tennis, Orlando, before the light goes." Esther always thought she looked best in her Yves St Laurent sweatsuit. Very me, she thought, on the way out through the garden.

❦ *CHAPTER 44* ❧

Jennifer watched her mother carefully that summer. Sexually she had much to think about. Caught between childhood and womanhood, but already awakened to orgasm by the molesters among her mother's friends, she was more aware than most girls of the power she held over Orlando. Passing him in the corridor, she brushed against him. When he sat in the huge, wicker armchairs on the porch, she sauntered by in tight, white shorts—her long, brown legs tapering down to fine ankles, her feet slipped into neat, navy-blue espadrilles, her T-shirt flat against her chest, the promise of breasts just starting to come.

Orlando lay and watched with amusement. Suddenly, when she least expected it, he would swoop down on her and tickle her until she cried out in ecstasy, throw her in the air, catch her, and then cradle her. "Really, Orlando." Esther was sharp one late-August morning. "If I didn't know you better, I'd think you had a crush on the child."

"But you don't know me better, do you? Anyway, I want to start painting you both tomorrow." Orlando and Esther were wandering naked around the jacuzzi in the pool-room. Esther knew that George was out of town. What she did not know was that Jenny was at her usual station at the top of the stairs. "That is why you find me so endlessly fascinating," Orlando continued, "because you hardly know me." Orlando knew where Jennifer was. As a child he too had played the onlooker in his family. He had watched out of his bedroom window in a jealous rage when his mother went skinny-dipping on the beach with other men.

"Let's go. I'm tired," Esther complained. "I've been shopping all day." She stood up and waded to the end of the pool and began to climb the shallow, marble steps.

Slowly facing Jennifer, Orlando stood up, slim and perfectly formed. He had very little hair, either under his arms or around his genitals. Jenny sat with her chin in her hands and grinned.

Nothing noteworthy happened until early December. Decorously, Jenny sat on a chair with Esther behind her for an hour each day while, equally decorously, Orlando drew and painted a mother-daughter portrait. "You can't see my legs," Esther complained.

"We don't care about legs, do we, darling?" he replied but he painted Jenny's legs, long, slim, and so smooth he wanted to smother them in kisses. Esther was cross. She broke up the sitting.

Jenny grinned. She did a lot of smiling. So did

Orlando. Jenny, at first unsure whether or not her feelings were reciprocated, watched for months the affection and love growing in Orlando's eyes. Now she knew all she had to do was choose the time and the place.

The garden was covered in snow, birds' footprints and rabbit droppings. Esther was furious. She had flu. She had the virus so badly she was confined to her room. Orlando absolutely refused to visit her. "I hate people who are sick," he explained patiently on the intercom. "I'll send you flowers. I'll write you poems. I'll even draw you a funny sketch. But I can't bear sick people. Your nose will be red and you'll sniff. Besides, you don't want me to catch flu, do you?"

Jenny was amused. No one disobeyed her mother except Orlando. George hated his beloved wife to be ill. He fussed like an outraged hen, his face red with worry. Finally, Esther ordered him to leave for Dallas. "Please, George," she pleaded. "Stop fussing and go to work." Reluctantly he left for the week. Jenny watched him go and then realized, as he walked through the door, that her security was gone, her father who loved her unconditionally.

She felt frightened but excited. She skipped off to catch the school bus which grumbled around Tesuque picking up the children of the rich and transporting them to the school which only accepted students after a rigorous vetting. Still largely the stranger, even among children of her own age, Jenny drifted through her days at school, impatient to return home to the good-humored joking and teasing to be found in Orlando's company.

The sittings continued without Esther. Shadows

merged in the drawing room. The Tiffany lamps showered greens and blues. The fire in the grate gave off fumes of piñon, juniper and oak. The ashes were piled high at the back of it because Maria had been given a week off. Orlando decided tonight that he would cook. Ah Ling was pleased. He needed a night off to organize the eventual overthrow of the rich white Anglos who were slowly moving to Santa Fe and buying up vast tracts of land, pushing prices beyond the limit that a cook's salary would ever stretch to for getting his wife a home. Ah Ling was a clever revolutionary. He watched and waited. Tonight he was going to a house in Chimayo where the post-revolutionaries had their meetings. He left Mandalay after serving Esther her dinner—rice and fish, as the doctor ordered. Esther ate very little. She was too ill to care.

With Nanny gone, it was Maria who now tended baby Max. He, still unwanted by his mother, lived like a small prisoner in the nursery. Maria, for her week away from Mandalay, had taken Max with her, knowing she could not leave the baby alone in the house with no Nanny and its mother sick in bed. Pushing aside her dinner tray and rolling on her side in bed, Esther did not think of Max or, for that matter, of Jenny. All she wanted was to get some rest.

Night fell on the great house. Orlando stood at his easel. The air hung heavy and thick between the man and the girl. Jenny decided the time was ripe, ripe for her first willing play for love. She sat looking at Orlando, her liquid eyes shining with permission. He stood, his groin waiting to explode. They waited.

Jenny decided that she should make the first move. Quietly she stood up and stretched her body sylphlike, her feet shod in ballet shoes. She wore black tights, over which she had pulled a pink, sun-faded T-shirt. Her graceful hands above her head, she arched her back. "I'll have a look at how you're doing," she said. The words from her mouth felt heavy. They felt as if they dropped like lead pellets onto the floor and lay there, bright silver, reflecting the firelight. The fires in Orlando's eyes were brighter.

Jenny stood beside him. She could smell the musk of her own sweat. On him, she could smell the familiar musty smell of a man in heat. She could see the bulge in his thin cotton jeans. He wore a white shirt with short sleeves and a round neck. Jenny was tall for her age. She put her still-sun-brown arms around his neck. She laid her auburn head upon his chest. "Kiss me, Orlando," she said with a tremble in her voice. "I want you to kiss me now."

With an unbearable dread, overpowered by an irresistible longing, Orlando's mouth opened upon hers. With a sense of a swirling vortex opening up under his feet, Orlando lifted Jenny and laid her on the huge, black leather sofa. He removed the slippers from her feet. Gently he pulled down her tights and with a sigh of pleasure he exposed the fold between her legs, innocent of hair but deadly in desire. The smooth body, still too young to be as frightening as the body of a woman, thrilled him. Slowly he lifted the pink T-shirt, and Jenny lay naked before him. Her eyes concentrated like a cat, she watched him remove his clothes. Finally he lay beside her, his fingers gently caressing her twin pink-flower nipples. Slowly he ran his hands over her eager body. "Faster," she said.

"You've done this before?" he asked incredulously.

Jenny laughed a bitter note. "This is the first time I've had a choice," she said. The mature woman left her face for a moment and Orlando saw the very hurt twelve-year-old.

"My God," he stopped and shook his head. "I can't do this," he said.

"Yes." She stared him in the eye, her own eyes steady. "You can." Then she laughed and Jenny, the woman-child, tickled him.

Orlando laughed as the young, lively fingers danced upon his neck, under his arms, down his ribs, across his belly. He squirmed like a child himself as waves of titillating tingles raised the invisible hairs along his bare skin. Within minutes, the tickling returned to stroking, and the stroking stoked the fire until Jenny took him in her mouth.

Satisfied and secure in the empty house, they walked to the pool and lay in its warm embrace.

Suddenly, the peace was shattered by the sharp, jagged sound of the telephone. "Where are you?" Esther demanded down the telephone's intercom line. "Where the hell are you?" Her voice, still hoarse from a fevered sleep, was irritable.

"Just having a swim."

"Jenny's not in her bedroom. I just tried her on the intercom."

"No, she's here. We're just having a late-night swim. Jenny couldn't get to sleep. She's been sitting for me like a good girl. So after she's had a swim, I'll make her a snack. And then I'll send her to bed." He winced as Esther sniffed loudly. "Don't do that, darling. It's a dreadful sound."

"Well." Esther was mollified. "I'm going to get up tomorrow."

"I shouldn't," Orlando advised. "Don't rush it. You'll relapse. Good night, dear. I'll call you in the morning. Okay?"

Esther put the phone down beside her bed. Something was wrong. She fell asleep.

As Orlando reached for a towel, he noticed how fast his shaking heart was beating within his chest.

Once dried, Orlando and Jenny pulled on their clothes and repaired to the kitchen. Ah Ling carried a good stock of wines for his dishes. He particularly liked to cook fish with a good Taittinger. There was always a bottle in the refrigerator with a silver spoon upended in the bottle to trap the bubbles.

"Champagne?" Orlando was nervous. He fought off a huge feeling of guilt. Child-molesting was not a crime he had ever considered committing. While he knew he was not guilty of initiating the loss of Jenny's innocence, he felt he had perpetuated the crime. He was still tremblingly aware that his orgasm was more intensely felt and more profoundly moving than any he had experienced before. It seemed to have come from a different part of himself, innocently lying on the beach in Portugal. This half-woman, half-cunning child, held him and his fate in the palm of her little pink hand and in the depths of her lovely, moist, soft mouth. This child, now looking at him through her gray eyes with her hair wet and dripping, could make him not only a prisoner in her life but also a prisoner in real life and a social pariah. The thought of the power she had over him gave him a curious sexual thrill.

Jenny watched through narrow eyes. She liked Orlando. The sex itself was only a means to an end: the power was pure bliss. Now she, Jenny, was in control—her mother, defeated and impotent. And Orlando, she thought, loved her. "Let's have a toast," she said sweetly, glass in hand. She stood, secure in her beauty as a woman, her power as a child and the world of money which cemented and fused her life. "To my future," she said and raised the glass.

Orlando raised his. "May you always have what you want."

Jenny sipped the champagne. "Ugh," she said. "It's gross. Would you mind getting me some Kool Aid?"

Orlando was glad to see the twelve-year-old return. "Okay," he said. "I'm off to bed." He stood awkwardly, unsure whether to kiss her good night avuncularly on the head or loverly on the mouth. He shrugged, adding, "I'm tired."

"I'll bet you are," Jenny said. She kissed him on the mouth but without passion, a child's kiss of affection and warmth. "Good night," she said and made a mock punch to his stomach. "Last one upstairs is a rotten egg."

They both raced up the stairs laughing. Jenny was well-pleased with herself. She lay in her big mahogany bed. Then, for a moment, she wished it was her little bed at Aunt Etta's house. Everybody has to grow up, she reminded herself firmly.

Orlando could not sleep. Normally, with a large amount of champagne buzzing about his head, he slept well whatever the perverse pleasure of the evening. But tonight, he lay for a long time trying not to think of what had just happened. Then he tried thinking of Venice and his old friend Julie.

The night hours limped to 2:00 A.M. and he suddenly felt the urge to telephone her, to confess. He quietly got out of bed and walked to the window of the guest room. The moon hung over the garden casting shadows over the snow-covered English lawn. This time Orlando did not marvel at the black, deep, star-studded night. He searched for Capella, his favorite star. He tried to sort out some of his confusion. "First," he said softly, "I shouldn't have done it."

But, said the little demon who caused him so much trouble all his life and seemed to live on his left shoulder, *you enjoyed it.*

"Well, that's true, but she is only a child."

More of a woman, really, the demon continued with his usual impeccable logic. *Anyway, someone else was responsible for seducing her in the first place.*

"I know," Orlando agreed. "She's no innocent. But why do I feel so disgusted with myself?"

You're growing older and so is your conscience.

Orlando felt physically sick. Now, the passion spent and the event relived, he felt not only self-disgust but also horror that he, a fully grown man, could be seduced by a girl of twelve. Suddenly, the true meaning of what he had done hit him with a blinding force: Orlando Machado was a child molester. Yesterday morning he was sexually delinquent. To that he would agree. "But no," Orlando argued, "I am not a child molester by nature."

He picked up the phone. He needed to confess. He was in a great deal of pain. The loss of her innocence—and his—made his hand shake. Nights with sailors or patrons who kept him had made him sick with self-disdain before, but now at 3.00 A.M., the hour passing so slowly, he trembled with sorrow. "Is that you, Julie?" He knew it was mid-morning in

Venice. She would know that it was still the middle of the night for him, but he knew he could count on her not being surprised. He often telephoned her at odd hours.

"Yes." There was a very thin rasp of a reply.

"Are you all right, Julie?"

"No," Julie said. "Orlando, I'm dying. I'm alone. Everyone else I know is dead."

"I'll come. I'll get a plane now . . . Don't die, Julie."

"I'll wait, Orlando. I'll try and wait."

"I have to talk to you," Orlando hesitated. "I've done something dreadful. I don't know if I'll ever forgive myself."

"We're all sinners," Julie said slowly. "Me the most."

Orlando knew he had to go quickly. He had to leave this house with its two women locked in mortal combat. He did not want to see the look on Jenny's face when she had breakfast with her mother. Such a battle between an ambitious mother and a sexually powerful daughter was a fight to the death, and he knew who the survivor would be. He also knew that he was a casualty, one of many, in the war that would rage for years to come, unnoticed by George Jensen in the multimillion dollar house which lay under the stars that night.

Orlando began to pack hurriedly and with a real fear that George might return unexpectedly to hear Jenny announce the outrageous events of the night. Her father would undoubtedly take his shotgun and blow Orlando off the face of the earth. His suitcase in one hand, his shoes in the other, he crept out of the house. Only the two women almost finished in his painting—one standing, the other sitting, a pair of brown eyes and a pair of gray eyes—watched him leave. He ran the last two feet to his car and was gone.

On his pillow he left a note saying he had been called away urgently:

> Julie is ill. Will finish the portrait some day but have urgent work in a gallery in Barcelona. Forgive me.
>
> Orlando

Esther was absolutely furious. "What the hell is all this about?" she screamed at Jenny. "I go to bed for a week and he leaves. You didn't fight with him, did you, Jennifer?"

Jenny lowered the lids of her eyes like drawbridges. It was a trick she practiced many years ago. This way, her mother, who could be a mind reader at times, could not see into her soul. This way she could also hide her amusement at her mother's defeat. Let her think we had an argument if she wants to, thought Jenny. She'll never know the truth. A sadness, too, was hidden in those eyes, for the child had been left by a man whom she believed to be an ally in her world. And now life would return to the strict regimen of Esther's world.

"Well, Jennifer, don't just stand there. Answer me."

Jenny shrugged her shoulders. "We had a swim and a snack—" With a twinge of fear, she remembered the champagne bottle.

"I'll go and ask Ah Ling." Esther stormed into the kitchen. "Ah Ling? Did you notice anything wrong last night?"

Ah Ling looked at his furious employer and then at

Jenny. His deep, intelligent eyes signaled Jenny. She was safe. "No, Madame," he said. "Nothing wrong. Mr Machado had dinner, I see Missy go to bed, and lock up myself."

Jenny's breath left her body. She knew Ah Ling had thrown the champagne bottle away in the dumpster behind the house. Ah Ling smiled. "Is Madame better now? Very good."

Esther was still angry. She marched into the drawing room. "Your shoes, Jennifer. Your shoes. Why do you always leave your mess about this place, huh?" As Jenny ran past her mother to pick up the offending ballet shoes, Esther raised her hand and caught Jenny's arm. "You're not going anywhere till I tell you to go." She slapped Jenny's face as hard as she could. "I'm going to knock some sense into you even if I have to kill you."

Jenny stood still. She could feel her cheek flush with pain. But, by now, mother and daughter were too far down the road of ambivalence and competition for Jenny to cry and let her mother see her in a weak moment. She had vowed long ago never to allow her mother access to her warm heart which was alive only because her grandmother and aunt loved her. Only there, in their houses, could she ever be vulnerable. Esther, in her anger toward her beautiful daughter, resented the girl her freedom, her money, her father who loved her. And now Esther's one source of perverse pleasure was gone. Now she was left with her husband George, a man she did not love, a man who bored her, who was not worthy of Esther's great talent. And Julie, her link to the Europe of her youth, was ill—maybe dying. "Jennifer," she said coldly. "Go to your room."

Alone in her room, Jenny had time for regrets. Regretting was far more painful than the slap her mother had just administered. Jenny was used to pain. Pain was a constant companion walking by her side, another girl who grinned and smirked every time her mother wounded her. Some days, Jenny felt she was a walking, open sore filled with puss which oozed and smelled of decay and death. Sometimes the burden of being unloved by her mother seemed unbearable. Sometimes, in Santa Fe, when she saw a woman and her girl-child at a soda fountain, smiling and giggling at a shared joke, her eyes filled with tears. A slight, golden haze of happiness enveloped the pair. Jenny had no golden haze of her own, just a deep, dark hole of pain and hurt. Alone, away from the accusation of her mother's stare, Jenny let her tears run freely down her cheeks.

Now, Orlando had abandoned her. Her female power had no chains to bind him to her. She was still only twelve years old. But the years ahead would bring her true maturity and in those years, she promised herself, she would be free of her mother. And some day, she prayed, she would love a man who would not leave her.

George was home at the end of the week, and Esther had plans to make George so happy she could wheedle some money out of him for a trip to Boston. She had seen in a catalogue that a rare fireplace and dining table with eight matching chairs were for sale at an auction. The dining table was from England, Regency period, elegant, and just right for her dining room. She wanted that table, and in order to visit Boston she must shop for a new wardrobe. Maria and the Salvation Army were always most blessed on these occasions. Esther gave away all her discarded clothes. Etta was too fat to wear her sister's clothes and Nora too unfashionable. So Maria delighted her young husband with a wardrobe fit for a queen. When they lay in bed making love, Maria's husband joked about the elegant lace nightie which lay in his arms. Maria smiled.

Maria knew all about Esther. She made it her business because she reported everything to the Party. Her father was the head man, and Maria resented Esther with all her money, her rich house, her private schooling for her daughter. Maria did not resent Jenny. She felt sorry for the poor little thing whose mother's sharp temper was often evident when Maria was there. If Esther stormed off after making a scene, Maria comforted Jenny. "Poor little one," she said. "If you lived in the Barrio, the social workers would come and take you away. Not on the North Side. Not in Tesuque." The social workers left the rich to their own desires.

But Maria could wait. Her father had plans. Even if he died before the time was ripe, there were younger men waiting—eager, like dogs, with their eyes shining and their tongues dripping, eager to fight the careless, the rich and the idle who usurped the city of Santa Fe.

While Maria dreamed, George was delighted. The trip to Dallas had been long and arduous. He lay on his first night home in his own big bath and watched his dainty, naked wife climb elegantly into the opposite end. That night, he lay his head in her arms, his lips on her breast, and he reckoned he was the luckiest man in the world. What other man had such a beautiful, intelligent, attractive wife who loved him and had sex with him whenever he liked? Well, almost whenever he liked. But she was delicate, he reminded himself. Esther's eyes, tight shut, decided that two thousand dollars was an excellent sum to charge at the Boston stores. Maybe a visit to the old restaurant, Emilio's . . . Perhaps Black Lewis had retired.

The next morning she woke, horrified. The dream had been a premonition. She picked up the morning paper which lay outside her door. George was snoring loudly. "Look, George," she said. "How awful." The headline on the front page of the Albuquerque Journal read:

BOSTON GANGLAND LEADER KILLED IN GUNFIGHT

Underneath the headline was a picture of Jimmy Delgado, a very dead Jimmy Delgado. Beside him lay Chi and Black Lewis.

"What? Hmm, what?" George was struggling out of a deep sleep.

"Nothing. Sorry, darling. Just some people I used to know a long time ago."

Esther got dressed and went downstairs to the drawing room. She put on the radio quietly. She called Ah Ling and ordered tea and toast, English style. She put her head back against the black sofa and shuddered inside. Middle age galloped toward her. Jimmy Delgado, like Julie Youngblood, was part of a past which had been her golden years. Now, that dream gone, Boston was like a theater with the lights suddenly out.

Esther lifted the telephone and had the operator

place an overseas call to Julie's palazzo in Venice. The line rang for several minutes. No one answered. Slowly, Esther placed the receiver back in its cradle. She held her face in her hands and wept, mourning for Jimmy, mourning for Julie, mourning for her own lost youth.

CHAPTER 45

The late 1950s hit Santa Fe like a tornado. The quiet little town reeled as the beatniks surged into the square, turning Santa Fe into a haven modeled on their mecca of Greenwich Village. They squatted dirty on benches and they howled Bob Dylan songs out of tune. They raided the shops with their checkbooks, having been paid to stay out of sight by embarrassed rich fathers and mothers back East. Private sex became public. Dirty books and obscene poetry were considered a religion, and the young people of Santa Fe were contaminated the most.

Jenny, beautiful, rich, talented Jenny Jensen, felt the world changing around her and, to her, the change came to signify freedom, freedom from her mother's rule. Orlando's departure had marked for Jenny the end of a life of outward subservience to her mother. Entering her teenage years, she transformed her life into one of open warfare against Esther. Recognizing her own power to be at least equal to Esther's (at the end of the day, had she now won

Orlando from her mother?) she no longer kept her will secret. She grew to do as she pleased, keep the company she chose, and Esther soon learned that the willfulness she had earlier discerned in her daughter was now completely out of hand.

Gradually Esther turned her dreams and ambitions from her daughter to her son. Max grew through the messy visceral years of infancy with Maria loving him as her own child. George, during the infrequent moments when he was not at the office, or away on a business trip, or relaxing in the evenings after days of overwork, doted over the son who, he was sure, would someday run his many expanding business ventures. When, however, Max outgrew his nappies, bottles and his inarticulate gibberings, Esther realized, as if opening her eyes for the first time, that in her family's midst was a beautiful child with blond hair and blue eyes; a quiet, well-mannered, happy, small boy whose bright face would peer smilingly over the edge of the dinner table. Here, Esther began to see, was her own male creation whom she could mold—the unfastidious years of cleaning up gone—to suit her dreams, an eager admirer, her own little man who would possess, she would ensure, none of George's more rough and boorish mannerisms.

To Max, his mother's affection was a treat. His first love remained Maria but when the beautiful woman—almost a stranger—who had hardly set an expensively shod foot in his nursery began to smile at him, pat his golden head and occasionally hug him to her fragrantly perfumed body, he welcomed the new attention in his own quiet, good-natured, uncomplaining way. After his father's attempts to show him how to hold a baseball bat or to give him a ride on the big swivel-chair behind the big desk in the big office at the Phoenix Company, his mother would take Max aside and straighten his collar. Then she would say, "Oh, don't listen to your father. You're not going to grow up just to become some baseball player. There are finer things in life waiting for you. And you certainly won't become a boring old businessman." Max was only barely aware of the look of sadness in his father's eye, as Esther walked the boy off by the hand.

George looked on helplessly through it all. How could he stop his wife from turning his son into a mama's boy? She was, after all, Max's mother, and George was glad to see her begin to love him. And what could he do about Jenny's increasingly outrageous behavior? Yes, from time to time he tried to put his foot down, but Esther only dismissed his efforts. "She's always had too much of a mind of her own," became Esther's habitual reply. Never mind, George comforted himself. It's just a phase. She'll outgrow it. His patience and love, he was sure, would triumph in the end over Jennifer's rebellion. In the mean time, he carried on with his diligent work as family financier.

As a teenager, Jenny came to regard her mother as the real-life counterpart to the Queen of Hearts from the Lewis Carroll story which Nanny had read to her years ago in the nursery. She saw Max as a poor duped prince, lapping up the Queen's whim as a complacent kitten drinks milk from a dish. Still, Jenny could not help but feel a real fondness for Max, so contented was his nature and so simple his needs. And George, Jenny believed, was the king who sat on a smaller seat beside the Queen's mighty throne. For all the conciliatory noises he made, for all his well-intentioned good cheer he was, in his own way, the family fool, the jester of the court, the laughingstock. A complicity spread through the family that George was not to be taken seriously. The sovereignty of Esther, Queen of Hearts Esther, was known to be uncontested by the effeteness of the King.

In Jenny's mind there was no doubt as to her own role. She was the rebel, the revolutionary who would not tacitly accept the omnipotence of the Queen. With each of her daily actions, each of her wild gestures of insubordination, she tried the Monarch's authority. And she knew she could count on her father to slip her—out of guilt—the odd twenty dollar bill to spend with the new friends she made, to provide her with reminders of his love despite her bad behavior.

At fifteen, her father gave her a Carmen Ghia, no pickup truck for his beloved, though rebellious, princess. At sixteen-and-a-half, she was picked up by the Santa Fe police for drunk driving and use of cocaine and marijuana. Two telephone calls and a check, and the policeman was told to let her go. George was angry but Jenny smiled prettily and promised, "I'll never do it again." What she meant was that she wouldn't drive her car. One of her many boyfriends could.

Esther, however, was not so easily won over, nor so content to accept Jenny's vows of improved behavior. Esther had had enough, her own will had been challenged too much. Using the drug-possession incident as her excuse, she persuaded George to send Jennifer to finish her high school education at a boarding school in New York state. "It'll be best this way," Esther explained. "They know how to bring a wild girl to heel." Her own mind was turned toward other dreams. Max, even at the age of five, showed promise at the piano. Indeed, he possessed a natural gift. And such talent cried out to be cultivated with lessons in technique, musical theory, and showmanship. At least one of her children, Esther told herself, would rise to prominence in the world and assume a high seat of fame.

Upon her return from high school at eighteen, George Jensen's daughter found the world to be a string of expensive pearls, each one there for the taking.

John Joseph Lipstone disapproved of Jenny's conduct. He was a year older than Jenny, gentle and kind—but a New Mexican boy. He thought mostly about horses, football and baseball. He chewed gum, wore a permanently grubby cap back to front and his face was a sunburst of freckles. He and Jenny were more like brother and sister. Really, J.J. bored Jenny. Her senses had been awakened by the probing hands of adult men and J.J. could not come close to giving her the same feelings. J.J. had first kissed Jenny when her front teeth were missing. Now he was appalled at what he saw. "Why'd you want to go to that silly old private school back East?" he said. "All you seem to do is take drugs and skip class."

"There's going to be a revolution," Jenny announced, back for the summer after graduating from the very private and very expensive Epsilon Community School. Suddenly Jenny was serious, her head still full of the exciting new theories she had discovered in the company of other rebels from wealthy families. "I learned all about it at school in our Social Affairs class. Do you know how many prostitutes are children?"

J.J. nodded. "Yeah," he said. "Dad says if your ma's a pro, chances are you'll turn out a pro, too. Look at Mabel from high school. She's turning tricks on the Plaza just like her mother."

"No, no, no. Don't they teach you anything at the University of New Mexico? Haven't any of your professors taught you a thing about social injustice, class discrimination, the wrongness of the world we live in?"

J.J. shrugged. "Some funny little guy with eyes like a ferret came to my dorm and asked me and Johnny Wheelright if we wanted to be commies. We threw him out. Johnny's the richest boy in New Mexico. He doesn't want to give all that stuff away. My dad's worked hard all his life. He's sitting on a fortune that'll be mine one day. I'm getting a Ferrari if I graduate *cum laude*, which I will."

"You don't understand, J.J. Really, you're just a country boy." Though frustrated by his evident incomprehension, a part of Jenny loved to tease J.J. She smiled to see the faded remnants of his freckles still lightly speckling the bridge of his nose. "Got a girl yet?"

"Nope." J.J. laughed. "I'm waiting for you to grow up, stop showing your panties and settle down."

She stretched in the early sun. They sat on the Plaza and watched people go by. Jenny shook her head. "I won't have to live like my mother or grandma or Etta. I'm a feminist," she announced.

J.J. blinked. "Oh no," he said. "We have those at school in Albuquerque. One thing going for them, they're all ugly, that's why they're feminists. But you don't hate men, do you, Jenny?"

Jenny laughed. "I love men and men love me, and women can do or be anything they like."

J.J. fell silent, letting the vigor of Jenny's words dissipate in the sunlit air. He looked at her seriously. The clothes she wore were disorderly and her jeans were frayed at the edges. But through the opening of her rumpled man's shirt he could see the smooth white skin between the roundness of her breasts. He noticed she wasn't wearing a bra. Looking sideways through her opened shirt, he saw the pink edge of a nipple. Her neck was slender, and the breeze innocently tossed a lock of her dark auburn hair across the neck's creaseless skin. In the simple beauty of her face, J.J. could still see a clean goodness which shone through, despite all her harsh talk and wild ideas. "Oh, Jenny," J.J. said, half-sighing. "This really isn't you talking, you know. Listen to yourself. All this talk about feminism and communism. None of it's you."

Hurt by his discarding of her newfound beliefs, but touched by the fondness in his voice, Jenny lowered her head. "Maybe you don't know me," she said. "I'm not sure I know myself any more."

"I know you." J.J. put his hand over hers. "I guess," he said with a small laugh, "I still think of you as the quiet girl grinding out good grades in the front of the class."

"I was silly, then." She shook her head. Her loose hair, J.J. noticed, fell beautifully around her face. "I didn't know I could run my own life. I tried to do all the right things just to please my mother. But—I don't know—maybe I could never really please her."

"And now you're trying to do all the wrong things just to bug your mother? Is that what you want?"

"Oh, J.J.," she said, an emotion between anger and despair in her voice. "How am I supposed to know what I want? I mean, you don't exactly have a lot of choice in my family. Just look at Max."

"Oh yeah, Max," said J.J., not terribly anxious to talk about Jenny's kid brother. J.J.'s thoughts were on Jenny alone. "How's Max doing these days?"

"Oh, he's just a typical six-year-old spoiled brat. Mom's spoiled him rotten lately, but then Dad spoils me." She paused. "Actually, that isn't really fair on Max. He's only six and already my mother hauls him around to more lessons than you could imagine. He has to take swimming lessons, karate lessons, fencing lessons and French lessons—on top of everything he has to do at school. Mom says it will make a Renaissance Man out of him. And he has his piano lessons."

"I hear he's pretty good," J.J. offered.

"Yes. Of course, he's only just started playing piano. But he really likes it. He sits there practicing for hours. Maybe it gives him a break from my mother. I don't know. And naturally Mom's already convinced that he has to be a world-famous musician."

"Mothers can be like that," J.J. said with a laugh.

"It isn't funny, J.J." Jenny was earnest. "I mean, in my family, you can't breathe without my mother telling you you're going to become famous for it. And I don't even know if I want to be famous for anything."

"Well, then. You don't have to be."

"That's easy for you to say. You said it yourself: you know what you'll do once you finish school. You'll go to work at your father's business. And some day the business will be yours. It isn't fair. You have your whole life planned out already."

"Yes, but . . ."

"But for me," Jenny continued, surprised to find how upset she felt, "it's different. My mother's always told me I'm supposed to become the Governor of this state. The first lady Governor." She pushed back the long hair which had blown into her eyes. "How am I supposed to know what I want to become? I don't even know what to do this summer. My mother thinks sending me away to school calmed me down. So now she's starting her plans to get me into politics. She's arranged with Senator de Chavez, my godfather, for me to have a summer job as a go-for in his office. I don't know. And then in the fall she wants me to go off to Wellesley, where she went."

"But what do *you* want to do?" J.J. knew what he wanted to do. He wanted to put his arms around the distraught girl beside him and kiss her forever on her invitingly soft lips.

Jenny lowered her face into her hands. "I'll tell you what I want to do. I want to go to sleep for the whole summer. I want to crawl into a cave and hibernate and not wake up again until I know who I am and where I'm going." She lifted her head and stared at J.J. "Wake me when it's over," she said with a small, sad laugh.

✤ CHAPTER 46 ✤

"Fine," said Esther coldly when Jenny told her she refused to attend Wellesley College. "That's fine with me. If you want to throw your whole life away, then go ahead. I won't stop you." Esther was giving up on her daughter. "If you want to be a casualty, then you can." Esther's voice rose and became sharper. "But you're not going to waste your life under the roof of my house. Tell me, where do you intend to live?"

"I don't know," Jenny said without raising her eyes.

"Of course you don't know," Esther continued. "You finished school in New York, but now you tell me you aren't prepared to work. Senator de Chavez will be very hurt, after all the trouble he went through to get that job organized for you. But if you don't care about his feelings (not that you ever care about anyone's feelings but your own), fine. I'll tell him myself. And since you won't be working, you won't be earning any money, so you can't pay for your own place to live. And I certainly won't throw away your father's good money getting you an apartment of your own in town just so you can party yourself stupid and get yourself thrown out by the landlord. Why, think of the public disgrace it would cause." Esther stared furiously at the top of her daughter's down-turned head.

In the end, it was decided that a cabana would be built for Jenny beside her own enclosed pool. Jenny could party all she liked with her outrageous friends, so long as they kept their dirty, unwashed selves out of Esther's house. Goodness knows what diseases these girls carried. And Esther's Max was not to swim in Jenny's pool. That was the deal made between mother and daughter. Max agreed. He agreed to do anything his mother wanted. Esther was queen for Max, and he was very happy to be her prince, even if he was almost permanently tired from all his lessons and allowed to play only with Lucienne Johnson—a suitable friend, Esther had decided; a girl similarly pressured by her mother Sonia.

Esther and Sonia were the best—or worst—of friends, depending on the competition. Both women were equally rich and they competed to buy the latest fashionable clothes for their children. Sonia's older girl Nancy, a disgrace to her family, graduated from the Epsilon Community School with Jenny. Both girls refused to spend money on decent clothes because the last thing they wanted to be was bourgeois capitalists.

"But, honey," George had tried to reason with his daughter throughout the summer. "I've worked hard for all I have. There's nothing wrong with enjoying the things you've earned." Jenny would not be reasoned with. She remained steadfast in the belief planted in her by her elite boarding school that capitalists and their money were the enemy.

Ah Ling smiled at all this. At last he had his wife and children with him. Mei Mei's graceful presence softened his heart. She immediately put up her statues of her lord Buddha. Being with her every day, Ah Ling stopped going to the meetings, feeling now a sense of gratitude to a country which took in his wife. He loved George, he decided. He, Ah Ling, had all a man wanted: a woman to love him. A man like George might have all the money in the world but Ah Ling knew Esther in a way George could never know her. Ah Ling ceased to hate. He felt sorry for George instead.

Jenny, once ensconced in the cabana built to order by a trustworthy contractor, closed herself off in a world peopled by the generation's refuse who gathered on the Plaza, their eyes always open for any opportunity to move in to someone else's comfortable wealthy home. Jenny's cabana became known locally as a good hang-out, a place from where no one was turned away and anyone could do anything they pleased. Surrounded by ever-present heaps of assorted bodies crashed out on various parts of the cabana's floor, Jenny pursued the one thing she had decided she wanted most: oblivion. In oblivion there was freedom from the pain of warring with her mother, the pain of facing decisions in her life, the pain of feeling trapped in a materialistic, bourgeois existence.

One day, toward the end of 1958's summer of discontent in Santa Fe, George had had enough. His home-life had become intolerable. Too many evenings had passed in which he sat at the dinner table, listening to Esther's endless interrogation of Max: how he was succeeding in all of his many classes. Any time George tried to mention Jenny's name, Esther stared at him with an icy indifference which seemed to say, "Don't talk to me about Jenny. She no longer exists so far as I am concerned." But George was not content to pretend that the cabana and his daughter existed in a different galaxy, a different universe, beyond his concern and responsibility. With each passing week, George realized that his daughter was not drifting through a temporary phase—she was rotting. And at last he recognized that if he didn't do something about it, no one else would. George's seemingly endless well of patience and forbearance had run dry.

On his day of decision, George stepped outside the kitchen door of his mansion. The smell of marijuana drifted across the lawn and with it came the sounds of a cabana full of people whom George did not know. That does it, he said to himself. He would take the law into his own hands once and for all. He walked across the garden with his shotgun in his hand and pushed open the door of the cabana. Inside, through the murk, he could dimly see bodies laid out like lethargically writhing animals, some dressed, some naked. "Jenny!" he bellowed. "Jenny, where the hell are you?" Through the thick smoke he saw Jenny in a heavy embrace with a dark-haired man who pawed at her breast. "What do you all think you're doing? Get the hell out of here, you dirty bums!" George was so angry he let fly a barrel of buckshot into the ceiling. A shower of plaster rained down on the inert bodies. "Get out of here!" George kicked at the bodies in an effort to get to Jenny.

Finally, he reached her and dragged her—so stoned she was mostly senseless—out onto the lawn. "The rest of you *leave!* You bastards! I'll be back and I'll shoot every damn one of you that's left! As for you, Jenny," George said, "I've had it with your behavior." He unceremoniously pulled a protesting Jenny into the house. "Get upstairs, take a bath, get yourself cleaned up and wait for me."

A black procession of Jenny's friends straggled out of the garden led by Nanny, whom George had summoned by telephone from next door as a reliable reinforcement. Nanny was now impressively fat and wore fatigues.

"Oh man, he's square, like not cool," floated across to George as he stood by the gate. George felt his anger rise within him. All summer his own daughter had jeered at all his values. She called him a male chauvinist pig. She told him he was oppressing Maria,

Ah Ling, Esther and Max. George was hurt, deeply hurt. And George would tolerate no more. Now he heard his principles questioned by an undistinguished piece of slime with legs. For a moment he raised his gun to his shoulder. No, he checked himself. Let the bastard just get the hell out of here and he can get on with his rantings in his own time. Putting down the gun, George chose to ignore the free-floating insult from the nameless face across the lawn but he decided to deal squarely with his daughter.

"What the hell is the matter with you, girl?" he said, sitting on her bed, that night. "I've given you everything you asked for, and you seem to hate me. I'm your father. I love you."

Jenny's head ached. Her eyes stung. She used mainly marijuana, so she was relieved she would be spared the pangs of withdrawal. But her sudden removal from what had become her way of life, she knew, would take more than a little getting used to. "You threw my friends out. You humiliated me," she sobbed. "They'll never speak to me again."

George sighed. "Okay, honey." He shook his head. "The subject isn't open for discussion any more." He looked soberly at her. "I've made a decision for you. You've graduated from high school now and you've made it good and clear to us that you don't want to go to Wellesley. But I'm not about to let you throw the rest of your life away by doing nothing. And you're not going out with that crowd anymore. I'm getting you the hell away from all of them. I'm sending you to England. You're a bright girl and you're just wasting your brain. I've got a business associate who's got a friend who's a professor at a university in England. I'm going to have you enrolled in a college there where you must behave yourself. Do you still want a career in politics?"

Jenny was quiet now. She knew when she pushed her father past his limits he could be no more yielding than a solid adobe wall. And this time she had gone too far.

"I know that's what your mother's always wanted for you," George continued without waiting for an answer. "You speak to your mother tomorrow. And we'll get you some decent clothes. I'll arrange everything." He spread his big capable hands. Jenny knew she was going to England. There was no point in arguing. All she had to do was say goodbye.

Only J.J. was happy for her. He looked at her miserable face and said, "Well, this is probably the last of your beatnik days. The university in England sounds wonderful."

Jenny drooped. "Me in college," she said. "Yuk."

∽ CHAPTER 47 ᲪᲜ

The arrangements to get Jenny into Wentworth University in Cambridgeshire were easily made. There was an agreed quota of students from America and two of them dropped out. Jenny took one place and Martin Archuleta took the other. They met at Martin's house in the Barrio area of Santa Fe. Jenny often drove to the Barrio to buy her plants at the Agua Fria Nursery, but she never stopped in the dusty streets to talk to the brown, cheerful children nor to the old grandmothers, rocking on their chairs on the little, white front porches, sorting apples and peaches, and cracking piñon nuts.

The Archuletas were a traditional Hispanic family. Martin's people originally left their village of Saint Martin in the north of Spain centuries ago, driven out by the continual warring in the border-country of Spain and France. Santa Fe, the City of Holy Faith, was their sanctuary but now, with the Barrio falling into the hands of property developers, the Archuletas were worried, anxious, and insecure. Money and greed now took the place of the fiercely tight community which used to lean over walls and talk the night away. Such problems, however, were pushed aside in the minds of the Archuletas when they learned of Martin's acceptance to Wentworth University.

Mrs Archuleta was thrilled that her only son, the cleverest boy in Santa Fe, was picked by the Governor himself to go to England. In honor of the occasion, she invited Esther and Jenny to lunch on Sunday after mass.

Esther made a face when she saw the invitation, a small letter of welcome from one mother of a future Wentworth student to another. "Go to a house in the Barrio?" Esther smirked. "I think not."

Jenny laughed. "Why not, mother? Do you think you'll catch the flu?"

"Be quiet, Jennifer. Very probably yes. I won't go. I can't stand the stink of the poor and their sour, unwashed smell."

"Well, I'm going. I do want to know at least one person at Wentworth." Inwardly, Jenny had to admit, the thought of going to England was beginning to grow exciting.

She was pleasantly surprised by Martin. He was taller than she had expected and more golden. His face was narrow and his hands long. His glittering eyes were hazel. He was lean and he was dangerous. Jenny had been around enough to know he was dangerous. She liked dangerous men. Orlando had been dangerous in his own way, but Orlando was not ruthless. This boy, about to be a man, was ruthless. Death lay in his eyes and flattery fell naturally from his lips.

Martin, upon seeing Jenny, sighed inwardly. Yet another pretty, promiscuous Anglo. At least she was clean.

Mrs Archuleta was surprised not to see Esther, but Jenny explained her mother was ill. The whole family sat down to eat. Martin's father was old. Martin had been a late but welcome arrival. He was horribly spoiled by his mother and sisters, and he remained an enigma to his father. Paulo Archuleta, Martin's father, was seventy. His world today in no way resembled the world he knew as a young man at the turn of the century.

His house, first built by his father and himself, was made with adobe mud bricks. Various male relatives helped them form the bricks and the women helped to mix the mud with straw. Then they surrounded the bricks with wooden strips specially made by his brother Tomas, and left the bricks to harden in the hot sun. Finally, the building finished, Paulo killed one of his bulls and collected the blood to paint the floors. Once that was dry, the bull was roasted whole on a huge spit, its testicles cooked in onion and garlic, then sliced. The tail was kept for soup and the horns for decorations. The village was invited and there were only three fights—two over women and one over a card game.

Those days were gone. Paulo knew and regretted it. "If God would only take me now," he was in the habit of saying, "before my heart is truly broken." His brother Tomas had just sold his house—his children's patrimony—to a property developer for thirty-six thousand dollars, a sum unheard of in the Barrio.

But today, with Jenny Jensen sitting at the table and his son leaving for England—a country he could only dimly perceive—Paulo Archuleta felt bereft. "What do you need with all this education?" he asked Martin. "Why? You have the sun, you have a place to live. You have your family here. Why not get married and have babies?"

Martin looked at his father and then at Jenny. "Dad," he said, "that's precisely why you live in the Barrio, in this house, on this land. Because that's all you did."

The various sisters were busy passing in and out of the kitchen, dishes in hand. Children ran about the garden and babies gurgled in over-stuffed chairs. The sisters' husbands, hair slicked back with Brylcream, talked furiously in the hall. "Come on, all of you," Mrs Archuleta called out. "Sit."

Jenny was listening to Martin's continuing argument with his father. "I don't want to live like this," Martin said. "I don't want to scratch a living with my chickens and my goats." He turned to Jenny with his peculiar golden eyes blazing. "I'll bet you don't have to milk cows and collect eggs for breakfast," he said loudly.

The family fell silent. "No, I don't, but sometimes

I wish I could," said Jenny, remembering the lonely breakfasts of her recent years. Then she remembered the breakfasts on Etta's ranch when, as a child, she would collect the eggs and milk the cow. All that seemed a lifetime ago. In her late teens, Jenny had drifted from her aunt Etta, almost embarrassed to observe the defilement of her own actions in the bright sunshine of Etta's innocence. But memories of time spent with Etta remained treasured, souvenirs of a golden age long gone by.

"And I don't suppose your mother does either?" Martin's voice broke into Jenny's faraway thoughts.

"Does what?"

"Collect the milk and eggs for your family."

"No," said Jenny. "The servants buy our food."

"Oh, I *see!*" Martin raised his voice and tilted back his head in an overstated nod, gazing at Jenny across his sharp cheekbones. "The servants."

"My dad made lots of money," Jenny shrugged, trying to dismiss the conversation.

"I'll bet he did." There was a jeering note in Martin's voice. It irritated Jenny. "And let me guess," he continued. "These servants of yours, would they happen to be Hispanic?"

"Well, yes. Maria is. But Ah Ling isn't. He's from Malaya."

"I get the picture." He seemed triumphant to watch his line of reasoning unfold successfully, like a prosecuting attorney in a criminal court. "So your people come with all their money to New Mexico— bringing with them, of course, their Oriental—and when they need more servants, there's always we New Mexicans, who will be only too happy to clean your house for you. That is the way the story goes, isn't it?"

"Listen," she said, leaning over the table. She could see Martin would not let the subject drop. "Don't give me all that baloney. We're all immigrants in this country. And even though you and your family might have been here a little longer than me and my family, you must still have come from somewhere else originally. And whether you came from Mexico or straight from Spain, the Indians were here first. And even the Indians are immigrants from Mongolia across the Bering Strait. So shut up." Jenny was surprised to hear herself. She was rarely that direct. And for a moment, as she heard her own voice, she thought she was listening to her father talking.

The room was silent. The family were used to Martin's polemics. He harangued them constantly, but to be rude to a guest in your own home was unheard of in the Hispanic community. "I apologize for my son," Paulo said. "He is overcome by the honor of your visit. Sophia." He beckoned his pretty wife. "Bring our guest some *posole* and tortillas. Say you are sorry, son."

Martin looked at Jenny. "I'm sorry," he said sullenly. "One day you will be too." But the old man did not hear him. Only Jenny did. Everyone else at the table chattered in Spanish. Martin's words trickled cold and threatening into Jennifer's heart and lay stored for many long years.

The day of leaving loomed, circled on Jenny's calendar by her bed. Her whole family were to spend a week in the town of Cambridge, then both parents and Max were leaving Jenny and touring France. George did not look forward to England. The English, he said, were too unclear about their politics.

Were they part of the free world or not? With the growing strength of their unions, George could not be sure. George was, in fact, hugely unhappy about the whole idea of traveling abroad, but his daughter was going to university in England and he wanted to check the old place out to see that those beatniks had not infiltrated yet another place of learning with their Commie muck.

Secretly, Jenny was pleased her father was taking the time off to take her to university. She wished her mother wasn't coming at all. She was worried enough to be seen by her future classmates with her father, whose Texan manners were dreadful and his attempts at arguing the most embarrassing thing in her life. But the thought of being seen in the company of her mother, with all her airs and graces, was truly awful. Jenny was at home in all strata of life: Ah Ling and his family felt like her own relatives, and Nanny too—happy, loving Nanny—on the next ranch. Etta had no airs or pretenses, neither did grandma Nora. Only Esther and her friends played the game. Jenny, laughing, ignored them. She was wary of leaving her friend Nancy Johnson behind in the hands of her ruinous mother, Sonia. "I'll write whenever I get a chance," she said the day before she left for England.

"I'll phone every week." Nancy was distraught. "I'll never survive without you, Jenny."

Jenny looked bleakly at Nancy, unsure why the girl seemed to put such weight on their friendship. "Nancy, you have to survive in this life. You have to." Her voice was as stark and uncompromising as Martin's voice had been weeks ago. Nancy sobbed but Jenny had to move on. She had so many goodbyes to say.

Last on her round of farewells was Aunt Etta, and Jenny arrived at the darkened ranch where Etta sat before an open fire after supper. She spoke with her aunt in the warm sitting room, at first feeling an awkward stranger. Then, as she discussed Wentworth and what she thought England would be like, she relaxed and found herself savoring the comfort and the perpetual tranquility which always seemed to hover around Etta. For a moment, the sullied memories of drugs, men and sex vanished from Jenny's mind, and she felt once again a clean, safe, cozy child.

Etta held Jenny's hand when she stood at the front door to say goodbye. "I'm glad you came," Etta said with a smile. "Thank you for coming before you left."

"Aunt Etta," Jenny began, then lowered her head with embarrassment. "Oh, Aunt Etta. I'm sorry I haven't come by to see you more often. It's just that—"

"You don't have to explain. I understand." She smiled. "I know life hasn't been easy for you lately. And to be a young person today, why, there are so many decisions to make. So many changes. And what does an old auntie have to do with all that?"

"Everything," Jenny said, returning the warm smile. "You know," she said. "I've always felt so safe here. With you, and the house, and the garden, and the animals. And now, I don't know. I have no idea what England's going to be like or anything." She looked seriously at the woman before her. "I'm frightened."

"Of course you are." Etta patted the hand in her own. "But don't worry. You'll be all right. You know, I've always known what a good girl you really are." Jenny let out a small laugh. "Ah, listen to me!" Etta laughed, too, catching herself. "I'm still calling you a girl. But you're eighteen years old now. A woman. And I know you'll be all right. And I'm always here if you need me." She held out her arms. "Now come and give your aunt a big hug."

Jenny felt a tear escape the corner of her eye. She was saying, she felt, a true goodbye. Goodbye to her past, goodbye to her childhood, goodbye to a life of knowing what comes next. She had been away to school before in New York, but she had always known she'd return. Now she was leaving for a different country, a different world. For the first time, she was leaving home in earnest. "Goodbye, Etta," Jenny said. She turned, walked from the house, and drove into the night.

The airplane took off from Albuquerque Airport and rose into the sky. Jenny was used to her father's light private airplane, the plane he flew himself to business trips in Texas and Oklahoma. Jenny had grown accustomed to the safe bulk of him at the controls. She did not feel nearly as secure on the huge plane which thundered across the airways and flew straight into the blue sky. The Jensen family, all four of them, sat in the first class cabin. Jenny could tell her father was nervous. The muscles in his face were taut and uneasy. He hated anyone but himself to drive any vehicle. She slipped her hand into his. "Don't worry, Daddy," she said. "We'll get there."

"Of course, we'll get there, little girl. We'll get there if I have to drive the damned thing myself."

"Champagne, sir?" The stewardess stood smiling at him.

"Well now," said George. "Aren't you a pretty

little thing?" The stewardess smiled. She liked Texan men. They took good care of their wives and children. "Hell, no," George answered at last. "Not that sissy stuff. Get me some coffee, honey."

Esther was perfectly aware that her husband was attracting attention. Around them sat gray, anxious business people dressed in gray with their gray minds checking bank balances. George's voice boomed against the cabin door then bounced back. He was wearing his favorite clothes, against all Esther's efforts—his brightly patterned red shirt and a turquoise and silver tie at the neck. His jeans were held up by a huge belt which strained to contain his stomach. His boots, made from rattlesnake skin, shone proudly. On his left little finger a massive diamond glittered, clasped in a yellow gold ring, and on his head he clamped a huge Stetson with a rattlesnake band. George had chosen the outfit that morning to make himself feel more comfortable, more at home as he ventured out into unfamiliar settings. Seeing the clothes laid out on the bed, Esther had simply shaken her head.

Now Esther wished she had tried harder. George looked completely out of place. His presence in the midst of the monotoned travelers seemed as inappropriate as a gorilla at a white-tie ball, a bull-moose among a herd of gazelles, a western saddle slung across an Arabian horse at a dressage event.

Esther, however—the experienced international traveler—was well-prepared. She wore her finely tailored traveling suit. Max was in expensive jeans and a striped T-shirt from France. Jenny, conservatively dressed in gray, was alive with anticipation and secretly pleased with the way her costly skirt and jacket felt against her skin. But already George was horrified. "Damn restroom," he said, striding up the first class aisle back to his seat. "All that money for the tickets and the damned restroom's small."

"Please, George," Esther hissed. "Can't you whisper, dear?"

"A man can't wipe his behind in a plane these days, they make the things so small," George carried on in a lowered voice.

Jenny was amused. The constant war between her mother and father gave her a certain sense of detachment. Her father never realized there was a war. He just boomed and bellowed his way through life and life was enormously simple for him. You were either a regular guy (in which case he liked you) or you were a Commie or a beatnik (in which case he would offer to deport you permanently to Russia). However, Jenny noticed, George treated women very carefully. His idiosyncrasy, well-known at the many bars he patronized, was that he would not do business with women. Neither would he discuss his money nor what he had in the bank with Esther or Jenny. Max was allowed to go to the office, but Esther was not. "My office is for men," he would say. "And when Max is old enough, if he wants to, he'll take over."

"What about me?" Jenny had asked on more occasions than she could remember. He loved his daughter, but he could see she was in danger of becoming just another loud-mouthed aggressive American woman.

"You'll get married and have kids and please yourself. Or," George always corrected himself, remembering Esther's wishes, "you can become a Governor. That's why we're going to England."

Jenny sighed now as she sat on the plane. Years of suffrage for women had not got through to her father.

George, sitting on the plane trying to get himself to sleep, was grateful for Esther. Dear, quiet, controlled Esther.

The journey was long and boring. After the night ended, Jenny left her sleeping family and walked down the aisle to the back of the airplane. Jenny felt cramped. Her tongue tasted sour, and she badly needed a shower. Suddenly she saw Martin Archuleta. She was disconcertingly aware of the fact that he was on the plane all along. She knew she had boarded first class with her parents, while Martin, surrounded at the airport by a bright gaggle of relatives loudly sobbing, waited with the rest of the people who made up the passengers in the uncomfortably crowded tourist section.

Great wealth had so far insulated Jenny from many issues. Great wealth meant that Jenny could cheerfully jostle with people at the Salvation Army Thrift Shop looking for quirky old clothes; equally she could take her outdated Bloomingdales dresses, her sweaters from Neimann Marcus and her designer jeans, and drop them all in the donations slot at the Goodwill Thrift Store. The great difference Jenny needed to learn was that she could brag of a bargain dress from the flea market, but she never bought her clothes at secondhand stores for lack of money.

Looking at Martin in his cheap, ill-fitting suit, she felt ashamed. Her gray jacket and her skirt, her cashmere sweater, her pearls and the diamond ring—a goodbye present from her father—would, she knew, probably pay for Martin's first semester of tuition.

Martin felt enraged at her standing beside him. She smelled of money, the white Anglo bitch. "What's the matter?" he said. "The lobster get to your stomach? Or are you just slumming?"

Jenny looked down at him. "I can't help it if my father's richer than yours. Anyway, I'm not slumming. I'm just stretching my legs." Martin had the capacity to make Jenny furious. Other people in her life had envied her, but Martin had a curious sneer in his voice which shook her gold-plated confidence—the confidence which belongs only to the magnificently wealthy when money is so vast and so piled that they have no need of envy, spite or malice. Jenny's crowd belonged there.

England, however, proved to be a shock.

Jenny supposed the car which collected them for the drive to Cambridge would be driven by a bright, cheerful cabdriver. She imagined the driver, like the New York drivers she had met, would chat about his country—with a cockney accent. Jenny, who opted to sit up front with the driver for her first introduction, found herself uncomfortable with the barely perceptible edge she detected in his voice. He chatted away pleasantly enough, pointing out passing landmarks and commenting proudly on the beauty of the countryside, but most of his speeches ended with, "I bet it's very different where you come from," and he would raise his eyes to look at George in the rearview mirror.

Jenny had seen the man wince when he first saw George. George's concerned face now loomed in the back of the car.

"Tell me," the driver said, as if casually, while the car raced down the motorway. "What did your old man do during the war? Wait. Let me guess. I'd take 'em for a marine."

"No," Jenny said nervously. "Actually, he worked for the army."

"Oh, yeah?" said the driver with an odd and exaggerated tone of interest. "And where was 'e sent? Come over 'ere to 'elp us out, did 'e?"

Jenny blushed. "He stayed in Santa Fe, helping out with the supply depot at the train station."

"I see," the driver said simply, but he drove the taxi faster.

George could hear the conversation from the backseat. He hated sitting there and he hated hearing himself being discussed by the driver. Nothing around him felt like home. The hills were smaller than those he was used to, and the sky unfamiliarly and threateningly gray. George could only sit and let himself be carried passively through this strange and different country.

He could see the driver's eyes watching him in the rearview mirror and he thought he saw a twinkle in the eyes, an impish delight at his own displeasure at being driven so fast and so helplessly. "All right, guv?" the driver called out, half turning over his shoulder, as if reading George's thoughts.

"To tell you the truth—" George began, hoping to persuade the driver to slow down. But Esther squeezed George's hand in her own, stopping him from saying anything out of place. "Yes," George said with a groan. "Fine. Great. Just dandy." He sat back in his seat and squeezed Esther's hand hard for comfort.

"Believe me, sweetheart, don't worry," George said as the taxi entered Cambridge. "I've made all the arrangements. My travel agent Billy booked us in and he says the hotel should be great."

Esther looked at George warily. She had hoped for a stay in the Savoy, but George had insisted everything was already taken care of. To Esther's knowledge, the town of Cambridge had no hotel to match the luxury of the Savoy. Still, she hoped, maybe Billy had found a gracious country house-turned-hotel to stay in. Maybe even a modernized castle. "All right," Esther said. "I'll trust you and Billy. I hope you're right."

"Don't worry," George repeated, patting her hand. "The hotel'll be fine." Frightened as he might be by the strangeness of the surroundings, George was pleased to see the inarguable beauty of Cambridge. And the thought of a night in a hotel bedroom with Esther excited him. It might be just like their honeymoon. Who knows? A pretty English town, a good meal, a huge, soft, feather four-poster bed, and maybe Esther would be in the right mood. Maybe this trip wouldn't turn out so bad after all.

When the taxi pulled up in front of the Hooded Raven Hotel, Esther's heart fell heavily to the floor of the backseat. The stucco on the hotel's façade was peeling, the flowers in the windowboxes were drooping, and the windowframes themselves seemed to tilt precariously. "Oh, George," she said in a soft whine.

"It looks very English," Jenny said, finding herself excited and genuinely pleased by the old inn's quaintness. Max ran ahead, and Esther walked silently past while George paid the cabby.

Inside the hotel the wallpaper held faded remnants of what had once been a flower pattern and the brownish carpet was worn and full of holes. Esther stared silently at George. The accusation in her eyes needed no articulation. "You never know," George offered, still hopeful. "The bedroom might be a real peach."

When George had signed in, a boy in his early teens with a profusion of pimples on his pale face loaded his arms with the Jensen family luggage and led the way to two adjoining rooms upstairs. He showed Esther and George into their room, grunted thanks to George for the shilling tip, then saw Jenny and Max to their shared room. When the door had closed behind them, George and Esther looked around. The floor sloped steeply to the outside wall, where the paint was coming off with damp-rot. George walked silently to one of the two single beds, separated by a darkly stained night-table in between. He sat on the bed and gave it a few sample bounces. No feather mattress, the bed squeaked loudly and accosted George's bottom with a rippled series of lumps. "Well," Esther said simply. "It certainly isn't the Savoy." George knew his hopes for the night, if not for the rest of the trip, were lost. He felt his mood turn as sour as the smell from the rotting wall.

The family went downstairs to the bar for a drink before dinner. George felt positively morose. He watched cautiously as his bright and curious seven-year-old son ran up to a policeman at the bar.

Max was thrilled to see a real English bobby. "No guns?" Max inquired.

"No." The Inspector was kind. "We don't need guns in England, and I hope we never will. We English are a peaceful lot on the whole. You know what my supervisor taught me years ago?"

"No." Max was enthralled.

"He said if a fellow's running down the road with a gun and he thinks of shooting you, he'll remember the rope and think again."

"What if he wants to die anyway?" Jenny asked, coming up to stand by her brother.

"Well, then I'm a goner. But I know my criminals, and I make my choices, so I'm still alive."

Some of the men in the bar, Esther noticed, were quite handsome in a very English way. Esther rather fancied a little liaison with a tutor, something that could be hidden carefully—little trips to her daughter's college, little romantic suppers by candlelight, intellectual discussions about Byron's incestuous sister, leading to a visit to her room, maybe coffee, a brandy or two, and then a look to check on the current status of the Great British Reserve . . . Yes. Life could get interesting once again.

Dinner was served in the dining room. George, still feeling foul with disappointment, picked up his pint of English bitter and led the family to his table, waved off with a friendly "Ta-ra" from the constable. At the table, George sat with his napkin under his chin and waited with a child's impatience for his dinner. The waitress, a bulging mass of fat with a dingy apron, pushed a rattling trolley full of plates toward them. They were covered with silver-plated warmers. She dumped the plates on the table and, with a titanic clash, gathered all the covers and threw them back on the trolley where they lay like a forgotten army. She wheeled the trolley away, its aged wheels shrieking in protest. George peered suspiciously at the plate.

He picked up his fork and poked the meat. With his knife he cut off a slice of the beef which lay in mourning in a sea of watery gravy. He put the beef in his mouth, chewed it and, with a great effort, made himself swallow. He tasted nothing.

The waitress returned and plonked down a bottle of yellow salad cream and left. George remained silent while, beside the single leaf of lettuce, he prodded with his fork a shy processed pea hiding under the Yorkshire pudding. Was this the country he was going to leave his daughter in? "You know," George said to Esther while Esther and Max began to eat. "I'm beginning to wonder if this whole thing is such a good idea."

"Don't worry, George," Esther reassured him, full of plans for future unaccompanied trips to Cambridge. "Everything will be fine. It's all for the best."

Later, George moaned and groaned all night in the small, bumpy bed. He hated being awake on his own. At 2.00 A.M. his dinner decided to attack his stomach from the inside. George rose from his restless bed to go down the hall to the lavatory, but as he went to walk through the bedroom door, he hit his tall brow heavily against the low doorhead. "Damn!" he hissed, rubbing his bruise.

"What's the matter?" Esther's voice was sleepy.

"Nothing. I just gotta go to the john. That's all. And they make the doors so damned low, I banged my head. Don't worry about it. Go back to sleep."

She squinted at him in the light from a street lamp outside the window. "Well, you certainly can't go without your bathrobe," she said. "You're not going to go down the hall naked."

George reached for his bathrobe from the arm of a chair and tied it insecurely around himself. His head still hurt. "This," he said, "has not been my day." He gave a small laugh at his own feelings of helplessness.

"And you watch. Once I get to the bathroom, that rusty, antiquated contraption of a toilet they got stuck up on the wall will probably come down on top of me and conk me again. It's only hanging by a single screw."

"Come on," said Esther wearily, rising from her own bed. "I'll walk you down the hall. I can't have you banging around all night, wrecking the whole hotel."

In the hall, Esther leaned back against the wall, hoping nobody would come by and wonder what she was doing outside the bathroom at 2.00 A.M. on a warm September night in Cambridge. "Are you done yet?" she said through the door.

"Almost."

Oh dear, Esther thought, and they don't have fans in England.

Later, by now fully awake, she lay in her bed and read. How like George, she thought. She looked at him, fast asleep, snoring like a walrus. And she smiled. Really, she thought. Sometimes George could be such a child.

❧ CHAPTER 48 ❧

Jennifer's tutor at Wentworth University was as famous for his rapport with his students as he was for his constant flow of erudite papers. Peter Stuart was tall and blond. He could trace his family back to the arrival of Vikings on the shores of a largely uninhabited Britain—Vikings who pillaged and raped. It was said in whispers in dark corners of the university that this peculiar talent had survived the many centuries and lay between Peter's legs. The women he compromised with his dark needs did not complain. Violated they might be, but to indict a senior don at Wentworth would mean that the university would unite against a lone student, all the great doors would shut with a final clang and hopes of a degree would crumble to dust. Peter Stuart smiled when he saw Jenny.

She was just his type. He thought the mother was nondescript, a little vulgar, and the father was a typical Texan. George thought Jenny's new tutor was a joke. "My dear Lord," he whispered to Esther upon the first meeting. "Is that supposed to be a man, or what?"

"Shhh, George. Be quiet. He's very famous."

"Very famous for what?" George was eager to know. "He's one of them queers. I can tell. Just look at the way he crosses his legs. I don't want no Nancy in fancy pants teaching my little girl. I want a real man."

"He is a real man," Esther rasped. "George, he's English. They're all like that."

"Oh." George looked at Esther. "Could have fooled me."

The introduction, the shaking of hands, the escorting of Jenny into Peter's office, the closing of the door behind her and the initial friendly remarks of "Tell me about yourself," had gone smoothly. Jenny found Peter to be an attentive listener and she felt the tightness in her stomach relaxing.

She felt at home with Peter. He lay back in his

professional chair and gazed at Jenny. He saw knowledge in her eyes which was rarely found in the eyes of an eighteen-year-old student. He grinned. His pale, sea-washed eyes lit up in the bleached beach of his face. Years of decadence had done their work well. His mouth had a castaway look; his teeth were bones upon a boundless shore; his hair was sun-blanched bladderwrack, drying on the sand. And his skin was as silky as the shore of the Caribbean, tinged with the pink of a silent sunset. Jenny chattered away innocently.

"I don't mean to seem rude," Jenny said after Peter had exchanged a few remarks, "but your voice is different from the English accents I've heard on television."

"No need to apologize." Peter smiled. "That isn't rude at all. I'm from Glasgow. We Glaswegians have a very different accent from the English. Don't worry. You'll get used to it in time."

He fell quiet and sat, staring at the young face before him, framed in hair of a lovely and enticing dark auburn. His fast eyes moved quickly over her and stole glances at the soft skin revealed in the opening of her shirt. Peter felt the lust rise between his legs and surge into his face, making his tongue thicken. He was aware of the growing, familiar desire to put his pale thin hands around the smooth skin of the throat. He lowered his eyes to his desktop and shifted in his chair. There would be time for all that later. First would come the thrilling months of seduction.

"Well, Miss Jensen," he said, realizing he had been silent for too long a moment. "Or Jennifer. May I call you Jennifer?"

She nodded consent. "My mother calls me Jennifer, but I'm more comfortable with Jenny."

"Very good," he said, pleased to see the friendly eagerness in her eyes. "And you may call me Peter. No need for formalities here. Tell me, Jenny." He accentuated her name as if making a point of familiarity. "What do you hope to learn here at Wentworth?"

"Well," she paused. "My mother's always told me I would grow up to be the first lady Governor of New Mexico. And I suppose that by coming here—"

"Ah," he interrupted. "Political aspirations? Very good. And is that what you want for yourself?"

She shrugged. "I'm not sure what else I would do."

"Well, you've come to the right place. And that would explain why they assigned me to be your tutor. Political science is my field. And did you read politics at . . . Let me see." He looked down at the file on his desk. "The Epsilon Community School?"

Jenny hesitated. "We read some political books, if that's what you mean."

"Forgive me," Peter said with a lordly bow of the head. "A Britishism. You see, here you read a subject. But in America, I should say, did you study politics?"

"A little," Jenny said with a slight laugh, charmed to discover the differences even in their shared language. "I mean, we didn't have to pick a major, not like in college. We had classes in everything. English, math, chemistry, history. But we did learn some politics in Social Affairs class. You know, we started out with Hobbs and Locke, then moved on to John Stuart Mill and ended up with some Marx."

"Good," he said, nodding. "And how did you find the Marx?"

"Very interesting," she said. "It gave me a lot to think about."

"Very good indeed." He smiled approvingly. "You should do very well here. You sound as if you had a good introduction to modern political thought. And I think that we have a good foundation to start on, with you as my student. Does that sound good?"

"Sounds good to me," she smiled.

"Excellent. We'll get you going on a reading list. I'd like you to read several books on English political history, particularly centring around the Industrial Revolution and the rise of socialism in England today. But what am I saying? This is only our first meeting and I don't want to overwhelm you with work. At least not yet." He laughed, and she laughed in return at his humor. "First, you must get settled in here. Get your feet under the table. And we can see to your reading the next time we meet. I'll see you . . . Let's see." He looked down at his appointment diary. "When are your parents leaving?"

"They go on Sunday."

"All right. How about first thing Monday morning?" Peter uncrossed his long legs. He was the only tutor at Wentworth to make a point of wearing jeans and a black turtle-neck sweater to his tutorial. He was the only don to immerse himself in his students' daily lives. There was nothing which Peter did not know about his students. Indeed, the casual clothes he wore made Jenny think of him more as a friend than as a teacher.

"I'll look forward to it," Jenny said, again with a smile which sent a tingle up Peter's legs.

"Wonderful. And in the meantime, I suggest you get to know the university. There's a special Student's

Night at the Student Union on Sunday evening. You can meet a lot of people and sign up for all sorts of activities. All of Wentworth's clubs and organizations will have tables there, and it would be a good chance to begin to get involved. You can go after your parents leave." He stood up from behind his desk.

"Great," Jenny said and, their first meeting over, she held out her hand.

Peter, upon seeing her out of his office, vividly remembered his own early days of recruitment into the cause. Now, with several British students recruited, he was ready to turn his attention to vetting the two Americans assigned to him. Martin Archuleta, he thought, remembering the name of the other American on his list. He would have to meet Martin to see what the prospects were for that young man.

Jennifer Jensen presented an interesting challenge but her intelligence and candidness would make the challenge exciting. Money was not a problem. Moscow knew, and provided for, his needs well. And he could always stay at the Ivy League universities whilst in America. They had been successfully infiltrated years ago. Now, through several simple phone calls, the various plants in America—some kept dormant for years—were activated, as Jenny began the steady process of her politicization.

On Sunday morning George and Esther settled Jenny into her dormitory room. The other half of her room was already apparently moved into, for posters hung on the walls and the bed was neatly made. The roommate, however, was nowhere to be seen.

George was eager to get back home. Already he felt

the familiar pain of separation from New Mexico. Now, the farmers were harvesting. Now, the many, brightly colored corn were tied in bunches and taken to the churches to lie with sun-ripened wheat in adoring worship of the Virgin Mary. George's hands twitched. Ah Ling would eat his radishes, those fine plump radishes he had sown. Before he left, they had poked out of the ground. To pick a radish, pop it in his mouth, crunch down on the white flesh and feel the stinging, sharp taste at the back of his mouth, that made George happy. Not England, with its weak, watery skies and its architecture, ornate and hard. George loved the adobe, the warm, soft, round, motherly architecture of Santa Fe. He missed the feeling of the great huge skies over his head. His missed interminable talks with Danny and Nora Gottstein, a chilled beer shared on the veranda with Etta. Here the English walked about as if there were a bad smell under their noses.

George spent the last night in England getting up the courage to tell Esther he had to go home. "You see," he said, "I can't even shit. Even if I go to France, I'm afraid I'll bust. I'm sorry, Esther. I really am. But Europe just makes me ill. I'm a man who needs my meat and potatoes, my baked beans and my beer. Here you can't even get ice. They serve the stuff warm."

Esther was gracious and relaxed. "Don't worry, darling. You go back. Max and I will have a wonderful time, won't we, Max?"

Max's eyes lit up. His mother could be the most wonderful fun. Max was extremely clever, and although he loved his father, his sensitive nature drew him to his mother's side, though her changeable moods always made him maintain his distance. Max kept a secret part of himself to himself. Esther, in Max, found someone to admire her appreciation of the finer things in life. If George tended to be a boor, Max, she had discovered, shared her aesthetic sensibilities. Max would love Europe. "Of course," she reassured George, "I understand."

Saying goodbye to Jenny on Sunday afternoon was difficult for George. He loved her very much. As a daughter she was all he wanted, despite the distress she had caused in her years of rebellion. She was beautiful, imperious and willful. He poured his heart out to her. He loved her courage and her sense of humor. He loved her strength. In her own way, she was as stubborn as he was. They had had their titanic rows but she understood him at a very deep level which was lost to Esther. She saw into his soul. His soul was, in its own way, subtly and oddly artistic. Scarred by Esther's indifference, George's soul hid from his wife's harsh words. But safe with Jenny, George and his daughter talked for hours.

He cried when he hugged Jenny goodbye and he was ashamed of the tears which spilled from his eyes to her shoulder. Jenny cried, too, not for herself but for her father's loneliness without her. For her mother, her feelings had hardened largely to indifference and, at times, to outright contempt. As for Max, well, she would miss his sometimes irritating presence, his good natured humor, his incessant practicing at the piano. And perhaps she would miss him. He was growing into a handsome boy and a better companion. "You be good," Jenny said, "or I'll tear off your head."

Max grinned. "You be good, or I'll tell your boyfriend you've been bad."

"I haven't got a boyfriend."

"Yeah, but you sure will soon."

Jenny made a face. "Naah. None of these English boys are any good. They're all wet and wussy."

Jenny grinned at her father. "I'm going to miss you, dad. They all seem so well-mannered around here. I'm a little afraid it will be like living in a morgue."

"Have to go, honey." George grabbed Esther by the hand. "Let's get out of here," he bellowed. "I've got a plane to catch."

Esther kissed the air beside Jenny's cheek. Jenny felt the chill between them bite into her bones. "I'll see you at Christmas, darling," Esther said.

"All right, mom. See you." Jenny turned on her heel and walked to her room in the corner of the quadrangle.

Her rooms, she found upon entering, were to be shared by a fierce-looking black girl from British Gambia. "Hi," she said. "I'm Jenny Jensen."

"Rich, I suppose?" The African girl's eyes glittered.

"Yeah. I guess so," Jenny agreed, surprised to be caught off guard.

"Capitalist!" She spat the words in Jenny's face.

Jenny shrugged. "My dad's a capitalist, but I'm sort of nothing."

"Just my luck." The girl stood up. She was tall, at least six feet. Her nose was flat and her mouth large. Her eyes were blank staring holes of rage. "Wouldn't you know I'd end up with a white oppressor for a roommate."

"Wait a minute!" Jenny was cross. "Hang on, lady. I'll have you know my people were Jews from Russia.

We were expelled and killed and murdered. We got to America with nothing. We were too busy getting oppressed ourselves to go around oppressing your people. Cut the crap, will you? If you don't want to share a room with me, that's okay by me. But you," Jenny put her finger to the girl's slim strong body, "you go elsewhere. I'm staying right here. Anyway, you haven't even introduced yourself. What's your name?"

"Hanna."

"Hanna who?"

"Hanna Entobe." She smiled. "And I think I might like you after all. Underneath all your rich, capitalist clothes, you're as tough as I am."

"Hey," Jenny smiled back. "Let's be friends, not enemies. Where did you get all this capitalist stuff from anyway? I heard it all before, you know."

Hanna frowned. "My father was trained in Russia as a student."

"Yeah. Sounds good." She looked at the poster which hung on the wall over Hanna's bed. Karl Marx's angry eyes stared at Jenny from the shaggy mane of his leonine face. "And I guess," she said with a sideways nod of her head, "that would explain the poster."

Hanna still frowned. "Listen. I'm sorry. I didn't mean to come on so heavy." She looked into Jenny's eyes and her own dark eyes revealed a depth of pain. "It's very strange to be here. It's such a different world. I mean, in the Gambia all you hear everyone say is anti-English and anti-American. And now I've been sent here. This is the best education my family could hope for, and they've sent me to learn all about this world. It's all so different." Hanna lowered her eyes. "We are a very poor tribe. Of course, my family couldn't afford to send me themselves. I got here on a scholarship from English missionaries. I hate them all. We dressed from the missionary barrels, and we were fed in the missionary schools." She sighed. "For that, we had to pray with them and," she looked down at her feet, "they squashed my feet into shoes."

Jenny put her hand out. "It's okay, you know. I'm terrified, too. We're in England now, and I can tell you, I'm going to cry myself to sleep tonight. My family just left and I miss New Mexico like I'm going to die. I miss my friend Nancy Johnson, and Ah Ling and all my friends. We'll just have to do the best we can and get on with it."

Hanna smiled. "Well, we might as well stick together. This is my first term."

"Mine too. Who's your tutor?"

"Peter Suart."

"Yeah?" said Jenny. "Well, we have more in common than I thought. He's good-looking."

Hanna laughed. "Yes," she said, "if you're interested in men."

"Oh, come on," Jenny laughed. "You mean to tell me you're not interested in them?"

"I don't know." Hanna shook her head. "My family tell me they have my husband all picked out for me when I finish my studies, but I don't even know the man I'm supposed to marry. And I don't know how I feel about the idea of meeting a man here. Whoever I picked, it wouldn't be the man my family have chosen. I don't know. I've been here a week now and all the men I've seen so far seem so immature and spoiled. I've met a lot of the women here, though. Some of them tell me I'd be better off with another woman."

Jenny laughed. "Men and politics will have to wait. Let's go and see if there's any edible food here."

"Okay," said Hanna. "But just remember—for some of us, our politics are the politics of survival."

"Fair enough," Jenny consented. "I'll remember that."

After a nondescript dinner of standard institutional food at the large refectory, Jenny and Hanna walked together through the autumn evening air to Student Night at the Wentworth Student Union. They had to ask directions from an upperclassman to the building but, having found it at last, they stood before the great Victorian stone edifice which, lacking a cross on top, appeared an impressive secular version of a cathedral. Or perhaps, Jenny thought, a castle.

Standing before the front steps and looking up at the turrets, jagged against the moonlit sky, Jenny sensed an excitement stir within her. For the first time, she felt herself to be a real university student. The building was more majestic than any of the homey structures in Santa Fe and it far outstripped the unassuming farm buildings which comprised Epsilon School. The Wentworth Student Union was strong, dark and grand. Its stones seemed wise, steeped in years of history and learning. This, thought Jenny, is academe. This is England. This is real life.

With the tremblings of a nervous subject entering the castle to stand before a mighty monarch, Jenny climbed the stone steps, opened the old and weighty wooden door and stepped into the cavernous main hall of the Student Union. Beside her stood Hanna, erect to her full height, no emotion showing on her face.

The hall was lit by many bright, bare lightbulbs which were covered by green, metal reflectors, hanging down by long, straight wires from the apex of the high and shadowy vaulted ceiling. All around the crowded room were groups of people standing, talking, leaning over the many tables set up about the perimeter of the cold stone floor. To Jenny's mind, everyone assembled seem to know each other already, for they all smiled and laughed to each other with confidence, familiarity and poise. Jenny felt like a small girl lost in a train station, looking for her mother's hand. "Where do you want to go first?" she asked Hanna, surprised to hear how small her own voice sounded.

Hanna looked down at Jenny. For all the stiffness in Hanna's face, Jenny could see the timidity in her eyes, too. "I don't know," said Hanna. "I guess we should just"—she shrugged—"circulate." Side by side, they walked forward and pushed their way into the clamor of voices and laughter.

The first table they came to had a sign which said, "Conservatives of Tomorrow." Beside the table stood a flock of people. They were, Jenny knew, of her own age, but somehow they all seemed much older. The men wore ties and jackets, and the girls (*women,* Jenny reminded herself) wore proper dresses. Jenny and Hanna stood, largely ignored, but they listened to the conversations around them. The voices were fine and refined. The talk was of parties, yachts and horses. Jokes were offered and appreciative laughter returned about various people who, Jenny gathered, were senior in the British government. The names discussed were as yet unknown to her, and the humor of the jests escaped her.

Through the crowd of the well-spoken and well-dressed moved a figure, conspicuous because of his incongruity. Her eye still not trained to the finer distinctions of English fashion, Jenny could see, however, that this young man's brown suit was shabby, untailored, and ill-fitting. His wrists stuck out baldly from his jacket's cuffs as his pale hand clutched a small glass of golden sherry. With the eagerness of a puppy-dog scuffling around party guests' feet, he intruded into other people's discussions, introduced himself loudly, and shook hands for too long. His accent, Jenny could tell from her experience of Peter's voice, was Glaswegian. And as he tried to win acceptance through his pitiable over-anxious attempts at conversation, Jenny could see the stiffening in the Conservatives of Tomorrow's cheeks and the subtle turning of their backs toward his face.

As Jenny watched, her eye caught Hanna's. Hanna's mouth gave a quick feigned yawn and her eyes rolled upward. Jenny laughed, pleased to feel her own tension breaking with the laughter. She accepted a sherry and then a second from a passing tray, and the pleasant liquid soon took the edge off her nervousness. These people, she recognized, were no different from the Country Club set in Santa Fe. Were she to join their group, she realized, she would soon find herself lonely and bored. The rich were fundamentally the same the whole world over. Putting down her half-finished third glass of sherry, she smiled and motioned to Hanna with her head, and the two young women left to visit other tables.

Through the evening, they wandered from one table to the next, listening to the conversation each group had to offer, drinking the different drinks each club had laid out. At the French Club they drank white wine and watched earnest black-bereted students smoke Gauloises and speak of Camus and Sartre. Their attempts to converse in French were halting and far from fluent.

They wandered through the hall past the Men's Crew Club, the Women's Hockey Club, the Track and Field Club. They moved on to the tables of the Drama, Arts, Music and Choral Clubs. After a brief drink, they left each table without leaving their names on the sign-up sheets. Jenny felt alone. Among the more artistically, literarily-inclined groups, the people all seemed pretentious, snobbish and, she decided, phony. Their posings and posturings all seemed affected, as if the students were pretending to be something they naturally were not. And those in the straighter, more conservative, groups she found boring. They appeared smug, complacent, and uninteresting in their predictably dull lifestyles.

As she looked around her, Jenny realized that not everyone belonged to a group. To be sure, most of the students looked as lost and confused as she felt. But toward these other new students, she felt no desire to introduce herself and make friends. To her they seemed plain and bland. Jenny knew what she would want for a club, and she could find nothing here to suit her tastes. What she wanted was to feel alive among a group of people, alive and awake to the more dangerous, more intense side of life. She wanted to find again what she had found in the guest houses at Mandalay among the Bohemian artists, the real artists, not mere students pretending to be artists. She wanted what she had found among her drug friends in Santa Fe. She wanted to be among people who knew the thrill of living on the edge of the darker side of life. Around her she could see only what she decided were three kinds of people: the Squares, the Phonies, and the Blahs. Jennifer felt lonely.

She remembered Hanna by her side, still an unknown quantity, and she walked with Hanna to the middle of the room. There, in between the heads and shoulders of many roving bodies, she spotted a familiar face, a face from home. Martin Archuleta stood awkwardly in the crowd. He held a drink in his hand and his head was turned, looking to see which table he should visit next. Jenny felt like laughing with relief to see another stranger like herself. His golden Hispanic skin did not blend at all with the pallor of the white English skin around him. He looked almost comically out of place, this New Mexican boy among the British. For a moment, Jenny's thoughts leaped to her home, to the sights which she and Martin were used to seeing every day. In her mind, she saw the vibrant blue of the New Mexican sky, the warm brown of the adobe buildings, the friendly homeliness of the Plaza in the center of town. For a moment, she wanted to hug Martin.

"Martin!" She called out and walked up beside him. "How's it going?"

"It's going fine," he said, squaring his shoulders and hardening his lost face to make himself look more of a man, more at home in the strange surroundings.

Jenny introduced Hanna and Martin, then said, "So, you having any more luck than we are, finding a good club?"

"Hey, I'm doing all right," he said.

"Yeah," Jenny continued, "but it's not easy to know what to join, is it?"

"Listen," Martin said, suddenly sharp. "Don't you worry about me. I can take care of myself, all right?" He looked over his shoulder as if seeing a club, calling to him urgently. "I gotta go," he said. "See you," and he walked quickly into the crowd.

Hanna turned to Jenny with a smile. "I may not be an expert on men," she said. "But I can tell you, that boy is keen on you."

"Oh, come on," Jenny shook her head. "Martin? He hates me."

"He fancies you is more like it."

"Fancies? Why, Hanna, only old ladies use that word in America. Is that the word they use over here? Is that the way they teach you to talk in Africa?"

"You're getting off the point on purpose," Hanna said with a laugh. "But that doesn't change the fact that Martin has his eye on you."

"That's completely ridiculous," Jenny blushed. "Be serious. Now, come on. Let's get another drink." They walked to a table, any table, just to get a glass which Jenny could quickly empty down her throat.

At last they came to a table which, Jenny noticed through the pleasant haze of her drinks, was surrounded only by women. Not a single man moved among the group. On the table, black lettering on a white sign stated simply "The Women's Group."

"Oh, look," said Hanna. "There's Professor Potter, but I hear everyone just calls her Pots. I met her the other day when I was going around and planning my classes. If you ask me, she's the most intelligent professor in the whole place."

A small group of serious-faced young girls clustered around a masculine-looking don in a severe shirt and tweed jacket. "Isn't she wonderful?" a young, pink, blonde-haired girl whispered to Jenny. "She's a very famous lesbian," she said in an even softer whisper.

Jenny looked at the woman. She was talking about Virginia Woolf's death by drowning as a result of Leonard Woolf's oppression of her talent. Jenny shook her head. The whole Bloomsbury set was one of her passions. In her bedroom at home she had almost every book written on the subject. "That's not right," Jenny said, intruding into the discourse. The words no sooner left her mouth than she regretted them, but the drinks seemed to have emboldened her. "That's not right at all. Virginia Woolf was molested as a child and she never recovered from the experience. Leonard Woolf adored her and cared for her through all of her breakdowns. You can't blame her death on him." The air turned slowly to ice.

The ice in the don's eyes were huge tundras of hatred. "And who are you, Miss Nobody with your horrific American accent, to correct me about my subject?" The question hung nervously in the air. "Well? Cat got your tongue?"

"No." Jenny whimpered. The other students stared with horrified faces.

Professor Potter smiled and began her well-rehearsed explanation. "It was the system which killed Virginia Woolf, the great, English, male-dominated, patriarchal bourgeoisie to which she so firmly belonged. In the end, she was destroyed by the disappointment and the realization that even with all her talent as a woman, she couldn't get the recognition she so badly craved, because"—Professor Potter's voice dropped and the young faces strained to listen—"because Virginia Woolf lived at a time when there were no choices. You," she pointed at the students, "have a choice." She pointed her finger at Jenny. "But you, you'll probably go home and waste your education and get married." She turned her attention to Hanna. "And what will you do?"

Hanna was thrilled to have all of this popular intelligent woman's attention turned squarely on her. "Go back to Gambia," she began, eager to say the right thing, "and work to liberate my people."

"Excellent," Professor Potter beamed with approval.

"And maybe get into Parliament," Hanna continued, encouraged by the obvious correctness of her answer. Her statement was met by small applause which began with the professor then spread to the other girls.

Jenny felt like a leper. And after all, wasn't it she who should be applauded for the political power she would some day gain? But she said nothing, and watched silently as Professor Potter spent the rest of the evening talking to the group, and mostly to Hanna.

Later that night, after Hanna was asleep, Jenny cried softly into her pillow. Why couldn't life be lovely and carefree? Why did the charismatic professor have to be a lesbian? Jenny wasn't frightened by the condition, just confused.

Jenny fell asleep remembering the fire which had leaped from Hanna's eyes and joined the revolutionary fire in the furnace of the professor's heart. Hanna was obviously going to be one of Professor Potter's favorite girls. Jenny was obviously not.

Jenny fell asleep wondering if anyone at all would ever accept her.

* * *

Monday morning changed all that. Peter Stuart was kindness itself. "Listen, love," he said in a soft voice, "don't worry about Pots. She's just a silly old lizzy, all dried up and looking for some young student to prey on." Jenny was shocked. She never expected to hear a professor at Wentworth criticize a colleague. "Besides, you're my student now." He smiled and pointed his finger at her. "You leave her alone. You have me now and I'll treat you as if you were my own daughter. Anything at all that upsets you, you tell me and I'll put it right."

"Well, to tell you the truth," Jenny began shyly, "I'm not used to homosexuality being so—I don't know, so open. We have them in Santa Fe, but I always thought it was all rather peculiar."

"Peculiar," Peter said, thinking what a lovely, soft peach of a girl. "Peculiar as in funny peculiar?"

"Yes, I suppose so." Jenny nodded. "Both really."

Peter smiled. "You're right. They are peculiar. But I'm afraid this university attracts them. We have an alarmingly high percentage of homosexual tutors and professors. All part of the administration's wish to seem liberal and unprejudiced." He frowned. "If you ask me, I think it's a bad thing. And it's particularly a bad thing when they get in and sexually pervert the students. Takes their minds off their studies and away from their ambitions."

"Like mine? To be the first lady of New Mexico?"

"Yes, something like that." Peter watched Jenny's face relax.

"And the last thing I need to know is, what's so terrible about being rich?"

"Nothing, dear. Nothing at all. Just that the clothes you are wearing could keep an Ethiopian family for a year, and the ring on your finger—which I assume is a diamond?—has already caused the death of several babies in South Africa."

Jenny's face frowned. She pulled the ring off her finger and dropped it to the table. "Oh no," she said, her heart in shards around her ankles. "Oh no. I've never looked at it like that."

"Well, my little one, it's time you did. Time you took a look at the real world." Peter got up and put his hand on her shoulder. "It is really," he said, "all a matter of distribution, you see . . . Don't worry about a thing. I'm here to teach you how to think. The world is like a prison, and the university is here to teach you all about the world." He slipped the ring into his pocket.

"I don't know why, but I'm beginning to feel very guilty."

"Guilty?" Peter was amused. "What about?"

"About everything, I guess. About my parents' money, the way I was brought up, how little I know."

"Well," he paused, choosing his next words carefully. "You have a lot to feel guilty for."

"What do you—?"

"Not you personally, of course," Peter interrupted, his tone fatherly and reassuring. "Your class, I mean. Look, Jenny . . . Your class, your family, your . . . No. Let me put it this way. Tell me, Jenny. What is history?"

Jenny hesitated, feeling very put-to-the-test. "I'm not sure I know how to answer that question."

"Then I'll answer it for you," Peter continued, assuming the voice of a lecturer at work, an attorney building a case before the court. "History is simply the struggle between the overprivileged and the un-

derprivileged." Jenny lowered her eyes. "I'm para-
phrasing Marx, of course," Peter went on, "because
I want to really get you thinking, get you to see things
a new way. But the evidence is in front of you. Your
roommate is Hanna Entobe—correct?"

"Correct," Jenny said, curious to see how this line
of thought would unfold.

"Now, Hanna—an African—is precisely your evidence of this injustice, this struggle. Hanna's people
have seen for themselves the rape of a continent.
They have witnessed the inexcusable invasion of
Africa by the Europeans. And what motivated the
European nations to perpetrate this shameful moles-
tation? Greed. For centuries the Europeans have prevailed. That is the overprivileged getting the upper
hand. But now the spirit of revolution is revitalizing
the African peoples, stirring them from their complacency, calling them to take up arms and demand back
what is rightfully theirs."

"That's why Hanna wants to get into the Gambian
government," Jenny offered. "To fight for her people."

"Exactly, Jenny. But unfortunately, your Hanna
has become sidetracked. I found a note from her
tacked to my door when I came in this morning. She's
transferred out of my tutorial, even before I had a
chance to begin working with her. It appears she's
already fallen under the influence of old Pots." He
shook his head. "Poor Hanna. She's missing the point
altogether. She's convinced her battle is against men
when it's really nothing of the sort. It's the Europeans
she needs to fight. The Europeans and their insufferable greed. She's fighting the wrong enemy. Only
when the united peoples of Africa fight their proper

enemy will the underprivileged truly gain the upper hand." He stopped and smiled. "But don't worry. This is simply a phase Hanna's passing through. You'll see. Some young man will come along and take her heart and she'll forget all about her battle of the sexes."

"But you," Jenny said, returning to the heart of Peter's discourse, "you're a European, aren't you? I mean, wasn't it the British who raped Africa the worst? Shouldn't you feel guilty too?"

Peter laughed. "But you miss a vital point," he said. "I am Scottish, and in the eighteenth century we Scots suffered the price of British greed at least as much as any other nation in the world. But your point is well taken. Collectively, we of the British Isles have every reason to feel guilty about our past. And it is this guilt which now demands change from us. This is why I do what I do, teach you what I teach you. Why, take a look at your own American history. Tell me why, in the late eighteenth century, did your founding fathers feel compelled to revolt against Britain?"

"They wanted freedom?" Jenny asked, feeling herself a schoolgirl quizzed in a basic class.

"Yes," Peter inclined his head, "but freedom from what?"

Jenny tried hard to find the right answer. "Freedom from British greed?"

"Precisely!" Peter cried with a pound of his clenched fist on his desk. The light of fervor burned in his eyes. Jenny found herself thrilled. "You see, Jenny, the taxes levied by the over-greedy, over-privileged British made life virtually untenable for the American colonialists. In response, they took the only natural course of action available to them: they re-

volted. The War of Independence was really a war
between the classes. And in the end, the colonialists,
by winning, secured for themselves a nation devoted
to freedom and equality."

"It didn't last long," Jenny said, half to pique
Peter's reasoning, half to prove to him her own powers of thought.

"How do you mean?"

"Well, less than a hundred years later they had to
fight another war because half the country had
become so good at living off the work of its slaves.
Now, there's underprivileged for you."

"Ah," said Peter, delighted with the sharp mind of
his eager student. "An excellent point. But here, when
we talk about your Civil War, we enter some very
murky waters indeed. Tell me, Jenny, why did America fight its Civil War?"

"That's easy," Jenny laughed. "Everyone knows
that. To free the slaves."

"It's as easy as that, is it?" Peter sat back, poised
like a fencer about to strike. "Then who started the
Civil War?" Jenny hesitated and Peter laughed triumphantly. "It was the South. Did you know that? You
see, with the advent of Industrialization, the North
became the industrial center of America. Certainly,
the South grew the cotton to be turned into cloth in
the textile mills of the North, but it was the industrial
North which kept the greater portion of the profits."

"Yes, but what about the slaves?"

"You're questioning. That's good—you're beginning to think beyond what your textbooks taught you.
You're seeing history for what it really is. Very good.
What about the slaves, you ask? Well, let's not forget
that Thomas Jefferson, your freedom-fighter *par excel-*

lence, was himself a slave-owner. Was the notion of slavery really so foreign to America, even in the North?"

"Yes, but Lincoln signed the Emancipation Proclamation."

"A political ploy," Peter said, with a shake of his head. "An artful stratagem. Yes, he signed the Proclamation, but why? Because the North was not winning the War as quickly as they had first expected."

"But you have me all confused," Jenny said, shaking her own head. "Are you saying slavery was a good thing?"

"Confusion is a good thing," Peter smiled. "It's healthy. Nurture it. Cultivate your own confusion. That's how you learn. Was slavery a good thing? Decidedly not. But I'm showing you it's not all as easy as you thought. The struggle between the classes never is easy. And as for slavery, you have Jewish blood in your family, don't you?"

"Yes. How did you know?"

"It's my business to know. Now, nobody knows more about slavery than you Jews. Why did Moses lead your people out of Egypt?"

"To free them from the tyranny of Pharaoh's greed," Jenny answered, now confident in the logic of this argument.

"You learn well. Exactly. Why, the entire Old Testament in its telling of the Exodus, if you view it correctly, is really nothing more than the history of an uprising, a revolt of the underprivileged, isn't it?"

"Well—"

"You see how far back it goes," Peter continued, "this struggle between the classes. And your father. He's a Catholic, right?"

"Yes."

"So we return now, Jenny, to your guilt. It's not your fault individually, Jenny, but do you see the injustice of it all? Your father sits on his millions while millions in the world starve. Really, Jenny, as a Catholic, he should know better."

Jenny stared back, feeling very guilty indeed. "But my father always says that if you gave the oppressed half a chance, they'd oppress everyone else as strongly as the next guy."

"Listen to yourself, Jenny," Peter said, almost pleadingly. "That's the voice of oppression speaking through you. Yes, I know. Too many times throughout history the oppressed have turned around, once in power, and become oppressors themselves. It's a disgrace when that happens. It shames us all, and it has happened far too often. But listen to me, Jenny. This time it will be different. There is revolution on the wind. Here. Now. Even while we sit and speak. Outside that window, the early gusts are blowing. The storm isn't far behind. And when this revolution comes, it will be the last, for never again will the slaves take up the whips of their masters. And do you know what will stop that from happening this time, Jenny?" Jenny shook her head. "Guilt. It is your guilt, my guilt, our guilt, which will keep us pure. We are the meek, Jenny. And we shall inherit the earth. Use your guilt, Jenny. Listen to it. Obey it always."

He fell silent and his eyes burned through Jenny. She sat dumbfounded as if in a spell. Peter smiled, looked at his wristwatch, and broke the spell. "And that," he laughed lightly, "is all the time we have for today." He stood and held his office door open for her. "Go along," he said. He gave Jenny an encouraging pat on the back. "You'll learn," he said. "You're already learning well."

Jenny, always curious, watched and listened as the first, then the second month at Wentworth passed. Obviously, her private schools in Santa Fe and New York had prepared her for nothing. Even the few beatniks who sat in their black berets in the corners of the Santa Fe cafés, loudly discussing existentialism and nihilism, knew nothing. Hanna agreed. "You're a baby," she said in the middle of November, as the two young women labored up the stairs, their arms piled high with books.

"But," Jenny argued, "if they want to kill all the capitalists, that means my dad, doesn't it?"

"No, not if he reforms." Hanna, deeply under Professor Potter's spell, spoke her beliefs with unabashed zeal and earnestness but she softened slightly, seeing the look of apprehension on her roommate's face. "Don't worry," she reassured Jenny. "Your dad will get a chance, just like everybody else. We all get to share."

"What about our house? We all get to share everything already. Ah Ling, our cook, and his family live with us."

"But in the servants' quarters, I'll bet," Hanna said. "When the Revolution comes, you'll all eat at the same table and live in the same rooms. No more servants' quarters. Just think of it, Jenny! Won't it be wonderful?"

Jenny laughed. "I feel like I'm listening to Peter Stuart—all this talk of the Revolution."

"Ah, but there's a difference," Hanna said. "Our Revolution, the one Professor Potter's been telling me about, will be the Revolution of Women. Can't you see it, Jenny? With women in power, everyone will live in equality. And that's when your family and your servants can sit at the table as equals."

Jenny frowned. "But we don't eat the same food. Dad hates Malayan food and Ah Ling thinks white people smell because we eat too much meat."

Hanna shook her head. "Oh, Jenny," she said. "Sometimes I think you're hopeless. I wasn't talking about food at all."

Jenny's head was too confused, full of too many new ideas to digest any more information. For the moment, she wanted nothing more than to change the subject. "Well," Jenny said, "at Christmas you can see it all first hand. Mom sent me the tickets for our holiday. See? I've got them. Here. She says she would love to have you to visit. Then you can see for yourself."

Hanna took the tickets away from Jenny. "Jenny." Disapproval was clear in her eyes. "We can't possibly travel first class."

"No, really. It's okay. We don't pay for them. Dad gets them through Billy, his travel agent. They're tax-deductible."

"Oh, Jenny. I can see change in you, but it's going to be hard. You live in such a mink-lined trap, don't you?"

"Maybe. I suppose so. But listen. Even if we could change the tickets, what would you want to do with the extra money?"

Hanna thought for a minute. "Well, if you don't mind, we need a largish donation for Professor Potter's fund for the university's Lesbian League. Professor Potter's in trouble because some of the parents aren't at all pleased that she is teaching lesbian literature at Wentworth. She said at my last tutorial that it's all very well to teach communism or any other "ism," but if women don't watch out, they'll get to drive the tractors while the men still make all the decisions. She says that happened in China, and when women get powerful, men make war to distract them and send them back into the home."

"Really?" Jenny was about to argue, then she remembered her guilt.

Hanna sighed. "Do read *The Well of Loneliness* by Radclyffe Hall, darling. I've just finished it. She is absolutely fabulous, and her love affair with Violet Dreyfus was so intense. You know, it's the intensity I'm really looking for. So romantic."

"Yeah. I guess so," Jenny said.

Hanna smiled. "Give me the tickets. I'm off." She lowered her eyes then raised them with a surprising girlishness. "You know, Jenny, I think I'm in love."

"Really?" Jenny raised her eyebrows. "A him or a her?"

"A him. I have no idea how I'm going to tell Professor Potter. She'll absolutely die. Pots says a penis is a symbol of male oppression." She giggled. "But I'm beginning to wonder."

Jenny laughed. "Where would you and I be without our fathers?"

"Clones, dear Jenny. Clones of our mothers."

Jenny giggled back. "I'd hate to be like my mother. Listen, you've got to introduce me to your guy sometime but I've got to run. I've got a ton of work to do on my final paper."

Jenny wrote her final paper for her first term at a fevered gallop. All these new ideas sent her into the library for most of the night. In her paper she attempted to bring together the conflicting concepts flooding her mind. In the end she decided on a title for her paper: "Socialism, Feminism and the Coming Revolution." There was little on modern feminism in the library but what existed was treasured and much thumbed by the students.

Jenny, lonely at first, found herself drawn to the political students. The intellectuals were, frankly, boring in their huge obsession with themselves. Jenny read Camus in the original French and thought little of him as a writer. But among the political students, Jenny at last found a group of her peers. The politicos, as they were known on the campus, held the thrill of dangerous living which Jenny had longed for. And in their seriousness, their commitment, their determination—Jenny believed—lay the true leadership of the future.

When Peter Stuart, in his languid, crystalline discussions, taught her the whole horror of the Victorian destruction of the lives of English working people, and the absolute cruelty which sent boys into mines, girls into factories, and little boys up chimneys, Jenny was appalled. "So all our school books lied?" she said.

"Yes. The rich have no conscience when they exploit the poor, nor do they have any qualm about rewriting history to suit their ends."

Again, she felt her guilt niggling. "Do you think we oppress Ah Ling and Maria?"

"Well," Peter's tone was delicate, "put it this way. Do you think a man of his age wants to cook food for other people?"

"We all love Ah Ling very much." She heard herself repeat her father's defense when she had accused him of oppression.

"Yes, but how do you think Ah Ling feels about you?"

"He's always loved me very much."

"Ahem. Don't you think he might have preferred his own house? Maybe, if he wants to cook, he might like to cook for a collective of people who have been growing food for him and his family, don't you think?"

"I suppose so. Do we have to get rid of Ah Ling?" There was anguish in Jenny's voice.

"No, dear. The coming revolution will do all that in good time. You, if you want to be the Governor of New Mexico, will see to that."

"But I'm still so confused. I mean, let's say for a minute I could become Governor. Should I run as a Republican or as a Democrat?"

"Well," said Peter. "Let's look at the possibilities. If you declare yourself a Republican, then you openly admit to your gladness in exploiting the under-privileged. And if you declare yourself a Democrat, then you only pretend to care about the poor. Wealthy Democrats stay wealthy. One way or the other, you're still oiling the grinding wheels of capitalism."

"Then maybe I should declare myself a socialist."

Peter laughed. "If you declare yourself a socialist, then you don't stand a hope in hell of getting into office."

"Now," Jenny shook her head. "I'm really confused. What am I supposed to do?"

Peter laughed. "It's really quite simple. First of all, don't publicly announce yourself a socialist. If you were running in England, you'd be fine. But in America, you'd disqualify yourself form the race before it even began. No. Declare yourself a Republican or a Democrat. It really doesn't matter which. What does matter is that you put the right kinds of policy into effect once you're in office. The best way to work, you see, is from within the system. Once you're in power, it's then that you must see that everyone gets what they need, that New Mexico is governed in a fair and good way."

Jenny smiled. "I'll certainly do that," she said. "And I'm trying to do my share already. Hanna's downgraded our air tickets so Professor Potter can have some money for her Lesbian League."

Peter felt his stomach tighten. He frowned. "You tell Hanna from me, no sexually delinquent people will be tolerated in the new society. You give that money to me. I have a student who needs some funds to go home for Christmas. You see, all those homosexuals carrying on about the place, they'll all be given a chance to reform. And if they don't, they'll go to work camps or get shot. You can't have homosexuals about the place. You watch, we'll subvert them and organize them into a cause. Then, when the time is ripe, we strike and they've all identified themselves. They've paid money into our funds for years, and they will for quite a few more." He grinned a dry, sand-bare grin. "Clever, aren't we? There are no homosexuals in China, are there?"

"No. I suppose not."

"Or Russia," Peter added. "Have you seen any evidence of homosexuals in Russian newspapers?"

"No, I suppose not."

Peter put an arm around Jenny. "Anyway, Jenny," he said, anxious to divert her attention. "I want you to know that I'm very pleased with your paper. The leanings toward feminism were perhaps a bit strong for my tastes but you argued your points well and showed some good, original thinking. I've given you an A+."

Jenny beamed. "Thank you," she said.

Peter bent his head and kissed Jenny on the lips lightly. A blue volt of electricity shot through Jenny's body. "And," Peter said with his sweet, little-boy smile, "I'll need that cash."

Jenny smiled. "I'll send Hanna over with it."

As the door closed, Peter stood in the middle of the room and congratulated himself. His next appointment arrived an hour after Jenny left.

Martin Archuleta had planned to stay in England to work with a revolutionary cell in Archway. "No," Peter said, handing him Jenny's money. "We have all the revolutionaries we need in England. We've been getting into position for years. England is a small country and it's organized from London. We'll take out the mines, the ports, then blow up London, and we have the country tied up. But your country is a different matter. I want you to go back and get to work in Santa Fe. I want you to do this so badly that I'm paying for your ticket myself. Here, take the cash."

Martin's eyes sparkled. For so many years, his family had been rich in worthless property but cash-poor. He watched his inheritance shrink back into the soil on which it had been built. For so many years he watched enviously as the white children played tennis and golf at the country club. He was the caddy to children his own age. He trailed them while they sauntered about in their expensive designer sneakers.

He watched his grandmother die in agony of cancer. His family did not have the exorbitant amounts of cash it took to keep her in the white hospital.

Peter saw the pain in Martin's eyes. "Don't worry," he said. "You'll put it all right in the end." Martin pocketed the money, but quickly his eyes looked downwards to his lap. "Martin," Peter said, a remarkable gentleness in his voice. "What is it? What's the matter?"

"I don't know." Martin shook his head sadly. "Don't get me wrong. Thank you for the money and everything. And it will be really good to get home. It really will . . ."

Peter reached across the desk and put his hand on Martin's shoulder. "I know what the problem is. You've been homesick, haven't you?" Martin nodded his lowered head and lifted a finger to wipe his eyes. "Ah," Peter crooned. "Poor you."

"I don't know," Martin said with a sniff. "I mean, I really appreciate being here and having the chance to study and all that. But my family's way back home. And my father never thought it was a good idea for me to come here anyway. And," he sniffed again, "I don't really have any friends here. I mean, I'm so different from everybody. I don't feel I'm one of them."

"Listen to me, Martin. Look at me." He waited until Martin's watery, golden eyes met his own. "Martin, I want you to listen to me very carefully. Never, never should you feel that you're not important. You're very important, Martin. And very special. You're probably one of the most important people we have here."

"Yeah?" Martin felt a faint hope begin to stir within. "Why?"

"Because you have a mission to be the instrument, the sword, of the coming revolution. For too long injustice has prevailed in the world. And it's our job, *your* job, to set that straight. And do you know who's been worst at spreading injustice throughout the world? America. I don't mean you, Martin. Because your people are not truly American. Your people have been hurt more than anyone by the Americans. For centuries now, the Americans have exploited the natural kindness and the industry of the Mexicans and—"

"I'm not Mexican," Martin insisted.

"What?"

"I'm not Mexican. The Mexicans are a mix between the Central American Indians and the Spanish conquistadores. But I'm not Mexican. My people came straight from Spain. I'm Hispanic. Pure-blooded Spanish."

"Of course," Peter said, thinking quickly, "but the Mexicans are your brothers. And why are they your brothers? Because in the eyes of the Americans, you all look the same. Do you really think the Americans care whether you're Mexican or Hispanic or pure-blooded Spanish?"

"No."

"And do you really think they'd exploit you any less if you were Spanish or Central American Indian? Of course not, Martin. The Americans have always exploited everyone. It's always been that way. Their imperialist greed is crushing the world now, as it has done ever since America first became a country. Why, look at the early history of America. Why do you think they rebelled against Britain in the very beginning?"

"They wanted freedom," Martin answered.

"Rubbish," Peter exclaimed. "That's your schoolboy textbooks talking. You know better than that, Martin. Think, Martin, *think*. The American colonialists wanted to break away from England because England was their conscience. As long as they were ruled by the British Crown, they had to behave themselves. They had to control their greed, their lust for taking over the world. So what did they do? They fought for their "independence." But it was no independence they were after; it was a licence. A complete and total license to take over all the people and all the land they could get their hands on. And it worked. As soon as they had broken from their English conscience, they set about stealing an entire continent. They stole the West from the Indians, and if the Indians wouldn't cooperate, they killed them. They stole half of the country from Mexico. Why, your New Mexico is really Mexico. It's only called *New* Mexico because the Americans stole it and made it part of their country. And what did your people, the Mexicans, the Hispanics, the Spanish—your brothers—get in return? You got the privilege of being their slaves. Tell me, Martin. How do you people live in New Mexico? Do they live as well as the white Americans? Do you live as well as, say, Jennifer Jensen?"

"That'd be the day." Martin smiled.

"It will be the day, Martin. That's what we're fighting for; for the day when you—the real New Mexicans—overthrow the tyrannical rule of the usurping white Americans and live as equals. That is your mission, Martin. That's what makes you so important, so very vital. Never let anyone make you feel you're not important."

Martin nodded for a while, considering the weight of his importance. "I see what you're saying," he said. "But shouldn't I be back there right now? I mean, with my family? Shouldn't I be with them, fighting, instead of sitting over here? I mean, sometimes, with them over there and me over here I get to feeling guilty and—"

"Stop." Peter held up his hands. "Stop right there. Never again, Martin, never let me hear the word 'guilty' come out of your mouth. Guilt is a wasted emotion. Nothing constructive ever comes out of guilt. And if you have any, Martin, get rid of it. Destroy it. If you ever feel guilt beginning inside you, stamp on it right away. We must remain guiltless, pitiless, merciless. You have no need of guilt because you're doing the best thing for your people here. Right here, even while I'm talking to you. You're learning, Martin. And everything I teach you will be useful to you someday. Someday you'll be in a position of great power, and then you can use everything I've taught you. You see? You must finish your education here, and then you can go back and make a difference. I'm sending you back for the holidays not because I want you to stay there. No, that would be a coward's way out. I'm sending you back because I want you to see—really see. You've seen it before, but this time see it even harder. See the difference between the way you live and the way people like Jennifer Jensen live. See what people like her family do to people like your family. See it and let yourself feel angry. Listen to me, Martin. Not guilty, but angry. Really angry. Then, when you return, I will teach you what to do with your anger. I'll show you how to set things right."

"I'm already angry," Martin nodded. He felt his heart beat faster. "And Jenny Jensen, part of me hates her. But another part of me—"

"Careful, Martin. In any war, you must always be careful. Jenny might be useful to us someday—you might need to work with her."

"Work with her? You must be kidding. She's got so caught up in this feminism crap I don't think she'll ever work with a man. And I don't know that I'd ever want to work with a woman's libber."

Peter laughed. "Yes, some of what she believes is feminist, but that too can be useful." He paused and smiled at Martin. "Let me tell you a little story." Then he shook his head. "No, I really shouldn't tell you."

"Go ahead." Martin smiled with interest. "Tell me."

"I really shouldn't." Peter's eyebrows were raised and a sparkle lit his eyes. At last he nodded. "Well, I wouldn't tell just anybody. But as you're so important to the cause, I'll tell you." He shifted in his chair and smacked his lips. "Let me see. Where should I begin? You see, I was recruited as a university student myself and I worked hard in the movement. The horrors of social injustice fired me then as much as they do now. I worked long and hard—as you will work—and I became, shall we say, highly regarded. Well, in the end, I had some very senior connections. In fact, my work took me all the way to Moscow."

"No kidding?" Martin was genuinely impressed.

"No kidding. You see, the Russians had their history of heartless imperialism too. But they changed all that. They worked for, fought for and, in the end, won their equality, their end to injustice. And now they know better than anyone just how much America needs to be brought to heel. Well, as I was saying, my work took me to Moscow, and with some very senior, very powerful people. Well, one night I was having dinner with some big men in the Russian government—the Minister of Defense, and the Prime Minister of Russia's wife, and . . ." he paused, "with the Prime Minister himself."

Martin's eyes widened. "Wow," he breathed.

"Wow, indeed, Martin. Anyway, it was during dinner that the Minister of Defense was discussing the best way to break down the capitalist stronghold in America. What was the heart of American strength? What would be their Achilles' heel? And then the Minister of Defense hit on the answer: the American family. The Americans treasure their family as a means of hoarding capital. The families in Russia and the new China had evolved past all that. They were willing to put country first and family second. And it was their work for the common good which made those countries strong. But the American family was the beating heart of American capitalism. So, what were we to do? What new psychology could we come up with to break down the American family?"

Martin shrugged.

"I'll tell you. It was actually the Prime Minister's wife who came up with the answer. Lovely woman, she was. And she looked at me while she spoke. I remember the exact words she said: 'You always subvert the women first, as in Africa, offering them contraception, free doctors, abortions and the rest. It was the women of the countries who adopted communism as a literary force in their lives. It was the French women in the French Revolution who finally went to the barricades and liberated France. It will be the American women, surely the most aggressive women in the world, who will take to the streets and force their men to share their politics. After all, American men are known for their cowardice where their women are concerned. Read Jung's speech of the thirties. He says it all.' "

Peter's voice dropped off, and his eyes looked into the distance. "And," he continued, clearing his throat. "That's how it all began. Such a brilliant plan. Of course, it would be a woman to come up with it. It takes a woman to understand the female mind. So you see, this feminism can be very useful to us."

"Come on," Martin cocked his head. "You're pulling my leg. You're really telling me the truth? I mean, about having dinner with the Prime Minister and everything, and his wife comes up with the idea of feminism to bring down America?"

Peter spread his hands. "Well, you can believe me or not. You're a freethinker, Martin. And that's why I like you. But think about it. It's beginning to work pretty well, isn't it?"

Martin had to nod. "But are you telling me all families have to go?"

"Not at all. Certainly not your family. I mean, you've got a good family behind you. I envy you that. It wasn't like that with mine." He lowered his eyes. "My father always assured me I'd never get anywhere. And even though I got a first from Wentworth, it never really made a difference to him—he just wanted me to work in the mines with him. And my mother never really noticed anything I did. She just wanted grandchildren from me. I suppose it never meant anything to them. What did my life at

Cambridge have to do with theirs in Glasgow?" Peter stared at the wall and for a moment he thought he saw his father's disapproving face staring back at him.

"But you know," he said, turning to Martin, "as I sat there at the Prime Minister of Russia's table, I thought, 'Now I've made it. Now I've gone somewhere.'" He put his hands together. "And you can feel that same feeling of accomplishment, too, Martin. Only you're lucky. You've got a good family to work with you. We need good, pure-blooded Spanish families like yours. That will keep us strong. No, it's the capitalist families we have to attack, families like Jennifer Jensen's. Remember this. If you ever need to really hurt someone, break apart their family. Hurt the people they love most."

"I see," Martin said. And he nodded.

"Listen, I have another student coming in soon, so we'll stop here. Take the money, get yourself a plane ticket, go home and look around you with open eyes. I want you to be very, very nice to Jennifer Jensen. I have plans for both of you. Long-term plans." He smiled at Martin. "And as for that other part of you, the part that doesn't hate her?" Martin blushed. "Whatever you do, you must never, never get into her bed. Is that a promise?"

Martin nodded. "That's a promise. A woman is never worth the price of a revolution."

"Good. That's what I want to hear. A revolutionary must be ready to kill and die for the cause at all times. He must even be prepared to kill his own mother if necessary."

Martin nodded.

Peter laughed. "Not *your* mother, of course." Peter was pleased. Martin was doing nicely, he thought, as he hugged the boy goodbye. "Have a good Christmas," he said.

"And you," Martin replied.

"I don't celebrate Christmas, Martin. There is no such thing as God. Religion, as Marx said, is the opium of the masses."

Martin left, puzzled by a vast blackness which settled on Peter's face. As Martin walked from the office, he quickly said a Hail Mary to himself to clear his soul from the sin of disbelief.

ᖇ᠍᠍᠍᠍᠍᠍᠍ CHAPTER 49 ᖇ᠍᠍᠍᠍᠍᠍᠍

Jenny sat by the window in the tourist section of the airplane. Her expensive cashmere coat contrasted oddly with Martin's jeans and his open-necked, checked New Mexican shirt. On the other side of Martin, Hanna lay asleep. Jenny envied Hanna her ability to fall asleep in any place and on any occasion. "It was the bloody missionaries with their incredibly long sermons," she once explained to Jenny. "I learned to sleep sitting upright with my eyes open." Now she lay languidly asleep, her long legs concertinaed against the seat ahead.

Jenny looked sideways at Martin. He had joined the girls at the airport in a very good mood. "Ah, I see we'll be traveling together, princess."

Jenny smiled. Martin in a good mood was irresistible. "Well," she offered, "it's ridiculous to spend all the money on a first class seat."

"Yeah, it is," Martin agreed amiably. "And it's even more ridiculous if you consider that the nose of the airplane is by far the most dangerous place to sit. You see, if the plane crashes, the nose goes down and the tail goes up. So the chances are that the proles like us will be saved and the fat-cat capitalists will drown." Jenny was entranced. She enjoyed sitting next to Martin. He talked nineteen to the dozen, his eyes alight, his Hispanic hands waving in the dim light of the cabin. Jenny felt she could listen to him forever. He wished, smelling her perfume, that he could lie back and slip his big fingers under her soft, sensual coat and under her skirt, stroking her gently until she flushed and came. They lay on the slightly tilted chairs next to each other, Jenny restraining a strong desire to run her hands down the long, lean thigh which pressed so close to her leg. Thigh to thigh they lay entwined in a forbidden, and unbidden, passionate embrace of the mind until they fell asleep, unslaked. Jenny dreamed of Martin's body in hers; Martin dreamed of Jenny's clear white skin and her long auburn hair aglow with the pleasure of his sexual love. But then Peter's face intruded upon Martin's dream and the excitement died away. A pity, Martin thought, as he awoke to the clatter of the early trolley pushing past. The stewardess had a nice ass, but Jenny had a blocked-off innocence and gave off a childlike vulnerability which Martin found exciting.

All his first semester at Wentworth he trifled with several of the sexually aggressive girls in the university. New ideas were what Wentworth was about. New girls demanded sex. Martin was a willing partner. But the girls, always looking for the new thrill, left him as quickly as they had landed in his bed, and in the end Martin invariably found himself alone and lonely.

Anxious not to be a complete social outcast, Martin hovered around the outskirts of a group called the Young Anarchists. Anarchy was such an attractive philosophy. Peter Stuart taught about the world of Emma Goldman and her crowd as if Emma had been his mother. Emma, born and raised in America, wrote revolutionary prose all her life, was expelled from America, welcomed in Russia and treated like the heroine which, Peter explained, she was. For Martin, the idea of a revolutionary woman was even more exciting than that of a revolutionary man. He had found the young socialist meetings often tedious and long-winded. The communists who merged with the young socialists, loved minutiae. They stood on street corners; they proselytized. Jenny, for instance, spent several hours on the plane explaining her new-found religion. But for Martin, still undecided on his precise political persuasion, anarchy was immediate. No thirty-year plans. No cells. Just big bangs and a lot of blood. Then change. The rich on the north side of Santa Fe would have to change their tune. They would have to lose the looks of disgust that they gave to the Hispanics, never truly seeing the wealth and tradition behind the Hispanic culture, the intricate details of the weddings, feasts, processions. On the whole, few friendships were made between the Hispanic and Anglo communities.

Martin's father preferred to run the politics of Santa Fe with an even, iron hand. Once, in Martin's childhood, his relatives lived on the ranch and he rode with his father and other cowboys to corral the cows. Now they lived on the family's old "in town" house in the Barrio. All other members of the family were in walking distance.

Martin knew, however, that all of this—the traditions, the families, the lifestyles—were being swept away by the coming wave of development. Martin did not want development or what the politicians in the state capital euphemistically labeled "community improvement." The developers, as far as Martin and his family were concerned, could keep their money, as long as the Hispanics could keep their ways. The Hispanics still treasured the system whereby, for a small fee paid to the Game Commission, they could hunt in the forests around Santa Fe and hang the freshly killed deer by their antlers, giving pounds of meat to the families. Another license fee paid, and trout, shad and bass were all hung in neat rows to be gutted by the women. Everyone had vegetable gardens and the traditional women took enormous pride in their jam-making. But change was coming, worst of all among the women.

As Martin sat and thought on the plane, he felt his anger growing and he prided himself on that anger. He smiled at the thought of using the feminists someday, all according to Peter's prophecies.

The girls Martin had met at the university were hard and aggressive. They argued with him. They contradicted him in public in a way which was quite unlike Spanish women. A Spanish woman never contradicted her husband in public. May he pray for protection from the Virgin Mary when he got home but, in public, respect from a woman meant she was modest at all times, even if everyone knew that behind her front door a woman like Martin's mother was the power, the center of everything. Outside, Paulo Archuleta might throw his weight about but inside, he was quiet like a dog. He loved his wife Sophia and she loved him. Martin loved them both and he swore that they would end their lives in the house the family had built together if not a better, wealthier house commandeered from the Anglos. The vow of the son to protect his parents was the most serious vow to be taken.

The airplane's breakfast trolley was now behind him. "Wake up." Martin tickled Jenny's nose with his fingers. Jenny woke up with a start. Hanna stirred. "Come on, Hanna," Martin scolded. "You'll miss breakfast."

The thought of missing food after years of semi-starvation caused Hanna to sit up. "Breakfast?" she said in her curiously English upper-class accent. "How lovely." She smiled at Jenny, having nearly forgiven Jenny completely for asking for the airfare money back. She was too excited about seeing America to hold a grudge.

All three of them sat munching toast and absorbing the smell of coffee. Jenny tried not to think of the breakfast being served in the front of the plane. The thick china, the huge reclining seats . . . Her back ached. The big silver jugs of coffee, the large white napkins . . . Never mind. Nearly home. At least the house wasn't hers, so not too many apologies to Hanna would prove necessary. She wondered how her family would take to her new conversion.

George was pleased with Jenny's grades from university. All he said was, "They're not teaching you all this Commie rubbish, are they? I didn't pay all that money to have them tell you I have to give it all to them Commie bastards." He was so nervous of Hanna he didn't bother to say much more on the first night they were home.

Later, when Hanna and Jenny left to unpack in the cabana, he complained. "She looks at me funny, Esther. I don't think I've ever had a black staying in my house." He looked doubtful. "I've read about the African blacks. Not the nice tame ones we saw on our honeymoon. No, I'm talking about the ones who live way back in the bush. Some of them eat people, you know." He smiled at his wife. "I hope Ah Ling has the cupboards full. I'd hate to see her go hungry." But George was altogether delighted to have her home, his daughter.

Later, after Esther was in bed, he toured the property, checking to see that all the doors were locked. Noticing a light under Jenny's door in the cabana, he stopped and knocked, pleased to see that Hanna's door was closed. Jenny was sitting up in bed, her knees under her chin, looking pensive. George sat heavily on the end of her bed. "What's the matter, honey?" he said. "Something bothering you?"

Jenny gazed at his face. "Yes," she said. "I'm different, you know, dad. All your life, you've had money."

"No, I didn't. I started off in a teensy-weensy store over in Lamy long before you were born. Hell, I worked my ass off night and day. Especially when I met your mother. I knew she had to have the best. Nothing but the best. So I sold up in the end and started up the Phoenix Company. It wasn't always so easygoing, you know. And then you came along, and then Max. Everything I do is for my family."

"I know. But don't you think the world is a big family?"

"No, I don't. I think there're those who work and those who don't. And I don't intend to pay my hard-earned dollars for those who don't, like the bums down on the Plaza or those welfare scroungers. What we need, instead of those Commie welfare workers lining their pockets with taxpayers' money, is the good old poorhouse. If you mess up, you go there and sort yourself out until you can get back on your feet again with hard work and maybe the help of a little charity. I don't mind charity. A little charity never hurt. But the way charity works is you get help from your friends until some day you can help someone else out. That's what we need, instead of the Governor throwing money at all the problems in the state. Every creep and panhandler in America comes to Santa Fe."

"Yeah?" Jenny was interested.

"Why?" George asked himself, then frowned. "Because we got a whole heap of Commies on the run from McCarthy. They wouldn't hack it back there in Washington or even in California, so they all come here to Santa Fe where they can get away with anything. And they don't do any of it properly. You see, welfare becomes a lifestyle. People get stuck in it. Charity's different. Charity just helps you out through the rough spots."

"But if the government was set up properly, then everybody's needs would be met and there would be no need for charity."

"Is that what they've been teaching you? Listen, honey. They've got it all backwards. That all sounds a great idea, but the problem with that kind of thinking is you have to assume that government's a good thing. But it isn't. You get a group of people together, call them a government, give them all the power, and—bang! They turn rotten overnight. Now, the US government knows this, at least the Republicans do. And even the government knows it's got to watch itself so it doesn't become too powerful and run around controlling too much of people's lives. That keeps it straight. Then there's room for charity. But you get one of your Commie governments, and charity takes a fast fly out the window. People's good nature goes down the tubes, and you're left with nothing but a bunch of nasty people walking around."

"That's absurd," Jenny argued. "How can you be so unidealistic. I mean—"

George yawned. "Listen, I gotta get some sleep. Let's not talk politics, darling. I've got you home now. Your Aunt Etta's dying to see you. And your grandparents are too."

"Dad," Jenny said, "I've got to talk politics. I want to be a politician. I want to be Governor of this state."

George blinked. "Well, that's what your mother's always wanted for you," he said. "But I've never been sure if it's what you want. I thought that was just when you were a little girl."

"No." Jenny shook her head. "You're miles out of line, dad. The world you grew up in doesn't exist any more. We have television now. The world is hooked up. What happens in Japan affects what happens in England. If children starve to death in India, it's my responsibility." She slipped her hand under the covers. "If we consume too much, the African nations do without."

George shook his head. "In my day," he said,

"women didn't discuss politics. That's all a man's world."

Jenny smiled. "That's why everything is such a mess. Women don't want to be protected. They want to cooperate as equals."

George looked mournful. "Just tell that to your mother," he said. "All my life, I've opened doors for women. I've always paid the mortgage. I always open the door for your mother, or any other woman. I give up my seat so a lady can sit down. And now you're telling me I've been doing it all wrong?"

"Right." Jenny nodded. "Hanna is going back to Africa to get rid of the British influence so that Gambia can be truly independent."

"How is she going to do that?" George asked nervously.

"They'll chuck them out with the help of the Russians."

"Oh," said George. "I see."

"And I will become the first lady Governor of New Mexico." She sat in bed, so tiny and determined, George could not argue.

He kissed her on the forehead and said, "Well, the old man, your father, better catch some shut-eye. I'm off to make some capitalist money tomorrow to pay for all this. Good night, honey."

"Good night, dad." Jenny fell into a deep sleep after realizing how much she had missed her comfortable bed, her deep carpet and her modern bathroom—above all, the bathroom, palatial compared to the dormitory bathrooms at Wentworth. Her last feeling before falling completely asleep was one of guilt that her bathroom should be so important to her. She felt so bourgeois, so guilty.

"I'll change," she promised Martin, who invaded her dreams.

The first few days home, Jenny dragged Hanna around Santa Fe. The whole town glittered with Christmas. The shops were bursting with produce, Kaune's, on the Old Pecos Trail, was piled high with wonderful boxes of biscuits. Ah Ling was busy and Esther frantic. Her mantelpiece was awash with invitations from senior Santa Fe politicians, including the Governor and Senator de Chavez, Jenny's godfather. Etta alone was giving a family party. Other friends were giving drinks parties. All over the north side of town and in the Tesuque Valley to the north of Santa Fe, life was now a huge social event.

Hanna found the luxury bewildering. She preferred to visit with Ah Ling's wife Mei Mei. In their simple servants' quarters, Ah Ling's smiling children lived a completely different life from the rest of the people of Santa Fe. It was the waste which broke Hanna's heart. When she heard that large boxes of fresh vegetables from the supermarkets were thrown away every day or given to the pigs, she burst into tears. When she saw the quantity and quality of clothes in the Salvation Army Thrift Shop, she was shocked and then angry. "You Americans are too careless," she said.

Jenny, having lived in England, could now understand Hanna's anger, for Jenny had seen that England no longer lived in the style of grandeur Jenny had imagined.

Hanna felt at home in the Barrio. "If these are your slums, give my mother a ring," she said. "Only we don't have a telephone."

Esther never felt very safe in Hanna's presence. Hanna stared at her intently as if she were looking at some exotic butterfly trapped on a pin. Indeed, for Hanna, used only to her family and friends, Esther was an exotic butterfly.

Christmas, on the whole, was punctuated by visits from briskly smiling door-to-door salesmen for the Lord clad in bri-nylon, buttoned cowboy shirts. The fact that God designed and populated Africa first never crossed their tiny, inch-deep minds as they tried to evangelize Esther's family and her African visitor. Only the Catholic priests, with their knowledge of mysticism, began to understand the whole, huge spiritual love affair between God and Africa. But no, here in America, Hanna felt the loneliness, the plastic.

If Albuquerque was America, America must be a giant shopping mall. Santa Fe was an exception. The little adobe houses stood in broken-down sincerity along the road which ran outside Kaune's shop on the Old Santa Fe Trail. Here, Hanna felt at home. All of the grocery store's staff were Hispanic and the food lay casually on the counters. Hanna missed her mother's cooking, but the New Mexico dishes of *posole* with green and red chilli, the hot spicy *Frito* pies, were a remembered taste. The Hispanic community was a warm community. Hanna felt less lonely among them.

Esther and George Jensen's house felt like a colossal wedding cake. The drawing room seemed an Aladdin's cave full of objects Hanna had never seen. The portrait of Jenny as a little girl hung, unfinished. "I don't know where he went," Jenny said, "but I heard the other day he's quite famous in New York." Orlando's story lay untold and all but forgotten, pushed down far into the melting pot of her childhood.

The distance between Jenny and her mother had grown so wide that Jenny now saw Esther almost completely as a stranger. Max, this Christmas, was busy with all his various extracurricular activities, and whenever he could find the time he sat in front of his piano and practiced with genuine love and devotion. If George pressured him too much during the holidays ("It just isn't natural for a boy to stay cooped up in the house all the time,") Max would gulp his breakfast and be gone, walking through the snow with his bike to visit his friend Lucienne. Esther despaired of never having time for the long, intimate talks they had on the Continent. Max took off with the healthy instinct of a border Collie. Two things filled the majority of his free time: music and exercise. Esther's interest in his affairs had become tiresome and his life, he decided—even at the young age of eight—was his own.

Life had begun for him this last summer. He was free and Santa Fe was a delightful place to live for a boy who loved the art galleries and the Indians outside the Palace of the Governors—all of whom had known Max from when he was tiny. He asked them all about their lives and listened to the Indian storytellers. He visited Frazer's Pharmacy and strolled the De Vargas Mall with Lucienne Johnson.

If Esther felt lonely within her own family, she did not share it with her daughter. Jenny, she knew, was not interested in what was happening in her life. She kept herself busy with one committee meeting after another. This year she was chairman of the local branch of the Republican Party. She was going to organize the primary campaign for the chosen Republican state senator to run for reelection. Besides, Esther's interests had veered in a new and secret direction, a direction which involved her family not in the slightest. And, Esther reassured herself many times, there's no reason for them ever to find out.

"One day," Jenny said, looking at her mother at lunch time, "I'll be running for office as a Democrat."

The gauntlet was flung, the glove down. Max and Hanna waited for the reply. "Well," Esther said coldly, "you'll have to run without my help. No child of mine running on a Democratic ticket could ever expect my support."

"Why not?" Jennifer's eyes were fierce. "Why ever not?"

"Because, my dear, you don't seem to understand much about politics in this state. Your father is one of the state's richest men. John Joseph Lipstone's father died while you were away."

"J.J.'s dad?"

"Yes, and J.J. inherited a fortune nearly as large as your father's. They got rich because they worked hard. There are people in this town, and they vote Democratic, who want to stop all that. Take away all your father's money and your grandfather's money, and give it to some mythical idea that doesn't work. I sit on the committees in this town. I know about every family who's on welfare. I know about the families who swap food stamps for alcohol and cigarettes, and the women who won't use contraception because more babies mean more money and more welfare workers. It's all very well to be nineteen and full of ideas." She looked at Hanna. "I'm sorry, dear," she said, "but I am not a woman to apologize for my way of life."

Hanna stared back. She thought of her own mother slaving in the small wooden shack in Gambia. She thought of the washing still done in the river. Of course there was now an affluent class of black people in the cities—some doctors, dentists and architects—but they conformed to the white man's image. They took off their cool robes and donned hot, uncomfortable suits and ties. Hanna's father had died before he could provide his family with sufficient money. He was a doctor, trained at the University of Moscow. His death in a typhoid epidemic left Hanna's mother with five children, a small house, a lush garden and the asinine faces of local Christian missionaries. The gap between the two worlds was too huge and too wide to even contemplate an understanding. Hanna decided not to try. "You have no reason to explain," she said politely. "You have a beautiful house and a husband who adores you. And Jenny, I hope, will be equally lucky."

"Except," Jenny said, "I don't need to be rich."

Max, bored by all this talk which seemed to go on endlessly, between the two girls, said, "Well, I want to be fabulously rich. And J.J. has the neatest Porsche in town. He said he'd give me a drive in it."

Lunch finished with a general discussion of who was invited for Christmas Eve. "Can I invite Martin Archuleta?" Jenny asked.

"Well . . ." Esther was hesitant. Martin and a few of his friends were known by those who ran Santa Fe to be a little wild. In his youth, Martin had often been in trouble with the police on the Plaza.

"He really has changed, mom. He's quiet and well-mannered now. Please?"

"All right," Esther agreed grudgingly.

* * *

Christmas Eve came in Santa Fe, announced by the usual "Ho Ho Ho" in the Mall as Father Christmas strode about. *Luminarios*—paper bags filled with sand and a burning candle in the middle—surrounded the city of Holy Faith. The great doors of the cathedral opened for Midnight Mass. The shops closed and the exhausted shopkeepers left their shelves empty and asleep. Jenny loved all this. The tall Norwegian pine tree they found in the Agua Fria Nursery was now decorated with ornaments from her childhood. Under the tree the presents kept their secrets until the next morning.

Now, in the rustle of cocktail dresses and general chatter of the Christmas guests, Jenny saw Martin coming across the room. Their eyes met in a savage embrace. Jenny felt as if she had been lifted above the crowd by an invisible force and deposited lightly by his side. "Hello." Martin's voice was warm. "Nice place you have here."

"Yes." Jenny was a little nervous. She had heard Martin's views on the subject of millionaires. "Dad didn't inherit the money," she blurted out. "He made it all himself."

Behind her, J. J. Lipstone loomed. "I've just inherited a huge amount of damned hard work looking after the show. I can see why my dad worked so hard. Hello, Jenny," he said, turning toward her. "Nice to have you back. You look lovely." He held both her hands in his and kissed a hello on her cheek.

To Jenny, J.J.'s presence felt like a comfortable, warm coat. If Martin felt excitingly dangerous, J.J. felt infinitely safe. He had known her since childhood and had seen her through all the varied, and sometimes rocky, stages of her life. J.J. was solid and consistent. Whatever changed in her life, she knew she could count on J. J. Lipstone to remain the same. Looking into his eyes, she was surprised at how glad she felt to see him again. At Wentworth she had never really been aware she had quietly missed this kind boy, now a genial young man. She could see in his eyes he held real love for her. For a moment, she forgot Martin at her side.

"You'll have to work hard," Martin said, his eyes cold and intense as he stared at J.J. The sharp voice brought Jenny quickly out of the cozy warmth of her thoughts. "You'll have to work hard to keep what was never yours." Martin turned on his heel and walked out of the house. Once outside, he leaned against the wall, shaking. Of course, J.J. did not recognize him. He was just a caddy making money to get to college. J.J. was the young boy with the heavy golfing bag who walked ahead of Martin talking to his friends. Now, J.J. was still ahead of Martin. To add to the insult, he saw J.J.'s new Porsche with its personalized license plates sitting in front of him, gleaming under the lamp. Martin went over and kicked the tire.

Inside the house, J.J. made a face. "I know him from somewhere," he said.

Jenny, shocked at Martin's reaction, stood still. Then, mindful of her manners as a hostess, smiled weakly at J.J. and moved off to circulate among the other guests. Too bad, she thought. Poor Martin.

Later, J.J. drove Jenny and Hanna to the cathedral for Midnight Mass. Jenny had no idea, as the bells welcomed Christmas morning after the service, that Martin was watching her with empty, desolate eyes from behind one of the pillars. As they walked through the doors, J.J. put his arm around Jenny. "Merry Christmas," he said and hugged her.

Jenny laughed. "Merry Christmas, J.J.," she said. With a sense of outright shock, she observed, as if from a distance, her own emotions at being held in J.J.'s arms. Her body felt warmed, as if by a large and steady fire. Yet could she really be feeling so much for J.J.? J.J. Lipstone, whom she had always taken for granted, assuming him to be as much a part of the Santa Fe scenery as the Sangre de Cristo mountains above the town. This, she was amazed to hear a voice in her head say, is where I belong. In Santa Fe, she thought, with J.J.

Quickly her thoughts returned to confusion. Good, old—by now familiar—confusion. It's probably just because I've been away, she told herself. And she found her confusion tinged with guilt. Shaking her head as if to clear her mind, she walked down the cathedral steps and into the icy air of the winter's night with J.J. by her side.

From his hiding place, Martin spat into a bank of fresh white snow.

CHAPTER 50

The years leading to the swinging sixties blossomed like an evil-perfumed flower. In Santa Fe, always well ahead of the trend, the degeneration of family life showed earlier than anywhere else in the world. To

Jenny, her first Christmas and the last innocent Christmas was now. The loss of her innocence was the knowledge that her mother was having an affair.

Hanna and Jenny were shopping at the mall for a final time two days before they were to leave for England. Hanna, over the weeks, was less angry than on her arrival. Now, she was more confused. The politics of her father seemed unassailable at Wentworth where the professors and the student body shared her left-wing views and encouraged her in the name of feminism to explore ideas. "Of course, lesbian behavior is a necessary part of a developing isolation from the dominating patriarchal world of men," Professor Potter intoned on a great many occasions. Recently, Hanna heard such words with her head lowered in embarrassment, guilty for her own growing feelings of love—for a man.

George and Esther Jensen were a puzzle to Hanna. George adored his wife to such an extent that Hanna had a disloyal thought: wasn't that exactly the way she herself wanted to be adored by a man? She explained her confusion to Jenny. "Of course," Jenny said. "But then, I suppose I've always taken dad's love for mom for granted."

"You mean," Hanna said, as they sat in the Dairy Queen in the mall, sipping ice cream sodas and resting their weary feet, "you want doors held open for you and everything carried?"

Jenny said, "Maybe manners are still manners."

Hanna sighed. "You know, maybe it's not such a terrible thing to love a man after all. And maybe I have the right to love whomever I want, not the man my family picks for me. I don't know. I think I've been hiding for too many years. I think that in order to run away from sex—no, not just sex, from lust, my own, another person's, I've been running away from all men. Like not always having to deal with the men in the party. Once it was decided that everybody had to sleep with everybody or you'll hurt their feelings, the men went wild. I guess I've been frightened."

"I know." Jenny looked at Hanna. "Nancy has had over a hundred lovers, mostly one-night stands." She sighed. "She thinks I'm too square. Actually"—she laughed—"I think I'm really cubed. I just couldn't do it any more. I did try it for a while, sleeping around. The first time, I mean the first time I really went all the way, was at school in New York. And then when I got back to Santa Fe, it just seemed the natural thing to do. And do," she laughed. "And do some more." She shook her head. "But it just doesn't seem right to do that, if not for my own self-esteem, but to dad. He'd be so disappointed if I went through life being the kind of woman who lets herself get used by men all the time."

"You're lucky, you know," Hanna said. "I know all about my dad's politics from his pamphlets and books, but he died before I had time to get to know him."

"Yeah. Your dad is sort of the first man in your life."

"He's important. You hear all about mothers in this country, and almost nothing about fathers. You're lucky to have a father who loves you so much."

"I know." Jenny laughed. "Even if he is a capitalist swine."

Hanna laughed gently in return. "Listen," she said suddenly. "These are my last days in America and I don't want to waste the whole time sitting in a mall. Let's get out of here."

"Great idea. Tell you what. Let's go and have a drink at La Fonda, a sort of Goodbye America, Hello England drink. Gee, I really hate to go back. I hate to say this, but I do miss the comfort."

Hanna grinned. "I must admit, I could get corrupted but then we'll soon settle in."

"Yeah. To the launderette. We can spend Saturday morning watching our knickers going round and round, I suppose."

Hanna was admiring the La Fonda dining room with its gaily painted flowers dancing their way across the walls, when Jenny saw her mother sitting in a dark corner with Jenny's godfather, Senator de Chavez. Her mother's back was unmistakable, the carriage of her head was poised and neat. Premonitions of the sixties' disheveled look did not affect Esther. She sat at La Fonda perched on her chair. She wore a neat suit but, bowing to current high fashion—as always— she wore no hat or gloves. Senator de Chavez, his handsome Spanish face alight, talked animatedly to Jenny's mother.

Jenny felt a great pang of sorrow at first to see her mother so obviously animated in the company of a man other than her father. Then, as she watched the exchanges of laughter and little touches on the hand, her sorrow became a welling sense of outrage. How could her mother betray her father so blatantly? The look on the Senator's face revealed knowledge of a rumpled bed, sheets dewy with desire, blankets abandoned. Senator de Chavez leaned forward and traced Esther's jawline with thick fingers. As his fingers passed by her mouth, Esther gave a fingertip a quick, almost imperceptible, kiss. Jenny felt as if her own heart would stop. But she could not explain away what she had seen: there was no denying their intimate knowledge of each other.

"Let's go," Jenny said. She pushed her chair back and walked out of the restaurant.

Hanna hurried after her. "What's the matter, Jenny?"

"Nothing." Always alone—feeling herself, in a flash, to be once again a child of secrets, a child with a double and hidden life—Jenny kept this secret to herself. "I've just got a headache."

"Oh dear." Hanna was sympathetic. "I'll drive you home."

Jenny didn't listen to Hanna on the drive home. She was occupied with an inner terror. What if her mother left her father? Max would probably go with Esther but she, of course, could stay with George. However much she might dislike her mother (now she felt a single-minded hatred), she knew George would die without Esther. He was getting on in years in Jenny's eyes. There was a gray in his face and hair which spoke of overwork. He had high blood pressure and there was always the danger of a heart attack. "George, calm down," was a frequent phrase both at home and at the office. Only her Aunt Etta could really keep George calm. Esther's uncertain temper kept him nervous and on edge at home. Placating Esther was like trying to soothe a rattlesnake. Personally, Jenny had always preferred the house when Esther was out. Then, the beautiful mansion breathed peace and security. When her mother returned from town after one of her many committee meetings,

Jenny remembered, George and the children had waited warily to see if the rat-tat-tat of her heels was a warning or a blessing. If the meeting had gone well, Esther would walk up the hall, her spiked heels pleasantly conversational with the tiles. If the meeting had gone badly, the machine gun sounds sent Jenny into where George sat, to try and divert her mother's anger. Max always scampered like a frightened squirrel to his room and Ah Ling melted like a pale shadow into the back of the house. In many ways, Jenny thought, we'd be much happier without her.

Somehow, even though she felt no love for the woman who had borne her, she, Jenny Jensen, was hurt at a very deep, baby level. Her family so far stayed, at least ostensibly, traditional—unlike so many others, who were rent apart by the various politics which demanded women be single, self-sufficient and preferably divorced, like Nancy's mother. The secure yacht lay becalmed in a world which seemed to have gone mad.

Recently, at Nancy's house, there had been no order. Nancy's mother, Sonia Johnson, seemingly threw her husband out of the house overnight, went back to school to get a career, drank heavily, cut her hair, and took to wearing what looked like flower bags. All night parties raged in the Johnson home. The house was dirty, the beds unmade. Nancy and her sister Lucienne were told that they could do whatever they liked. This Christmas Nancy's mother decided that they would not have a Christmas tree, and Jenny and Hanna were introduced to the new lover. Nancy was enthusiastic in her newfound freedom, but Jenny, always a little aloof from her friends, disliked the smell and the mess.

Would Esther now end up like Sonia Johnson? Would Senator de Chavez be only the first in an endless line of lowlife lovers? Jenny sat in the car and shook with fear. Would all order she had known in her life be shattered irreparably?

Jenny's way of life, the ritual of breakfast and lunch served on proper plates, a cup of English tea served at four, and then dinner, was deeply ingrained. Both she and Hanna agreed, when they first shared a room together, that they were not going to degenerate into untidy, dirty student living. To be in politics and to study history, one did not have to be dirty. They disagreed over the question of shaving. Jenny refused to sport hair on her legs or under her arms. She didn't care if the other girls called her reactionary. "I shave my legs for me," she said defiantly.

Now, as she sat in the car on the way home, she felt as if her brain and her heart had been given a mighty blow. Her heart lurched and hardened. Everything she had held in trust all her life was torn apart. Her foundations had crumbled: her mother was having an affair. Of course, Nancy would laugh if she knew how shaken and shocked Jenny was. Sonia Johnson openly had affairs. Different men inhabited the house at different times. Nancy considered herself bisexual. She took sex, along with all her needs, casually. The familiar smell of pot was always in the air at the Johnson house. Jenny did not think Esther would recognize a chalice if she saw one. George frequently cursed the flood of drugs. Santa Fe was the armpit of the drug market.

For the capital of New Mexico to have no international airport was a pity, but it was whispered that if Santa Fe ever had an international airport, the private planes which landed at irregular hours would be subject to search, and some Santa Feans might lose an income. Johnny Mulhoham was an angry man. It was said he made a living with a string of prostitutes and was now impoverished except for special favors. The women of Santa Fe gave away for free what they had previously sold to men for marriage and children.

The men of Santa Fe were delighted, except for George Jensen and Danny Gottstein. *"Oy,"* Danny complained to George. "They can hardly wait to get undressed. I have to keep my nurse in my office all the time."

"Yeah," George agreed. "I got a new secretary. She put her hand on my crotch. I told her to get out, the dirty bitch. She screamed at me. Told me I was discriminating against her. 'You're ugly,' I said."

When Hanna parked the car in front of the house, she leaned forward and opened the door for Jenny. "You go in and get some aspirin. I'll take the car to the garage. Lie down in your room and I'll call you at dinner time."

"Okay." Jenny walked slowly through the front door. She did not have to worry about her mother's whereabouts. She knew where her mother was and had been. She wished she had made a mistake but she knew Esther too well. The only other time she remembered that light about her mother's figure was when Orlando lived with them when Jenny was twelve. The two events closed in her heart and, deep inside her, the monster awoke. She must get even for her father's sake. She must avenge the crime perpetuated by her mother and her godfather. Jenny was planning revenge.

❦ *CHAPTER 51* ❦

Once back at university, much to Jenny's surprise, she saw little of Martin. Both girls were very busy after the Christmas break. Hanna was studying the history and rise of the American superpower, and British imperialism in Gambia. Professor Potter taught the girls in her classes that African women, like the men, expected to be liberated once the British left, but when the British did leave, the men in the families would continue to expect their wives to stay at home, have babies and cook the supper. If women tried to have careers, the men would still expect them to make all the child-care arrangements and cook and clean. "But," Hanna said, "that's not just Africa." And then she laughed. "You know, Jenny, it's happening to me, too." A mischievous spark glinted in her eyes.

"Hanna," Jenny said, "are you trying to tell me something?"

Hanna giggled like a naughty schoolgirl. "You know the fellow I've been telling you about? The one named Prince? The one I've been racking my brains about for months now?"

"Yes."

"Well, in the end I thought: why fight it? Why not let him love me. So . . ."

"So?"

"So . . . Oh, I might as well just say it. We're together. We are now an item, a couple, a pair, a whatever you want to call it."

"You really love him?"

"I really do."

"And he really loves you?"

Hanna giggled. "He really seems to. I find it a little hard to believe but he treats me like a goddess." She wrinkled her nose and laughed.

"Oh, Hanna! I'm so happy for you!"

"But you haven't heard the worst part. He's so—so—unfeminist. He expects me to get him meals round his place. He won't lift a finger to cook. God knows what he ate before he met me." She looked at her hands. "Old Pots is furious. I told her about it yesterday and you know what she said? 'Get rid of him!' she told me. 'If all women left every male chauvinist pig in this country, we'd have a feminist revolution overnight.' But, Jenny"—Hanna's eyes glowed warmly—"I really don't want to get rid of Prince. He's kind and gentle. He treats me so well. I've never had a boyfriend before."

Jenny grinnted. "Better a chauvinist pig in the hand than Professor Potter in the bush."

Hanna laughed. Since she visited Santa Fe and saw how Nancy lived, proclaiming her sexual delinquency as a religion, like her friends, Hanna decided that would not be her life. Whatever Professor Potter's teachings and her feminist beliefs, Professor Potter's private life was her own. If gossip-mongers gossiped and said Pots was living with another woman, it was still none of anybody's business. But Hanna was truly in love for the first time in her life.

Jenny was sincerely pleased for her. She had noticed the quickness in Hanna's step and the light shining in her eyes, the sudden warmth in her smile. Now she knew why. "Does this mean you've slept with him?" Jenny asked.

Hanna shook her head. "I'm not going to sleep

with him. Not until—that is, *if*—we end up getting married."

"What does he say?"

"Well, he was quite surprised, but I explained I don't want to be like other girls." She shook her dark head. "I must be the only virgin at Wentworth."

Jenny laughed. "We'll get you bronzed and sit you up on a mantelpiece. So tell me, what are you doing tonight? Are you going out with him?"

"Oh, we're off to a pub."

"I'm off to see Peter. He's asked me to supper in his rooms."

"Hmm." Hanna grinned. "Suppose he seduces you?"

"Suppose he does?" Jenny shrugged her shoulders. "At least he should know what he's doing. It feels like I've been sitting on the shelf so long I'm afraid I'm beginning to rust. Anyway, what am I talking about? He won't."

Hanna smiled at her friend, a questioning look on her face.

Jenny very quickly found out that love and sex unmixed could be a nightmare. On entering Peter's rooms, she felt a strong current of expectation. Peter had his scout lay a card table out in the small sitting room. A plate of pink, juicy, moist ham sat on the white tablecloth. Beside the plate, a thinly sliced pale green cucumber lay and beside the cucumber was a plate of thick red tomatoes, sliced and sugared. The salad lay in a big brown bowl, curly green leaf upon curly green leaf. Jenny was thrilled. A decent salad was hard to find and, in the sauce boat, a freshly made yellow mayonnaise sat waiting.

"Hello there." Peter came out of his room carrying

two wine glasses in one hand and a bottle of white wine in the other. Expertly, he popped the cork. The smell of the vineyards of France permeated the air. "Can't get good French wine like this from California, you know."

"Oh yes you can," Jenny retorted. "The Pinot Noir is just as good as anything you can get in Europe. It's a nice wine."

"Since when did little American girls know anything about wine?" Peter teased.

"Ah Ling and my mom are both experts. We haven't all just come off the cattle boats." Jenny enjoyed sparring with Peter.

After dinner, Jenny sat, hazy with wine and sleep in the light of the candles, a Cointreau in her hand. Peter looked at Jenny. Jenny looked at Peter. That he had noticed her since she first walked into his office at the beginning of the year seemed undeniable. The fact that he was intelligent seemed indisputable. The idea that he might actually love her still remained a mystery. As Jenny sat on the sofa she debated furiously with herself. You never know, she told herself, he might be different from all the rest. I've changed since my slummy days. I'm ready for a real relationship. Maybe he really does love me. Maybe we could make it work. Maybe he wants to be with me forever. Maybe I want to be with him . . .

"Shall we?" he said suddenly, and Jenny half-jumped.

Here goes nothing, Jenny thought. "Why not?" she said, in an attempt to sound worldly.

Peter took her and led her to his bedroom. The room was sparsely furnished, more of a cell than a bedroom. The bed, she found, was hard and Peter quickly proved himself even harder. Though when they first lay down together Jenny found herself shaking with excitement, Peter's roughness turned her titillation to authentic fear. If this is his idea of making love, thought Jenny, forget it. Her only thought became how to survive the experience, now a living nightmare.

She was biting her lips in an attempt not to scream. Peter was pounding away at her. At one point in the maelstrom of that night, he had her legs over his shoulders. His face was black, his eyes were bulging, and his tongue was hanging out of his mouth as he glared at her. "You bitch," he said. "You whore. You little prostitute. I'll fuck you to death." Finally spent, he rolled over. "Get dressed and get out," he said and closed his eyes.

Terrified, Jenny collected her clothes. She saw she was bleeding, but she didn't care. She ran out of the college and headed for home half-dressed and in bare feet. The night sky looked down in sympathy at the young girl whose hopes for real affection had been so cruelly smashed.

After a bath and some aspirin, Jenny was still crying. She wished so much she could tell her mother but her mother would only laugh. She couldn't tell her father, and Max was too young. Aunt Etta would never understand. Aunt Etta had had one man in her life, and in those days, women didn't fool around, Jenny was sure of it.

As she lay in her bed, she felt a very old pain. Once again she was a child, a girl of twelve, mourning the loss of a man she thought had loved her. But Orlando hadn't loved her, and neither—very obviously—did Peter. What an idiot I am, she thought, to imagine that Peter would ever love me. And all I got was used. Again.

To Jenny the whole world felt like one huge, aching wound. The empty universe was full of pain. Would any man ever love her, she wondered, as she cried. Were all men the same? Had it been Martin or J.J., would it have been any different?

She fell asleep begging God not to make her pregnant. He heard her prayer.

The university years passed but the pain did not. Jenny felt the essentially trusting, childlike side of her was dead. However much the next tutorial left her trembling with fear, she had to go. She needed her degree, she decided, if she wanted a career in politics and it must be a first class degree. Now, after the event with Peter, she felt betrayed—both by him as a man and a mentor, and by his politics. Maybe Professor Potter had a point. If socialist men treated women like that, then there had to be a revolution, not what Peter preached but a revolution among women so they would not be decimated and defiled by men ever again.

To Jenny's surprise, Peter greeted her quite warmly, as if nothing had happened. She was just another student, a girl to use. And now she was dependent on him for her degree. That ensured her continued silence. But what Peter did not know was that the newly blooming women's movement had just attracted one of its fiercest supporters.

Professor Potter was pleasantly surprised when Jenny turned up in her class. The new Jenny, the angry Jenny, the Jenny abandoned by Orlando and betrayed by Peter, this Jenny was ready to take on the world—the world of men.

* * *

Hanna, very much in love with Prince—an African medical graduate like her father—was going back to Africa to be married. "You know what?" Hanna said on their last evening together in their room. "I'll even wash his socks."

"Oh, Hanna you big baby. There'll never be equality if you don't make men responsible for themselves."

"I know," Hanna sighed. "Isn't it awful? But I like washing his socks and sewing on his buttons. I like the look on his face when I make him fresh pizza. It's true. You know what they say about men."

"What? That a woman without a man is like a fish without a bicycle?"

"No." Hanna rolled over on the floor, her chin in her hands. "No, no, silly. A man wants to make love and then have his wife turn into a pizza."

Jenny snorted. "Preferably both at the same time. And smoke a cigarette. And you mean to tell me you still haven't slept together yet?"

"No. I told you. I'm going to wear white with a clean conscience. We both prefer it that way."

"Okay," Jenny said. "Have it your way. Oh, Hanna, I'll miss you very much." Jenny hugged Hanna—dear, kind, dependable Hanna.

Hanna hugged Jenny. "I hope you'll be happy."

Jenny looked at her. "I hope so too." She leaned against her friend and began to cry. "But I'm really beginning to wonder if I ever will. I just don't know anymore. I really don't know."

"Shhh," said Hanna, not knowing what to say. "It will be all right. You'll see. Everything will work out all right."

Jenny cried and cried.

❧ CHAPTER 52 ❧

"Marry him." Etta's statement was simple.

"It isn't as easy as all that," Jenny sighed as she sat back in a large armchair in the sitting room at Etta's ranch.

"Why isn't it that easy?" The look on Etta's face was more direct than Jenny remembered ever having seen before. "What else are you doing with your life? You're twenty-four now, you graduated from college two years ago and you seem to be just waiting for something wonderful to come along. And I promise you nothing more wonderful than a proposal of marriage from a good man is going to come your way. So marry him."

Jenny leaned back against the headrest. "Aunt Etta, I don't want to get married just because there's nothing better to do."

"That isn't what I said." Etta remained firm. "Or if that's the way it sounded, that isn't what I meant."

"And I certainly didn't get a degree in political science just to become a housewife."

"Jenny," Etta's voice softened. "Listen to me. What I mean is this. You went away to England, you got your degree, and that's good. But that doesn't have to say very much about how you want to spend the rest of your life. The *rest of your life,* Jenny." Etta had passed her fiftieth year four years ago. Her face was round and worn with experience. Her intelligent eyes stared at Jenny with deep and intense concern. "I mean, yes, you have your politics and everything but politics don't bring you happiness. A good marriage does. I know you might be sitting there thinking, "What does an old woman on her own know about marriage?" But I tell you this: yes, I've managed fine, living on my own. But it isn't the same. Life is meant to be—I don't know—shared. And for all I've looked after myself for so long, there's hardly a day that goes by when I don't wish I had someone, that one special person, to share it all with." A silence fell as, in her mind, she saw Tom Harding's face. She wondered how he would have looked in his fifties, had he lived.

"But that's just the point." Jenny sat forward. "I don't know what would happen if I had to share every day of my life with a man." She shrugged. "I might lose myself. Look, I spent four years at university trying to find out who I am, and now you're asking me to give all that, and everything I believe in, away? Don't you see? I don't just want to be an appendage to another person, just a half of a couple. I don't want people to know me only as "Mrs John Joseph Lipstone." I have to be a person in my own right: Jennifer Jensen. A woman, a whole person—not just a half."

"Do you think your grandma Nora is any less of a person just because she's married to your grandfather? Do you think she's only "a half" just because she can spend her whole life loving the same man?"

"No," Jenny said, looking out of the window as the last beam of sunlight settled behind a mountain. "Of course not."

"You know, even as a child, I watched my parents' marriage, and that's what I always wanted for myself." She lowered her eyes. "Certainly there's no great horror or shame in spending life on your own, but let's not go trying to make a great virtue of it."

"But look." Jenny turned back to face her aunt. "I'm not trying to say there's anything wrong with the way grandma and grandpa live, or the way you live, or the way anybody else lives. I'm just trying to figure out how I want to live. It was different for grandma when she married grandpa, and it was different when you were growing up and mom married dad. Today, women have so many more choices. I've learned so much and I don't just want to throw it all away. I want to fulfill myself as a person."

Etta laughed. "Oh, it might look different, I know. But relationships are always the same, no matter how modern life seems to get. Jenny, you say you want fulfillment. Fine. You could become the Mayor of Santa Fe, or the Governor of New Mexico, or the President of America. Wonderful. I'm sure all those jobs have their rewards. But if you don't have anyone to share it with, what does it really mean? It's what you come home to at night that really matters."

"Listen to yourself, Etta. That's the voice of oppression speaking through you. That's like saying it doesn't really matter what a woman does. Whatever she does, it'll just be a "little job". Men's work is important but a woman's work isn't."

"Jenny." Jenny could hear the sternness in her aunt's voice. "I don't think you came here to discuss politics and whatever your books say, marriage is not a political arrangement. We're talking about the meeting of two hearts, "becoming one flesh," as the Bible says; going through the rest of your life with the one person you want to be with more than any other person on earth. Politics have very little to do with that. And if it's fulfillment you're after, what could be more fulfilling than loving and being loved by someone completely?"

"But you said it yourself. 'One flesh.' " Jenny leaned forward and covered her eyes with both her hands. "Do I really want to be half of one?" she said, her voice muffled in her hands.

"Well," Etta raised her eyebrows, "think about it for yourself. Why did J.J. ask you to marry him in the first place? Does he just think you'd make a good other half? Or does he see all of you, a whole person, all of Jenny Jensen, and love all that he sees? Maybe he loves all of you for what you are."

Jenny slid her face up through her hands and rested her chin on her fingertips. "Maybe he does. But I'm not even sure what all of me is. I mean, maybe, unless I do become something great, like becoming Governor, maybe I'm nothing."

"I don't think J.J. thinks you're nothing. Maybe he sees more in you than you see in yourself." Pushing against the arms of her chair, Etta rose, walked to the hearth, and poked the fire. "Do you love him?"

"I'm not really sure I know what it means to love a man. What's love anyway? If it means you enjoy being with a person, and feel good about him and about yourself when you're with him, then yes. I suppose it's hard not to love him. He's thoughtful, and kind, and says he always wants to make me happy. 'What's not to love?' " she said with a laugh, mimicking the Jewish lilt and intonation of Nora's voice in a phrase that both Etta and Jenny had grown up hearing from Nora's lips.

Etta laughed, too. She turned her back to the fireplace and smiled at her niece, the young woman she wished had been her own daughter. "Jenny, I've never really told you to do anything before, but I'm telling you now: marry him."

"You should be pleased," Jenny smiled. "My aunt Etta has told me to marry you." She sat in the corner of the large leather sofa in J.J.'s house. In the years since his father's death, J.J. had directed his father's company to even greater success than it had enjoyed before. When he bought his own house, he bought a spreading, comfortable old adobe, spacious enough to hold a family. The rounded walls in the sitting room were freshly painted white and warm rays from a pine fire glimmered on the newly polished panels of the aged wooden floor. Jenny sat at one end of the generous sofa with her bare feet tucked under her. J.J. sat at the other. In their hands they each held snifters of their after dinner brandy. "And my father," Jenny continued, "says that if I have to marry any man, it might as well be you."

J.J. laughed. "So," he said, "what are we waiting for?"

"I guess," Jenny set her brandy down on the coffee table, "we're waiting for me to make up my mind. And I'm waiting for my mind to tell me the right thing to do." She stretched out her legs until her feet rested in J.J.'s lap.

J.J. put his brandy on the table and reached to touch her toes. They were chilly, he noticed. Taking her small feet between his large hands, he rubbed them warm. "And what's your mind telling you right now?"

"My mind," she said, shifting in her seat to lie fully back with her eyes closed, "is saying, 'Be careful.'"

"Be careful of what?" He smiled and carried on with warming her feet.

"Be careful of you."

He looked at her face with her eyes closed. How he loved that face—the full soft lips, the graceful nose, the dark, alert eyes. "You don't have to be careful of me," he said. "I've told you already. All I want to do is to make you happy for the rest of our lives. I'd never hurt you."

"Yes," she said, breathing out deeply and feeling herself relax. "But I shouldn't need you to make me happy. I should be . . . I don't know . . . more self-sufficient than that, and I don't know how happy I could make you."

"Don't worry about that." He laughed. "That's for me to worry about. And I've already decided that I would be happy just to be with you."

"No, really, J.J." She opened her eyes and put her arms behind her head so she lay on her crossed wrists. "It would be such a responsibility having to worry about another person's happiness when you're not even sure how to make your own. And I don't know if I can do it. I don't know if I'd be any good at, or if I'd even want to, spend my time looking after you. Having to deal with another person's moods, cooking for you . . ."

"Are you complaining about the steak I cooked for you tonight?"

"Of course not." She laughed. "It was a perfectly good steak and you're a perfectly good cook. But that's not what I'm talking about. I'm just worried . . ."

"I know what you're talking about. You're worried about giving away your whole life. Just handing it over to another person and you're not sure how much of yourself you'll get to keep for yourself."

"Yes," Jenny agreed. "Exactly. Have you been worried about that too?"

"Of course, I've thought about it." He paused, nervous at making her feel too much of a stranger, too much of an object of contemplation or, perhaps, of doubt. "I thought about it," he continued, "and I decided this is definitely what I want. You're what I want. I mean, look around you." He lifted a hand from her warm foot for a moment and waved his arm around him. "Look at this house. Look at the way I live. It's a very nice house and I'm very happy in it. But there's only so much I can do to make this feel like it's really home, not just the place where I live. I sit here at night sometimes and wonder what's missing. Something really is missing—in my house, in my life, in the whole world for me. I realize what's missing is you. With you and me together always, everything would feel"—he shook his head—"Full. Complete."

She pulled her feet away and sat up quickly with her legs crossed beneath her. "But that's exactly what I'm so frightened of, J.J. I don't want us to be together just out of need. Just because we're afraid to be alone."

"I'm not asking you to be the stucco to fill the cracks in the wall. Sure, I have my cracks but I can take care of those myself. Maybe they'll never go away, I don't know. But I just want you to want to be with me, cracks and all, and I just want to be with you. Don't worry—I'll never tie you down. You can do anything or become anything you want, so long as I can be there with you."

She sat quietly, staring at him. What are you waiting for? she asked herself. What more could you want? What better guarantee? Suddenly, in an instant, there appeared before her the images of faces: Orlando's face, Peter Stuart's face, the vague faces of many half-known men in between. "Why," she said at last, "should I trust you?"

His voice was serious. "Why shouldn't you?"

He's so innocent, she thought and, remembering her past, she suddenly felt very old and soiled. "Maybe," she said, "I have more reason to be cynical than you do. Maybe it's because——"

"Jenny," he said, with a decisiveness verging on impatience in his words. "We can go through the 'because's and the 'but's and the 'what-if's forever. But at some point, you can stand on the dock and stare at the lake for only so long, until you just have to hold your breath and dive in. There comes a time when you have to put aside all your doubts and go ahead and do what you know you're meant to do, what feels right, what's natural. Jenny, I want you to marry me."

"J.J.," she started, then paused. "J.J.," she began again but found no words. He seemed so good, so safe, but why should his love for her be any different? Why would it, why should it, last? "J.J.," she said again, "will you make love to me?"

Smiling, he leaned forward and put his hand on her knee. For a moment she looked like a child to him, a small, hurt child. He wanted to love that child until he could take away all her pain forever but he was frightened of hurting her even more. "You don't want to wait until after we're married?"

"No," she said. "I need to know now. I need to see if you'll still love me."

The look on his face was at once loving and confused. "Is this some kind of a test?"

"Yes," she said. Then, "No. Oh, J.J., I don't know. Just, please, love me."

Silently, he stood, lifted her from the sofa and carried her to his bedroom. And J.J. loved her with all of his heart and all of his body. He was delighted to find in Jenny the fulfillment of every passionate dream he ever had dreamed. He learned the deep satisfaction of loving every part of a woman's body as if each part held her soul. He fell in love with her round, neat body; her soft, small buttocks; her warm, moist, welcoming vagina. For years he had loved her intelligence and sensitivity, her ability to make him laugh until he cried. Now he loved her heart and her body in union. Jenny relaxed, responded, joined him. She let herself be loved.

When they had finished, J.J. felt as if it were April—spontaneous, bud-busting April. He stood up from the bed, walked naked to his study, and returned with something in his hand. On his knees he asked her to marry him. "Please," he said. "Please, Jenny." He slipped the family engagement ring onto Jenny's left finger.

On the day of George Jensen's fifty-sixth birthday, Jenny married John Joseph Lipstone. She stood beside her husband wearing a long white gown, surrounded by a flock of bridesmaids, swearing to love and honor this man for the rest of her life. The word "obey," omitted from the service at Jenny's insistence, lay quietly neglected on the ground.

The sun shone on George with the same intensity which had warmed his broad shoulders all those years ago at his own wedding. Head bent, George tried very hard to keep his tears from falling down his face. He wanted to howl like a wolf and tear up the pews to hurl them at the assembled, well-dressed and ever-so-polite crowd of Esther's friends. Most of all he felt the oddest impulse to kill J. J. Lipstone, the man who was taking away his daughter and the man who was going to defile George's precious flower, his virgin.

Jenny said, "I do," and J.J. kissed his bride. George's fingers curled. He liked J.J. well enough yesterday. He was glad the man was rich enough to give his daughter anything she wished for, and he warned J.J. before the ceremony what would happen if Jenny were ever to suffer even the slightest moment of sorrow. "Oh, Dad," Jenny had sighed. "You're always so extreme." J.J., upon hearing George's plan, was white. "Don't worry, darling," Jenny had said. "His bark is always worse than his bite."

"Yeah," J.J. had muttered, "but it's who he's going to bite that bothers me."

Now the long bridal train turned and Jenny, aglow, followed by Nancy Johnson, her chief bridesmaid (who wore a dress for the occasion) walked down the aisle. Pictures were taken on the steps, a slight breeze swayed, the soft dresses billowed and fluttered and, for the first time, Jenny felt at peace. She watched Esther through narrowed eyes.

Esther stood beside her daughter, her elegant figure giving no clue to her age. Her face was unlined and her mouth dropped only slightly. At fifty-four Esther gave off a curiously sterile air. She was, Jenny thought, like a fly stuck in amber: perfectly preserved, but no life shone in her eyes—no seeds nurtured her soul. On the surface, Jenny's mother had everything a woman could want: a loving husband, two adorable and successful children, and as much money as anyone could possibly spend in a lifetime. Still, to Jenny, Esther appeared as a crisp, empty, corn husk.

One by one the guests walked down the receiving line, shaking hands with the groom, kissing the bride, hugging the relatives on both sides. With a profusion of hugs and squeezes, Etta wept happily, greeting Jenny like Danny and Nora Gottstein did. A minute later, Jenny felt her cheek tighten as Senator de Chavez pushed his mushy lips against her skin. She stood silent. Then she watched as he moved to Esther, kissed her on the cheek, and told her how proud she must be. Only Jenny noticed the small blush on Esther's cheek, the quick flash of the eye that coyly said, "Move on. Don't let anyone see." And de Chavez moved down the line.

Esther clucked and chatted to all the passing guests and exchanged longer conversations with Sonia Johnson and her old friends, Emily and Gaston St Honoré. When, at last, all guests had offered their congratulations, Esther turned to Jenny beside her. Her face seemed fixed in a frozen smile. "Well, Jennifer," she said, mostly through her teeth, "you should be very pleased with yourself. Today you become a housewife."

"Mother," Jenny half-pleaded. "Please, not today."

"I knew you'd never become anything important," Esther said, her voice part-whisper, part-hiss. She shook her head. Her eyes were as hard as quartz, but her mouth still smiled frighteningly. Jenny, staring at the mouth, noticed a small ring of tiny wrinkles around the painted lips. "I wasted my dreams on you,

Jennifer. I was foolish to ever imagine you had it in you to become Governor." She leaned forward and pressed her lips hard against Jenny's cheek, close enough to the ear so that Jenny could hear the loud smack of the lips' kiss. Esther stood back and smiled harshly at her daughter. *"Mazel tov,"* she snapped.

Jenny felt stung by the irony of her mother's remark—the sour sarcastic remnant of a discarded Jewish past. Bitch, she thought. Horrid, horrid bitch. For a moment, Jenny felt like ruining her mother: now, at once. She wanted to raise her hands, quieten her guests to attention, point to her mother and Senator de Chavez now standing a distance away and talking to his friends. She wanted to denounce them both, point them out for what they were—adulterers.

"Here," Esther said suddenly, reaching behind her own neck to unclasp her necklace. "I want you to have this." She looked down at the small, heart-shaped locket in her hand. Its gold glinted sharply in the sunlight. She lifted her eyes to Jenny. "This belonged to my grandmother Lilla. And it was her mother's before her. She brought it with her from Russia. You know," she looked down again at the piece, almost tenderly, "I got this when I was a little younger than you are now, and it's always been very special to me. Your great-grandmother was a woman of great dreams. I always thought I was very much like her. And I had hoped," she stared at Jenny, "you'd be like her too. It seems I was wrong. Here." She lifted her hands and clasped the chain onto Jenny. "Wear this around your neck."

Jenny opened her mouth to say something. What, she did not know. But she felt J.J.'s comforting hand on her shoulder and heard his friendly voice whisper in her ear, "How're you doing, Jenny? Lot of guests . . ."

"Ah!" Esther cried, a little too loudly, with raised arms. "Here's my new son! What a proud mother I am!" She reached her face to J.J.'s and kissed him on the cheek. "Oh dear," she said, standing back. "Look what I've done now. I got some lipstick on your cheek." She reached up and smeared his cheek with her thumb.

Jenny—now Jenny Lipstone—sighed.

From only a footstep away, Esther's son, her *real* son, looked on. Now, at twelve years of age, Max was old enough to bitterly resent his mother's emotionally incestuous needs. Music was his only love, and in recent years he noticed that Esther spoke of his music almost jealously. Today—a handsome young man dressed in his black tuxedo—he arrived a few days before the wedding. By now, Max was a nationally renowned prodigy, playing his beloved piano in concert halls all over the East Coast. To get away from his mother, he applied for, and was granted, early acceptance to the New England Conservatory of Music in Boston, and he stayed on the East Coast as much as possible. Now, standing next to her, he felt angry and ill at ease. During the picture-taking, he pulled away from Esther, but Max was glad of the day for his sister.

His understanding of emotional situations was precocious. He had a simple brother's love for Jenny. Her hard exterior, her political convictions, all hid a softer gentle Jenny whom he watched, over the years, pick up a small bird and feed it until it could fly again; caress a cat; or visit the hospital to push a trolley of library books. Max knew the private Jenny, the wounded Jenny, unloved by her mother, the abandoned Jenny, the betrayed. Sometimes Max felt that Jenny had the better end of the bargain. Ignored himself as a baby and infant, then suddenly, as a child, becoming the brunt of her overpowering attention, he wished his mother had neglected and abandoned him always. Sometimes, the cloying pressure Esther put upon him was all too much. Even the smell of her perfume made him want to throw up.

But J.J. was a good fellow, and tonight there was the wedding party. Max was looking forward to that. Lucienne Johnson, home from boarding school for the wedding, was going to be there. Max knew the feelings he had for Lucienne were beginning to grow beyond friendship. Lucienne, once a little tomboy, was changing into a lovely, surprisingly womanly, teenager. And Max, for the first time in his life, was falling in love.

Now, Lucienne stood by Nancy, tall and blonde, the summer freckles still across her nose, her green eyes fringed with double lashes. She looked coolly at Max. A slight, flirtatious smile played on her lips. Max smiled back at her and in her smile he could see a whispered promise for the party that would come tonight.

Esther was very pleased. After the wedding party she sat on the big, black sofa and looked at the unfinished portrait of her daughter and herself. The two faces set in mutual antagonism were well caught. Orlando had telephoned just a week before the wedding. He offered to finish the painting for Jenny as a present. Now, tonight, her daughter married and out of the house forever at last; George asleep and miserably drunk on unaccustomed champagne; Esther contemplated the future.

Max had asked if Lucienne could spend the night. George had raised a suspicious eyebrow, but Esther had reassured him, "Oh, he's only twelve and she's just his friend. Let her stay." Now upstairs in the guest bedroom Max, having tiptoed, lay in Lucienne's bed. "Does this feel good?" she whispered.

"Yes," said Max.

"You sound surprised." Lucienne gently caressed Max's body, slowly moving her hand down from Max's stomach. "Touch me as well." Lucienne took Max's hand. "There. How does that feel?"

"Exciting," Max said, his voice hoarse with desire. Suddenly Max came. "Oh, I'm sorry," he said, dreadfully embarrassed. "I'm really sorry."

"Don't be," said Lucienne. "This is your first time. Just lie quietly in my arms and we'll go to sleep. I'm too drunk to come anyway."

Max felt slightly disconcerted by the evident knowledge and experience in Lucienne's voice. But given the company Lucienne's mother kept, he figured that anything went in Lucienne's house. He lay in her arms and felt peaceful.

George had lately grown to frighten Max. His fierce bear hugs disturbed the boy. Now that he was growing up, George's overwhelming back-slapping, shoulder-punching form of loving just hurt. Max inherited his height from his father, but he inherited his slim body from his mother. Tonight, he slept safely in arms which were kind and gentle. To Lucienne's surprise that night, the precocious girl—a stained reputation left behind her at her boarding school—fell in love with the boy in her arms, a love which was to last all her life.

Jenny made love to J.J. in the honeymoon hotel in Aspen, Colorado. J.J. slept soundly while Jenny lay awake and hoped she had done the right thing, that this was not a marriage she would regret for the rest of her life. George was an easy bet for Esther. He was as simple and as clear as a pane of glass. Esther could guide George through life as if she were training a horse. J.J., Jenny knew, was another matter. He was a king in his office. He was brilliant at the negotiating table. He was intuitive, perceptive and disciplined. What he did not know about could be held on the end of a fork. But where women were concerned, he had no knowledge at all.

J.J.'s family was patriarchal in the extreme. His father, right up to his death five years ago, had ruled with a rod of iron. His mother died when he was very young, and he lived in this house of men, looked after by his older brothers who flew one by one from the family home and business and their father's strong hand. From the age of fifteen, J.J. accompanied the old man to his lair in the office, and by the time his father died and J.J. left university early to take over the business, J.J. was in immediate control. The youngest businessman in New Mexico was now in command of his father's millions.

Jenny liked her husband. She felt a deep and sensuous passion for Martin which she knew must remain always a secret and unrealized. Martin kissed her formally after the wedding, a dry kiss on her cheek. His eyes, fathomless and empty, burned a hole into her breasts. The look traveled through her body and burned between her legs. His eyes stayed with her through the journey to the Lear jet. His body lay beside her as, at midnight, she lay in J.J.'s arms, having shared her orgasm—guiltily, not meaning to—with Martin before J.J. fell into a deep sleep. Now, she finally fell asleep but Martin's eyes stayed open and watched the young couple with hot, burning hatred.

The night died and the new morning was trembling in the wings. In the summer dawn of Aspen, Colorado, the locket lay in a jewelery box beside the marital bed. The past lay sleeping in the hollow of the heart. A silent accusation, encased in velvet, the locket waited for the future to unfold.

❦ CHAPTER 53 ❦

Early in Jenny's first year of marriage, her aunt Etta died of a heart attack. The shock was enormous for Jenny. Years of running the huge ranch had taken their toll early on Etta. Jenny cried for her aunt who had loved her like a daughter all those dark years when the pain left in her soul by her mother sent her flying to Etta for comfort. "She really loved me," Jenny sobbed in J.J.'s arms.

"I know she did," said J.J.

"And I loved the ranch. Aunt Etta was so soft, so warm. Now she's gone. And the ranch, my safe place . . ."

"No, it hasn't gone," J.J. whispered lying in bed with his beloved wife. "Before she died she asked me if I wanted to take the ranch over. I said 'Yes,' because I knew how much you loved the place. If you like, we can live there."

"Are you sure, J.J.?" Jenny sat up in bed. "I'd love to live at the ranch. But this is your house. I mean our house. And . . ."

"This is just a house," he said. "The kind you buy and sell. But the ranch belonged to your great-grandfather Reuben. It's part of your family. It's where you belong and I know it would make you happy to live there, for it to become our own."

"Thank you, darling. Thank you. You're so good to me. I'd love to live at the ranch. Then I'll feel near to aunt Etta." This time Jenny made love to J.J. with her whole heart.

J.J. smiled contentedly. He too had always loved the ranch. He would see his children playing on the porch.

At the ranch, she gave birth to her son after a year of marriage and lay back peacefully with her baby at her breast. The huge family gathered at the christening and among the various fairies who danced joyfully, only one could be said to be bad. Her black dress and wand, silently and invisibly, cast a shadow on the baby's head as he lay contentedly cooing in his proud father's arms.

The baby Benjamin's fat, joyful, little feet acknowledged the love which surrounded his baptism. Everyone was pleased, including Orlando, who stood at the back of the church. His presence, to Jenny, was certainly unexpected. Willfully she refused to look him in the eye throughout the entire service.

The baby smiled when the priest put salt on his tongue. "Always a good omen," Ah Ling said to his wife, who stood beside him. Ah Ling had good reason to be pleased. At last, his children all gone, he had his own house and he lived quietly with his wife. Occasionally, he helped out at the big house, but he did so out of love for his master, George. There was no love for the mistress. But now his days were long, as long as the rows of potatoes planted in his garden and as fulfilled as the fat-bellied jars of salt pork which stood in his larder. Today, Ah Ling was happy. There was a new baby in the family: Benjamin Lipstone, born to a wealthy house and the ancestors honored by the birth of a male heir. Ah Ling was well pleased. Benjamin waved his fist and gurgled all through the day.

During the reception at the ranch following the service, Orlando chose his moment, when Jenny was alone in the kitchen, to approach her. "Jennifer," he said, standing before her. He merely stood, not sure what to say.

"Orlando," she said simply. "I'm surprised to see you here. I didn't expect to see you again."

"Jenny, I—"

"What are you doing here?" she continued. "In Santa Fe, I mean." She stared at him. He was older indeed, but his face retained its eternal boyishness and his skin, still smooth, seemed to have lost only the tautness of youth.

"Well, actually, I'm here for two reasons. Didn't your mother tell you? I spoke to her a year ago about finishing that painting I never finished. Kind of a wedding present for you and your husband."

"No, she didn't tell me. But it doesn't really make a difference. You can finish the portrait of her if you want to, but not me. She can keep the picture. I really don't need to be reminded."

"Jenny, I—I—It's not just the portrait which isn't finished. I mean, I ran off, ran away, and I never could explain . . . I'm sorry. I—"

"Please, Orlando, don't." She looked him directly in the eye. Her eyes, he could see, were older and deeper than they had been in childhood; warmer. "I don't want to talk about it. There's no need to. I'm a grown woman now. I have a husband and a son to look after. It really doesn't matter. And if it does, it was too long ago to worry about now. But if you came to apologize," she paused, "then I accept. Maybe it was brave of you to come here today, I don't know." Her voice showed no emotion.

She looked at him and he lowered his eyes. For years she had thought of him as her enemy, her user, her betrayer, her abandoner. Now, as she saw the hair thinning on top of his lowered head, he looked pitiable and pathetic. "Orlando," she said with a marked gentleness in her words, "if you came to be absolved, then consider yourself forgiven." Inwardly, Jenny felt herself relax as if, by forgiving Orlando, she had forgiven herself.

"Really?" His voice was small.

"Really." She smiled and put a hand on his shoulder. "Everyone needs the slate wiped clean from time to time." Her smile widened and he laughed, relieved. "So tell me," she said, talking as if to no one but an old friend, "what was the second reason you're in Santa Fe?"

"You'll laugh," he said, "but I'm here to paint a

portrait of the new Governor's wife. You know, when I received the letter asking me to come to New Mexico to paint the first lady"—he chuckled—"I was sure I'd be painting you."

"Surprise," Jenny said with a queer half-laugh, and she held out her hands, indicating the kitchen and the ranch around her. "This is where I am."

"My God," Orlando stood back, still smiling, but with his eyes narrowing and his head nodding in a distinctly European way, an artist appraising the composition of a scene. "Who would have thought that this is the same little girl I knew who assured me she would be the Governor one day?" He laughed, but heard his own laughter grow thin. His absolution was still too fresh and the subject of Jenny's youth still taboo. Jenny lowered her eyes. "I'm sorry, Jenny," he tried to recover. "I only meant, with all your mother's talk, I never imagined I'd see you married and settled."

"I know what you meant," she said. "And you're right. I never imagined that this would be me either."

But he could hear the distance from him in her voice. I deserve that, he thought. He felt foolish to have expected that she could be his friend after what he had done. He would content himself to be, if anything, her acquaintance. "Well," he said quietly and he took her hand in his as if saying goodbye, "as long as you're happy."

I am happy. I really am. Jenny said this to herself with a mixture of genuine surprise and vague, unsettling doubt. She told herself this when she fed and changed Benjamin, when she tended the kitchen garden once Etta's, now hers. She reminded herself of her happiness when she cared for the animals on the ranch; when she swept and dusted the house; when she cooked dinners for J.J. made from her own chickens and her homegrown vegetables; when she went with J.J. in the evenings to the homes of other members of Santa Fe's wealthiest set.

Happy though she might be, she also found herself tired. Looking after everyone and everything—the baby, her husband, the house, the animals, the garden—was simply too much. J.J., seeing her strain, suggested they hire help. A nurse from England, Abigail, was duly appointed to help with Benjamin. Strict in her uniform, Abigail replaced the long dead Nanny who ruled Jenny's nursery with a firm but kindly hand. Abigail was trained in a college. Her knowledge of children came from books. Smart during the day in her well-cut uniform, she was a tramp by night, unknown to Jenny for Jenny had enough on her mind running the sizeable ranch.

Jenny was pleased to be pregnant again. She was even more pleased to follow in the family tradition by giving birth to a girl. I'll call her Sarah, she thought. J.J. was delighted and George overwhelmed. As much as he loved his daughter, his granddaughter was a special star in his universe. He passed by the ranch daily and stopped to kiss his little granddaughter good night. When Danny Gottstein died quietly in his sleep, it was Sarah—a great-granddaughter!—who gave Nora something to live for. Frequently, Jenny took Benjamin, a busy two-year-old, and Sarah for visits to their great-grandmother's house.

* * *

The two children grew and the years passed. For Benjamin and Sarah, life was like a golden, glowing honeypot. They were loved and cared for by the large family who surrounded them. And if their nanny Abigail gave distasteful parties, attended political meetings on her nights off, and filled her small cabin on the far edge of the ranch with dirty friends, then the Lipstone family took no notice, so complete were they and, in a way, remote in their happy familial duties.

Jenny was too absorbed in her own domesticity to notice a lot of things which went on in the old bunkhouse on the fringe of her property and to feel deeply the tremors which shook America. 1966 passed and Jenny cared for her two infants. The next three years came and went. The nation was at war with itself. Youth rallied against age. Black demanded freedom from white. The wisdom of the country's foreign policy was placed, irreversibly, into the gravest darkest doubt. Women became a nationally recognized force in politics, a force which could not be ignored. Mankind, humankind, placed one of its own on the moon. All existing order was threatened by the tidal waves of change, rebellion, dissension and, to some minds, anarchy. Remnants of sleepy American passivity dissolved, as protesters—some quietly, some violently— warred for peace and freedom. Two generals were assassinated in that war, but Jenny's political activism only took the form of reading newspapers and watching the television evening news. There were chickens to feed, children and a husband to mind, and nursery schools to arrange.

Was Jenny bored? At times she began to wonder, but whenever the thought arose, she reminded herself once again of her happiness. How lucky she was to have such a good and loving husband and such beautiful children. Certainly, there were moments when she marveled at her own complacency, but life on the ranch held for her an almost magical quality. In many ways, the changes in the nation were precisely the changes she had hoped for so passionately at university. Why was she not more pleased, more thrilled, more charged with the exhilarating electricity of change? In her own way, Jenny had found her sanctuary. Her daily chores at the ranch returned her to those distant sunlit moments of peace by the side of her matronly aunt. Secure and cozy in the arms of her marriage, her home, her children, Jenny felt strangely and happily childlike once again.

Only one thorn niggled at her satisfaction—guilt. It was the guilt of feeling herself complacent, nourished in her by Peter Stuart years before. "Cultivate your guilt," he had said. "Use it." The guilt made her uneasy, and brought with it its friend—Jenny's old friend—confusion. Confused in her happiness, Jenny felt herself in a dream. Her life was real, her husband real, her children real, but sometimes (only at times) everything seemed so unreal.

Santa Fe, like the nation, was hit by the storm of change. The town itself became divided. The Spanish mostly held to their old ways. The Anglo ranchers and farmers too scratched their heads, bemused. The new young whites, however, brought with them the germ of discontent. Most Hispanic women of Jenny's age were married to traditional Hispanic men, who had largely ignored the feminist movement. They expected their wives to have their tortillas fried and dinner on the table. The older women shook their heads. The younger ones did not know what to think.

The face of Santa Fe changed, as what had been a relative trickle of beatniks onto the Plaza of the fifties became a torrent of hippies in the sixties. Those who had been artists were now activists. Leading them all was the far-from-dormant figure of Martin Archuleta.

At the height of the storm, Martin called a conference at a local college which was a hotbed of left-wing propaganda. As usual, the keynote address had taken a hostile turn. The anarchists, led by Martin, physically attacked the socialists who were taking an inordinately long and boring time in an attempt to filibuster a resolution exhorting all the factions on the left to cooperate with each other to overthrow the government of New Mexico and to declare it the first revolutionary state in America.

The rest of the conference was mostly chaos, when no clear settlement could be agreed as to the proper voicing of demands. Demands were made in the words of compassion: money for the old, the poor, the homeless, and the sick. That most money never reached the battered wives and their children as they fled to shelters, nor the homeless who roamed the streets and were driven from state to state, was not discussed. That most money lined the pockets of the people who attended conferences, ostensibly about social issues went unnoticed. The real issue was politics.

Even as a good anarchist, Martin was frustrated by the chaotic outcome of his conference. Despairingly, he placed a late-night call to Peter Stuart, still his mentor. "We're getting somewhere," Martin complained down the bad telephone connection, "but not fast enough. These people just don't know what's good for them. They're all too happy to let life go on as always."

"And Jenny Jensen?" Peter, still groggy in the early morning hours of English time, sounded half-asleep.

"Lipstone, you mean." Martin shook his head. "She's the worst of all them. Like I told you in my letters, she's married to the most rampant capitalist in the state and from what I hear on the grapevine about her, she doesn't even seem to mind."

"Don't worry," Peter assured Martin, his voice waking up. "I've planted a pea far under the princess's mattress. She won't sleep for ever. Believe you me."

In the first September of the new decade of the seventies, Jenny Lipstone watched the second of her two children begin school. In the days, weeks and months which followed, Jenny found herself facing more empty hours than she had ever known before. She still had the garden, the animals, the house to look after but without the children as the central focus of her daily activities, it all began to feel pointless. Jenny felt she was playing house.

J.J. remained as loving as ever. In the evenings after work he always discussed with her avidly the movements and decisions of his business ventures, and he always valued her sound advice. His attentiveness never dwindled. Still, increasingly, Jenny felt envious to see him go off to his daily exciting world of business. He had his own life, his own world, apart from the family. And the family, the children, were away much of the day.

In some of her free hours she read, but more and

more she sat quietly in a rocking chair by the window, gazing out at the tranquil, unchanging ranch. In her hand she rubbed and turned over the locket. She opened it and became lost in her thoughts as she stroked and plaited the lock of her great-grandmother's hair. Even when she put the locket down on the table, it seemed to glower at her. It pointed at her and laughed. When she put it away in the jewelery box at the back of her bottom drawer, she knew it never slept. She could not hide from the locket, her eternal irrepressible reminder.

She became undeniably aware of her own loneliness. Moreover, her two inescapable companions—guilt and confusion—gave birth between them to a new emotion: failure. Maybe her mother had been right at the wedding. Maybe her becoming a wife, a mother, a housewife, was a change to be mocked. What happened to my ambitions? she often asked herself. What have I become?

She half-trembled when a voice inside her head answered her own question. "You," the voice said in a tone which sounded frighteningly like her mother's, "have become nothing. You," the voice accused, "have failed."

ᏚᎥ CHAPTER 54 ᏚᎥ

"J.J." Jenny's voice was still soft and breathless from making love. "I'd like to ask you something."

Completely satisfied and nearly asleep, J.J. murmured, "Ask away."

"J.J." She leaned herself up on one elbow. "I've been thinking lately. I'd like to go back to school. I'd like to get a job."

J.J. opened his eyes in the dark. Jenny's words frightened him, but he was even more frightened by the thought of what he knew would happen if he tried to hold on to her too tightly. Never did he forget just how independent her nature really was. "Well," he said after a pause. "That's not something you have to ask me. I'm not here to give you permission or to forbid you from doing anything."

"You mean that?"

"Of course I mean that." He hoped his voice did not give away how nervous he really felt. "I've always made it clear to you you're free to do whatever you want. And if going back to school and getting a job will make you happy, I think: sure, go ahead."

"Oh, J.J." She kissed him on the cheek. "Thank you for being so understanding."

J.J. relaxed a little. Maybe her going back out into the world wouldn't pull her away from him after all. "I mean, look," he went on, feeling more confident by the moment. "The kids are at school most of the time and if you ever need to work late or something like that, Abigail will always be there to pick them up, right?"

"I love you," Jenny said, feeling truly blessed to have married such a man. She put her head against his chest and listened to his steady breathing until they both fell asleep.

Jenny signed on for courses in social work at the Community College of Santa Fe. She found the studies exciting and she was pleased to see, with life-experience now under her belt, how quickly she excelled in class, how much easier learning new ideas seemed than it had been when she was young. The other students in her class, mostly young women, were thrilled to see a woman in her early thirties return to college. Jenny became a living proof to them of their theory that it was never too late for any woman.

Her first semester at college, she passed her exams with brilliant grades and by her second semester, she declared her field of specialty to be in two subjects. Child development was one, and political science, her first academic love, the other. In no time Jenny found herself to be well on her way to a double masters degree, and what started out as volunteer work at the Police Department, training young officers in the field of child abuse, soon became a well-paid, part-time job. Jenny began to feel fulfilled.

Almost always she came home in time for the children's dinner, and she relaxed in the bubbling torrent of words from Benjamin and Sarah. She sat by the bath and watched them play. She tucked them up and kissed them good night. On the occasions when she had to attend a lecture at night or work overtime at the Police Department on one case or another, Abigail never failed to pick up Benjamin and Sarah from school, feed them and put them to bed. Abigail proved herself to be a real rock.

It was really on a dare that Jenny attended her first political meeting. Jenny loved the feeling of sitting in her classes surrounded by eager, intelligent, politically-minded young women. She was vital again. She felt her old enthusiasm and sense of involvement, like hot embers beneath cold ashes, stir once again, enlivening her, returning to her life an intense passion which she had not even noticed herself missing. The students in her class respected her thoughts, and it was one of them who invited her to attend the meeting one night. Jenny laughed at first when she heard the name of the group. "WAMP?" she asked.

"Yes," the bright-faced young girl explained. "Women Against Men in Power."

Probably silly, Jenny assured herself as she left J.J. and Abigail to give the children dinner that evening, but she drove herself to the meeting anyway. Despite the absurdity of their name, however, she was surprised to find herself enthralled by the group's earnestness and moved by the powers of their free thought. These young feminists, she thought, had actually realized much of what she had hoped for ten years ago. These were the daughters of her early dreams. These were the new leaders. Being with them, Jenny felt her old sense of healthy outrage return to her. She smiled. It felt good to be back amid the fighting and the fevered arguments. Is the old me, she began to wonder, really so dead?

She went a second time to the WAMP meeting and then a third. Soon her attendance became a weekly event. "Fine," J.J. always said to her as he came out to the car to kiss her goodbye. "It's fine with me." She was only away, he reminded himself, one night a week. And it would be selfish of him to keep her all to himself. Anyway, it was only a local women's group, not some national movement. What could be the harm? "Have a good time," J.J. said, with a little knock on the car door. "It does you good to get out and meet some new friends." But why, he always wondered when he walked back into his house alone, did he feel so worried?

At one meeting, a young woman—the same who had invited her to begin with—asked Jenny to share with the group some of her early experience as a feminist in the late fifties and early sixties. Jenny, nervous about addressing a crowd (even a small crowd) after so long, steadied her voice and told the group about what she thought would interest them: her views on England, on America, on being a young student herself, on the pleas for social justice she had learned under Peter Stuart's tutelage. When her talk was finished, Jenny blushed to hear the thunder of their applause and to see the audience rise to their feet. They hailed her as their elder friend, their mentor, the mother of their movement.

Indeed, Jenny herself felt quite motherly toward many of the younger, more lost, WAMP members. She made it her habit to take up old friendships which had fallen by the way. Regularly, at least once a week at lunchtime, she sat with Nancy Johnson having croissants and cappucino at a Santa Fe outdoor patisserie.

Nancy Johnson now lived in a commune. She hailed herself as a radical lesbian. Her sister Lucienne lived in New York. Quietly, Lucienne abhorred her older sister's strident sexuality. She and Max lived a calm, civilized, unmarried, "new" life of their own. Their opinion was that if they chose to live together, that was their business. Not even Esther dared intrude. The subject was never mentioned. Lucienne managed Max's career, and Max, at the age of twenty, was now an international success. They were a happy, independent young couple who loved and took care of themselves. And even though Nancy Johnson disapproved loudly of Lucienne's heterosexual preference, Jenny had to laugh. She liked Nancy and found her company stimulating.

When, during their lunches together, a fellow student or member of WAMP came and sat down at their table, crying before Jenny because of a relationship gone wrong with some man or woman, Jenny very much played the part of mother, comforting and offering well-appreciated words of advice.

Before she knew it ("Could two years really fly past that fast?" she asked Nancy one lunch), she had earned her masters degree. This fact received another standing ovation at the next WAMP meeting, for the members always applauded each other for the triumphs they announced from their daily lives. Jenny loved their praise.

Jenny was the only member truly surprised when, at their meeting to elect the new year's officers, she heard her name announced as a nominee for the chairpersonship. After the vote of raised hands was tallied, Jenny fought back tears of pride and joy. She, Jenny Lipstone ("You really should think about using your maiden name again," her sisters frequently reminded her), was WAMP's new head.

Between parent/teacher conferences at her children's school, continued seminars at the Police Department, weekly WAMP meetings and her regular duties as wife and mother, Jenny found herself attending meetings for one new caucus then another, joining one coalition then the next, and standing at the head of a posse of women activists. The group regularly picketed the state senate, lobbied for women's rights issues, and fought for votes in the elections. They knew they had a long, dark road ahead. Though the men of Santa Fe might appear to be the last guard of male supremacy, it was the women of Santa Fe who were the hardest to convince of the virtues of today's womanhood. The women of Santa Fe were largely Hispanic and traditional. Jenny was learning to her cost just how traditional the Hispanic women of Santa Fe could be.

Though Jenny still dressed and gestured according to the old school of femininity—unlike Nancy, who wore jeans with a man's shirt and a tie—she found herself repeatedly frustrated in her efforts to get the older Hispanic women to see the light. She tried, on many occasions, to enlighten the older women working as caretakers for the community. She tried and she tried. They never seemed to listen. Was it then her fault in the end when, almost overnight, native Santa Feans found themselves pushed out of their jobs as social workers? Could Jenny help it if the new freethinkers coming in from out of state told the elderly women of the community to mind their own business and go home?

Santa Fe was changing and, for better or worse, change was becoming an unstoppable force. The communities found their village schools closed, their churches locked, and their traditional way of life—their centuries of family tradition—broken on the wheel of modern convenience. Slowly, the history taught in the schools was the history of Marxism. The children were taught that their parents were capitalist swine, that the police were pigs and that family life was a way of keeping the rich rich and the poor poor.

Jenny, to the increasing displeasure of the more

radical groups around town, still managed to stay, at least by their measure, largely traditional. She was, however, unaware that Abigail was a member of one such radical group. She didn't really have time to notice. Too many demands were made on her time already by committee meetings, WAMP board meetings, pickets, seminars, lectures . . . Without really noticing, Jenny was becoming decidedly skillful at fielding difficult questions and handling dissension both from the right and left.

There were afternoons after school when Benjamin, especially, missed his mother. And it would have been nice if J.J. had more time to take him to league games and cub scout meetings. His father, Benjamin understood, was away running the empire. But Benjamin knew there was no point complaining so, on the afternoons when Abigail didn't seem in the mood to play with him and Sarah, he looked after his younger sister and took her to all his secret hideouts on the ranch.

The steady growth of Jenny's political status and influence did not go unnoticed by Esther. Though a confirmed Republican herself, she watched with a certain pride as, on occasion, Jenny's face appeared on the evening news leading a group of picketers, the chosen local spokesperson for the voice of today's woman. Jenny's politics remained, for the moment, outside the standard party system but Esther did not mind. Maybe, Esther hoped, Jenny was coming to understand why she had had such ambitions for her. Their relationship was still cold beyond description and Jenny never telephoned or invited her mother to lunch. But soon, Esther reassured herself, someday soon she'll understand.

Martin Archuleta, too, though himself sitting on the opposite side from Jenny on many issues, watched her rise in prominence. Martin was pleased. She would indeed be useful some day, and that day appeared to be approaching with increasing momentum.

J.J. found himself disgruntled with life. But who could he turn to? He certainly did not want to complain to Jenny, for she seemed so happy. He would not dream of taking her happiness away from her. But who else would understand? George had retired from the Phoenix Company to play golf and drink with his buddies. J.J. would die first rather than moan to George, particularly after his promises to keep Jenny always happy. And as for Esther, when she wasn't spending her time with Orlando and his crowd of painters and friends who claimed to be poets, she was wrapped up in her own political "do's." Besides, J.J. knew what a betrayal it would be to Jenny to discuss her with her mother. What was he to do?

The answer came to him in the spring when Benjamin was nine and Sarah was seven. Max and his girlfriend, Lucienne, were in for a visit. They stayed at La Posada. Both Max and Lucienne enjoyed Jenny's company, and J.J. enjoyed theirs. They brought with them news of the outside world. They brought gossip from New York and tales from London.

The two young lovers (J.J. had reconciled himself long ago to the fact that they were living in sin) came over to the ranch one night for dinner. J.J. had spent his day watching the ticker-tape tap out symbols of wealth from New York, Paris, Tokyo and London. It was when Max told an amusing backstage story about his last concert at the Royal Albert Hall that J.J. found his solution: a trip to London. Never mind England's economic difficulties, J.J. decided. A trip to London would be a good chance to scout out new business prospects and, more importantly, it would give him an excuse to take Jenny with him, away from it all. Abigail could look after the kids, and he could have Jenny all to himself . . . The more he thought about it, the better he liked it.

"Look," he said a week later, as he undressed to get into bed beside his wife. "Look what I found in my jacket pocket." He reached into his pocket, pulled something out, and tossed it gently onto Jenny's side of the bed.

Curious, she lifted the envelope and opened it. "J.J.!" she exclaimed. "Are you serious?" In her hand she held two first class plane tickets for a round-trip to Heathrow.

Wearing only his shirt and his boxer shorts he fell across the bed and lay with his head on Jenny's stomach. "What do you say," he said, "we take a little break? Just the two of us, huh? I hear Kensington Gardens is beautiful this time of year. What do you say?" Without words, Jenny expressed her enthusiastic reply.

To J.J.'s disappointment, they never actually made it to Kensington Gardens. In fact, just the two of them spent remarkably little time with each other. On their luggage, their initials intertwined, but J.J. and Jenny hardly had a free moment to intertwine themselves. They stayed at the Savoy. J.J. loved the room and everything else about the hotel but he quickly found himself caught up in an endless series of business meetings.

Jenny told him not to worry. There was a lot she could do to fill her time. She spent very little time shopping, and mostly she visited the British Museum. She spent long hours in the London Library drinking up the English constitution and English history. Then, having refreshed her memory from her university days of the intricacy of English governmental procedure, she sat many days in the gallery at the House of Commons. She listened to the debates. Some were excellent but none were like the glorious oratory of Winston Churchill whose books she treasured, the adagios of Bevin's pleadings for the poor now silent, the rich thick voice of the past now dead. Jenny was disappointed, but she attended and learned. She watched. She listened. On several evenings J.J. dined alone in the Savoy's River Room, for Jenny was off, engrossed in a late session at Parliament.

One day, a week before their scheduled return, she attended a Buckingham Palace garden party. She was presented with J.J., being a prominent American businessman, to the Queen. Jenny resolved after that experience that she would run her government (that is assuming, of course, she ever decided to bid for a position of real power) with the grace and the elegance with which the Queen elicited the love, respect, and obedience of her people—without any need for words or commands. Jenny decided that good old, back-slapping, under-the-table New Mexico politics would have to go. Instead, an elegant, quiet, restrained manner would be her style of government—should, of course, she ever choose to run.

After her return from London, Jenny took her first step into the full and public arena of politics. There was to be a debate, and she set to her preparations with the entire strength of her diligence and studiousness. As she prepared, she felt within her the fierce flame of ambition begin to glow with a greater intensity than she had experienced for years.

Terrified at the thought of being caught off guard by any surprise question on any detailed point of argument, she did her preparatory homework well. She read all there was to know about New Mexico. She watched television avidly. She immersed herself in the history of this rugged, dangerous, relatively new-born state—unlike anything or anywhere else in America—with its massive, windswept deserts, cold and silent under a full moon, its great, green cactus standing still and foreboding. The canyons were alive with long-dead Indians, their ghosts silently stalking General Kearney and his men, also dead. They still wandered, dripping with blood and bandages, along the highway which leads down the Old Santa Fe Trail to La Fonda, the center for all travelers, burned down and then rebuilt. Apache Canyon was dark and dangerous as the Apaches themselves. The huge forests of piñon and spruce were filled with game. Bobcats, mountain lions, the cough and high singing voices of the coyotes, the deer, the racoon, were all living together in an unparalleled harmony. Jenny studied all of it.

She knew that if she was going to take on a public battle, she would be safer in the night of the forest stalked by a mountain lion than in the Capital Building stalked by Martin Archuleta, for he was to be her opponent in the debate. The forest had rules. The animals shared a code of honor; Martin obeyed no rules, he had no code of honor. Martin carried years of vengeance on his shoulders.

As she readied herself for her test, the first, full airing of conflicting political views held by the growing New Mexican factions, she found her dreams haunted by a vision which nightly gained clarity and color. In her dreams she saw herself living in the Governor's Mansion, a house which for now she only visited with J.J. by invitation. Also in her dreams, sometimes as a friend and sometimes as a villain, she saw the sharp, hard face of Martin Archuleta.

The night of the debate approached. The forum was to be an assembly of politicos representing all aspects of New Mexico's political life. Jenny was to speak on the subject of the suppression of women in politics. Martin was speaking against her motion that women must be given an equal place in the legislature. The Press awaited the debate with great anticipation. It would be, as they called it, "some fight," and all the newspapers knew that covering it would make for exciting, controversial reading.

On the day of the debate, the men met at the Bull Ring to have lunch and discuss tactics. The women met at Nancy's house. They clutched their lunches in brown bags and sat cross-legged on the floor. Jenny wished her group would be a little more professional. Jenny felt secretly that the women in her group let the case of all women down with a huge thump. The feminist propaganda was cranked out on the oldest of smudged paper. The rhetoric was at times hysterical because equality and revolution meant that there were to be no power struggles among the workers. Jenny, still wounded by the double-edge of her experience with Peter Stuart, refused to allow Nancy to call her comrade, refused to be suitably cowed because she kept servants and a nanny for her son. Jenny's place of leadership in the group was at times precarious, given the scope of beliefs held by incoming WAMP members, but she trusted Nancy. "I'll kick anyone's face if they upset you," Nancy said, and today of all days, they sat in Nancy's house among the stench of the dirty plates and roaches, and they planned.

"No, no," Jenny said wearily at the end of the session. "Monica, if you insist on a picket to force the government to pay for all women's sanitary towels, I'm not speaking. You'll just make an asshole out of yourself as you usually do. Please, not a Tampax and sanitary towel sit-in. I read the cuttings from a march in Bristol, England. It didn't raise anybody's consciousness. It just made everyone on the march look ridiculous, and people howled with laughter."

Monica scowled. She was small and fat with protruding eyes. She lived with her girlfriend, Robyn. They fought together in their relationship and side-by-side for the coming female revolution when women would dominate the world. Men were expendable. Men, Monica explained loudly and at inopportune moments, had no seed. Men, she said to Jenny, very earnestly, on their first meeting, not only have no seeds but also they are only catalysts. Jenny had tried not to laugh.

But today, she tried not to get provoked. Her thoughts, like those of a boxer about to enter the ring, were focused solely on Martin, a well-known, brilliant speaker. All of Santa Fe chose to hear this debate and there was standing room only available in the forum. "For once in your life, Monica," said Jenny, "keep your mouth shut. I don't hate men. In fact, sometimes

I think men aren't the problem. Women are. Men at least cooperate. You lot just compete."

Monica looked at Jenny. "Well, we can't all be rich bitches like you."

Jenny laughed. "My dear Monica, we can't all be poor and ugly like you," and she gracefully left the room.

Martin looked wolfishly at Jenny across the room. He smiled and raised his hand in a cool practiced wave. Jenny acknowledged the wave as calmly as possible. She saw her mother and father move slowly down the aisle. Her widowed grandmother Nora, now eighty-four years old, needed George's arm. Nora strongly disapproved of her feminism but, as George said, "Ah well. I love my little girl. Give her a batch of young hens and she'll be too busy to go to all those meetings with all those ugly ladies."

J.J. walked behind the family party, proud in one way but worried sick in another. His beloved wife was about to be put publicly on display. He hoped dearly she would not find herself on a civilized gibbet. Her growing political involvement left him increasingly confused. But how could he complain? Even if she were preoccupied with her politics, she kept a lovely home, and Benjamin and Sarah seemed to be turning out well enough. Maybe Benjamin was a bit withdrawn, and maybe Sarah's teachers were worried about her because she was shy and so often appeared depressed, but they were good children, and they both loved their mother very much. As J.J. found his seat, his main concern was that Jenny's feelings should not get hurt in the cruel, gladiator-like battle of public debate.

"Women have no place in government. A woman belongs in the home." Martin started his speech. He originally arranged his speech to annoy the feminists but, the more he worked on it, the more passionately he felt about what he was to say.

There were awful arguments within the anarchist group which met at his house. "You can't cook. You can't sew. You live in a pig-sty. You smell," he had finally shrieked at a girl in his group.

"I don't want to do any of those things!" the girl screamed back.

"But then," Martin interrupted, "what can you do, eh? You are illiterate. You can't write a report. You whine about PMT. All you're fit for is to make a cup of coffee, and even that's lousy." The other men in the group quietly agreed. If the men of the group really wanted to plan, they met surreptitiously. If they did not want their plans to be in the latest piece of gossip on the Plaza, they kept their plans for themselves. And all of them knew that never, never, never would they marry any of these "new" women. In their heart of hearts, they agreed that their wives would be virgins and cook pizza and *posole*. Except for Martin. His heart was taken by a woman who could never be his wife.

The knife turned as he began to speak in anticipation of Jenny's passionate attack. "Of course, women must make decisions about their own lives. But traditionally and historically, when women have become powerful in the marketplace, civilizations have fallen. One need only remember the fates of ancient Greece and ancient Rome, and the lesson is learned. Surely, it was the very notion of a higher position for women which brought about the demise of those great civilizations." Martin was pleased to hear himself use the educated voice he had learned in England.

"Why, we ask," he continued, confidently, "is this so? Women are subjective creatures. Biologically they have the hormonal mechanisms to kill in defense of their children. Men die defending territory. Objectively men will cooperate and plan to protect their group. Women, on the other hand, never cooperate; they compete."

Jenny's head was spinning. She had to out-match this attack on women, but she felt torn in two. All she believed that women could be and could do lay smashed, months ago, as she watched the women at various conferences tear each other apart. Her own group hardly ever held a meeting which did not degenerate into an uproar. She remembered the nights she and Hanna had fantasized about the birth of the New Woman . . .

It was Jenny's turn to reply. She faced her audience and breathed deeply. Then, steadying her voice, she began. "I would like my worthy opponent," she inclined her head but not her eyes in Martin's direction, "to analyze his remarks concerning what best serves the interest of the majority. The fact is, women are a majority in this country. My opponent, however, seems to imply that women, by virtue of their biological destiny, are unfit for positions of power."

"I object!" Martin rose to his feet. The moderator nodded. "Women do have power—absolute power. A matriarch stands in equal position to the patriarch. The man has power in the marketplace, and the woman has absolute power in the home. Ask my father," and he winked at Paulo Archuleta, who blushed and nodded. The entire auditorium clapped and cheered.

Monica and Robyn stood up and bellowed, "Male chauvinist pigs!" They clenched their fists and stormed out.

"If I might finish my analogy, Mr. Moderator," Martin continued calmly, "a woman takes her centrality into the boardroom where she then attempts to run the boardroom as she runs the family. When she reaches for male power, she is confounded. Men think linearly, we do business linearly. Women don't—they treat the boardroom like the coffee shop."

By now, Jenny was furious and her previous plans to maintain her composure vanished. "How dare you generalize like this!" Her voice was raised and her cheeks flushed. The audience fell silent as the battle raged over their heads.

Martin—cool, calm and cruel—was largely backed by the audience. The men of Santa Fe, unlike the rest of the country which cowered and wilted in the heat of angry women, hated the new women who strolled the Plaza in their stained shorts and grimy T-shirts. Silently they applauded Martin.

Jenny passionately and lucidly fought Martin. Their voices intermingled, and in their opposition lay desire and attachment. J.J., with Nora on one side of him and Nancy Johnson on the other, sat and watched, impotent. Jenny, he had to admit, was holding her own pretty well. But was this what she did at her nighttime meetings? All this battling with words and platitudes? Was this what she wanted for herself?

Nancy leaned intrusively across him. Her face

glowed with enthusiasm. "She'd make an excellent Governor, you know," she beamed in a loud whisper.

Nora snorted. "Too much of her great-grandmother in her for her own good."

J.J. put his hand on Nora's knee. "I'll look after her," he said. "But she's free to do what she wants."

Esther tapped J.J.'s shoulder from behind and put her head between his and Nora's. "Well, she's a good speaker. I'll give her that."

George grunted. "She's damned marvelous, Esther. Marvelous." He was almost in tears. He was not actually listening to the words. He gave up arguing with Jenny years ago and now he tried not to pay too much attention to the content of her beliefs. He was just pleased to see so many people looking up at Jenny with such obvious admiration. "To think that's my little girl." He blew his nose.

Jenny, hearing the trumpeting even from the podium, smiled. Dad, she thought.

The smile infuriated Martin. She can afford to smile, he thought. She had a tart of a nanny, servants, a fine house, and a millionaire for a husband. All her politics were just a gloss, a screen. Anglos like her pushed his people out of their historic heritage with a few signatures on a piece of paper. Families like hers came into town and stole vast stretches of adobe houses on Canyon Road, on the Old Pecos Trail. In those days they paid the Hispanics a pittance and now Santa Fe, New Mexico was one of the cultural capitals of America, and the money did not go into the hands of the Spanish settlers or the Indians. It went into the hands of banks owned by outsiders and into the hands of millionaires, white millionaires. There were so many of them on the north side that nobody bothered to count. Slowly, Santa Fe's warmth and intimacy were turning into a lustful greed for money, restaurants and malls—not for the locals, too poor to contemplate the luxurious dresses, weaves, and artefacts, but for the rich with their jets neatly parked on the Santa Fe Airport. The careless, idle rich who did not even spend the bulk of their money in Santa Fe. If they wanted to spend, like Esther liked to spend, they bought their shoes in Italy, their suits and dresses in Paris, and their furniture in Boston. No Hispanic carpenter would ever be asked to Esther's house . . .

No, Martin realized, after this obsessive litany churned in his head, if he and Jenny were to race for the top—for the role of Governor—his game had to be very carefully thought out. When he needed to destroy her, he must look for the one thing she could not bear to lose, and that thing was not her husband.

Slowly the debate came to an end. The vote showed that the audience was overwhelmingly in Martin's favor.

"Only in Santa Fe," Nancy comforted Jenny as she stepped off the stage. "Good old, patriarchal Santa Fe."

"Yeah. Only in Santa Fe. But, Nancy, some of what he says is right, you know. Nothing ever seems to come out of our meetings except petty jealousies."

J.J. pushed his way through the crowd. "Well done, darling. Well done." He hugged her.

Her family crowded around her. She saw Martin stalk from the podium. He glared over his shoulder at her. The look cut her to the quick. Oh why, she thought, must he both love and hate me? She did not hate Martin, but she certainly did not like his politics.

Bombs and guns seemed an unnecessary violence, and from his early talk at Wentworth she knew that terrorism was more his style than diplomacy.

"You know J.J.," she said much later that night, inspecting the nail polish on her toes, "I think I'm going to resign officially from the feminist faction. I really don't know that it does me any good to be publicly associated with the kind of crap Monica and her set spew. I can't really go on pretending that women are somehow superior to men. That kind of position narrows one's political possibilities so much. And anyway, I shouldn't have to defend my right to paint my toenails or wear perfume."

"Thank goodness." J.J. let out a gigantic and relieved sigh.

Jenny lay back against her pillows. "I tell you, J.J., it was quite a feeling being on that stage tonight."

"I'm sure it was." He pulled the blanket up under his chin. The emotional strain of the evening had left him exhausted. His body felt like collapsing hours ago, and his mind switched itself off after his second gin-and-tonic at the congratulatory party which had followed the debate.

"I really felt important, like I was doing something important. I felt prouder of myself than I have for a long time." She looked at J.J.'s turned back.

"You should feel proud of yourself anyway," he mumbled, genuinely too tired to talk properly. "I'm always proud of you, Jenny."

"A person could get very used to that kind of renown."

"I'm sure they could." He yawned.

"Yeah. You know, Senator de Chavez came up to me tonight after the debate at the cocktail party in the lobby. Oh, don't worry, I know him for the son of a bitch he really is. I have no illusions about that."

"Glad to hear it." J.J. rolled into his pillow, anxious to get to sleep.

"But that doesn't mean he couldn't be useful, and it doesn't hurt to be seen to have the endorsement of your godfather—bastard that he is." J.J. let out a small half-asleep snore which Jenny mistook for a grunt of agreement. "And we did have a surprisingly pragmatic talk," she continued. "It's all been pie-in-the-sky until now, but he seriously thinks that a dark horse candidate would stand a very good chance. I mean, I hate the man but he does have his finger on the pulse of New Mexico. I can't argue with that, however much I despise him personally. He says everybody is fed up with seeing the same old names of the same old people, and that they'd welcome a total unknown. He says the time is ripe for a drastic change. He thinks the chances would be very good." She waited for a reply. None came. J.J. had one foot in the land of sleep and the other was about to follow. "I think," she said, "I'll surprise everyone and run on a Republican ticket." She laughed. "It's been a while since New Mexico had a Republican for a Governor."

"I see," said J.J. His eyes snapped open. Desperately he wished that he was waking to a dream, a very bad dream, but he knew what he had just half-heard was real. His back turned to Jenny, he lay with his eyes open. He wanted to cry.

Jenny lay back and almost at once fell into a deep sleep.

Across town in the Barrio, Abigail, the nanny, was rapidly getting drunk. Martin sat silent and smiling.

He listened to every detail which fell out of her lascivious mouth. Ply her the right way, and she could tell him anything he would ever want to know about life inside the Lipstone residence, and she was, apparently, a well which would never run dry. In return for the information, all he had to do was to fuck her. She paid for the alcohol and he paid her back by the pain he caused her. Both were mutually satisfying events.

◈ CHAPTER 55 ◈

Jenny set about preparing herself meticulously for the responsibilities she aspired to assume. She still raised her children and looked after her husband, but always kept a hand in the running of the state and its capital city. Her friendships grew among a group of handpicked, powerful members of the legislature. She attended parties. She entertained—always with the right people.

During the years leading up to the election, Jenny laid a careful trail. While Martin ranted and raved about social conditions, abortions, welfare housing, Jenny knew that the women of Santa Fe rarely voted. She spent her time in the hospitals by bedsides, in the old folks' homes listening to what women wanted, in the coffee shops, in the pastry shops, in churches, at women's luncheons. Through it all, Jenny was building a constituency for herself.

She tuned her ear to hear which issues her people

wanted pursued. Abortion was a sticky issue. The town was so Catholic and the feminists were so strident. Jenny made her position clear: she was a Catholic, therefore abortion was never an option for her. If, however, an abortion needed to be arranged, it was a matter between a woman, her partner and her doctor. As Jenny spread her views around the town, people on both sides of the issue tended inevitably to agree. The mid-seventies had a certain buffering effect upon America, rounding off the sharper edges of social dissension, merging most factions toward a largely accepted middle ground of vague liberalism, relatively innocuous compared to the vehemence of the sixties.

Only the most radical remnant factions and their members took offense to the platform Jenny was building. "You can't say that." Monica, still as militant as ever, heckled Jennifer wherever she went.

"I can and I will." Jennifer, remembering the Queen's calm demeanor, never raised her voice.

"What about a woman's right to choose?" Monica dogged.

"What about the father's right to an opinion?" At times, even in defense of her middle-of-the-road line, Jennifer found herself booed and jeered by extremists on either side. The Moral Majority was fiercely partisan, as opposing groups met to fight and to picket the local abortion clinic. The hopeless, white-faced victims of their anger were caught on Channel 4 television.

Jenny was tired and despondent. She lay in the armchair of her ranch's sitting room with a drink in her hand as she watched the television. She saw the hatred on the faces which yelled and screamed at the frightened women. J.J. was away. The children were out with their friends. The house was quiet. Jenny watched and found tears running down her face. She knew those hate-distorted faces personally. She also knew, in as small a town as Santa Fe, these people used their own internally violent families as a launching pad to justify their politics.

As Jenny reasoned her way back to sanity, she saw Martin's face on the screen. For a moment the camera captured him so that he was glaring at her from the television set. Jenny jumped up and turned off the television.

How she wished she had someone to turn to, to talk to. But J.J. was out of town, her sensible father would, no doubt, be out playing golf, and Nancy Johnson certainly would not provide any comfort: Jenny felt in no mood to be on the receiving end of a tirade concerning further proof of men's oppression. And she didn't want to trouble her grandmother Nora. How could she explain to the old woman her pain at feeling mauled in the cruel, machine-like teeth of heavy political PR career-building? Nora, she knew, never understood in the first place why a woman would want to choose such a life for herself when she already had the sort of wonderful husband other women would die to marry. The person she really wanted to talk to was Etta, but Etta was long dead. Those soft arms and that pillow chest existed no more for Jenny in the world.

For lack of a better alternative, Jenny considered calling her mother. Esther, in the recent years since Jenny's decision to run for office, appeared to stand at somewhat less of a distance from her. Jenny's hurt and betrayal from her knowledge of Esther's relationship with Roberto de Chavez was no less intense now than it had ever been, and by the exchanged glances between the Senator and her mother at various public political affairs, Jenny had every reason to believe the nature of their liaison was still intimate. In moments of hard anger, she rehearsed in her mind scenes of exposure, various ways to ruin her mother's reputation by public announcement of her infidelity. But Esther, for the moment at least, remained useful, a political imperative. It was through Esther that Jenny gained many introductions to people of power and she was fully aware that, when election-time came, a scandal on her mother's part would be held directly against her. Jenny walked a careful line with Esther. She socialized with her little, mostly at carefully chosen public events.

Jenny thought about the expediency of her relationship as she stared at the telephone. No, she realized, her real feelings were deeper than that, though she could not say for sure, even to herself, what her real feelings were. Lately, she had to admit, she thought she detected a look in Esther's eyes, as she sat at various fund-raisers' head tables beside her daughter—a look which seemed to verge on pride. Etta's death had left a hole in Jenny's life. Nowhere in the universe was there a woman to appreciate Jenny fully, just for being herself. Despite her growing popularity, there lurked inside Jenny the taunting childhood demon of failure—so deep inside she was not aware of which devil she ran from. It was as if an imperceptible voice within Jenny told her that only by winning the election would she escape the demon once and for all. The small hints of Esther's pride, her mother's approval, seemed to keep her one step ahead of failure—life-threatening, world-destroying failure.

"Mom," she said on the phone for comfort, then was not sure what to say. "Did you see the news?"

"Yes." Esther was preoccupied. "I caught some of it. So silly, isn't it, darling? All that fuss over a mere abortion. Really, I think they do it just to get themselves on television."

"I guess so." Jenny realized her mother had not heard the desperation in her voice. Why should she? Jenny told herself. I didn't really tell her anything. But the strain of explaining her morose feelings to a woman who was obviously busy with her own life was more than Jenny wished to attempt. Jenny made brief small-talk and hung up.

She went to bed early, took two sleeping pills and dived into oblivion.

Oblivion was beginning to be a regular refuge for Jenny. Oblivion was a reliable friend, a predictable port in a life which felt increasingly stormy, unsafe and hurtful. She had sought oblivion in drugs as a teenager and it called to her once again. It took the edge off life, numbed her pain. When Jenny could anaesthetize the part of her vulnerable to pain, she felt she could handle anything. After coming home from the police academy or from campaigning, she went straight to the drinks cabinet. A quick shake of the martini shaker, a little pearl onion or a small green olive, and she sat watching the news on Channel 4, searching for oblivion.

J.J. was almost always absent. The children had begun at boarding school. When they were home, they lived in the peculiarly insulated cloud of young American friends. The noisy, chattering crowd invaded Jenny's house, dive-bombed the freezer, filled her microwave with popcorn and played music loudly. If she was lucky, Sarah came to kiss her good night. Occasionally, Benjamin asked a favor. Usually he was gone. Jenny realized she was lonely.

Her friends talked about their families, about who slept with whom in the endless Santa Fe merry-go-round of bed-swapping. Jenny had no desire for another man. By now, she and J.J. had drifted so far apart they rarely spent time together any more. They hardly ever slept together. Jenny felt her sexual urges pushed further and further away as she struggled to balance her home life, her working life, her marriage and her children in an endlessly futile attempt to keep all these brightly colored balls in the air. Slowly, Jenny lost her quick laugh, her sense of humor, her patience, her warm smile. Soon, the cocktails were followed by a bottle of wine, then pills for sleeping, then blessed oblivion. Tonight was one such lonely, oblivious night and Jenny slept a dreamless sleep.

J.J. saw the change in Jenny. He was painfully aware of the cold distance, but felt unable to do anything except helplessly watch Jenny's heart float away from him. He scolded himself regularly. He should have put his foot down earlier. He never should have let her go back to college. He should have tried harder to dissuade her from getting a job. He should have been more attentive. He should have bought her more presents, taken her on more trips. He should have made her feel more loved so that she would not have had to turn in new directions to feel good about herself. He had seen the hurt child in her even before they had married, and he had tried to love that child well enough. He should have been able to love her into happiness. Obviously, he told himself, he had failed.

But what could he do now? He had released a half-tamed horse too early onto the open prairie, and now he had no way to bring it back home again. And even if he could, how could he expect his beautiful creature, having known unlimited freedom, to be content again with the burden of a saddle on the back, the rubbing of a bit in the mouth?

One night, just as the hoary-fingered frost froze patterns on the windows, J.J. asked his secretary to attend a conference in Alaska with him. She often traveled with J.J. She was twenty-five and married to an Hispanic carpenter, whose hours were flexible as he worked from home. Her baby girl was cared for by her grandmother, so Martina was free to work in order to pay her uncle for the acre of land and the new trailer.

Martina was soft and dark and round. She smelled like chocolate-chip ice cream. Her presence gladdened J.J.'s heart. After lying next to his wife's drugged body, he looked forward to Martina's bright face and her happy smile. He liked to look at her little, apple-tight breasts as she leaned forward to put his papers before him. He enjoyed her solicitous attention to his well-being. She brought him dishes for lunch—tortillas, *posole* with pork and green chilli, refried beans, home-made *sopaipillas*, puffed white and delightful. She gave him honey and fire-red chilli to pour on the *sopaipillas*.

Soon J.J. was hopelessly in love with this girl. Or was it lust? J.J. wasn't sure. But the thought of her body curled next to his own tormented him. Then, close on the torment, lay guilt, with its long green sticky fingers.

For a year J.J. had fought with the demons of temptation. Then the business trip to Alaska came up.

Soon, Jenny was ready to challenge the other runners for a place—her place—the Governorship of New Mexico. She was enmeshed in running the gubernatorial race. Her only opponent was Martin Archuleta, who had leashed himself to a Democratic ticket. The other candidates dropped back long ago in the primaries. Jenny was too preoccupied to care about J.J.'s frequent absence.

In the Florentine Hotel in Anchorage, Alaska, warm with wine and good French cooking, J.J. kissed Martina's hot, wet mouth. Finding her willing, he picked her up and carried her into his bedroom. He made love to her with all the intensity he was capable of. In his passion he felt the brief, yet merciful, easing of his pain. Martina responded like a small tiger. She rode him to ecstasy. Then he fell like a log, replete and satisfied.

The morning found J.J. with an aching head in his hands. Martina smiled, amused at this man's anguish. "We'll tell no one," she said, snuggling up beside him. "Your wife doesn't need to know anything. Besides, we can always book two rooms." J.J. groaned again. Guilt, remorse, sorrow, dishonor all gathered around the bed.

After that trip, he tried to keep his hands off her, but Martina refused not to tease and taunt him. J.J., over the months ahead, began to feel less guilt, less remorse. Jenny had her own life, her own friends and her politics. All he was doing was taking a little pleasure for himself, a little solace, a small comfort. And then they got careless.

"Do you know," Orlando asked Esther, "that J.J.'s having an affair?"

"Really?" Esther raised her beautiful eyebrows. "How do you know for sure, Orlando? This is probably just a bit of vicious Santa Fe gossip put out by Martin Archuleta."

"No, it's true. I heard the rumor a while ago. They were seen together in Hawaii. What they were doing on the beach was hardly secretarial." He laughed. Orlando was now a well-preserved sixty-five. His days of success as a painter sat well with him.

Esther frowned. She would have to tell Jenny. The threat of a last minute scandal could ruin Jenny's career. And for Esther, Jenny's career was all-important. Max escaped his mother. Occasionally she was allowed to attend one of his concerts, but Lucienne was always there to see that Esther's claws did not reach the man she loved. Lucienne understood Max in a way no one else did. Max, when he played the piano, exposed a raw nerve. He quivered and shook in the total concentration of his playing. Cruel, jealous people always surrounded him. They tried to harm him but Lucienne was always there, an impenetrable rock. Jenny, however, was far from impervious to her mother's cruel ways.

"I think, darling," Esther said down the phone, "we should have lunch today."

"I'm awfully busy, mom," Jenny said.

"Well, I think this is important enough for you to put everything else aside and meet me at the Patis Corbae."

"Okay. If you say so." Jenny liked the Patis Corbae. The chilly winds of late September promised an early winter. The Patis Corbae was warm and cozy. It would make up for the iciness she could already hear in Esther's voice.

"Do you know, darling, that J.J. is having an affair with his secretary?" Esther leaned forward with her knife poised for the kill.

"Oh really?" Jenny, a superb politician, raised her eyebrows and leaned back in her chair. A long time ago, Jenny learned to suspend herself in an abyss, to leave insults and hurts alone on the crags, to deal with feelings later in the privacy of her own home. And today, Jenny had armored herself with a generous dose of tranquillizers, protecting her in advance from the pain. She could tell from the edge in her mother's voice on the telephone that this lunch would not be pleasant. "Well," Jenny sighed and smiled a small, resigned smile, "the wife is always the last to know."

Esther frowned. "Jennifer," she said, "you must take this seriously, dear. If the news leaks out, you won't make it to the Governor's chair."

Jenny smiled emptily. "Don't worry, mom. J.J. can leave. I'll be a single-parent mother with two children to support, and I'll get the single-parent vote. Goodness knows there're enough of those in Santa Fe." She gave a small laugh, wrinkled her face, and looked toward her lap.

Esther could see the pain beginning to show through on Jenny's face. Esther had, in fact, been pleased to hear the news from Orlando. J.J., she had always felt, was an encumbrance on her daughter, and getting rid of his domestic ties would remove from Jenny the final obstacle to total, single-minded commitment to entering the office of Governor. And for too long she had watched as Jenny seemed intent on running her own life, even her own campaign, her own way. Telling Jenny the truth would bring Jenny closer and back under her control, a control she had lost more than thirty years ago. But the hurt in Jenny's eyes was more than Esther had anticipated. She knew if she did not handle this correctly, her plans could backfire dreadfully.

"Jennifer," Esther began with a tenderness in her voice Jenny could not remember hearing any time in the last thirty years. "Jenny, I feel terrible about this. I know what your marriage means to you."

"I don't." Jenny felt the pressure of unwanted tears begin to push at the back of her eyeballs. "I haven't known what the marriage has meant for a long time."

"And I know what the election means to you," Esther continued, her voice soft and warm.

"You do?" She blinked hard to push the tears back inside her head. "Then maybe you could tell me?"

"Well," Esther smiled, "I can tell you what it means to me. You know, it's funny, we haven't really talked this way since you were a little girl. And I used to talk to you so much, even when you were a tiny baby but children grow up, I guess, and they outgrow their parents—but they don't have to outgrow their dreams. And that's what this election means, Jenny. Our dreams. I've told you all this before." She shrugged. "Maybe you don't remember." She looked at the locket hanging around Jenny's neck. "No. Maybe you still do. My grandmother Lilla—and I see you're still wearing her locket—was a great artist, a very great artist. And she tried so hard to be recognized, to become somebody important but there just wasn't room in the world for a great woman."

Jenny listened to her mother's words. Somewhere inside her a memory stirred, a memory of this repeated litany she had heard as a little girl. The feeling of being a little girl merged with the agony of J.J.'s betrayal, and Jenny sniffed, a child wanting to sob.

"And when I grew up," Esther went on, "I had my own hopes for myself. My mother never really saw why I couldn't be happy to live her kind of married life, but I didn't let that stop me. You know, Emily and I were the first women from New Mexico to be accepted to Wellesley. Did you know that? It's quite an accomplishment. And I went to college, and I traveled, and I saw the world." In her mind she saw Jimmy Delgado's face smiling at her as he showed her out of his front door and never saw her again. Esther's voice dropped. "And I failed." She shook her head. "I've never told this to anyone before, but I failed. I don't know exactly why or how. It just happened. I just didn't fit into the world out there. I wasn't even sure what I wanted to become—a doctor, maybe, or a lawyer, or a writer. But I didn't make it. The world let me down." She leaned forward and took Jenny's hand. "So, I got married to your father, and then you were born."

"Then I was born," Jenny repeated mechanically, wishing she had never been born. Again she felt the urgent weight of expectation which had pressed so heavily upon her in her youth. She sighed.

"When you were born, I felt like I was being given a second chance." Esther's face lit up. She held Jenny's hand tight. She laughed. "You know, it might sound silly now. A young girl's fantasies, really, but when I got back from Boston, I made a vow: my daughter would do it for me. I'd have a daughter and she'd be my sword, I promised myself, to take on the world and change it so women like me would never fail again." In her eyes burned the passion of that promise long ago. "And I did have a daughter. And now you're so close, Jenny, so close. You're little more than a month away from being the first lady Governor this state ever had. You can do it, Jenny, I always knew you could. And now this has happened to you—J.J.'s been unfaithful, but you can't let this get in your way, Jenny. Why, there isn't a woman out there who hasn't been hurt by a man. This can make you strong, Jenny, don't let it stop you now."

Jenny stared at her mother. The face was a naked portrait of ambition. Jenny felt no ambition of her own right now, only pain. Quickly, she pulled her hand away from her mother's and reached into her purse. "Well, mother," Jenny said and she knew her hand was shaking as it searched inside the purse, "that was a good speech. You really ought to write it down."

"Jenny." Esther pulled her hand back, offended. "I'm not giving you a speech. I'm telling you the truth."

"The truth, mother?" Jenny's hand found what it was looking for. Just the feeling of the pill bottle in her hand began to comfort her. "It's funny to hear you talk about telling the truth." With both hands she struggled with the childproof lid of the pill bottle then, popping off the top, poured three valium into her palm.

"Jenny," Esther began, she saw Jenny put the pills in her mouth and reach for a glass of water on the table. "Jenny, don't."

Jenny held up her hands for silence as, with a difficult gulp, she swallowed the tablets. "You know," she said, "it's truly ironic—almost laughable, come to think of it—that you should be the one to tell me about J.J." Even to say his name hurt. "Strange to get a report of adultery from you."

Esther folded her hands in her lap and sat up straight. "I'm sure I don't know what you mean."

"Don't you?" Jenny sensed her agony turn to anger, and anger was safer, keener, stronger. "Senator de Chavez does, I'm sure."

Esther felt the blood flee from her cheeks. "Jenny, I—"

"Don't, mother." She shook her head sharply. "There's no point in explaining, no point at all. But you see, I know you for what you are and nothing you could say would change my mind." She glared at Esther and felt her eyes narrow. Then she smiled. "But don't worry, mother. I'm not about to tell anyone. I've certainly been tempted to, and I've spent enough hours just dreaming about the day I'd ruin you. You see, I've had my little dreams too, and I took my own vow: the day I saw you with Senator de Chavez, I swore I'd ruin you and let everyone see the real you. But now, I won't." Her eyebrows wrinkled as she felt the tears threaten again. "Now I know how much it hurts to be hurt by someone you love. And I could never do that to dad. He doesn't deserve to be hurt that much." She stared at her mother and felt her eyes squeezing at their corners. "He might be an idiot to love you so much, but he does. And I can't take that away from him."

Esther could not tolerate being so much at her daughter's mercy. "Jenny," she said, keeping her voice straight. "You're upset. J.J.'s upset you very badly—"

"Save it, mother. You enjoyed telling me about him. You relished every minute of it."

"That's not fair."

But Jenny did not want to talk or listen any longer. The valium, thank God, were beginning to do their job, and she could feel a welcomed exhaustion start to make her head heavy and her thoughts slow. She put her hands over her face and shook her head.

"That's not fair at all, Jenny," Esther persevered. "I'm not trying to hurt you. I just don't want anything to stop you. You've come too far."

Jenny dropped her hands. Her face was white and bleak. "Don't worry." Her voice was very weary. "I won't stop now." Esther sighed. "I'll still make it to Governor." She fixed her eyes on her mother's face and could see the relief it held. When she spoke, her voice was small. "What else," she said, "do I have in my life now?"

"I hear," Jenny said at one o'clock in the morning, thoroughly insulated by alcohol, "you are having an affair with your secretary."

J.J. stood in the doorway with his briefcase in his hand. "Who told you that?" he said.

"My mother." Jenny lay in bed, her auburn hair loose on the pillow. "Don't make it worse. Don't lie." J.J. looked at the ground and mumbled a confession. "Okay." Jenny was very business-like. "You get packed and leave. I'll send the rest of your things to the office in the morning. We were finished a long time ago anyway." J.J. tried to interrupt. "I don't want to hear it. I'll tell the children when they come home for their Thanksgiving break. The election will be over by then, and they can stay with me." Jenny swallowed her two usual sleeping pills and a third for added security. She turned over. "Shut the door behind you," she said.

J.J. packed. He walked down the drive. He heard the scrunch of the pebbles under his feet and he wished he were dead. He knew he still loved Jenny, but he knew her well. Her absolute, unbending integrity and her devotion to the truth at all costs meant he would never get back into her life again. Jenny reminded him of a huge vault. Once the door slammed on a situation or a person, it stayed shut.

❧ *CHAPTER 56* ❧

J.J. was right. Jennifer Jensen made sure she had no time to grieve. Through all of October, the voting for the governorship approaching, Jenny traveled. She went to small towns and villages. She was a Catholic, she was a woman, she cared about women's issues, but she knew just as well about the farmers' lives and their need for more support. She truly cared about their opinions. She listened. She came home every so often and collapsed. Then she got back on her feet and talked and talked and talked.

In November the day came when the votes were counted. The campaigners who traveled with her, supported her and loved her, wept with joy. "You've made it," Nancy said. "Oh baby, you've done it!"

Martin, her opponent, came across the floor. "You won the fight," he said bitterly, "but you haven't won the war."

Jenny looked at him. "There is no war, Martin," she said and she smiled. "I want you to seriously consider being my Lieutenant Governor. I know it's unusual for a Republican to appoint a Democrat as Lieutenant, but I'm all in favor of a bi-partisan approach. Together we could really clean this place up. I'm an Anglo, you're Hispanic. Your people are far more likely to listen to you."

"I'll think about it."

"Okay." Jenny put her hand out. "Friends?"

"Yeah," Martin said. "Friends." Martin had a new plan, a gem of an idea, and he smiled at Jenny. "Good night," he said. He couldn't wait to discuss it with Peter Stuart on the telephone. Peter would be proud. Martin would do something important after all.

Jenny attended the victory party for a short while. In the middle of all the hand-shaking, revelry, and loud band music, Esther rushed to Jenny and hugged her tightly. Pulling back, with her hands still on Jenny's shoulders, she glowed, her face more excited than Jenny had ever seen before. "We have triumphed!" Her words were slow, deliberate and joyful.

Jenny pulled her mother's hands off her body. "Have we?" she said drily. Then she nodded. "Maybe we have, maybe not." She turned quickly and walked away.

"Benjy," she said, finding her son. "Take me home. I'm exhausted."

Benjamin, who looked so like his father, smiled. He

got a special leave of absence from his college in New England to be at his mother's side for the election. When he surprised Jenny by arriving home early, she told him of her forthcoming divorce. Benjamin was crushed, shattered but he tried to be strong, for his mother's sake. He explained everything down the phone to his younger sister Sarah, finishing her work at her boarding school, and it was he who talked her through her tears.

As Jenny lay in bed that night, she considered her position, for the first time. She had won. She was the incumbent Governor of the state of New Mexico. Her dream was secure: she was to be the First Lady. All that she had hoped for, all that her mother had hoped for, was now fulfilled. Jennifer Jensen (for she had decided to use her maiden name early in her campaign) had what she always said she wanted.

Jenny sighed. The struggle was over. Now she could enjoy the fruits of the long battle. She wondered why she felt so bereft, why it would have felt so good right now to have someone to share her victory with her. Probably just exhaustion, Jenny assured herself, refusing to confront the pain and the emptiness J.J.'s absence left in her life. I'll feel happier about everything in the morning. She took the usual sleeping pills and lay back on her pillow.

Jenny fell asleep. Her victory tasted perilously like ashes in her mouth.

Jenny gave her inaugural address with Martin beside her. Her first appointment had been Martin Archuleta as Lieutenant Governor. Her second was JoAnn Sandoval, an Indian Mexican, as adviser. She had a good record of service in the state senate and, to Jenny's pleasure, JoAnn was a middle-of-the-road moderate on virtually every issue. Though JoAnn lacked charisma, her steady diligence could always be relied upon.

Jenny knew she had won the race as a dark horse. She chose to ignore the usual route which was endless politics in the state senate, endless debates which changed nothing. Jenny preferred her own approach: to spend her campaign and her term among the people of New Mexico. Her idea proved to be an excellent choice. New Mexico had voted for a change of leadership. Roberto de Chavez turned out to be right.

Now, as the sun streamed down and a huge fluffy cloud passed over the dome of the State Capital Building, Jenny began to feel her life might be truly blessed after all, that maybe it *was* a good thing to be Governor. While she was speaking her first words to the assembled houses of the New Mexican government, she reminded the men that her administration would not reflect her role as a woman. Rather, the fact that she was a woman would prove immaterial. She could and would rule as a *person*. She acknowledged in her speech she needed to get to know all the people who would help her take New Mexico from its present poverty-stricken state. "I intend," she announced, "to improve education, social services and the medical system."

Martin smiled. She could intend all she wished, he thought. New Mexico's underbelly ruled New Mexico. Gangs, factions and old family ties—these were the true New Mexican powers. Banks regularly went bankrupt. Loan officers made loans to uncles, cousins, and friends. No matter. One bank closes, another opens. Hotels, malls, you name it. It had a family name on it. Either Anglo money or Hispanic, no one cared.

While Jenny spoke, JoAnn Sandoval shuddered. An Anglo Governor in an Hispanic state, she knew, had a difficult task before her. Though happy to work with Jenny, JoAnn knew how many of her own people did not share her spirit of cooperation. Keep New Mexico beautiful. Shoot a Gringo, she remembered. On her reservation, that slogan was hung on trees.

"I want to see that we have a balanced budget," Jenny's voice rang big and clear in the enormous room. "Most of all, we must encourage the growth of light, smokeless industry in our state. We cannot be known solely as a tourist attraction. A man or a woman cannot live a life of serving tourists summer and winter. We must have proper, steady jobs to generate income from within, not from without, New Mexico."

The mayor of Santa Fe frowned. He had every intention of turning Santa Fe into a better version of San Antonio, Texas. For the moment, the Santa Fe River ran—or straggled, in the heat of summer— through the center of the city. Only bums and a few tourists hung out along its weed-infested banks. The mayor had other ideas. He wanted the river to represent the focal point for the city. He and the Santa Fe Improvement Committee met regularly to devise their hopes of swelling the river with a downstream dam, then lining its banks with long pavement walks, warmly glowing lamps, and more tourists, more bars, more boutiques, more gift-shops, more money. And if all went well, the second stage of the plan would entail extending the development downstream, right into the heart of the Barrio. The mayor was a greasy, fat man with an unpleasant wart on the side of his nose. He had already received money from contractors he already had chosen to build up Santa Fe. James Agate, an Anglo, was to be the chief contractor in charge of the town's revitalization. Much money was riding on this plan. Now, thought the mayor, that stupid bitch Jenny Jensen is going to sell me down the river.

The director of Human Services winced as Jenny spoke. Santa Fe Human Services always ran on the *mañana* principle: leave a problem alone, and it will go away by itself, eventually. The director of Human Services had taken a long time to get to her elevated position. She was all for leaving well alone. She arranged conferences, flying in the luminaries of the conference circuit, all espousing one central philosophy regarding family matters: if a woman was hit, the man must be arrested and punished. Now she looked at Jenny through narrowed eyes. The bitch, she thought. She and Jenny had clashed before.

"I intend," Jenny continued, "to audit Human Services" spending and to lead an investigation into the whole department. I intend to close down the rape crisis project, and those child-abuse programs which prove themselves ineffectual, and other wasteful organizations in our state. If we can streamline our costs and develop an efficient department of Human Services, we obviously would have no need of the other organizations.

"I intend," she said, smiling at the chief of police, a huge man much loved by everyone, "I intend to put the funds freed by this streamlining into our excellent police force." Chief Angelo grinned back. "We need better equipment," Jenny explained, "better cars, and better pay for the police.

"I also intend to see that every teacher in this state is tested for proficiency. The education standard here ranks among the lowest in the nation." She frowned at the director of the Education Department. She knew him from the old days, a hard-line, bitter communist. He must go, she thought.

Slowly, her speech came to an end. When she finished speaking, an uproar filled the assembly. Some people shouted and some booed, others clapped. Chief Angelo came up to Jenny and hugged her. "Thank God you're in," he said.

"Thank God I've got you." Jenny smiled.

The director of Education came scuttling across the floor. His pink nose twitched. "All I have to say—"

"Don't say it. She's tired. Leave her alone." Chief Angelo pushed him. "Get lost." Angelo hauled the man off, bellowing a hearty rendition of "I'm in the Money."

Jenny suddenly felt exhausted.

Martin Archuleta saw her to her car. He pushed his way protectively through the television cameras, past the out-thrust microphones. "Tell us about your marriage." One pushy interviewer from the East Coast had done her homework well.

"There is nothing to tell." Jenny, more used to the media than she had been in her early days, stood still. Used to them or not, she suddenly felt surrounded by barely human people, all of them on the attack. "I don't see what my marriage has to do with my position as Governor of this state." Inwardly, she kicked herself. She'd have to work on keeping her cool, but their badgering was getting out of control.

"Did he leave you or did you leave him?"

"Why did he leave?"

"Is there another woman?"

"Are you dating?"

The questions came like gunfire. Because of her extraordinary position as woman Governor of a state, press from across the nation had come. The reporters from the East Coast were particularly numerous. Many well-known journalists, foot-in-the-door, faces carved out of rock, voices harsh from years of dealing in the more sordid scenes of other people's lives, pushed into her.

Then she remembered Martin beside her. "Help me out," she whispered to him.

Martin was amused. She has a lot to fear, he thought, a lot. Martin nodded. "Okay, boys and girls. Give the lady a break." He pushed his way into the crowd and got her safely into her car.

Jenny drove back to the ranch. She had several months before she was to move into the Governor's Mansion. The State Senate Budget Committee had allocated a grant to remodel the Governor's Mansion for its new mistress. All the way back to the ranch, the television cameras followed her. The relentless clicking of the journalists pursued her. Even once the gates of the ranch were closed behind her, she felt invaded. She asked cook for a light omelette and a green salad, and she pulled the curtains across the windows even before the sun set. She felt as if a thousand eyes could penetrate her walls and leave her bare, naked of body and soul. Maybe, she thought, the Africans were right. Maybe a camera does take your soul.

The phone rang—a sleek, humming purr. "How does it feel to be First Lady?" It was her mother.

"I don't know," Jenny confessed. "It hasn't really sunk in yet."

"Your father sends his love." Esther's voice stopped. "We're going to the de Chavez house to celebrate." Then she said, as if to explain, "Just as friends."

A knot of anger tightened in Jenny's throat but what was the point of opening that wound again? "They haven't invited me."

"Oh, they assumed you'd be too tired."

"I am." Jenny could not help but think of her mother in Senator de Chavez's arms. "I'm going to bed after dinner. Benjy'll be in later."

"All right, darling. Your father sends you his congratulations."

Suddenly, Jenny desperately wished she was little again, leaning against her father's big, strong chest, listening to the boom his voice made in her ears. Esther put the phone down and Jenny was left alone in the room. Of course, there had been invitations for dinner for this great night in her life. Jenny refused them all. This night she felt was one she wished to spend taking stock of her situation.

So far, and until this day, she had refused to think about her husband. The shock of his betrayal was so deep and the agony so great that she felt, if she allowed it to surface, she might be washed away into a dark never-never land. She heard on the grapevine that J.J. was in bad shape. He had been seen in town, gaunt and unshaven. Jenny knew he must be feeling bad. Normally he was meticulous. She also heard the girl had left the office.

Jenny sat. She looked at the wedding ring on her finger. So far she had agreed to stay married for political convenience. J.J. indicated through his lawyers that he would like to seek marriage counseling, but Jenny knew all the counselors in town were a rag-bag of failures. The few shining exceptions were her friends, and she did not want to expose her very private life to them. For now, anyway, Jenny preferred to throw herself into her new life and work so hard that all pain and feeling could be pushed aside. J.J. was a problem which might have a natural solution: a quiet, uncontested divorce several years down the road.

Benjamin did not come back that night. Jenny assumed he was staying with his friend Jim, but she was wrong. Ben was asleep on the floor in the Barrio. He was at the house of a man who had just introduced him to the biggest high of his teenage life. "Wow," he said, before he passed out.

Wow, indeed. The drug dealer smiled. He picked up the phone. "He's out cold."

On the other end of the phone, Martin grinned. "Take a picture," he said, "and drop it by my office."

The drug dealer nodded.

The Governor of New Mexico slept soundly, aided by her sleeping pills. Her son slept as if dead.

J.J. by himself sat outside the little chapel in Chimayo, New Mexico, twenty miles to the north of Santa Fe. He was spending time with his old friend, the Catholic priest. Behind him squatted the *morada*, the meeting house of the Penitente Brotherhood. Many of the men had grown up with J.J. They all knew of his shame and disgrace. Father John sat beside him and tried to comfort him.

After the initial shock of leaving, J.J. had time to think, particularly about Jenny. The pools of sorrow and outrage which were her eyes haunted him. If Jenny had shrieked or hit him, J.J. could perhaps have reasoned with her. As it was, the professional coldness she had shown him on the night of their separation left him no room for discussion. J.J. found no more success with Jenny's family. George was no help. He threatened to shoot J.J. if he ever saw him again. Esther just smiled her thin, mean smile. "I can't see what the fuss is all about," she said. "Leave Jennifer alone. She'll come to her senses."

Tonight, the priest was tired. Easter was approaching. The annual pilgrimage to the church in Chimayo was almost organized. Juan Herrera had been chosen to be the Cristo this year. A dozen men were selected to do the ritual penance. Father John looked at J.J.'s ashen face. "You know," he said, "sometimes a man must do penance to feel himself a man again."

J.J. nodded. "I feel so unclean. I can't wash it away. I've tried confession. I've said Novenas. The feeling won't leave me."

"Why don't you ask the Brothers if you could follow the procession? I know it's unusual for an Anglo to be given permission, but they all know you. You know, Pedro has asked."

"Yeah," said J.J. "I heard he molested a little girl."

Father John nodded his head to the side. "Yes. But this way he'll change. Prison never touches the soul."

J.J. walked across to the *morada*. The simple room inside the adobe building was lit by lamps, and the walls were hung with the stations of the cross. A tall, gaunt, hooded figure knelt before the altar. Above him was a painting of a lamp, the lamp carried by each participant. One side of the painting showed the whip of sorrow, and across from it was depicted the chain of shame. The man before the altar, unknown to anyone but the Brothers, kept a nightly vigil for the safety of his soul, atoning for the murder of his mother. Undetected by the police and confessed over to God, this man prayed through the night that his promiscuous mother might rest in God and that a path in heaven be laid for his own soul.

J.J. knelt beside him and asked humbly if he might confess his sin with the Brothers. The man listened and then looked at J.J. A murderer and an adulterer knelt side by side. The man's brown eyes were luminous. *"Sí,"* he said and returned to his devotion. I hope, J.J. thought as he left the *morada*, my eyes will one day look clear again. That night, J.J. slept well for the first time in months.

❧ *CHAPTER 57* ❧

A special conference was held in Washington, DC. The President was so concerned over the levels of violence in American families that he called all the Governors together, along with selected members of both the US Senate and the House of Representatives, to try to agree on policy which would provide results. "You will never change violent families until you get them into residential care." Jenny was adamant. "I've looked at my state's budget and we've been throwing money at social problems as if money were a solution. It isn't. Rich families on the north side of Santa Fe can beat each other up and molest their children and no social agency will do a thing to stop them. If you are a child in a violent family, at least in the Barrio you will be heard but"—she shook her head—"on the north side, who hears the child? The walls are thick, the grounds immense. Violence and incest, as we all know, are a learned pattern of behavior. We have a few families in Santa Fe where we can trace the bulk of the violence and delinquency in town directly to their door." So Jenny spoke to the politicians from around the nation on the first day of the conference. Her views were largely well received. She had grown cynical, however, that her speech would produce any real change, anything more than well-meaning congratulations.

Washington was at its best. The White House, heavily guarded, was as white as Jenny remembered from a trip with her father when she was a very little girl. At dinner—an enormous banquet in honor of the President and his wife—Jenny dreamily sat looking into the flickering candle in the middle of her table. Demographically small as Jenny's state was, the President's wife was particularly kind to Jenny, making special efforts to come to her table and talk, both women united in their cause of child protection.

Jenny sat that evening, watching everything around her like props in a dream. This, she knew, was the best part of her work. This was when reality matched fantasy. This was the sort of evening people dreamed about. This was as good as it got.

She had learned already that the rest of the work, the daily meetings back home, were a grind. It might be one thing to be Governor, but to have absolute power to execute your will and your convictions was quite another. Change, she could see, would be slow. Individual efforts produced very little result. Every new idea, innovation, or aspiration became bogged down in an insufferable string of committee meetings. When a problem arose, a committee was formed to investigate. When that committee needed more information, it appointed a sub-committee. When the sub-committee wished to get to the heart of the issue, they selected a task force. The task force sat through endless hearings then, finally, reported its findings back up the ladder. In the end, opinions were formed in the minds of the original committee and they, in turn, relayed their opinions to the state senate. The houses of the state senate argued the matter at hand, debated, voted, debated some more, revoted, resolved. Ultimately, the resolution went before the Budget Committee and they never seemed to have enough funds to approve anything anyway. The lengthy procedure of checks and balances, more often than not, came up with nothing more than a round of disgruntled faces on all sides of the issue.

Jenny breathed in deep the air of the White House. She had to admit to herself that she did not look forward to going back to New Mexico. Glamor existed only in fleeting seconds such as this. The rest was drudgery. Already, Jenny noted with an immense sense of anticlimax, being Governor felt like just an ordinary job.

After the conference, a reluctant Jennifer returned to Santa Fe. Never mind, she told herself as she got off the plane, one has to keep up appearances. Though feeling futile, she made a show of ruling with an unwavering determination.

After more uncountable weeks passed, Jenny noticed her drive was working, if not for her state, then at least for herself. Her loneliness, like her boredom, she managed to push aside. She regarded her work as the only reliable force in her life. Political observers marveled at her energy, not knowing its true source: the high of rage and pain.

She attended the Good Friday service at Chimayo, walking the last few yards to the church with the pilgrims. She did not see J.J. He was in the mountains behind the church. The little procession began its pilgrimage away from prying eyes.

Women were not allowed to attend this ceremony, the secret ceremony beyond the procession, and Jenny left before it began.

Slowly and quietly, the hooded men merged into the failing light as they began the long walk out of the mountains, down the valley, and into the church. Only the swish of the whips as the backs of the penitents were lashed broke the eerie silence on that Good Friday night, when their *Cristo* paid the price for the salvation of all mankind. Juan Herrera was raised on the cross and hung suspended before the processional left the mountain. The moment was solemn and silent. Gently, the cross was lowered and Señor Herrera, honored by sharing the cross of his Savior, joined the procession. J.J. prayed for true repentance. Soon the pain of the whips went unfelt.

Slowly, the Brothers walked through the village of Chimayo and into the church. A Brother waited for them there. Most of the village stayed away, the young ones not understanding the need for this confession. They had not suffered yet.

In silence, the procession entered the church. When the great doors swung shut, the flames of the thirteen candles were extinguished one by one until the little church was dark. The *santuario* stood silent, except for the ritual prayers and the moans of the *penitentes*, on their knees. J.J. found himself prostrate on the floor.

The doors behind him opened slowly. The night crept in to say its prayers. The wind swept through the church and the elder villagers stole away.

J.J. walked home, his back smarting, but his head high. He had hope—hope that if he were man enough and loving enough, he could get Jenny back again. He knew he would have to be patient, he had learned patience: he would wait.

CHAPTER 58

The first two years of Jenny's reign passed steadily. Trying to remain true to her campaign promises she found, in rare moments, the satisfaction of seeing some of her original intentions find their way to becoming (after laborious procedure) state policy. Teachers who were illiterate or who pushed their political views on the children were thrown out of the schools, whether the politics were of the left or the right.

Martin was secretly horrified, though he always appeared to do his best to support Jenny's bills. His best recruits came from the high school: anarchy was so popular among adolescents, and he hated to lose his stronghold there. But politics, he knew well, demanded certain sacrifices, and he was happy to give Jenny these relatively minor victories so that someday he would enjoy his own.

Most mornings, Martin had breakfast with Jenny. Three times a week they had a working dinner. JoAnn was often asked, but she usually had to refuse politely, for she was too busy working overtime at her desk. For many years, Martin relied on Abigail for information. In the last years, a nanny was no longer needed. Now he need not rely on anyone for information. He was at the heart of the power. He knew Jenny better than she knew herself.

What was happening in Benjamin's life was a mystery to Jenny. Because of her own drug experiences, she would have recognized the red eyes of a dope addict but this new drug, this highly refined cocaine, showed no signs. The insidiously rotting brain cells lay, a silent pool of stagnation in Benjamin's head though, to his mother, he looked perfectly normal from the outside. He was occasionally miserable and angry but Jenny was too busy to pay much attention.

Her daughter married at sixteen, in Jenny's second year of office. She married in Peru where she had gone when she left high school. Jenny could not attend the wedding. The schedule of office left no time for a few days away. Jenny was sorry, but Sarah forgave her. "You'll love him, mom. He's wonderful. He teaches the farmers here how to rotate their crops without the help of the Western World's chemical fertilizers." Jenny was glad for her daughter.

After a great deal of controversy, Jenny and her supporters within the state senate finally managed to close down the Human Services administration completely. Martin encouraged her. The unions tried to fight back but Jenny laid down stiff penalties. She was backed by the Republicans who agreed that far too much taxpayers' money had already been swallowed by the merchants of human misery.

Instead, Jenny opened volunteer-staffed sanctuaries with a few, highly paid people who had a caring vocation. Overnight, those who abused the taxpayers left for El Paso, famous for its handouts. Those who needed help attended the twenty-four-hour crisis centers where they found food and shelter. Every night, the crisis vans visited the supermarkets and collected sufficient food for the hungry. The women at the sanctuaries ran a restaurant in town, serving a one-price meal.

Slowly, in gradual stages, the improvement of Santa Fe began. For all the usual frustration of dealing with the various committees, Jenny did find a certain pride in the fact that she remained as true as she could to her principles. Child abusers went to halfway houses where Jenny devised a scheme which monitored their whereabouts at all times. They went to work, came back and paid restitution for the children they abused. Several times a day, a computerized telephone system telephoned them at work and at home automatically. If the criminals were not there to recite a voice-coded message back to the machine, the police were alerted immediately, and Police Chief

Angelo more than happily sent his men out on a roundup. This last piece of legislation pleased everyone, Democrat and Republican, and because of it Jenny stood through one of the few standing ovations she was to receive during her term.

But a thorough vetting of all politicians by polygraph pleased no one. "I don't care," Jenny said firmly. "If a person wants to stand for office, he—or she—has to have clean hands. I'm tired of all the payola that goes on in this town."

JoAnn Sandoval sighed. She knew Jenny would get nowhere with this one.

"Why change something that works?" Martin said in yet another hostile staff meeting. "We've always lived this way. You're an Anglo come into town . . ."

"I am not an Anglo who has recently come into town." Jenny's voice was sharp. "I am as much a Santa Fean as you are. Just remember that."

Martin bit his tongue, and at the end of the meeting waited for the rest of the staff to leave quietly. Martin looked at Jenny and smiled suddenly. "No hard feelings," he said. "All part of the business."

Jenny nodded wearily. "No hard feelings," she said.

"You look tired," he said. "Come on. We can sort out your friends' problems in the Barrio while I drive you home."

"Do we really have to tackle that one tonight?"

"Yes, tonight. The proposal goes to the committee tomorrow, and it's such a good idea." Jenny groaned. Housing was not one of her strong points. So many square feet per person . . . Rules, regulations . . . Jenny did not much like the nitty-gritty details. She usually left them to JoAnn who was magnificently meticulous and glad to do it, but Martin had made the wording of this new proposal his special business. "If this project gets off the ground," Martin said, gunning his Porsche, "and if we do get the bill passed through the legislature, the poor people of Santa Fe will have much to thank you for."

Jenny nodded. "Yeah. If we discriminate in favor of young married couples with incomes less than $25,000 per annum, we'll keep the Barrio in the hands of the people. We'll give them a good low-interest, fixed-rate mortgage, and we can keep Santa Fe for the Santa Feans, and out of the hands of the developers. Who knows? If it works, maybe we could try a similar program down in Albuquerque."

"I like that," Martin said. "Keep Santa Fe for the Santa Feans." Hmmm. We could always use that as a slogan. Very good."

"Glad you like it." Jenny laughed. "Anyway, Martin, if I just sign the bill, can I leave all the details to you? I have so much work, I just don't ever get the chance to go down to the Barrio."

"Sure," Martin said. "I'll be glad to take over."

Later that night, after dinner, Jenny relaxed with a generously poured snifter of brandy. Martin sat comfortably in Reuben's chair—now ensconced in the palatial Governor's Mansion—holding a club soda. Always wanting to be sharp, he made it his practice never to drink in Jenny's company. His long legs stretched out in front of him. "You know," Jenny said, "we go back a long way. All the way back to when we were students. I had a letter from Hanna the other day. She's a grandmother now and living in great style in St. Loup in Africa."

Martin raised his eyebrows. "Well," he said slowly, "we've all aged. I've been told your ex hasn't done too well."

"I know." Jenny's voice was tinged with sorrow. "He's had a rough time. I hear he's filed for a Chapter Eleven bankruptcy, but that ought to hold the creditors off his back long enough for him to reorganize. You know," she said, "there was a time, right after the divorce, when I would have been glad to hear the news. I was so hurt then. The bastard deserves everything he gets, I used to think. Now, I'm not so sure. I hope he'll be all right, and I think he will be. He's a good businessman and he always comes out on top."

"I think you're letting him off easy," Martin prodded.

"I can't hate him," she said seriously.

"That's not what you say about some of your political enemies." Martin shrugged. "I wouldn't want to cross you."

"Then don't." Jenny looked across at Martin. She heard in her own voice her acquired hardness, her professional habit of stating forceful sentiments strongly. "I make a good friend and a dreadful enemy." Listening to her own voice she suddenly felt herself tremble. She remembered the stories Nanny used to read to her. She remembered how she once thought of her mother. My God, Jenny said to herself, *I've* become the Queen of Hearts. She looked down quickly and finished her brandy in one mouthful.

Martin smiled. This is like taking candy from a baby, he thought.

The third year was as hectic as the previous two. Jenny was often called to give evidence to various commissions, mostly convened in the Eastern states. She traveled to meet her peers and to exchange ideas. She was well liked and popular with the press, but she was lonely.

At the end of the year, she looked at the results of the Barrio Housing Project. The ground was broken and the foundations laid. She was pleased. Christmas arrived unusually cheerfully. The nineteen-eighties had struggled successfully by now to loose themselves from the grip of the sixties and seventies. The young people of the eighties were smartly dressed, and it seemed to Jenny that overnight the people of Santa Fe cleaned up their act, drank Perrier, and decided to make a million. All except for Benjamin—her gentle, gregarious son. Officially he transferred his college credits to the Community College of Santa Fe. He wanted to stay, he explained, close to home. He was studying, but only fitfully. She hoped that Benjamin was beginning to pull himself out of his hole.

She heard that J.J. had made an effort to be with his son, and Benjamin had gratefully accepted the gesture. J.J., having endured the roughest of rough spots, was beginning to get back on his financial feet. As a secret, silent partner, he was buying his way into the Phoenix Company. George was still furious with J.J. for betraying his daughter. Though officially retired from the Phoenix Company, George maintained his role as chairman of the board. A series of minor heart attacks, however, had put George out of operation for many months. He was pleased, from his bed, to hear his board members' reports that an anonymous investor was keeping the company buoyantly liquid.

Jenny was relieved to find her father looking

healthy and calm when she attended Christmas dinner at Esther's house. This, she knew, would probably be the last year of her grandmother's life. Nora Gottstein was in her nineties. She clung to life bravely, but in her own way she was eager to be with her Danny once again and for eternity.

The meal was excellent and George bellowed as they all sang carols. Benjamin left to spend the night with his father. Sarah had telephoned from Peru earlier in the day to send her mother her love. Jenny went home to the Governor's Mansion alone.

Here I am, she thought, in my forties. Everything at my feet and no man to love. The thought escaped before Jenny had time to quell it. Since her divorce, Jenny had resolutely warned any man who showed interest, "I'm not the marrying type." Nor was she promiscuous. The Governor of New Mexico must be without reproach. Only Martin was allowed into her inner sanctum. Now, the passion which had colored their early years together had become calmer. The tiger which once stalked in his eyes became tame. Jenny felt comfortable in his presence, relaxed and unwatchful.

As Jenny fell asleep, James Agate, the mayor, Martin Archuleta, and a carefully selected handful of Barrio gang leaders were deep in conversation. A bottle of whiskey stood on the table. The mayor was drunk. "She'll never know what hit her, the bitch," he burbled. He scratched the wart on the side of his nose.

As the housing project went up, the young people of the Barrio became aware that what was being built was not housing for the poor. Instead, they saw shops erected for the tourists, condominiums for the single rich, houses within walking distance of the Plaza—a new Plaza. Quietly, James Agate approached the elderly of the Barrio. They were confused. They did not want to live in boutique-land with loud noise leaking from the restaurants and newly opened nightclubs. They wanted their peace and quiet. When James Agate offered them half the appraised value of their property in cash, most of the elderly took the money, glad to have got out so easily. Then, deflating his net worth through a number of various names and small daughter companies, James Agate applied for the special fixed-rate mortgages on these properties to finance his building schemes. Approval of the applications was a doddle: he could make himself look as poor as he wanted to on paper. If anyone on the approval committee asked any questions, their curiosity was quickly laid to rest with a donation to their campaign funds, and if any newspaper threatened to print an editorial about what was really happening in the Barrio, a bit of cash bought their silence too.

Those on the housing committee who were politically motivated to get rich said nothing. The others, busy with their jobs by day and meetings by night, read the falsified reports, oblivious. Jenny was in trouble.

Having left the whole project in Martin's hands, she had spent much of the year crisscrossing the country on a fact-finding mission. Between fulfilling her social functions as Governor and trying, without success, to balance the state's pitiable budget, Jenny was tired. So tired that she paid little interest to Martin's reports. JoAnn constantly handed her fact sheets which she almost reflexively threw into the bin. She did not hear the angry rumors. She did not see the young men afire with rage, the young girls betrayed by their Governor.

Martin did his job well. Quietly, in secret meetings, he informed the people of the Barrio that they had been tricked by their white Anglo Governor. "Why should we trust the Anglos?" he said tonight to the gang leaders. "Who lives on the north side? Do we? Does your mother?" he said, pointing to a twenty-year-old. "Heh, Ramon? You, all of you. You're in trouble. No jobs. Your mother's on the streets." Martin knew Ramon's reputation for violence. He knew the crowd Ramon ran with. "Our time," he said, "has come. Our time is now. It's up to you," he said. "All of you."

"That's right," the mayor slurred drunkenly. "It's up to all of us. I mean you."

"Listen to me, Bro," Martin said to Ramon, dropping his educated political voice and using the words of the streets. "I want to tell you something I learned in the Anglo school. If you want to really hurt a person bad, hurt a person they love. That's a lesson I never forgot, and I want you to remember it, too, *si?*"

Martin smiled at the sober figure of James Agate. Both men knew the mayor would remember little, if anything, of this meeting. "I am having dinner," Martin said to Ramon in particular, "with the First Lady, her son, and her parents. We'll be at the new restaurant in Agua Fria. La Mama's, it's called. We'll be there Friday night at nine o'clock. There is an eclipse of the moon that night and I will see the street lamps are not lit. The rest I will leave to you." He reached and shook the young man's hand.

"Bueno," Ramon said with a nod.

CHAPTER 59

Jenny dressed carefully for the dinner on Friday night. Apart from an early visit to break the ground in the Barrio for the newspapers, she had not been there at all. Guiltily, she promised herself she would take more interest from now on.

Benjamin looked handsome in his jacket and tie. "It's a long time since I saw you with a necktie," Jenny said.

Benjamin smiled. "I know," he replied. "Santa Fe's gone straight."

Jenny put her hand on Benjy's shoulder, so tall and so straight. "Darling," she said. "I've been thinking. Let's go to Peru next month and see Sarah. Let's just have some family time together."

Ben's eyes lit up. "Mom, I'd love that. I'd really love that. Promise?"

"I promise." George's car came up the drive. Mother and son went out to greet Jenny's parents. George, feeling much better and fully recovered, sat behind the wheel.

"I must say," Esther said nervously, as they drove through town, "it's awfully dark in these little streets." Jenny hardly listened. She made a point of ignoring most of what her mother said.

Benjamin laughed. "It's an eclipse of the moon, grandma."

Jenny lay back in the car. It was dark. The street lamps were out. Jenny assumed the electric company had not yet managed to hook up the lights for the newly developed part of the Barrio. She could see vague outlines of buildings, lights in windows. To her, the adobe boutiques looked like homes. She smiled. How wonderful, she thought. The young couples can have a good start in life.

Esther never went to the Barrio. She was full of fear. To her, the people of the Barrio were wild animals. George drove up the road and stopped at the top. "There it is," he said.

La Mama's had huge floor-to-ceiling windows opened wide to let the night air fan the cheeks of the guests. Tonight, Martin had closed the restaurant and explained to the staff that for security reasons no other customers were allowed. He would, of course, see that the management lost no money. The staff were delighted. "No chatting to the Governor," Martin had advised. "This is just a quiet, family affair." For the meal, Martin had chosen a traditional New Mexican selection. The price on the menu which Martin had had specially printed to disguise the usually exorbitant costs designed for wealthy tourists, was $3.00 per head.

"Marvelous." Jenny was impressed. "That's marvelous. Everybody can afford $3.00. And all the local families can come and get a good meal inexpensively. We're keeping Santa Fe for the Santa Feans after all." Martin sat opposite Jenny. Suddenly, she was aware of a heat in Martin's eyes. She looked at him. "Anything troubling you?" she said.

"No." Martin shook his head, the tiger roaring to get out. All these years he had disciplined himself not to let Jenny know of his hatred for her and her way of life. Soon the tiger could run free. His Porsche was waiting and then a plane. In one hour, he would be gone.

The hour ticked by unbearably slowly. Jenny's back was silhouetted against the window. Next to her, Ben sat silent, riddled with guilt, but now a new hope lay a month away: no drug dealer tracking him with threats. He would spend a month with his mother and his sister, and maybe he could confess to his mother and shake his habit.

George was busy shoveling the good New Mexican food into his mouth. Esther sat nervously on the edge of her seat, trying to figure out who had sat there before her.

Over Jenny's shoulder, Martin could see figures moving. His heart was in his throat, beating wildly. He saw the edge of the pale moon creep from behind the eclipse. "Now!" he screamed silently. "Do it now!"

The crack of the bullet repeated five times and caught the family unaware. Martin, at the first peal, leaped to his feet and was gone. The last Jenny saw of him was his contorted face, his eyes shining, white froth on his lips. A last, mad look of triumph, and Jenny knew she was betrayed.

Everyone dropped to the floor. Jenny, lying under the table, listened to herself breathe. Time stretched to a weird, contorted slow motion. Jenny found herself surrounded by stillness. No noise from anyone else reached her ears, which roared like the hollow echo of the ocean. She could feel her heart beat in every part of her body. Amazed, she discovered she was still alive. She lay and waited to become aware of pain. Her body was numb with fear. But no pain arrived. None of the bullets, apparently, had succeeded in finding her out.

Putting out her hand to prop herself up, she felt a

warm, sticky pool of blood forming under her hand. She raised her hand quickly to her face. Maybe she had been hit. Maybe she was simply too numb to feel it. She wiped her hand on her shoulder. The blood came off easily, and her hand showed no wound. She looked up quickly. The blood wasn't hers. It was Benjamin's.

In a horrible instant flash of understanding, Jenny realized all: the one thing that would have hurt her most had happened. She recognized Martin's plan. The bullets had not been meant for her; they had found their target accurately, and by hitting her son, they wounded her most deeply of all. Her son lay beside her, quite still. She slid to him and hugged his head to her chest. She rocked his head like a baby and crooned to him.

Outside there was pandemonium. People, lights, the restaurant staff rushing to and fro, car horns blaring. Eventually, the police, an ambulance, and Chief Angelo himself arrived. Jenny was in a state of shock when Chief Angelo found her—face white, hands shaking, still hugging her dead son.

He crouched beside her and put his arms about her. "Come on," he said. "Come with me. Let me take you outside."

Mechanically, unaware of any sensation, Jenny stood and let herself be led.

"Listen," Chief Angelo said when he got Jenny outside. "We'll take care of everything here. I think you ought to go home and try to get some rest. I'll come by in the morning to check on you." He shook his grizzled head. "Poor boy," he said. "Poor boy."

George held Esther in his arms. She fainted. "I'll

take her to the car." George felt as if his universe had gone with his grandson but, like any old hunter, he kept moving. "Bring Jenny to the car," he said to Chief Angelo, carefully carrying his wife through the crowds.

Jenny faltered, but automatically she walked through the crowd outside with her head held high. I'm the First Lady of New Mexico, she heard her voice ring repeatedly within her head. First Ladies don't cry.

George drove home. Ah Ling was waiting: he had heard the news on the radio. Ah Ling helped Jenny to her old bedroom, the nursery she had had as a small girl. "Here, Missie," he said. "Take this powder. Good Chinese remedy. You sleep. You cry tomorrow."

But even the medicine did not touch Jenny's broken heart. When she lay on her bed the numbness vanished and more pain than she had known in all her life seized her at once. She rolled on the bed and writhed. She hugged herself and banged her head again and again against her pillow. If she hit her head hard enough, she prayed, she would wake up. But she knew this was no dream. She had been given a son, had loved him, and now he was gone. She would never have him back again. Had she loved him enough? The thought tortured her. Had she ever loved anyone enough? Had she ever really loved?

She cried all night. The next day, George would not let her give the official signature identifying the body. "No," he said. "I'll do it. You remember him before he died."

"I can't." Jenny wept. "I'll never forget. I'll never forgive myself." The memory of Benjamin's broken body bleeding on the floor of the restaurant and then the shock—the shock the next morning of the photographs of another Benjamin—all across the newspapers and magazines of America—a Benjamin snorting cocaine, a Benjamin passed out, a Benjamin staggering down the road on the Plaza. These pictures greeted Jenny during the days after her son's murder. Martin had done his work well. The dark seeds he had planted were blossoming.

Jenny, as the days passed, knew she would have to resign. She wearily showed her speech of resignation to her father. "I'll make my announcement to the press after the funeral," she said. "I'll appoint JoAnn as my successor. She's good and steady." Then she laughed at the wretchedness of the irony. "New Mexico will get to keep a woman Governor after all." Her laugh quickly became sobs, as she hugged her father. "I failed," she said. "He fooled me. I should have known that he'd always hate me—I thought these last years that we were friends. And now . . ."

George nodded. "Well, that Archuleta fellow's gone. They traced him to Mexico. He disappeared—they'll never find him." George felt very old and very despondent. "It's my fault," he said. "I should have tried to stop the whole damned thing years ago." All he could do now was to hold his daughter while she wept.

Flowers for the funeral arrived along with cards, phone calls, well-wishers, sympathizers . . . But the damage was done. The Barrio was lost. The last piece of Santa Fe had been given away to strangers. Jenny was in a trance. She shook hands. She kissed cheeks. She wrote letters. And the day of the funeral dawned.

CHAPTER 60

Ben was to be buried beside Reuben in the family graveyard at the ranch. The funeral was a family affair. Nora, in her wheelchair, chanted to herself the *Kaddish*, her Jewish people's prayer for their beloved dead. Sarah was on the plane, flying in to join her family after the funeral. George held up Esther, dressed in a well-tailored black dress. A bereft Max stood beside Lucienne. Ah Ling and Maria were there. Jenny, wearing a black veil, stood across the open grave from J.J.

J.J. looked like a dead man himself. When the coffin sank slowly into the ground, he suppressed a groan. Jenny, trembling, shut her eyes and, with her hand on the locket which had belonged to Lilla, she looked into the past.

The short ceremony was ended, and slowly the guests began to walk toward the house. The setting sun turned pink the land of Reuben's ranch. "You coming with us?" George asked Jenny as he held Esther's hand in his own.

Jenny shook her head. "I want to stay here for a while. You go on. I'll be up soon."

George put his hand on his daughter's shoulder. He looked across the open grave to where J.J. stood and for the first time since the separation looked J.J. directly in the eye. He said nothing, just stared. Then, one man to another, he nodded his shared feeling of loss. He turned and squeezed Esther's hand. Esther put her hand lightly on Jenny's arm, but Jenny stood rigid. "Come," George pulled his wife away.

Jenny on one side, J.J. on the other, they stood for timeless moments and looked at the polished lid of their son's coffin. Slowly, J.J. walked to Jenny's side. "May I?" he muttered, and he raised an arm behind her waist.

"Oh, J.J.," she said as she turned to him, "I'm so sorry." Anguished tears ran down her face. "I'm so sorry. It's all my fault. I never should have . . ." She sobbed as if her heart would break.

J.J. held her as he had longed to do for lonely, empty years. "Don't, darling," he whispered. "Please don't blame yourself." He bowed his head over hers and he, too, shook with sobs.

Jenny whispered bitterly as she clung to J.J., "I will never forgive myself."

J.J. shook his head. "It's as much my fault as it is yours." He pushed himself away from her. "You know, Jenny," he said slowly, "I'll always love you. Even if I have to wait all my life for you to forgive me."

Jenny dried her eyes and stared silently into the grave.

"I promised you that you could trust me," J.J. said. "I let you down."

Jenny put her hand to her throat, took off the locket and held it in her hand. She gazed at the mound of red clay which rested beside the grave.

She said, "I should have trusted you. If I had from the beginning, none of it would have happened." She looked up into J.J.'s face. "You're a good person, J.J."

Jenny looked down at the golden locket. She opened it and, with a distracted finger, stroked her great-grandmother's hair. Her thoughts, however, gave her peace. From the past, Jenny had demanded her answer. From the past, and from the locket, Jenny had received her answer. She was not alone at the grave.

"You know," she stared at J.J. with burning eyes. In his face, behind the immeasurable depth of his pain, she could see his forgiveness and his love. "You know," she repeated, "this is never what I wanted to become. This isn't me." The tears once again poured down her face. "I never wanted any of it." She sobbed like a child. "I wanted to please my mother, and I never could. I wanted her to love me. I wanted to be important enough. But none of it means anything." J.J. held her.

"Jenny," he said, "my darling, beloved Jenny."

"I want you back, J.J." She hugged him tightly. "Please, take me back."

"We were never really apart. You were always in my thoughts, in my heart. I know we can get our life together again."

"I hope so," Jenny said. "God, how I hope so. I know how much I want to try." She looked down at the locket for the last time. Then she threw the golden heart onto the pile of red, rich earth.

Jennifer Jensen put her hand into J.J.'s and turned from the grave.

Erin Pizzey is the author of four novels. *The Snow Leopard of Shanghai, The Consul General's Daughter, In the Shadow of the Castle,* and *The Watershed.* Well known for her work with battered wives and their children, she is an accomplished journalist and has written a number of nonfiction books as well. She lives in Cayman Brac with her husband and children.

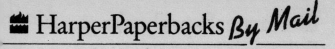